He stood just within the room, watching her, his legs apart, his arms folded casually across his broad chest. He wore high boots over his tight-fitting black breeches, and a silken shirt open at the throat. The soft evening breezes stirred his burnished hair, like pirate's gold in the glow from the sconces.

Through the open doors, bright rays of the moon shone against his back, and haloed his tall form. He seemed a thing of the night, an astral creature, charged with the luna-light. He did not move, but continued to gaze upon her. And she could not draw her eyes from his reflection, lest he dissolve into a pool of pure radiance. She dare not turn, dare not look at him directly. The silver moon-aura held her fast.

She watched as he walked toward her. He came to stand at her back. She felt his fingers in her hair, and then his lips whispering against its silkiness. "Hello, little gypsy."

At his touch, the chrysalis of pain and regret fell from her; her dormant senses blossomed anew. Was he real, or was she now part of the illusion? "Rudolph, I don't understand. I . . . I . . ."

"Not now, ma petite, not now."

GABRIELLE DuPre

Forget Me Not

CHARTER BOOKS, NEW YORK

Special thanks to Charlyn
Kelleher and Carol Hobson for
their patient and loving assistance
with the typing and proofing of
the manuscript.

FOR NANCY
. . . who saw and remembered.

FORGET ME NOT

A Charter Book/published by arrangement with
the author

PRINTING HISTORY
Charter edition/August 1985

ISBN: 0-441-52092-8

Charter Books are published by The Berkley Publishing Group,
200 Madison Avenue, New York, New York 10016.
PRINTED IN THE UNITED STATES OF AMERICA

"Even as a broken Mirror, which the glass
In every fragment multiplies—and makes
A thousand images of one that was
The same—and still the more, the
        more it breaks;
And thus the heart will do which not
        forsakes,
Living in shattered guise; and still, and
        cold,
And bloodless, with its sleepless sorrow
        aches,
Yet withers on till all without is old,
Showing no visible sign, for such things
        are untold."

George Gordon, Lord Byron

BOOK I

New Orleans

~❦~

"And who dare question ought that he decides?
That man of loneliness and mystery,
Scarce seen to smile, and seldom heard to sigh, . . ."

George Gordon, Lord Byron

~ *Chapter 1* ~

Simone Montpellier stood in the shadows, waiting, the sounds of revelry a counterpoint to the drumbeat of her heart.

"Mon Dieu!" How she loved New Orleans, and at no time more than Mardi Gras. If the cruel Fates had deprived her of family and identity, they had at least shown mercy in depositing her in a city so suited to her temperament. Would the Comus parade never come? she wondered, as she nervously fingered the small packet of sleeping powder in the folds of her full skirt. Madame Felice's request for the draught tonight had eliminated the final obstacle in the bold plan that had taken form only this afternoon.

Simone had sat reading aloud to Madame Felice when Yvette, fresh from the day's festivities, had burst gaily into the room.

"Grand-mère! Simone! What a day it has been! New Orleans and the Mardi Gras will never be the same."

As Yvette babbled on about the triumphant Rex march through the Vieux Carré, and of the Russian grand duke who had been in attendance, a subtle change was taking place within Simone. The resolution which had been growing through years of discontent now crystallized into a silent vow—no longer would she live vicariously. She must grasp every chance to live life to the fullest and she must begin at once.

For all but the briefest part of her seventeen years she had lived in the Crescent City, while its gay cornucopia of life spilled all about her; she was always an observer, never a participant. This isolation was in great part due to

5

Simone's peculiar circumstances. In the year 1854, a steamboat towing a sailing ship into the Port of New Orleans exploded, destroying both vessels. There were pitifully few survivors. One of these, an unidentified infant, was taken in by the Ursuline nuns. The good sisters dutifully made inquiries in France, from whence the ship had sailed, but there was no record of so young a child among the passengers. As there seemed nothing further to be done, the child's origins remained a mystery. They christened her Simone, as she was almost certainly French, and Montpellier, because Mother Superior harbored fond memories of that region of her native land. And so the infant girl grew to young womanhood within that sheltered environ, protected against everything but that great well of unknowing which lurked within her secret self.

Who was she? Who were her parents? What had they been like? These and a host of equally unanswerable questions rose up time and again to haunt her as she lay sleepless in her small bed, or dreaming over her chores. She often envied the girls sent to the convent to be educated by the nuns. If her romantic heart yearned for a more exciting life, so did her restless mind often times covet the security of their backgrounds and well-planned futures.

Always introspective, Simone was at this very moment reflecting on why she so loved the Mardi Gras. It was surely the blurring of identity which appealed to her. A masker could be who and what he wished. At this insight, her full lips curved in an ironic smile. In her frequent daydreams she was ever the highborn lady, yet her present attire belied this fantasy. A young lady unescorted at this hour would certainly be noticed, but not so a gypsy wench! As such had she clothed herself, gypsies being in no way remarkable in cosmopolitan New Orleans, since the famous voodoo queens often wore colorful gypsylike garb.

A clever touch, she mused, congratulating herself on the success of her bold endeavor. It had been simple, really. After the Durands had left to sup with friends in anticipation of the night's events, she had given Madame Felice the draught. Then she had informed Dorrie, the servant girl, that she herself felt ill and would retire early. There was little danger of anyone other than Dorrie discovering her absence. On the evenings when madame took the sedative, she invariably slept the night through. As for the rest of the

Durands, they would scarcely return before dawn, it being their custom to breakfast on *beignets* and *café au lait* after the ball. So, donning her gypsy disguise, she had slipped over her balcony and climbed down the trellis to the moonlit courtyard below.

It was a long walk to Gallier Hall from the Durand residence on the Rue Royal, but Simone was determined to see the Grand Duke Alexis. Rumor had it that he had become enamoured of the exquisite Lydia Thompson after hearing her sing "If Ever I Cease to Love" in the New York comedy *Bluebeard*. So he had followed her to New Orleans, where she had a scheduled engagement. All New Orleans was agog over his unexpected visit. It seemed fitting that the duke's arrival should coincide with the height of Mardi Gras fervor. Today's Rex parade, the first in history, had been hastily organized by some of the city's most prominent men, and a holiday declared in his honor. And now, tonight, Comus would salute the duke as well.

Simone was standing across the street from this august personage, though she could not see him in the crowd that thronged the platform fronting Gallier Hall. Complete with crimson canopy and a thronelike chair erected especially for him, the semicircular platform was decked with evergreens and small flags at its railings. Larger flags of the United States, Russia, France, Prussia, and Britain, and the Confederate Stars and Bars graced the entranceway. An archway of gas jets, complete with crystal shades, surmounted all. The New Orleanians had gone to great lengths to please their royal guest.

A delighted gasp rose from the crowd, ending Simone's reverie. The Mystic Krewe of Comus had at last arrived. Eagerly, she stepped from the shadows of the grandstand, confident that none would observe a lone gypsy girl.

Comus, the first of the Mardi Gras krewes to parade, had started this tradition in 1857. Except for the years of turmoil during the Civil War, Comus had been delighting the people of New Orleans with magical processions, and the aristocratic Creoles with glittering *bal masqué*. Tonight's parade was no exception. It was heralded by a cavalry unit briskly keeping pace with a brass band. Always inspired by ancient mythology and classical literature, the Comus revelers had constructed colorful floats depicting these themes. Flanking each float were *flambeau* carriers, young Negroes hired for the evening to carry torches to illuminate the way. Interspersed among them were costumed walkers adorned with enormous papier mâché heads. Spontaneously joining the procession, they lent an air of mischief and gay abandon.

If Simone thought a lone gypsy girl would go unnoticed in the crowd, she was mistaken, for at least two pairs of eyes had caught sight of the captivating picture she presented. One pair recognized her as Simone Montpellier; the other saw only a beautiful, carefree gypsy. In the flickering light of the *flambeau* she appeared as some exotic doll. Simone was a perfect blend of Creole heritage. She bore the delicate bone structure of a French beauty and the dusky coloring of a Spanish madonna. A mass of raven hair fell from beneath her crimson tignon. Her almond-shaped eyes, the color of polished ebony, often betrayed the depth of her emotions. A delicate nose and a full, sensuous mouth completed her perfect face. Though petite and fine boned, her womanhood was evident. The loosely draped peasant blouse could not hide the high, full breasts which rose above the tight cumberbund at her waist. And the yards of crinoline only accentuated the well-formed hips.

As the Comus parade marched toward its glittering finale, Simone realized that her masquerade was drawing rapidly to an end. All too soon, she would once again become Simone Montpellier, companion to Madame Felice. Nothing had really changed. Simone, gay gypsy maiden of the Mardi Gras, would quickly disappear into the recesses of memory. Why did the magic have to cease? Simone's spirit now began to imitate the somber mood of the fast approaching Lenten season. What grand fun it had all been! Yet, like the homes which would soon be stripped of their carnival bunting, Simone would be stripped of her fantasy identity.

As she turned toward home, Simone strolled to the lazy rhythm of passing carriages. Suddenly a pair of strong arms encircled her. As she was whirled off the ground, hungry lips sought hers. The searing kiss was impatient as the tongue sought her open mouth. Pressed intimately against a muscular form, she sensed its smooth hardness through the rough cloth. She felt bruised and burned by this heated passion. Mon Dieu! she thought, I'm going to die. I can't breathe! Simone began to struggle against a broad chest —pushing, pressing. All at once the arms released her.

Startled, she fell backward as male laughter echoed caustically in the now quiet street.

"My little gypsy, my kisses have never brought such a response."

"It is perhaps that a kiss given is only as good as a kiss received, monsieur."

He laughed, folding his arms across his massive chest, his mocking eyes reflecting his amusement.

Simone looked up into a remarkably chiseled countenance. The handsome features were somewhat distorted by a hardness and cynicism revealed in his eyes. Were they blue? It seemed as though they had paled quite suddenly into the gray of a mist. He was tall, seeming to tower over her in his military costume, his very size intimidating. In her narrow world she had felt competent to meet all challenges, but her limited experience had little prepared her for this blond demon. Yet she was extremely pleased with the audacity of her bold retort. He must not guess her naiveté.

"Perhaps I need more practice, ma petite. Will you be my teacher, or does your expertise lie solely in fortune-telling, little gypsy?"

"Monsieur, I am not prepared to give you lessons in amour."

"Oh, I am heartbroken . . . no love, no secret glimpse of my future?"

"I will gladly read your fortune, monsieur, if you will meet me at Madame Ninon's tomorrow morning at eleven o'clock on the Rue St. Anne. Madame Ninon is a renowned priestess of voodoo and her establishment is known to all. Everything that I know of the black arts, I have learned from her. Now as to improving your amatory abilities, I will leave you to your own devices. Nouvelle-Orleans is a city of love, monsieur. I am sure there are many willing teachers." Not waiting for a reply, Simone ran quickly down the banquette, leaving the tall stranger behind.

Approaching the Rue Royal, she slowed her pace, and was relieved that no menacing footsteps followed. Opening the lacy wrought-iron gate, she turned into the gaslit courtyard of the Durand residence. It was quiet, and only the sound of the bubbling fountain invaded the peaceful night. A number of large palms stood sentinel. The gentle breeze stirred their fronds, which cast eerie shadows over the cobblestones. Quickly she moved into the darkness and edged her way toward the beckoning trellis. How relieved she felt in having escaped that arrogant stranger. She was quite pleased with the manner in which she had met his sarcastic verbal challenges. But her masquerade had been the most fun. A gypsy, indeed! A rendezvous to tell his fortune! She had to stifle the laugh that filled her throat. However, it had been wonderful to play the gypsy for even a few moments longer, to stave off the realities of her life as Simone Montpellier. As she climbed gingerly up the trellis and angled her body over the balcony railing, she was assaulted by the familiar images of her life.

Her life with the Durands, although hardly fulfilling, was not unpleasant. Madame Felice Durand had been so kind to her these last three years, and the opportunity to help the dear invalid was a welcome escape from the rigid discipline of convent life. A frown crossed Simone's pretty face as she realized how deeply shocked madame would be should she learn of her adventure. Madame Felice must never discover Simone's secret self.

The room in which the girl now stood was small, but the furnishings were of excellent quality. It was in marked contrast to the bare cell she had shared with Aimee at the convent. And more than the rich appointments, she valued the privacy it afforded. For though her room immediately adjoined that of Madame Felice, many were the uninterrupted hours she could call her own. As Simone slowly removed her gypsy costume, her hands lingered over the bright fabric of her skirt, and her eyes held a wistful expression. How delightful it would be to keep tomorrow's appointment and live the gypsy life but one more time. Even to see his face from some hidden vantage point when I didn't appear, she mused, might be almost as satisfying. She moved toward the cheval mirror and looked innocently at her own body. Simone was intrigued by her image now that she had reached womanhood. She had no real idea of the standards which measured beauty in a woman. She knew that she was not ugly, yet she believed herself not especially pretty. Simone's hand moved to touch the mole above the nipple of her right breast. A beauty mark, some would have called it; Simone doubted its beauty. She cupped her breast and felt its firmness. The nipple grew taut. In the dim light of her room her pale olive skin took on the luster of antique ivory, and the virgin down between her legs shone darkly.

Simone knew little of the secret couplings of men and women. Closing her thickly fringed eyelids, she wondered what loving a man would be like. Her head fell back as though in a trance.

Without warning, a light knock on the door broke the spell. Before Simone could completely close her hastily donned wrapper, Maurice Durand entered the room. He did not fill the doorway, for he was a man of slight build. His curly brown hair tumbled over eyes that drank hungrily of Simone's young body, watching as she clutched at the opening of her wrapper. A lascivious smile curled about his thin lips. He had begun to perspire under the satin folds of his costume.

Simone had never liked the foppish Maurice, who had always made her feel inferior in the Durand household. Now recovering, she hissed angrily, "What are you doing here, Maurice? Why are you not at the Comus ball?"

Ignoring her indignant query, Maurice ventured nearer, and loosely fingered one raven lock which had fallen carelessly over her breast. His breathing quickened subtly as he whispered, "My dear Simone, I do not know which I find more pleasing—your present charming dishabille, or the gypsy garb."

"What do you mean, Maurice?" she said, his words chilling her heart.

"Do not be obtuse, my pet. Did you think a mere costume could hide your wild beauty? You were easy to discover from my perch atop the float. I am sure Grand-mère would be most interested in the escapades of her little nurse."

Her emotions barely in check, Simone voiced her deepest fear, "So you plan to tell madame."

Maurice smiled as he laconically reached inside the wrapper and pinched the rosebud that was a nipple. "Mais non, ma chère, I think we can make certain arrangements so that Grand-mère need never know."

Recklessly, Simone struck Maurice sharply across the face, all thought of possible consequences driven from her mind. Cruelly clutching her wrist, he spoke in icy tones, "Have you forgotten who I am, and who you are?" Before Simone could make a reply, he inexplicably released her wrist. And running a thin finger across her tremulous lower lip he whispered, "But I am a forgiving and patient man, ma petite, we shall speak more of this later." With a wicked smile he crossed the room and was gone.

Grasping the brass bedpost, Simone pressed her feverish cheek against the cold, smooth surface. If this is what it means to be with a man, I want no part of it. And yet with the stranger, it had been somehow different.

~ *Chapter 2* ~

Rudolph Nikolaivich Balenkov stood in the Bourbon Suite of the St. Louis Hotel awaiting Alexis's arrival.

It would be good to see his friend again, he mused. Idly, he glanced around the room, his alert, gray eyes taking in the sumptuous surroundings. Even by the standards of the Imperial Court, the room was impressive. The French Creoles had certainly never forgotten their heritage. Tracing one finger across the back of a chair, Rudolph noted the damask rose pattern bursting forth from the fabric which stretched across its delicate curves. The design must have - been a favorite of the Court of Louis XIV, he thought, for it also bloomed profusely on a matching chair and settee.

A large, pastel-hued carpet covered the highly polished oaken floor, and seemed to give an openness to a room threatened by too much gilt. It seemed like a woman's room, Rudolph thought as he walked to the heavily draped windows and looked down into the street. And yet, how well such opulence suited Alexis! A soft smile curved upon Rudolph's lips as his gaze moved across the room to a painting of satyrs and wood nymphs frolicking in a glade. Very appropriate! Certainly the duke's reputation had preceded him. As if conjured up by these musings, Alexis himself appeared in the room.

"Ah, Rudi, my old friend, how good it is to see you again! It has been too long!" cried the duke. In two quick strides Alexis had crossed the room and embraced the taller man in an affectionate, bearlike hug.

A deep chuckle escaped Rudolph's throat. "Come now, Alexis, the day has not dawned that you would pine for any but a lusty wench."

It was now Alexis's turn to laugh. "I surmise that you have been apprised of my latest romantic escapades, Rudya."

"I could hardly fail to take note of them, Alexis, since those adventures have most recently led me from New York to New Orleans. Indeed, only our friendship, and the command of your brother Crown Prince Alexander could have induced me to cross the Atlantic with my ship at this time of the year."

"My brother!" said Alexis, his tone at once becoming more serious.

"Yes, I have a letter from Prince Alexander which he instructed me to deliver personally." With this, Rudolph reached into his uniform, withdrawing an envelope affixed with the royal seal.

Taking the letter from his friend, Alexis broke the seal. Unfolding the parchment, he rapidly scanned its contents. Finishing, Alexis glanced up as Rudolph queried, "Any problems, my friend?"

"Nothing which requires my immediate attention. In fact, your transatlantic journey was indeed unnecessary. My brother is quite impulsive."

"Don't apologize; we have been friends far too long to bother with explanations," answered Rudolph.

"Ah yes, my friend, what good times we have shared and can still share. Your trip need not be in vain. New Orleans is filled with beautiful, loving women awaiting two such cavaliers as we."

Rudolph laughed at this term, *cavalier,* as applied to himself, and said, "So it is true that the beautiful Lydia Thompson no longer intrigues you."

"Not so, dear Rudya, but Lydia is not the only flower that blooms in the garden of amour."

At Alexis's words, an image of the wild gypsy flooded Rudolph's mind, and a smile came unbidden to his lips.

This softening of his countenance did not go unnoticed by the astute Alexis. "I see you have already encountered at least one blossom," he said.

His thoughts broken by Alexis's quip, Rudolph replied, "Not a blossom, Alexis—more the elusive firefly."

Alexis's face became quizzical, one eyebrow arching upward at this uncharacteristic remark. Rudolph had never before spoken so poetically or introspectively about women. In fact, it had always seemed to Alexis that Rudolph was almost cynical in his treatment of the fairer sex. Certainly all outward signs pointed to the fact that women filled only a physical need for Rudolph. Could some wench have succeeded in penetrating that iron control which had characterized his friend since their university days? Ever the student of human nature, the probing Alexis asked pointedly, "Who is she, Rudi?"

Laughing, Rudolph answered, "I don't know, Alexis. Only a beautiful gypsy maiden who promised to tell my fortune. I spied her among the revelers last evening."

"I have never known you to play hound to the fox before; ever have you been the pursued. But the hour grows late, let me not keep you from your destiny. Fly to your gypsy maiden!"

"Alexis, you are making too much of this. Unfortunately, I must return very soon to Russia. Let us enjoy each other's company before I depart."

"Russia—so soon?" questioned the duke.

"Yes, unless Pavel completely usurp my position with our uncle."

"Pavel, ah yes, Pavel. The dark cousin who plays so well the jackal to your lion. You must not let him proceed unchecked. As for our being together, there will be time enough this evening. I am to accompany Monsieur Georges Toussaint to supper at the home of one of the city's prominent Creole families—and you shall come as my guest."

Leaving the St. Louis Hotel, Rudolph stepped into the bright sunshine of a crisp, late winter's day. Breathing deeply, he walked briskly toward the Rue St. Anne and Madame Ninon's. How different New Orleans was from St. Petersburg. This city was young, vibrant, lusty, yet she wore well many of the old traditions of her French and Spanish heritage. As he glanced up at the lacy balconies making interesting patterns against the sky, Rudolph thought how like the city was the gypsy—so alive, so unpretentious, yet . . . He pulled himself away from his musings. He was no poet, and certainly no romanticist. Why was this city mesmerizing him?

Reaching Rue St. Anne, he looked about for someone who could direct him to Madame Ninon's establishment. A praline mammy stood not far away, hawking her delicious confections. As he approached, the sweet aroma of her pecan and coconut candies filled his nostrils.

"*Pardonnez-moi,* can you direct me to Madame Ninon's?"

A deep chuckle arose from her expansive bosom and split her broad black face into a grin. The grin remained, and twinkled in her eyes as she answered in her rich Creole patois, "You want that your fortune be told, m'sieur? Madame Ninon eez the one for you, all right. She lives but three blocks down. You will see *le crucifix noir* over the door."

Thanking her, Rudolph dropped a coin into her basket and proceeded toward the house. Upon reaching his destination, he noted the small, well-kept structure. Except for the black cross dominating the threshold, there was nothing sinister about the house. Like the other residences on the street, it stood flush with the cobblestone banquette, its brick facade broken by shutters and a heavy cypress door.

Rudolph knocked. After a few moments the door was opened by a young, lanky Negro boy, a bright cloth, wrapped turban fashion, about his head.

"Is your mistress in?" inquired Rudolph.

Without a word the boy closed the door. Almost immediately it was reopened. Standing before him was a woman of late middle age, her unlined bronze skin and high cheekbones betraying her *os rouge* heritage. Madame Ninon was only half black. Her mother was a full-blooded Choctaw Indian who had left her tribe near Bayou Lacombe to marry a free Haitian black.

Breaking the silence, Rudolph ventured, "Madame, I was to meet your gypsy girl here this morning. She is to tell my fortune."

"My gypsy girl? No gypsy girl lives here. It is just me and

the boy. But I will gladly tell your fortune, m'sieur. No one sees the future more clearly than Madame Ninon."

As the fortune-teller spoke, Rudolph realized that he had been played for a fool. What more should he have expected, especially from one of her kind. Always he found women to be weak like the mother he had hardly known, or ruthless like the aunt he knew too well.

Feeling Madame Ninon's penetrating gaze upon him, he was drawn back to the present. He thanked her for her time and turned to leave. This whole incident was becoming boring and rather tiresome.

"You do not wish Madame Ninon to throw the bones for you, m'sieur? I feel they will say much good for you."

Intrigued by her words, and with a rare free afternoon before him, Rudolph acquiesced, and was led through a front parlor into a second darkened room. Coming in from the bright sunshine, it was a moment before his eyes could adjust to the gloom imposed by the heavily shuttered windows. The room was filled with a pungent odor, an aroma Rudolph had never before experienced; its cloying essence repulsed him.

Sauntering easily into the chamber, the Negro youth began to light the black candles of a low-hanging chandelier. The candlelight showed the room to be sparsely furnished. A heavily draped circular table surrounded by four straight, austere chairs were the only real furnishings. A small cabinet held a curious collection of things which Rudolph surmised were some of the elements of the fortune-teller's trade. The walls were whitewashed, and bare as old bones except for a picture of *le sacré coeur* surrounded with aged palm fronds. The Jesus image at first seemed no different than those Rudolph had seen depicted in many Russian icons. Upon closer inspection, however, he was somewhat shocked by the incongruity of the inverted position of Christ's heart. Rudolph began to feel ridiculous in such surroundings. He was ever the man to deal only in reality, yet the fine blond hairs at the nape of his neck had involuntarily risen.

Madame Ninon quietly asked Rudolph to be seated. At this the boy surreptitiously departed, and the two were enclosed alone within the circle of candlelight. Reaching into the folds of her red apron, madame pulled forth a black

leather case. With one swift motion she unfastened the
restraining ties and flung forth an array of bones. In the
flickering light the skeletal pattern played curiously upon
the inky cloth of the table. The bones spoke in the
mysterious language of the voodoo arts. As she sat completely mesmerized by their silent message, Rudolph sensed
that the medium had momentarily forgotten his presence.

After a time, a soft moan issued from Madame Ninon's
throat, and though her eyes remained glazed and unseeing,
she began a soft chant. The words, incomprehensible at
first, became clearer; in spite of himself, Rudolph moved
closer in order that he might better hear them.

> "... Rudolph Nikolaivich Balenkov, you are
> a great man, yet to become a greater man. You
> will be a man of vast wealth and hold
> cherished lands. And love will come to you,
> the love of a highborn woman. Yet I see many
> trials before you. I see two—the light and the
> dark. The light and the dark are one. Yet
> 'darkness in the light' shall triumph.''

With this, Madame Ninon's eyes slowly closed. When
they reopened it was to see the unmoved face of her
observer. His calm demeanor belied the fact that Rudolph
had been startled by her use of his name and baffled by her
strange allusions to light and dark. Cynically, he discounted
her prophecy of wealth and marriage in view of the present
uncertainty of his inheritance. Certainly Pavel might be the
undoing of such a future.

Brusquely, Rudolph rose, bringing the bizarre encounter
to a close. Following his lead, Madame Ninon stood, and
was opening her mouth to speak when Rudolph abruptly
thrust several gold coins upon the table.

Affronted by his manner, Madame pushed the glittering
pieces away with a fanning motion of her long, thin fingers.
"M'sieur, your gold I do not want. My stories are for those
who see with the eyes of children. I sense you do not
believe. I cannot accept that which I have not earned. Go
and make your own future.''

Knowing that he had been dismissed, Rudolph left,
tossing a coin to the Negro youth who opened the door for

him. The bright sunlight and cold air presented a refreshing relief to the oppressive atmosphere of the fortune-teller's salon. Rudolph walked on. Above the steel-gray eyes, furrows formed in the high forehead. Unwittingly, Rudolph felt unnerved. Hailing a carriage, he barked instructions to the driver to proceed to the Townsend Mansion on Basin Street.

Kate Townsend was the gregarious and lusty proprietress of the most luxurious brothel in New Orleans. Her fame spanned two continents. She was the darling of the aristocracy who sought forbidden amusement in the arms of some of the most beautiful women in New Orleans. And Kate's girls were refined—educated in the arts of pleasing even the most discriminating male. This tone of refinement, however, did not extend to the decor, which though costly, could hardly be called genteel. Kate's room was the showplace of the establishment, although few patrons were privileged to cross its threshold. The remainder of the three-story marble and brownstone mansion, however, suffered little in comparison. Each room held a white marble fireplace, and the flames were reflected in polished black walnut floors. Most of the furnishings were upholstered in ornate, red damask, and the windows were shrouded in heavily tasseled drapes. Mirrors gleamed on every wall, and a profusion of plate glass abounded. Ormolu clocks chimed the quarter hour, and cupids smiled slyly from gilded cornices. Even the chamber pots were lined in gold.

The drive through the French Quarter was swiftly accomplished, and now Rudolph tugged at the bellpull of the bagnio. The beveled edges of the leaded-glass doors caught the early afternoon sunlight. The door opened, and a small, neatly uniformed Negress appeared. A somewhat astonished look crossed her brown face as she surveyed the tall, uniformed figure who towered over her. She was about to inform him that gentlemen were not welcomed before eight o'clock in the evening, but the regality of his demeanor and the assurance in his handsome face quickly forced her into the house to seek out her mistress. After a short time, the maid returned and ushered him into an elaborately appointed anteroom. Seated on a gold brocade settee was the famous Kate herself.

"Come closer, m'sieur. I would see the man who can put my dignified Sarah into such a tizzy."

A half smile pulled at his lips as he crossed the room. He stood before her, legs apart, arms folded across his chest.

Kate was eighteen when she arrived in New Orleans. She was reputed to have been extremely pretty, and the most popular harlot of her day. Now at thirty-three her once fine figure could only be described as overripe, and one suspected that time would not deal gently with her. Rudolph's appraisal, however, went beyond her physical appearance. He was drawn to the charming, yet shrewd personality that was revealed in her candid smile.

Kate's eyes were dazzled by one of the most magnificent men she had ever seen. The trim cut of his uniform only enhanced his maleness. His broad chest rose above firm muscled thighs, which were clearly defined in tightly fitting breeches. His face was angular, and there was nothing of softness in it, except perhaps for the mouth, which was slightly full and sensuous. The eyes were gray, almost clear, and they were so penetrating that Kate thought she must be blushing—something she had not done since before her dance-hall days in Liverpool. This man was a lion, she thought, an untamed lion. She liked him immediately.

"I begin to perceive why you so unnerved my Sarah, m'sieur . . . ?"

"Rudolph Nikolaivich Balenkov, Madame Townsend. I am sorry to intrude upon your privacy at this hour, but I shall not be long in New Orleans, and thought it unseemly to depart without partaking of the renowned pleasures of your illustrious home."

"Let it not be said that Kate Townsend violated the Creole code of hospitality." Motioning him to be seated, Kate herself rose and retrieved paper and pen from a brightly hand-painted desk. Scribbling a hasty note, she rang for Sarah, who appeared almost instantly. After receiving softly murmured instructions, the maid exited.

"Share a glass of wine with me, m'sieur," said Kate, as she poured the ruby liquid from a fine crystal decanter. Without speaking, Rudolph reached for the proffered glass and sampled the wine appreciatively. Before he had finished, Sarah had reappeared. Her whispered words met with Madame's approval. Turning to her guest, she said, "M'sieur Balenkov, if you will follow Sarah, I feel that you will find that the reputation of my house is not without foundation."

With a slight bow to Madame Townsend, Rudolph followed Sarah up velvet-carpeted stairs to the second floor. She led him to the room at the end of the hall and vanished.

Rudolph slowly opened the door. He found himself in a pink cloud of a room. Organdy curtains hung from the canopy of the huge four-poster bed that dominated the chamber. The windows were swathed in rose-colored organdy and damask. A slight movement behind him caught his attention. He turned to behold a titian-haired nymph who stood near the marble fireplace. Wrapped only in a fringed shawl emblazoned with cabbage roses of pink and mauve, she appeared a rosy Venus. Dropping the shawl, she walked gracefully toward him. Her body was lithe and supple. The flames of the warming fire had imparted a faint blush to the porcelain skin. As she came before him, she turned her delicately featured face upward. Cornflower blue eyes looked appraisingly into Rudolph's, as she pressed her small pouting mouth up to his. Slowly Rudolph warmed to the pressure of her lips, and gently pried open the full mouth with his searching tongue. Untwining the slender arms from around his neck, he released her. Gazing intently into her eyes, he stood immobile. Expertly, the young girl unbuttoned his jacket and opened his shirt. Her soft fingers teased the golden down of his chest; she ran a pink tongue across one nipple. He led her hands to the waistband of his breeches. Suddenly kneeling, she slipped the pants downward over the tensed muscular thighs. A thin white scar shone livid against the bronze skin below his abdomen. Slowly, she traced a finger across the mark and gently caressed his now quickened manhood. Impatiently Rudolph drew her up. Quickly, he finished undressing and carried her to the bed. Dropping her onto a mélange of cushions, Rudolph lowered his body over hers. His strong fingers coiled into the masses of her hair, causing the tresses to fall down across her milky breasts. Roughly brushing the concealing locks away, he savagely bit into one rouged nipple. A small cry that was more of pleasure than of pain escaped her lips. Iron fingers kneaded the flesh of her young body as if he sought to mold her into some image of his own. His hand desperately sought the soft mound between her slim thighs. She thrust her body upward, feeling wave after wave of warm liquid passion. Suddenly he drew away, his face contorted by some overpowering emotion. His lips stretched tightly across his white teeth, his eyes darkened dangerously. Viselike, his fingers gripped her quivering shoulders and turned her abruptly onto her stomach. Ignoring her cries, he entered her in a way she had hoped no man ever would. His powerful thrusts culminated in his cry of pure anguish.

~ *Chapter 3* ~

The evening was cool and clear. A full moon bathed the Vieux Carré in silvery illumination as the carriage bearing the Durands' guests for the evening pulled before the Rue Royal residence.

Simone, who was perched upon the window seat in Madame Felice's room, began hurriedly unfastening the latch which held the shutters.

"Simone, it is cold. Why do you open the window?" Madame Felice gently scolded as she drew her shawl more tightly about her shoulders.

"*Pardon,* madame, *un moment;* I must see the royal guests," explained the girl. "The servants have chattered of nothing else the entire day," she continued, as she leaned forward for a better view. The carriage door opened, and Simone recognized Monsieur Toussaint, a frequent visitor to the Durand household, as he stepped onto the banquette. Following him was a uniformed figure who turned abruptly and held open the door as the magnificently clothed Duke Alexis alighted. Never before had Simone beheld such splendor. Not even Comus in all his regalia cut a more dashing figure than the blond, mustachioed duke. Unconsciously, Simone's attention was drawn to the man closing the carriage door. As he turned, the moonlight touched his face. A gasp of recognition issued from her lips.

"Petite, is something wrong?" queried Madame Felice.

"No, madame," answered Simone as she mechanically refastened the shutters.

Downstairs, after brief introductions had been exchanged, the family and their guests proceeded to the parlor. Pouring wine into crystal glasses, Monsieur Durand spoke, "Your Highness, how do you like New Orleans and the Mardi Gras?"

"I find both quite charming," responded the diplomatic Alexis, noting that this reply obviously pleased his host.

Armand Durand was an aristocrat of Creole extraction, an attorney who took more pride in his reputation as a breeder of the finest gamecocks in the South, than in any of his other accomplishments. The ravages of Reconstruction had touched him less than most of the members of his class. Unlike the majority of their contemporaries, the family had not bound its fortune exclusively to King Cotton. The Durand family had always had extensive holdings abroad; over the years, Armand had tampered little with these profitable enterprises. Typical of most Creoles, the genial and portly Armand was imbued with a joie de vivre, and little in life troubled him overlong. Characteristically, his family was the center of his life; he was an indulgent husband and a doting father.

Accepting his claret, Georges Toussaint added gallantly, "If the duke loved New Orleans and the Mardi Gras, they loved him no less in return. With your presence, the carnival has truly been a success."

"Oui," affirmed Maurice, "the Mardi Gras can only gain in magnificence from the blending of Russian nobility and Creole aristocracy. Do you not agree, Your Highness?"

The duke, who had ignored most of the ostentatious speeches in which the status-conscious Creoles had sought to involve him, parried, "My dear sir, I feel you have made far too much of my presence at your Mardi Gras."

At this the petulant Maurice fell silent. He remembered that the duke had quoted from the Declaration of Independence, and had insisted on standing with the other parade goers instead of occupying the thronelike chair prepared for him. The duke certainly fell short of Maurice's expectations of nobility.

Breaking the strained silence, Yvette began timidly, "M'sieur Balenkov, how does our New Orleans compare with your St. Petersburg?"

Rudolph politely answered, "They are quite different, mademoiselle. A comparison would be most unfair."

Feeling somewhat rebuffed by this noncommittal reply, the pretty Yvette subsided. How different this man was from the Creole gallants who filled her busy life. The very picture of femininity, with soft blond curls framing lively blue eyes, Yvette was unaccustomed to such aloofness in a male. His lack of social art was in stark contrast to the gay banter which characterized Creole life. Unaccountably, she was not repelled by his coolness. How this man attracted her!

Yvette's contemplations were interrupted by the appearance of Moses, the butler, who announced that supper was being served.

As the group proceeded to the dining room, Madame Cecile Durand turned to the duke, "Your Highness, I must apologize for the paucity of the fare this evening. It is Ash Wednesday, and I'm afraid that the sacrifices of the Lenten season are upon us."

"Please, Madame Durand, no apologies are necessary. We, too, have our Lenten customs in Russia."

"We must also offer our regrets that my mother is unable to join us this evening," added Armand. "She has been unable to walk these many years due to an accident. She dines in her room with her young companion, as is her custom, but she extends a most warm welcome to you."

"Please convey my best wishes to your dear mother, and thank her for the graciousness of her hospitality," replied the duke.

After everyone was seated, supper began with bowls of steaming gumbo over fluffy rice. The pungent brew, redolent of filé and other spices, contained a variety of Louisiana seafood. This course was followed by a salad vinaigrette of winter vegetables fresh from the city's market. The entrée was pompano *en papillote,* fish from the nearby Gulf artfully prepared in oiled brown paper by the Durands' competent Negro cook. Served with this was baked eggplant in a smooth cheese sauce. A light white wine of excellent vintage accompanied the meal. Over a dessert of *baba au rhum,* the conversation, which had been somewhat desultory throughout dinner, became livelier, with the tempestuous politics of Reconstruction dominating the greater part of the dialogue.

Politely interrupting, Madame Cecile offered, "Gentlemen, can we not talk of more pleasant topics? I find local politics most distressing." Directing her attention to Rudolph, she asked, "And what of your family, M'sieur Balenkov? Are you married? Have you children?"

Quite suddenly, Rudolph had become the center of attention. Alexis looked intently across the table at his good friend. He was interested to see the effect Cecile Durand's words would have upon him. One other at the table waited anxiously for the reply. Yvette peered obliquely at the Russian from under lowered eyelids.

"My parents are dead. I am unmarried," answered Rudolph.

Disconcerted by his terse rejoinder, Madame Durand began nervously to finger the lace border of her napkin.

Almost immediately, Rudolph felt remorse for the curtness of his answer. How easily wounded she was, he thought. And how like his mother.

Armand Durand broke the awkward silence, suggesting that the gentlemen retire to the parlor for brandy and cigars. Tactfully, the women excused themselves and bid their guests adieu. Cecile Durand graciously proffered her hospitality to the duke and his guest for the duration of their visit.

In the parlor, the conversation swiftly turned to male interests. Easily, M'sieur Durand veered the talk in the direction of his favorite topic—cock fighting.

Alexis had always been fascinated by games of chance, and relishing a new challenge to his betting skills, he expressed great interest in the subject.

"Would you care to see my prize cocks tomorrow, Your Highness?" inquired Armand, eager to show off his champions. "My plantation is near the city, and it is only a short journey on horseback."

"What a pity," replied the duke sincerely. "I have many appointments tomorrow that require my personal attention.

It is a most kind offer. Perhaps Rudolph will accept your hospitality."

Maurice, ever ready to play the role of gracious landholder, offered, "I will be most honored to show M'sieur Balenkov our prize gaming cocks, mon Père."

"Splendid! Rudi, you must go!" cried the duke.

His face showing no emotion, Rudolph impassively accepted Maurice's invitation.

The details of the morrow's country excursion were quickly settled, and the guests bid their host good night.

All evening, Simone had kept company with Madame Felice, often reading aloud from Francois Rene's *Atala*. Her lips formed the words, but her thoughts were elsewhere. She regarded the advent of the arrogant stranger into the Durand household with ambivalent emotions. Most obviously he posed a threat in that he could reveal her Mardi Gras escapade. On a deeper level, conflicting feelings plagued her. She knew she disliked this conceited man, but she also longed to see him once again. He was something exciting to Simone, and excitement was the thing most lacking in her often drab existence. She was relieved when madame had finally nodded off to sleep and she could retire to her own room. Her perceptive mistress had apparently sensed her discomfiture, and Simone was grateful for the reprieve. No sooner had she reached the haven of her bedroom than an eager knock sounded on the door. Without waiting for permission, Yvette entered the room.

"Oh, Simone, what a night it has been! If only you could have been there." As the impetuous girl rambled on about their royal guests, Simone once again reflected on the blank spaces in her life. Having no identity, she was forever condemned to the role of outsider. She fit in nowhere. Yvette's next words, however, abruptly ended her reverie.

". . . and the duke's handsome friend, he is so cold, and yet . . . Oh Simone, he intrigues me. So tall and unfeeling, like some Greek statue. Only his eyes seemed alive, their color constantly changing. The duke introduced him as his closest friend. Rudolph Nikolaivich Balenkov is a captain in the Royal Russian Navy. And, Simone, he is from a noble family too! Oh, I do hope I see him again."

As Yvette chattered on, Simone decided that she, too, would like to see Rudolph Nikolaivich Balenkov once again. What fun it would be to fool nobility. After all, she thought, he doesn't know who I am. Could the gypsy live again?

~ *Chapter 4* ~

The River Road stood bathed in golden sunlight on this crisp, late winter's morning. Flanking the narrow dirt highway which ran north to the capital at Baton Rouge were high rolling levees. These levees seemed as innocent hills challenging the idle stroller to climb their dewy slopes. What a panorama would greet him as he reached their pinnacle! For below the grassy incline lay the fabled Mississippi stretching and curving sensuously as it lapped hungrily at the embankment.

The high levees gave clear evidence that New Orleans and much of southern Louisiana lay precariously below the level of the sea. These mounds, not unlike the dikes of the Netherlands, afforded the area protection against the often turbulent weather rising from the nearby Gulf. The destiny of New Orleans was bound inextricably to the water.

Across the roadway, the ancient bearded oaks watched in stately silence as two horsemen cantered leisurely down the path. The flashing hoofs of their spirited mounts churned the dust, filling the still air with billowing clouds.

The voice of Maurice Durand sounded above the soft clopping of the horses. "M'sieur Balenkov, as you can see, the South is not so uncivilized as some critics may report. We, too, have our estates. Our plantations, I am told, are not unlike the great manors of Europe." Pointing to a neoclassic structure, its Doric columns partially obscured by arching oaks, Maurice continued. "There stands Columbine, the home of M'sieur and Madame Lucien Rousseau, our close friends and neighbors."

Since no response was forthcoming from his traveling companion, the remainder of the journey was passed in silence. As he followed Maurice's abrupt turn into an intersecting lane, Rudolph was surprised by a sight for which he had been totally unprepared, in spite of the younger man's pontifications. The carriage drive was lined on either side with magnificent oaks, whose intertwining branches embraced in Gothic arches. Sunlight filtered through the leafy canopy overhead, dappling the flanks of the steeds, who, sensing the nearness of a warm stable and a bag of oats, now quickened their pace.

The plantation lay ahead—stark, white, pristine. If the land was the essence and soul of a family, then a home such as this was its purest material expression. Rudolph could at least understand Maurice's pride. Did he not feel the same for his land, his home?

"Welcome to La Rochelle," exclaimed Maurice.

As they dismounted, a small Negro boy ran hurriedly to retrieve their reins, his eyes widening as he took in the tall, uniformed stranger. Noticing his obvious curiosity, the Russian smiled at the gawking youngster, who acknowledged this friendly gesture with a flash of white teeth.

"Bo, what are you doing standing around? Can't you see those horses are in a lather?"

"Yassuh, Massah Moreese," drawled Bo, shuffling off toward the stables.

Facing Rudolph, Maurice noted sarcastically, "Thanks to Mr. Lincoln, it's harder than ever to get things done properly. But enough of this. Come, let us go in and refresh ourselves."

As they crossed the portico and reached the massive door, it opened unexpectedly. Filling the opening from side to side stood an expanse of black bombazine and starched white cotton. Alma's ready smile broke the polished ebony of her face. If not for their bright sparkle, her eyes would have been lost behind her prominent cheeks.

"Well, if you ain't a sight for sore eyes, boy! Yo must be wantin' sumptin' to come way out heah and leave all yo prissy city friens behind, Mastah Maurice."

Before the discomfitted Maurice could venture a suitable retort to this singular tirade, the woman's attention fell on an inwardly amused Rudolph. "And who be this fine gentleman? I ain't nevah seen the likes of such a tall man in all ma born days."

"Rudolph Nikolaivich Balenkov at your service, ma'am," he announced, smiling and inclining his head.

"Lawsy me, what a name! You sounds important. You all come in and let my Joseph fix you up a hot toddy."

The foyer in which Rudolph found himself only emphasized the simplicity which crowned the home's exterior. The cypress floors were golden-brown mirrors, and the pleasant odor of beeswax attested to their constant care. An oaken staircase spiraled upward about a crystal chandelier, its rainbow prisms creating complex patterns on the oriental carpet. A gallery of French ancestors watched from their lofty heights as Rudolph moved into the parlor. In contrast to these dark and staid visages, the focal point of this room was a large portrait of a woman whose vital beauty seemed to infuse the very atmosphere with life. She was a delicate creature, yet behind her virginal beauty one could sense a shrewd intelligence, the pale blue eyes seeming to appraise one from their canvas depths.

"So you have noticed Madame Felice Durand," declared Maurice, observing Rudolph's absorption. "It is a lovely painting, is it not? It was a wedding gift to my grand-père. *Quelle dommage!* What a pity you were unable to meet her. Since her unfortunate riding accident many years ago, she rarely sees anyone except family, and of course, her young companion, Simone. She was carrying her second child at the time. My father has always regretted his lack of brothers and sisters."

"She is indeed a lovely woman; she seems to belong here," noted Rudolph.

"She does, indeed! La Rochelle was her family home. However, my father wishes that she be with us, and as he prefers life in the city to the role of country squire, for most of the year, we reside in town. In the summer La Rochelle is a refreshing haven, and unequaled for entertaining."

Joseph, bearing a tray with two steaming mugs, entered the room. He was tall and erect. The grizzled head spoke honestly of his many years, and his face was a tracework of lines defining his noble character. He was a product of the old South, the faithful black who had served a good master well. As many treasured house slaves throughout the South,

Alma and Joseph were integral parts of the Durand family, and there was mutual respect and love between master and servant.

"Thank you, Joseph, that will be all," said Maurice, dismissing the butler.

Rudolph sampled the heated brew appreciatively, and commented on its unique flavor. Maurice explained that the heady concoction was Joseph's winter specialty. In the summer his talents with bourbon produced an unparalleled mint julep.

Warmed by the drinks, the two men stepped outdoors and walked toward the pens which were at some distance behind the home.

"The house is only one part of a working plantation. Sugar cane is our principal crop, though many acres are still planted in cotton," intoned the young Durand.

"It would seem that your family was spared much of the hardships of your recent war," commented Rudolph, his attention engaged by this talk of land.

"Yes," agreed Maurice, "as did many of our friends. Thankfully, New Orleans escaped the tragic fate of many of her sister cities."

Shrill crowing alerted the two that their destination had been reached. The birds were noisy, high-strung creatures who strutted nervously about their individual enclosures. At the pair's approach, Isaac, the handler and trainer, greeted them, and proceeded to feed his restive charges.

"These birds, like fine thoroughbreds, are raised for one purpose only. The horses to run, the cocks to fight," declaimed Maurice, as preamble to a detailed pedigree of his father's champions. "A combination of English and French lines has been carefully interbred with local stock to produce a bird with compact body, long, prominently spurred legs, and an indomitable fighting spirit." Expounding on the long history of the sport in New Orleans, Maurice grabbed one of the feisty roosters, pinning its flapping raven wings to its body and turning its leg upward to display the lethal spurs. He called to Isaac to bring out the metal spikes worn by the bird over his own natural armament when in mortal combat. Receiving the sharp device, Maurice began to run one slim finger down the barbed instrument, and delicately stroked its wicked point. Caressing it, he spoke almost feverishly of the thrill of seeing the birds charge, propelling their streamlined bodies into the air, their flailing legs attempting to score a deadly strike. As he spoke, Rudolph noticed with distaste that Maurice's face had flushed slightly, his unfocused eyes had glazed, and a thin line of perspiration moistened his upper lip. Clearly this bestial duel to the death was more than a game of chance to this pretentious fop.

Recovering, Maurice resumed his explanations in a more controlled manner. He gave Rudolph an exhaustive discourse on cockfighting, including a detailed description of the betting procedures.

"My father is eager to learn of your impression of his birds, and would like you to accompany us to a match tomorrow, so that you can experience the sport firsthand," concluded Maurice.

"Unfortunately, I must leave New Orleans very early in the morning. I regret that my sojourn in your city has been so brief. I hope to return some day."

Maurice, desiring to exploit his acquaintance with the Russian to its fullest, had planned to play gracious host and parade Rudolph before his fun-loving friends. Crestfallen at first, Maurice countered, "Oh, but surely you can spend one more evening with us. You must dine at my home tonight; my father would insist."

Although Rudolph would have preferred more stimulating diversions on his last night in the Vieux Carré, good breeding dictated his courteous acceptance of the kind invitation to dine.

Since the subject of cockfighting was not considered a suitable topic for feminine sensibilities, the men had spent a comfortable hour in the drawing room before dinner, discussing the sport at length over Madeira and cigars. Armand had expressed his particular disappointment that his guest would be unable to see his beauties in action. Rudolph promised that, should he return to New Orleans in the future, he would be delighted to attend a match.

Madame Durand and Yvette appeared promptly as the clock in the parlor chimed the accustomed dinner hour. In the Creole tradition, the women, as on the previous evening, were elegantly dressed. Madame Durand wore a claret-colored velvet gown, which stood in vivid contrast to

her alabaster skin. Ecru lace bordered the décolletage and
the trimmed puff sleeves which fell slightly below her white
shoulders. The tight-fitting bodice gave way to yards and
yards of velvet skirting, which was scalloped at the bottom
to reveal ecru lace between moss green rosettes. Yvette's
gown, however, proclaimed her passion for the newer
Parisian mode of dress—she had forsaken the hoop for the
bustle. She wore an ensemble of ice-blue silk consisting of a
skirt and tunic, the latter cleverly caught up in back to form
the bustle. The front was draped in soft folds over the
flowing pannier. Ruching in the court style of Louis XVI
accentuated the lines of the elaborate garment.

Rising at the entrance of this elegant pair, Armand
tucked his wife's arm in his, saying, "Shall we dine?"

With good grace, Rudolph offered his arm to a beaming
Yvette, as the company moved to the dining room.

Conversation around the table was of a more relaxed and
genial nature than on the previous night. Their Russian
guest, if not totally animated, seemed somewhat less taci-
turn to the gregarious Durands.

The sounds of male and female voices drifted up to the
small figure huddled in the shadows of the second floor
landing. She had listened intently, especially concentrating
on the comments made by the foreigner. Simone knew it
was childish to eavesdrop, but her compulsion to live
vicariously was strong. How surprised the arrogant Russian
would be to see her there. Surely the shock of seeing the
wild gypsy in the Durand household would arouse some
emotion in that smug face. Straining again to catch the
murmurings of the conversation, she idly stroked one raven
plait. As if mesmerized, she began slowly to unbraid her
hair, softly fingering its silkiness. The glorious mane fell full
across her shoulders and breasts, a soft smile played upon
her lips, and her black eyes danced in anticipation.

As the Durands and their guest dined, the capricious New
Orleans weather changed. The clear crispness of the day
gave way to a murky night whose gusting breezes blew
balmy from the Gulf. Dark clouds like black galleons
scudded before the full moon. There was a promise of rain
in the air; one could almost smell the moisture. The
fountain babbled monotonously, and the ripening fragrance
of the first camellias of the season spiced the wind.

Rudolph emerged into the courtyard, his thoughts entirely focused on preparations for his departure.

"Bonsoir, Monsieur Balenkov," sounded a musical voice in the shadows.

Turning toward the source of the unexpected greeting, he beheld a specter in the dimly lit recesses of the patio. The small figure was partially bathed in the cold light of the moon. The face seemed to radiate as the silver rays played upon its smooth planes. Long hair blew wildly about the milky shoulders, and a glimmer of gold, teased by a moonbeam, shone as she moved slightly in the half shadows. She seemed the embodiment of the earthy languor that had invaded the night. As he walked closer, the apparition resolved itself into the familiar figure of the gypsy.

"So it is you," Rudolph uttered, a bit too sharply.

His tone forced Simone to seek his eyes, wondering if their color betrayed his mood. She laughed nervously, but sauntered easily through the iron gates into the mellow glow of a gaslight. Rudolph slowly followed the girl into the street, her laugh unconsciously irritating him. Her use of his name had convinced him that she and the fortune-teller were, after all, allies. It clearly explained the voodoo woman's apparent clairvoyance. He ignored the question of how the gypsy had come to learn of it.

"Do you always fail to keep your appointments? I would think that would make for poor business," he said acidly.

"Do you not know we gypsies have a reputation for lying?" she toyed with the Russian.

His look held no humor. The gaslight clearly revealed the icy gray depths of his eyes. For the first time this evening, Simone began to ponder the possible consequences of her rash impersonation. Belatedly, she realized that this was not a man to play games with. She must soon regain the safety of the courtyard. Even as desperate plans for escape flitted through her mind, something within her sensed that it was already too late for vain regrets. The old Simone and her secluded life had been doomed when the gypsy had first taken fire within her.

Had the light been brighter, Simone would have realized that more than his eyes had undergone a transformation.

His body had become rigid, and the smooth muscles along his jawline contracted involuntarily. Rudolph had never enjoyed the inane banalities of courting, and teasing women such as this were meant for only one thing. Characteristically his anger and passion became one.

A scream died in Simone's throat as he lunged forward and cruelly assaulted her open mouth. He pressed her body against his, and she felt the rippling muscles of his chest and the urgent tightening in his loins. He twisted his face from side to side, bruising her lips with his tongue and his teeth. His fingers dug deeply into the soft flesh of her arms. She tried to fight his growing desire, but her movements only inflamed him the more. He seemed to be so hungry, so angry, so desperate. His fierce Mardi Gras embrace had been fervent, but this was a brutal attack. The small knot of fear which had been growing within her blossomed into terror. Overwhelmed by this paralyzing fear and some other emotion which she could not name, Simone lost consciousness.

Rudolph felt her grow limp in his arms. Slowly some measure of control returned. Hailing a passing carriage, he wrapped the insensate girl in his cloak.

～ *Chapter 5* ～

The dock was strangely quiet and peaceful. The crew had either bedded down early, or had not yet returned from one last evening of carousing on lusty Basin Street. Rudolph's arrival at the pier was observed by the lone sailor who stood sentry duty. If he noticed his commander's peculiar burden, he said nothing. The amorous adventures of a captain and a prince were not to be questioned by a simple Russian seaman.

Shifting Simone's weight to one side, Rudolph gingerly opened his cabin door. Walking over to the large bed, he casually relieved himself of his gypsy captive, releasing her onto the yielding cushions. Removing his jacket, he once more became the dispassionate observer. She was so petite, smaller than he had first realized. Although her body was fully ripened, Rudolph saw with some surprise that his gypsy was more of a girl than a woman. A fragmented image came to him, an engraving he had seen long ago in a children's book—an illustration of the sleeping princess who could be awakened only by a kiss. Her breathing was regular now, and her full breasts rose easily. She had been so frightened earlier; now she appeared like a child. Child, thought Rudolph, no child filled him with such feelings. As he watched, Rudolph began to experience the familiar, restless passion, and yet, in this passion there was no anger.

The laughing grew louder; it became a hideous cacophony raking her senses. It had all been so gay and beautiful—the carefree maskers in a long queue weaving sinuously through the narrow alleyways. Now it had all changed, the faces of the revelers growing grotesque and threatening. She ran, but their clamoring footfalls echoed after her.

"Oh Mother, oh Mother, help me!"

"I am here child," answered the gentle voice.

Turning quickly, Simone dashed into the comforting arms of Mother Superior. She felt the rosary pressed into her hand. "Thank you, Mother," she breathed, beginning her fervent Hail Marys. As she looked down at the beaded chain it began to writhe. It was a holy thing no more! The individual beads had fused into the segments of a hissing serpent which encircled her small arm. She screamed and flung the evil creature from her body. Suddenly the strains of a haunting melody filled the air, and she was propelled into the arms of a harlequin. It was a bal masqué, and they were participants in a hectic quadrille. As the frenzied dance mounted to its climax, she passed from partner to partner: a dazzling knight who bowed to her regally, a

swarthy gypsy who whispered, "Beware the lion!"
Finally, as the clock began to strike midnight, she found
herself in the arms of a tall soldier. It was time to
unmask! Gaily she pulled the concealing fabric from his
handsome face. "No, no!" she cried, as the countenance
of the arrogant Russian stood revealed!

Since the gypsy had proved so uncooperative in the past,
it was Rudolph's plan to undress her as quietly as possible
before she regained her senses. Surely when presented with
a fait accompli, the silly girl would stop her futile struggling
and welcome the prospect of a pleasant interlude in his
luxurious captain's quarters. Did not vagabond females find
such things romantic? Deftly, he unloosened the wide
cummerbund, and unfastening her skirt and petticoats,
expertly stripped them from her slim body. The peasant
blouse presented little problem, and he easily slipped it over
her head. As she lay revealed in her corselet and pantaloons, Rudolph marveled at her tiny waist and perfectly
rounded breasts. With her raven tresses tumbling carelessly
about the porcelain face, she looked like a doll impudently
discarded by some fickle child drawn to another fanciful
toy. The small mole above her right nipple fascinated him.
Lightly he stroked its surface, causing her breast to ripen
quickly. His mouth ached to kiss its tautness. Checking this
impulse, he began to pull at the laces of her corselet. It
released her easily. Anxiously, his hands sought the narrow
ribbon fastening her pantaloons. Pulling the waistband free,
and using the palms of his hands, Rudolph gently rolled the
fabric down her thighs. The flat abdomen begged for his
touch. Artfully, he ran his hand over its ivory contours. The
mound of shiny black hair between her legs was so soft to
the touch that Rudolph's breathing quickened at the promise of what sweetness lay within. Resisting his mounting
passion no longer, he lowered his face over hers. "No, no!"
she cried, as her eyes flew open, focusing full upon his face.
The steel-blue eyes pierced her consciousness. This was no
dream. This was real! At her unexpected outburst, his lips
curved into a cruel smile. She began to struggle, but his
large body covered hers, and his searching tongue softly
encircled the inner moistness of her mouth.

Unexpectedly, he casually drew back and stared intently
into her face. His gray eyes were almost transparent, and

their coldness evoked an unconscious quivering in her naked body.

"What's the matter, ma petite, do I frighten you? Or do you grow tired of your little game? Your fortune-telling abilities remain unproven, but perhaps, after all, your true talents lie in the art of love."

Enraged by his sarcasm, her temper momentarily overcame her fear of him, but, perversely, the angry words that sprang to her mind would not come forth. Like a frustrated child, she beat with tiny fists upon his broad chest. Laughing dryly at her impotent fury, Rudolph clutched the flailing arms and pinned them above her head. A sob wracked her throat, and angry tears spilled from the corners of her tightly closed eyes. Yet her tears only seemed to stimulate him. Using his free hand, he held her face firmly, and began to rain feverish kisses about her eyes, ears, and neck. With his searing lips, he branded her wet face over and over again. Finally his mouth came to rest on her own. He seemed to draw the very life from her body.

Simone was in a frenzy of despair. She must escape this writhing blond devil. But there was no escape. Her mind was a kaleidoscope of shifting sensation and erratic emotion. His kisses burning into her flesh . . . if only he would stop . . . just for a moment, let him stop!

Quickly his hand moved from her jaw and reached for her breast. Gently he began to move his expert fingers across the white flesh—stroking, pressing, teasing. His leonine head moved from her face, and adeptly he ran his tongue down her arched throat, between the soft mounds of her bosom, to finally receive one hard pink nipple between his open teeth.

Simone's shocked consciousness searched for some island of stability in this raging turmoil, and found none. A sharp pain at her breast alerted her that some new violation of her body was beginning.

Releasing her arms, Rudolph shifted his massive body as if to move from the bed, yet the pressure of his powerful form returned almost immediately with a new urgency.

No escape . . . the crush of his body was weighing her down . . . down. Her nerves were inflamed and her skin seemed to burn under his warm flesh. What was happening to her? Why did she feel so strange? But the heaviness was tugging at her body again, and her tortured mind let go and floated free. Her will was a thing detached, and her body had a mind of its own.

Rudolph planted his muscular thighs on each side of her rounded hips. Prying open her slender legs, he lowered his golden body onto hers. Faltering only slightly, he entered her deliberately. Deeply his ready manhood penetrated her silkiness.

Simone was shocked by this violent intrusion. The pain of his entry caused her to thrust upward. Her arching body relaxed slightly, and she concentrated on the aching fullness which she experienced between her quivering thighs. The heavy languor had taken full possession of her now. She was sinking down, down into some sweet stupor. Her flesh was dissolving, and paradoxically, also becoming heavier. A rapturous pressure welled within her, and now her desire for escape was transformed into a desperate need for release from the unbearable tension. Her traitorous body flew upward to meet its tormentor.

Piercing and thrusting with uncontrollable frenzy until he could no longer endure the sweet tension, Rudolph surrendered to his demons.

As if of one body, one will, one spirit, the two lovers came together on that island of ecstasy where time and its mandates have no meaning. Rudolph cried out intensely; Simone moaned softly in defeat and triumph. His body fell heavily onto hers. He breathed deeply but irregularly, as if he had fought gallantly. And yet, had not won total victory.

The moment was over. Their bodies glistened with the honest moisture of loving. Their labored breathing was now soft and rhythmical. They lay together untouching. Simone's eyes remained tightly lidded. She was afraid to open them, sure that the world would be somehow alien. Surely she was a far different creature than the careless child who had dallied in the moonlit courtyard. She had always felt that life had been cruel—giving her few choices to make, offering her few dreams to realize. But this, this was something completely beyond her understanding. She hated this man who had used her so wantonly. Had not the nuns warned her of the evils of the flesh? Yet she could not understand her own reactions. Her body had betrayed her in its surrender.

Rudolph looked at the ceiling, studying the beams he had seen a thousand times before. His leaden gray eyes moved mechanically down the straight wooden lengths. Rudolph had always felt that he had mastered life, certainly he had mastered women. He was a man of indomitable control. He took pride in his realistic approach to living, and accepted cynicism as a necessary evil. Yet this girl had fooled him! She was so openly free, her gypsy fire had burned so brightly. But a virgin! Prince Rudolph Nikolaivich Balenkov did not see himself as a despoiler of virgins. Was this another mystic gypsy ploy? He smiled at his own gullibility. Turning slightly, Rudolph looked down at the gypsy. Her beautiful body still glowed from their lovemaking.

"Well, you are full of surprises, ma petite."

Opening her eyes at last, Simone looked up into his startlingly handsome face. It was the first time she had really observed him closely. The tousled hair shone burnished in the lamplight as it tumbled over his high forehead and curled lazily about his temples. She had dared to look into his eyes only once during their coupling. Their deep blue color suffused with passion had burned into her consciousness. Now they had become the unreadable flat gray of slate. Where before they had warmed her, she now felt chilled. Instinctively she pulled the cloak on which she lay about her.

"Little gypsy, your body lies as cunningly as the sweet mouth. It spoke to me of passion, not purity. Or are you like the mythical Aphrodite who renews her maidenhead after each night of love?"

This last was too much for the overwrought Simone. He had ruined her life, and now he dared make light of it. Her black eyes blazed with suppressed violence as she fairly screamed, "How dare you! What do you know of me? You care only for yourself; you care nothing for my feelings! You care not that I am ruined!"

Her outburst was greeted with mocking laughter which filled the small cabin. Rising easily from the bed, he walked casually to a fine mahogany credenza. "If not I, then inevitably some other. Why do you grieve, my gypsy? You have had the best of teachers, and you proved a most exceptional pupil." As he spoke, he poured a fine burgundy into two crystal tumblers. Returning with the wine, he continued, "Ruined? It is rather a cause for celebration. Let us toast your newfound womanhood."

Seating himself on the edge of the large bed, Rudolph passed the girl the sparkling crystal. Simone gazed intently into the wine's crimson depths. The smoldering anger which had roiled within her exploded, and she flung the glass and its glistening contents at his mocking face. In its wild trajectory it missed its intended target, but collided instead with the small bachelor's chest at the bedside. The faceted tumbler shattered instantly, a jagged sliver slashing the Russian's cheek. A scarlet rivulet marred his chiseled face.

Simone's breath caught in her throat. Already she regretted her rash act. Rudolph lightly fingered the small wound, his wide mouth curved in a brittle smile; his gray eyes had turned to ice. Deceptively indifferent, he turned away from Simone, setting his glass upon the small chest. Only momentarily did his finger trace the pattern of the crystal. Suddenly tensing, the knuckles of his right hand turned white. In one swift motion his pent-up fury was unleashed. His open palm crashed into Simone's startled face, his fingers leaving ugly red marks against the creamy skin. The girl crumpled into the cushions, silent sobs wracking her naked body. Rudolph's gaze could have been called disdainful, had it not been so detached. Regaining his control, he walked toward the bath.

Simone teetered on the brink of despair, but her defiant nature would not allow her to give up. She lifted her head to brush aside the ebony locks that had fallen over her eyes. As she smoothed the heavy waves from her forehead, Simone glimpsed her clothes lying in a crumpled heap upon the floor. The red skirt like a wilted poppy, caught her interest. Ruefully, she turned to make certain that he had not returned. Stealthily, she crawled out of the bed and grasped the crinoline skirt. It has to be here, she prayed, as she nervously plunged her hand into the deep pocket. Please . . . please . . . Yes! Simone's fingers gratefully encircled the tiny packet. She slithered across the length of the bed. Reaching the edge, she knelt before the small chest; her trembling fingers fumbled with the ties of the packet. At last they came free, and furtively she emptied the entire contents into his waiting glass.

The soapy water stung the open cut. Rudolph passed the towel across his face, and examined himself in the oval mirror. The face which looked back at him was . . .

strange. Some trick of the light had clothed his features in an alien darkness. His hair had lost its golden glints, his blue-gray eyes were lost to shadow. Rudolph ran a firm hand over the corded muscles of his neck. Abstractedly, he rubbed the hard expanse of his chest. Deliberately, almost methodically, he began to undress. Rudolph moved like some golem, controlled by unknown forces. His eyes stared ahead, but were focused on some inner vision. At last he stood naked, clothed only in the natural grace of a healthy predator.

Some primitive instinct alerted Simone to her captor's return. Her hand jerked convulsively away from the crystal tumbler. Rudolph stood in the doorway, his naked body pure in its maleness. Her eyes widened, the pupils dilating in fear, her bare breasts heaving with her ragged breathing. She wanted to run, to escape, yet she could not. Her eyes had become transfixed on his form. It was splendid in its perfect symmetry. He was Orpheus coming for his Eurydice. But no, that was wrong. She must run *from* him, not to him. Slowly, he strode to the forgotten glass of wine and drained it neatly. His thirst slaked, he reached for Simone. Desperately she leaped from the bed, struggling toward her discarded costume. He must not catch her, he must not. In a few easy strides Rudolph crossed the room, and his powerful arms encircled her. "No, no!" she screamed, "not again. Please!" Unhearing, he flung her facedown on the bed. Frantically, she scrambled to her hands and knees, and tried to crawl away. His heavy body fell full upon her, knocking the air from her lungs. Her scream sounded only in her mind. She clawed at the coverlet, gasping for breath. Quickly he mounted her, his chest pushing against the soft surface of her back. One free hand slipped beneath her abdomen, and reaching lower, he cupped her soft, curling mound. He entered her swiftly, his burning shaft once again finding her hidden recesses. Then the tortured cry came, and the powerful body quivered violently as he reached imperfect fulfillment. Spent, Rudolph tumbled on his back, a growing lethargy beginning to claim him. Almost immediately, he slipped into unconsciousness.

Simone moved gingerly. Slowly withdrawing from his side, she noted that the drug had begun its work. If she had not felt so defiled and miserable, she would have congratulated herself on her cleverness. As his breathing became more regular, she moved cautiously from the bed. Slipping hastily into her clothes, she moved to the cabin door. Her hand clutched the brass knob. Anticipating her freedom, she attempted to turn it. It would not move! It was locked!

Drained momentarily of all hope, Simone sank to her knees. Pressing her forehead against the cool knob, she found herself on a level with the keyhole. The key! It must be here in this room! Rising to her feet, she surveyed the cabin, making a mental inventory of its spartan furnishings. Surely the most logical place would be the captain's desk. Walking softly across the hardwood floor, Simone reached the handsome desk and pulled open its large central drawer. Stacked neatly were a variety of parchment: letters, documents, maps. Shuffling through the vellum, Simone found nothing. Disappointed, she rummaged rapidly but silently through the remaining drawers. No key! Her attention then focused on a small compartment nestled beneath a maze of pigeonholes filled with navigational charts. A tiny brass key protruded from the diminutive lock. Had it not been for the bright tassel which depended from the key, the compartment itself would probably have gone unnoticed. Carefully she twisted the shiny instrument, and the drawer opened easily. Sliding it toward her, Simone examined its contents. As she moved aside a solitary leather volume, an exclamation of delight escaped her—the key! Grabbing it, she clasped the treasure to her breast. With its possession, hope returned.

As Simone reached out to close the secret compartment, her natural curiosity intruded, as the book within caught her eye. The cover was embossed with the gilt letters R.N.B. in a Romanesque scroll. Rudolph Nikolaivich Balenkov. The book was his. Haltingly, Simone touched the fine leather and felt the suppleness that comes with constant use. It opened readily to "Cain," by George Gordon, Lord Byron. Simone's eyes were immediately drawn to the boldly underscored lines. She read:

> Lucifer: *I pity thee who lovest what must perish.*
> Cain: *And I thee who lov'st nothing.*

Although intrigued by these lines, Simone could tarry no longer. Cautiously, she moved to the door, the precious key clasped tightly in her fist. She thrust it impatiently into the lock. Hearing the familiar metallic click, she was rewarded as the knob turned easily in her hand. Opening the door, she was dismayed to hear the sound of heavy boots moving down the narrow corridor toward her. Swiftly, she closed the door in aching frustration. Closer and closer the muffled footfalls came. They trod abruptly to a halt before the captain's cabin. Simone ceased breathing. Only inches of wood separated her from this new threat. A paroxysm of apprehension gripped her as she frantically scanned the chamber in search of a place to hide. Her mind raced with hideous thoughts of what her discovery might mean. An eon seemed to have passed, and still neither she nor the unknown foe outside the door moved. Then, to her enormous relief, the footsteps retreated down the hallway. Waiting only a moment, Simone decided she must try an escape once again. As she clutched the knob in her moist hand, she unconsciously turned to view her sleeping antagonist. Perversely, her feet took her closer. He lay sprawled upon the rumpled counterpane, an aura of peace making the usually arrogant features appear boyish. At the sight of his naked body Simone blushed, remembering what had gone before. Angrily, she spun away, returning resolutely to the door. As she opened it, a sudden lurch rocked her against the wooden frame. Mon Dieu, the ship was moving!

~ Chapter 6 ~

A sharp rap echoed distantly through the fog of Rudolph's ragged consciousness. The insistent knock came again, this time with heightened clarity. Rudolph opened his eyes, straining to focus in the painful light. He sat up reluctantly and swung his leaden legs over the side of the bed. The knock sounded again, causing him to flinch involuntarily. Ignoring his nakedness, Rudolph padded across the room and opened the door. Standing in the passageway was his first officer. As always, his uniform was impeccable. With practiced control, Vladimir Shenkerenko held his eyes level with Rudolph's. If he was distracted by his captain's nakedness, his characteristic restraint did not betray him. Saluting smartly, he spoke. "I apologize for waking you, captain, but since you did not appear at the ship's sailing or this morning, as is your usual custom, it was feared you might be ill. I felt it my duty to inquire and to report on the status of our voyage."

"Don't apologize, lieutenant commander," Rudolph's voice cut in sharply. "What is our status?"

"We are on schedule, captain, and our charts indicate that this leg of our journey should go rather smoothly. We are nearing the mouth of the river where the sand bars can be most treacherous. However, we shall soon be navigating in the open waters of the Gulf."

"Thank you, Vladimir. I shall be on the bridge shortly," said Rudolph, closing the door.

Rudolph's head pounded; slowly he began to massage his throbbing temples. Closing his eyes, he allowed his aching

head to fall backward. Where was Yuri, anyway! Breathing
deeply, he tried to recall the events of the previous evening.
Vague flashes teased at the edges of his consciousness.
Bright colors burned vividly against ivory skin. A cloud of
raven hair flew in billowing masses, as a sensual form
whirled to wild music. Throwing back her head as she
abandoned herself to the haunting beat, the moonlight fell
full upon her upturned face. The plaintive strains of the
gypsy music grew louder. Gypsy music? Why gypsy music?
. . . *The gypsy!* His hand flew to the cut on his cheek. The
spiteful bitch had wounded him. What time had he put her
off ship?

Pushing these confusing images aside, he determined to
call the cabin boy and have his bath. Perhaps things would
be clearer after a hot soak and a hearty breakfast.

Rudolph walked distractedly to his armoire, retrieving a
silken robe. He reached for the bellpull to summon Yuri.
As he drew the cord, a patch of color caught his eye. He
moved closer to the mass of tangled fabric. Surely this was
but another phantasm of a sodden brain. But no, this rag
doll of a girl was all too real. Vaguely he recalled fragments
of the night before. Could he have drunk so much that even
the keen sensations of his animal passions could seem so
remote? What was this gypsy vixen still doing aboard his
ship? Rudolph did not like surprises, and especially, he did
not like this one. Looking down disdainfully, he nudged her
rudely with his foot.

As the ship had sailed irrevocably down river, all hope of
escape had ebbed from the weary Simone. A thousand
times she upbraided herself for the fool's game she had
played. She had courted disaster, and it had claimed her.
She thought about the Durands. How puzzled they would
be at her strange disappearance. How dear Madame Felice
would miss her ministrations. All, all for naught. They
would never know of her plight. But perhaps that was best,
for she could never face them with the knowledge of her
shame burning within her. Finally, totally spent in mind and
body, she had sunk to the floor in despair. Would that she
could sink into oblivion, never to rise again. Exhaustion
overtook her, and she slept.

Lost in the depths of a fitful slumber, Simone was
suddenly roused to full consciousness by the thrust of

Rudolph's foot against her. She gazed upward, and their eyes locked in silent combat. Trying to gain some semblance of dignity, she straightened her back and haughtily brushed her tousled hair from her face. With a sure hand, she pulled up the blouse which had fallen from one shoulder. She would not have him think her completely wanton. She gazed unafraid into the icy depths of his eyes. The cruel set of his jaw gave his face an almost sinister expression. His wide mouth was fixed, and his eyebrows were drawn together above the bridge of his straight nose. The blue robe had fallen open to his waist, revealing the blond down of his tanned chest. He was full of contradictions, this man. A golden beauty masking an inner darkness.

"What am I to do with you, gypsy?" inquired Rudolph contemptuously, her defiant stare provoking his ire.

"Captain Balenkov, since you brought me here against my wishes, I believe that is your problem," countered Simone sarcastically.

"Mais non, ma petite, the problem is yours. I hope you are a strong swimmer."

With more courage than she felt, Simone cried, "I demand that you return me to New Orleans immediately!"

His anger dissolved in open amusement at this obviously ridiculous suggestion. "Consider yourself fortunate, little gypsy," he exclaimed. "You shall soon see *Mat Russkiya*, my Mother Russia!"

Yuri Yesenin hurried down the long hallway, responding to his captain's call with some bewilderment. Although Captain Balenkov was not perversely occupied with schedules, he was, indeed, excessively late this morning. Yuri felt subconsciously responsible for his captain, and in fact, took great pleasure in his yeoman's duties.

Yuri was only sixteen, but had developed a keen sensitivity far beyond his years. Even his physical appearance bespoke his poet's soul. Of medium height and slender frame, his finely chiseled features were dominated by his large hazel eyes. These remarkable eyes registered his instant response to every experience. And if Yuri was vulnerable, it was because his eyes constantly betrayed his ready emotionality. Thus did they betray his obvious surprise as he opened the stateroom door. Even his captain's erratic moods and often singular behavior had not prepared him for the scene which greeted him.

Standing arrogantly in a corner of the room was his captain, his hands on his hips, his legs spread wide. Yuri had always thought that Rudolph Balenkov could dominate a room by his sheer physical structure, and his presence had never seemed more awesome than at this moment. For now he towered over the small figure of a beautiful girl who sat on the floor, looking up at this giant with frightened eyes. She seemed to Yuri some fantasy creature. Was it a costume she wore?

"Must you gawk, Yuri? Haven't you seen a woman before? This little gypsy princess, it seems, will be sailing with us to Russia. Well, don't just stand there, Yuri. I am in sore need of a bath," Rudolph continued, irritation seeping into his voice.

Hastily, and in great dismay, Yuri retreated. He recognized this strange interlude as a possible harbinger of the old pattern—*toska!* The renaissance of the black melancholy which periodically took possession of Rudolph filled the yeoman with deep apprehension. And this girl, who was she? But such questions were fruitless. Yuri had long ago abandoned his attempts to fathom his captain's motives, especially during these irrational cycles.

Simone sat staring vacantly into space. The sound of Rudolph's ablutions in the adjacent room scarcely registered in her consciousness, so absorbed was she in her impossible situation. She logically accepted her condition as hopeless. Yet her fiery emotional nature refused to recognize that thoughts of escape were futile. Maybe the cabin boy, she thought, could help me? He seemed nice enough. Almost as soon as the thought had crystallized, Simone attacked her naiveté. The cabin boy, indeed! He was obviously the captain's man. He could be more of a problem than an asset. Her musings ceased as Yuri's voice intruded, "What is the attire for the day?" she heard him ask. Such devotion, Simone thought sarcastically.

A short time later, Rudolph re-entered the room fully dressed. He wore a dark blue jacket which tapered at his waist and fell to midthigh. The jacket fitted snugly across his broad chest, and its high collar circled his throat tightly. The

slim trousers were white, and fitted neatly into calf-molding
black boots. He wore little military decoration and, indeed, little was necessary, as the man exuded power. This
picture of sartorial splendor, however, was lost upon the
brooding girl, who saw only the embodiment of her cruel
fate.

With catlike grace, Rudolph crossed the room and exited
without once looking in the girl's direction. Yuri had not
failed to notice his captain's apparent indifference. Hesitantly, Yuri approached the girl. In a faltering voice he
offered, "The captain has ordered that a bath should be
prepared for you."

Simone momentarily pushed all thought of her predica-
ment from her mind, and surrendered herself to the steaming water. The tension eased slowly from her cramped
muscles. She remained almost stationary for a while before
lathering herself liberally with the rich soap. How good this
felt!

Yuri had certainly been most solicitous, offering to wash
her crumpled costume, and supplying her with a pair of
britches and a shirt. Plainly, these clothes belonged to a
much smaller man than Rudolph, most likely to Yuri
himself.

Like Aphrodite newly born, she rose from the water. Her
body glistened, and her usually ivory-hued skin had taken
on a pink glow. Reaching for a towel, Simone ran it across
her breasts, peaked from the slight chill of the room. Her
hands moved to dry her abdomen and slim legs. Standing
before the cheval mirror, she looked critically at her
reflection. Did her body now look any different than it had
that night in her room, when she had first appraised its
womanhood? Nothing seemed to have changed physically,
yet how changed was she. She had experienced the ultimate
union between a man and a woman. Unlike her romantic
daydreams, which had promised the fulfillment of sanctified
love, this encounter had been a brutal violation of her body
and spirit. Yet she had survived. Or had she? She stepped
closer to examine the face which peered intently from the
glass. The eyes which stared into her own were blacker than
she remembered. The lips had become fuller, perhaps at the
expense of the face, which seemed to have lost some of its

soft contours. She looked away, breaking contact with the intense stranger who confronted her. Finally, she donned the male garb, and decided that she could pass for a yeoman if not for the flowing hair and the rounded hips; certainly her breasts were well camouflaged by the full shirt. Simone again inspected her image and frowned slightly. Her hair was a tangled mass of wet curls. Walking to a nearby chest, she hoped that the brute had a comb or a brush, so she could rectify her dishevelment. The top of the small cabinet held an array of toiletries. Simone was somewhat taken aback at their luxurious refinement. The boar bristle brushes were encased in silver, and were engraved with an ornate crest. A family crest? wondered Simone. She ran a finger lightly over the fine patina of a matching silver shaving cup. In the shadow of a ceramic ewer she espied the object of her desire—a large ivory comb mellowed with age. She held it in her hand, examining the lovely design on its intricately carved spine. As she worked it deliberately through her tangled hair, she contemplated the convoluted personality of her captor. Who was this man, Rudolph Balenkov? Could the owner of these aesthetic objects be the same insensitive savage who violently possessed her body and sought to enslave her mind as well? Debasement and refinement seemed at war within that strange being.

Yuri's knock brought an end to these disturbing speculations. At her invitation, he came in with a luncheon tray. The food was basic shipboard fare, but a small decanter of white wine promised to make the meal more palatable. In any case, Simone found it delicious, as she had eaten little in the past few days. How far away the fateful night of the Comus parade now seemed, yet it was but three days ago that her masquerade had begun.

As she ate, Yuri's eyes quickly took in the metamorphosis that the simple seaman's clothes had wrought on this young beauty. Her tomboy appearance was somehow more endearing than the vivid gypsy guise in which he had first beheld her. Yuri's appraisal did not go unnoticed by Simone. She immediately detected the glint of appreciation in his expressive eyes. But they were only a man's eyes, she thought, looking easily on the pleasing form of a woman. Perhaps these clothes did not hide her femininity as well as she had supposed. She wondered further what he really thought of her. Who does he think I am?

Yuri was pulled away from his ministrations around the cabin by Simone's voice.

"Thank you, Yuri, for the meal, and, of course, the hot bath and clothes."

"You are quite welcome, mademoiselle . . . mademoiselle . . .?"

"Simone, my name is Simone."

"Simone, that is a French name, is it not?"

"Yes, and I notice that you speak the language quite well."

"Merci beaucoup, Mademoiselle Simone. For that I have my captain to thank. He is also teaching me English. He says I have an exceptional aptitude for languages," finished Yuri, his soft voice alight with pride.

"I see," murmured Simone, thinking to herself that this was but another guise—Rudolph Balenkov as benevolent mentor. "So, you have known the captain for some time?" she gently queried.

"Oh yes, Simone. The Yesenin family has served the Balenkovs for generations. In fact, my grandmother, Mimka, has been the only mother Rudolph . . . Captain Balenkov, has ever really known."

"Mon Dieu!" exclaimed Simone to herself in utter exasperation. This was too much! Must she now think of Rudolph as a poor, motherless orphan? Never! Not even the gentlest of mothers could have tamed the savage that was Rudolph Balenkov!

~ Chapter 7 ~

The waves rolled heavily, spewing their foam into the salt-laden air. The spray leapt eagerly upward, misting the pensive face at the open porthole.

Had the circumstances been different, she could have allowed herself to surrender to the sea's tranquil rhythm. Strange how water in all its manifestations called to her. The mighty river lapping hungrily at its banks, the silent bayous disturbing in their fecundity, and this boundless rocking ocean—all evoked a similar disquieting emotion. What siren voices did she now hear?

She turned abruptly from the porthole, rubbing the prickled flesh of her arms. She was cold. And, she admitted to herself, she was lonely. Neither Rudolph nor Yuri had returned to the cabin during the day, and now it was late afternoon. Her eyes wandered to the cache of books nestled on a shelf in the corner. Earlier in the day, she had discovered them in her explorations of the cabin. The small collection offered a surprising array: French novels, English poetry, and Russian histories shared the shelf with naval manuals and charts. At least this pirate was well-read. Later, she knew, she would be grateful for the diversion the books would offer on the long voyage, but just now they were powerless to soothe her. How she hated the forced circumstances of her life! She certainly had made few choices about her destiny in New Orleans. And now this . . . She finally acknowledged consciously what her inner mind had known all along—her situation was, indeed, hopeless.

She still sat deep in introspection when the cabin door opened to reveal Yuri with her evening meal. He seemed as preoccupied with his own thoughts as she was with hers, and little conversation passed between them. Instead, Simone turned her full attention to her tray, as the welcome aroma of food assailed her nostrils. Her depression had not stunted her appetite. Eating heartily, she offered a grateful prayer that she had not been plagued with *mal de mer*. Captain Balenkov, you don't control everything, she thought with satisfaction.

Simone sat reading, a small circle of light illuminating the pages of a book which tonight held little interest for her. The walls of the cabin seemed far away in the darkness. Silently, she rose from her curled position and moved to the beckoning porthole. Outside, a cold light iced the undulating waves. The crescent moon shone intermittently through the ragged edges of gray clouds blown like torn banners across the velvet sky. She was peaceful now; she could sleep. As she turned toward the bed, her body tensed, and her tranquil mood was shaken. His bed—no, she would not sleep in that bed ever again. Almost savagely, she tore at the coverlet and flung it into the corner. The floor had served her before; it would do so again.

Nestled in the warm folds of the quilt, and lulled by the gentle rocking of the ship, Simone soon succumbed to the latent weariness within her. Yet if she yearned for peaceful repose, she was not to be so blessed. Her body contracted, her knees drawing tightly to her chest as she struggled with her dreams.

A soundless wind blew the filmy veil against her white face. It molded against her rigid features as it streamed backward into enveloping mist. A long aisle stretched before her. Why was she being carried? She could walk. "Please, let me walk!" she cried. Why is Madame Felice weeping? "Please, madame, don't cry; weddings are a time of joy." Look at the beautiful flowers . . . but they are all calla lilies. Too white, and cold like marble. Where are the jonquils, hyacinths, and violets? Is it because of the coldness; has this unnatural frost prevented their blooming? Yes, that must be it. For I, too, am chilled.

At this thought, she began to rock back and forth in what seemed some bizarre dance executed in a queer tempo. She should move her feet; she should flow with the rhythm. But the confines in which she now found herself prevented this. She was in some sort of boat. So small, she thought, a tiny vessel fashioned solely to bear her body. "How charming!" she murmured, as she touched the polished ebony side of her tiny craft. Her hand moved to its interior to stroke the blue satin lining on which she reclined.

Unexpectedly, the monotonous cadence of the waves became more and more agitated, threatening to capsize the curious vessel and thrust Simone into the frigid depths below. With horror, she sensed the growing hunger of the rising water as icy tongues of salty spume licked at her face. She felt her body grow heavy, her veil and gown becoming soaked with the ocean's raging torrent. Her eyes began to sting as her tears melded with the sea's. About to be engulfed by the chilling waves, she opened her eyes once more . . .

Rudolph Balenkov stood above her, his clear laughter ringing in the stillness. In one hand he held a single glass of claret, in the other a half-filled decanter. Amused, he surveyed the wine still dripping from the girl's startled face.

"Do you prefer this cold corner to my bed, ma petite?" he queried mockingly.

Gathering her shattered senses, Simone realized that she was no longer dreaming. "Rather the rat-infested hold below than your bed," she spat.

"Splendid idea, little gypsy, but it is I, and not the rodents, who require your company this night."

Tensing, she countered, "Take me if you so desire, but I shall not come willingly." Expecting to be swept from her position on the floor, Simone was astonished when the Russian simply lowered himself beside her. Casually he placed the decanter and his glass upon the floor. Simone's nerves were stretched to their limits as he observed her languidly from his couchant position. Without warning, he lunged, and with one huge paw ripped open the silken shirt to reveal the ripe body beneath the concealing folds. Pinning her protesting body with one strong forearm, he reached for his half-emptied glass with his free hand and offered sarcastically, "More wine, ma petite?" Not waiting for a reply, Rudolph artfully dribbled the red liquid over her form. Simone's body, stained by the sparkling liquid, became instantly chilled. Her tawny nipples signaled the arousal of her senses as the wine slowly rouged the soft contours of her breasts. Humiliated by her powerlessness she shrieked, "You are a beast!"

Thoroughly amused by her childish outburst, his reply was punctuated by raucous laughter. "And you, my dear, put on airs."

Lowering his leonine head, Rudolph stared intently into Simone's apprehensive eyes. Opening his sensuous mouth, his long, soft tongue slid from between even white teeth to lap the fruity essence from her glistening flesh. Slowly he traced the ruby patterns as he moved his mouth under each soft mound, missing no droplet, teasing each nerve. Expertly, his tongue circled her aching peaks, crying to be suckled more earnestly. Abandoning the nippled hills, his burning lips moved from the sheltered valley at their base to trace the course of the scarlet rivulet and drink deeply at her brimming navel. His thirst only partially slaked, he moved lower to drink more deeply of that other sweet wine which awaited his eager mouth.

Buffeted in the riptide of her surging emotions, her hands grasped his neck, the fingers buried in the hair at the nape. Sinking deeper into the seething passion of her own body, the young nymph tightened her grip on the golden mane. Simone began to sway to the erotic rhythm which Rudolph orchestrated upon her flesh. Fighting her insistent body no longer, she could *drown* now. A strangled cry escaped her—"Please . . . yes . . .

Abruptly, the sweet assault ceased. Jolted by this abandonment, she raised her lids to meet his cold appraising stare. What lay behind those suddenly graying eyes, whose opaque gaze seemed to pierce into the very depths of her soul? Without a word he rose and moved away. She heard him stir the dying embers of the fire. As she listened to him undress, her mind dreaded the possibility of his return, but she knew her treacherous, unfulfilled body would welcome such a prospect. She felt so empty, so hollow. In relief and despair she heard the bed boards give under the weight of his body. From the cold floor she listened to his regular breathing.

The lemon-yellow sunlight of late morning streamed through the open porthole. Simone arched her young body languorously, and breathed deeply of the salty air. As she opened her eyes she became aware of the comfortable bed beneath her. How had she come to rest here? Who had carried her from her hard pallet on the floor? She had little chance to speculate further, as there came a knock at the door. Drawing the covers up to her chin, she wished for a mirror. She smoothed her tangled hair as best she could and called imperiously, *"Entrez!"*

Yuri entered with her breakfast, his eyes nervously seeking a comfortable place to rest. Simone almost giggled at his obvious discomfiture.

"Mademoiselle Simone, I thought perhaps you would like breakfast," he ventured with some embarrassment. "While you eat, I shall draw your bath," he continued, "and afterward you shall be able to wear your own clothes. That should please you," he finished proudly.

"Oh thank you, Yuri, that would indeed be marvelous," she answered him.

As soon as the cabin boy retreated, she scurried from the bed and retrieved a fresh shirt from the armoire. It was one of many which hung there, and she donned it hastily. It fell to her knees. Though self-conscious, she was at least covered. She had almost finished her breakfast when Yuri returned, bearing buckets of steaming water. Leaving the boy to his yeoman's duties in the captain's quarters, she entered the bath. The hot water soothed her as she briskly lathered her limbs with fresh-smelling soap. Her body frothy with suds, she stood and reached for the bucket of clear water which waited beside the tub. As the hot rinse water cascaded over her, she squealed with delight. Quickly she toweled herself to a healthy glow and reached for her familiar costume. As she touched the colorful fabric, thoughts of her foolish masquerade flooded her memory; she resolutely pushed them from her mind. The past is best forgotten, she resolved, as she passed into the bedchamber. Thanks to Yuri's efforts, it was in perfect order.

"Vous êtes très belle ce matin, Mademoiselle Simone," Yuri saluted her as she entered.

"Merci, Monsieur Yuri," she returned graciously with a smile. Simone felt more herself after a sound sleep, breakfast, bath, and the restoration of her clothes. The old confidence began to return. "Well, Yuri, as I am on this ship, I might as well see as much of it as I can."

"Oh no, mademoiselle, I am, indeed, sorry; the captain has given strict orders that you remain in the cabin," he lamented.

"What! He can't do that," she railed, her voice rising with anger. "I am not here by choice. Am I now to be a prisoner? I'll show him. He'll not have his way in everything!"

As she spoke this last, she stalked toward the door. Yuri moved quickly, blocking her way. He continued, pleadingly, "Mademoiselle Simone, please, you must not. The captain is in one of his black moods!"

"Black mood! I'll show him a black mood if I don't get out of this room," she cried, stamping her small foot.

Yuri cringed at her vehemence, but stood firm. He admired her spirit and wished that he could please her. He did not blame her for resenting her confinement, but it would not do for her to be seen by others on the ship. What circumstances had brought her here? What role did his captain play in this strange drama? In any case, he dared not oppose Prince Rudolph Balenkov. Sensing that Simone was not likely to relent so easily, he sought to stop the beginning of a new tirade. Holding up his hand he began earnestly, "You do not understand, Simone. It is not a good thing to challenge the captain. He is used to obedience, and it is accepted by all that it is especially dangerous to cross him when the darkness descends upon him."

"Darkness? You make it sound like some ancient curse. I'm not afraid of your captain's darkness," she averred flippantly.

"Oh but, mademoiselle, you are not Russian. You do not understand. It is *toska!*"

Yuri had tried to explain *toska* to the young girl. But *toska*—the dark moods, the black melancholy—was something more to be experienced than explained. And his master's *toska* . . . well, it was something special that even Yuri did not quite comprehend.

Yuri Yesenin had been with Captain Balenkov since he

was twelve years old and, of course, Rudolph had known the boy since his birth sixteen years ago. Perhaps Yuri's best insight into his captain's character came through Yuri's grandmother, Mimka, who understood Rudolph better than anyone. Although only twenty-four, Rudolph had been matured rapidly by rank and family circumstances. Prince Rudolph Balenkov was of one of Russia's ancient noble families. When not managing his country estate near Moscow, Prince Balenkov assumed the title of Captain Balenkov in the Russian Royal Navy. It was in this capacity that he could best execute sensitive diplomatic missions for his tsar. This naval career meant that Yuri Yesenin became more to Rudolph than simply his old nurse's grandson. Yuri had become Captain Balenkov's trusted yeoman, accompanying him on his many voyages over the last four years. Yuri deeply respected, and was entirely devoted to, his captain. Yet, during the "dark times," Rudolph made it difficult for Yuri to love him.

And now this new twist—this gypsy girl—this enigma! Who was she? What was she to the captain? Yuri had seen the captain with his many women, and it always seemed to him that there was never any love involved. Yet, this one was somehow different. Certainly they appeared to hate each other. Perhaps they hate each other too passionately, contemplated Yuri. She seemed so innocent. But, if she were, what was she doing with the captain? This was so strange, this beautiful young woman sailing with them to Russia. It was a dangerous situation for Prince Balenkov. It was, indeed, important that her presence be kept secret, for there were those who would use this information against him.

"Yeoman Yesenin, you seem preoccupied of late." Yuri turned abruptly, his coursing thoughts interrupted by the critical tones of Vladimir Shenkerenko. "And our captain seems in the blackest of his moods," the lieutenant commander resumed. "It must be most difficult for you, yeoman, as you are with him more than any of us. And such a voracious appetite our captain has displayed of late, so many trays of food. You must spend much of your time in the galley."

"Like you, lieutenant commander, I find it always a pleasure to serve my captain. My duties I perform most willingly. If you will excuse me, sir. I must return to my tasks."

Vladimir's eyes narrowed as they followed the retreating form. This brief interview had only enkindled his already awakened suspicions. There was intrigue here, and he was a master at that game.

Unlike Prince Balenkov, Vladimir Shenkerenko, as so many others of his class, had gained his title and rank through the civil service. In short, he had earned his title; Rudolph Balenkov had inherited his. From the beginning, he was determined not to remain merely an inconsequential member of the service nobility. To improve his position in the rambling bureaucratic hierarchy, he was prepared to do whatever was necessary. His unscrupulous nature did not balk at even the most unethical of activities. His noble captain was hiding something, of that he was certain, and he, Vladimir Shenkerenko, fully intended to ferret out his secret. A smile crossed his sharp features as he congratulated himself on his cleverness. At last, he was sure, he had found bait for his trap.

~ Chapter 8 ~

Throughout the long day, Simone paced the cabin, a caged animal. From time to time she gazed out the single porthole. The vista, however, remained unchanged. The day was overcast. There was no horizon; the leaden sky melted seamlessly into the molten sea. She seemed a captive of the endless void, poised within infinity. But infinity was not her immediate domain, Simone reflected realistically, this ves-

sel was. And she did not even know its size. Yuri had
identified the ship as a screw corvette, but that left her
totally unenlightened. She was surprised to learn that a full
crew consisted of fifteen officers and over two hundred
noncommissioned officers and men, although the crew
numbered considerably less at this time. When she had
questioned him as to the length of their voyage, he had
replied that it could take from three to four months to reach
St. Petersburg, depending on the weather. It was then that
she had decided that she would go quite mad within the
confines of this cabin. And yet, what did Russia hold for
her? What would happen to her at journey's end? Would he
simply abandon her in a foreign land? Well, she had wanted
excitement, but how the mocking Fates had toyed with her.
How she hated this man!

Yuri entered the room. His cheerful greeting went unheeded as she continued to pace the floor. Yuri, however,
was not offended by Simone's indifference. He smiled to
himself as he continued with almost pompous ceremony to
set an elaborate table. He left a tray of covered dishes
complete with a magnum of champagne, and discreetly
excused himself.

Simone refused to turn when she heard the heavy door
open. She did not have to see him to know that Rudolph
Balenkov had entered the room. She could sense his
presence; she could hear his deep regular breathing and
inhale the salty smell of him. It was strange how familiar he
had become.

"I thought we might dine together tonight. Surely you
must be hungry, ma petite, since Yuri says that you refused
lunch. Perhaps tonight's repast will be more to your taste,"
he said mildly. Without waiting for a response, Rudolph
strode past Simone and entered the bath. As she listened to
the splashing of water in the basin, Simone's eyes blazed
with suppressed fury at his nonchalance and insensitivity to
her misery. Where was the black mood of Yuri's dire
warnings? And what new tactic expressed itself in this
sudden gentility? It mattered little what he intended; she'd
have no part of it.

Refreshed, Rudolph re-entered the room. Walking to the
table, he graciously offered her a chair. Unaffected by this
display, and filled with loathing, Simone remained where
she was. "Suit yourself, mademoiselle. *My* appetite is

excellent." With this Rudolph took his own seat and began to dine heartily, with exaggerated manners and movements. Intermittently he glanced up at her with a tolerant smile for her childish pique. Unable to endure another moment of this insulting charade, and overcome with hunger, Simone walked imperiously to the table. With deliberate care she seated herself, placing the elegant square of white linen primly in her lap. She served herself generously from the array of dishes before her. Ignoring her dinner companion completely, she concentrated her attention on the smoked fish, roasted potatoes, pickled beets, and crusty black bread. She was especially delighted with the superb champagne with which Rudolph had silently filled her glass. He, however, scrutinized her closely. Who was she? *Simone* Yuri had called her. Her French was impeccable, not the patois of the lower classes. Her features were delicately chiseled, her lovely hands were unscarred by the ravages of hard work. True, her skin was tawny, but not from the sun; her dusky beauty came naturally. She sat regally at his table, using the proper utensils, relishing the fine champagne. All of this, and more that was indefinable bespoke good breeding—everything except the circumstances of their meeting. She was undeniably refined in some ways, but she *had* to be what she had at first appeared—a common girl of the streets.

The clink of a glass brought him back to the present, and focusing on her again, he noted the glowing animation in her face. The gypsy fire was being rekindled by the sparkling wine. "More champagne?" he asked, refilling her glass.

"It is an excellent vintage," she acknowledged, finally speaking.

"I am so glad you approve, mademoiselle, you seem to approve of so little," he replied archly.

"Only because I have found so little worthy of approval, *mon capitaine.*"

"Touché," he laughed, raising his glass in salute.

The remainder of the meal passed in an amiable silence. Simone drank liberally of the fine champagne, Rudolph keenly aware of the amount she consumed. He watched with amusement and anticipation. Perhaps she would be more pliant in this condition.

Becoming aware of his regard, Simone looked up to see

his hunter's eyes upon her. She realized the trap had been sprung. She had drunk too much; her head was decidedly light. She must get away and think. Abruptly, she rose, her napkin sliding to the floor. As the room swayed violently, she clutched at the back of her chair. Instantly, Rudolph was at her side; she was in his arms. She threw her head back in giddy laughter and felt his lips at her throat. Her arms entwined about his neck as all thoughts of escape vanished. She felt him sweep her up, as he carried her to the waiting bed. Her next awareness was of her nakedness and his. For the first time fear did not cloud her appraisal of his body. He seemed all of one color—his skin, his hair—all burnished gold. His muscles rippled just below the surface of his taut skin. His broad chest tapered to a small waist and flat abdomen. Simone's eyes traveled to the thin, anomalous white scar above the golden fur of his groin. She wanted to touch this fascinating flaw, but her arms were leaden. She could not move. Without shame she gazed wonderingly at his large, ripened manhood. He was so astonishingly different than she. He was beautiful, she decided, all of him.

Simone watched as he moved to the foot of the bed and knelt at her feet. Slowly he separated her slim legs and angled his body between her thighs. Gently he opened the sweet flower of her womanhood and entered her between soft, moist petals. Simone moaned, her breathing quickening as she instinctively matched the rhythm of her body to his thrusts. They rode the crest of their passion together. And when they had reached love's perfect fulfillment, it was a moment of total surrender. As her body arched toward him in her ecstasy, he fell forward to meet her, his face buried in her hair. Rudolph quivered convulsively. Above her drumming pulsebeat she heard his husky whisper. "Simone, Simone."

The sound of her name still ringing in her ears, Simone slowly awakened. The cabin was flooded with bright sunlight, and the busy noises of the deck drifted in through the open porthole. He had said her name for the first time last night as they came together in that furious moment of passion. It was as if he had finally accepted her as a person—no gypsy girl of the street—but Simone, a woman!

What was she thinking? What kind of trick was her mind

playing now? First her body had betrayed her. Now, her mind! To Rudolph Balenkov, Simone Montpellier was simply an object of pleasure. How she hated this man, she reminded herself. Nothing he could ever say or do would change that. Restless and resentful, she cursed her fate. Why did this have to happen to her? In fact, why had the whole of her life happened as it had? Life was cruel . . . pointless. All hope of a simple, decent life was certainly gone, and any romantic dreams of an aristocratic existence which she had once nurtured, now seemed ridiculous. What man would ever want her now?

Realizing that such unanswerable questions could contribute little toward improving her situation, Simone desperately sought some diversion for her tortured mind. It was in a similar state of desperation that Simone had discovered Rudolph's hidden volume of poetry; it was probably for this reason that she remembered the book now. In a matter of moments, she held it once again. This time she could examine it at leisure. Turning to the frontispiece, she perceived that it was a volume of English romantic poetry including the works of Byron, Shelley, and Keats. As she leafed through the closely printed pages, she noted that it was Byron whom the owner most often read. This was apparent from the obviously worn pages and underlined passages in the section devoted to this poet. Stopping at a page, she read a stanza in which some of the lines were boldly marked.

VIII

And who the first that, springing on the strand,
Leap'd like a nereid from her shell to land,
With dark but brilliant skin, and dewy eye
Shining with love, and hope, and constancy?
Neuha—the fond, the faithful, the adored—
Her heart on Torquil's like a torrent pour'd;
And smiled, and wept, and near, and nearer clasp'd
As if to be assured 't was him she grasp'd;
Shudder'd to see his yet warm wound, and then,
To find it trivial, smiled and wept again.
She was a warrior's daughter, and could bear
Such sights, and feel, and mourn, but not despair.
Her lover lived,—nor foes nor fears could blight

That full-blown moment in its all delight:
Joy trickled in her tears, joy fill'd the sob
That rock'd her heart till almost heard to throb;
And paradise was breathing in the sigh
Of nature's child in nature's ecstasy.

Simone was not familiar with this work. She wondered about the maiden Neuha and her lover Torquil. Seating herself in a nearby chair, she decided to read the tale from its beginning. The poem was "The Island," a romantic story relating how an island girl had saved her English lover Torquil, a seaman seeking refuge from a despotic captain. Enchanted by the poem, she lost herself in the complex narrative. As she read, Simone stroked the fine leather cover of the beautiful volume. Subconsciously, she could sense Rudolph as she held his book and read his poem. Unwittingly, she cast Torquil in his form.

She had sought solace, and momentarily had been seemingly transported out of her own dismal situation. But this proved a cruel illusion. As she reached the story's end, the happy resolution of the final passage mocked her. With some irony she reread the lines.

XV

Again their own shore rises on the view,
No more polluted with a hostile hue;
No sullen ship lay bristling o'er the foam,
A floating dungeon:—all was hope and home!

What kind of escape could she expect from *this* floating dungeon? There was no hope or home for her. There never had been.

Her head tilted against the high back of the chair. Wearily, she closed her eyes, suspended in time, a captive of myriad conflicting emotions. Unable to deal with these complexities, she retreated into a void which they could not penetrate. Thus it was that she did not hear the door when it opened.

Some subtle change in the room alerted her. Her heavy lids opened slowly to behold a dark idol towering over her. There was no mistaking the pent-up fury that so suffused his being and communicated itself to the very atmosphere. But this anger was more than the dark moods which she had witnessed previously; this was something different. He was a madman stripped of all reason. He was a primeval thing, his raw naked emotions exposed. He had been violated in some way, and he knew only that he must strike back, hurt his enemy.

Simone watched intently as he struggled with this animal force within himself. It was as if he were waging a deathly battle that he had often lost, a battle with another being, a dark demon which had defied exorcism. She felt she had intruded into a private world where no one had ventured before. She had somehow become part of this titanic struggle. Tired and worn, she was frightened beyond all comprehension.

An eternity passed. There was a knock at the door. The prince supplanted the fiend. His voice was low, almost calm as he spoke. "My book, please."

Yuri's knock had saved her, she thought, as she watched the captain slip the slender book into the pocket of his jacket.

Later, once more alone, Simone reflected on what might have happened had not the interruption come. Who might have been the victor in that strange internal conflict? Was this *toska?*

~ *Chapter 9* ~

As one day blended into the next, Simone's life settled into a bizarre routine, which was largely fashioned by Rudolph's variant moods. Many of her solitary hours were spent in contemplation of this complex man, who had reduced her to an imprisoned concubine. Some days she saw him not at all. He came in after she was asleep and left before she had arisen. The only evidence of his having been there was a slight depression in the mattress and the lingering scent of him. She no longer struggled when he took her; she knew it was hopeless to resist. Ashamed of her body's wanton response to his lovemaking, she armed her mind against him. She was always on guard, lest the rare pleasant moment which they shared blind her to what this man really was. But who was he? Was he the sensitive man who read and enjoyed the poems of Lord Byron, or was he the uncontrollable savage who cared little or nothing for anyone, perhaps not even himself?

The tiny cabin had become her world. Outside the single porthole was an endless stretch of water. Occasionally, she glimpsed schools of flying fish as they skimmed the waves, their winglike fins reflecting the sun's bright rays. Once she had seen the far-off spout of a whale. But on most days, there was only the illimitable ocean rolling on without change. Yuri, who had experienced the sea in all her moods, assured Simone that this benevolent aspect was to be cherished. If this fair weather persisted, they could reach St. Petersburg sometime in May.

Yuri, kind and gentle Yuri. Without him she surely would have gone mad. He was the best of friends. Invariably cheerful, he was ingenious at coaxing her out of her depression and lightening her ennui as he worked about the cabin. He had even consented eagerly to teach her Russian, and spent his every spare minute coaching her in that alien tongue. Yuri took great pride in his own linguistic ability, and was clearly delighted in her aptitude. With little else to do, she was making rapid progress; many of their conversations were now in Russian. She had asked Yuri not to inform the captain about her lessons. She was sure the boy believed that it was her wish to surprise Rudolph with their accomplishment. He therefore obliged, innocent of her deeper motive. Instinctively, she sought some advantage over her enemy.

Unfortunately, these sessions with Yuri, although educational and certainly enjoyable, shed little direct light on her captor. Yet Simone was perceptive enough to realize that she had fallen into the hands of a very rich and powerful man. Surely she would hold little interest for him after reaching Russia. He would have to send her back to New Orleans. New Orleans! She mouthed the words silently. She could easily have become melancholy at the thought of her beloved city, but she checked herself and tried to determine objectively what she might do when she did return. Of course, going back to the Durands was out of the question. Perhaps she could return to the convent. Surely the good nuns would not turn her away. But what then?

It had been days since Simone had last seen Rudolph, and in spite of herself she looked forward to the time when he would again return to the cabin. However, she quickly discounted her eagerness, and attributed her anticipation to boredom. It was understandable that she would have ambivalent feelings about being in his company. For in his dark moods he was grim and unapproachable, and when he was in the deepest throes of *toska,* Rudolph Nikolaivich Balenkov was dangerous.

That very evening Rudolph entered the room unexpectedly, and seemed in an amiable mood. The two enjoyed a pleasant dinner, and for the first time he seemed genuinely interested in how she had passed the day. Spurred by his interest, Simone became animated, talking freely about the book she had begun that afternoon, Flaubert's *Madame Bovary.* She conveyed to him her excitement at discovering this particular work, and admitted that its controversial reputation had piqued her curiosity. So far, she declared, she had found little in it to invite censure. It seemed an honest attempt to portray a woman's inner feelings. It was surely a unique work, and she for one felt that the author deserved praise for his literary daring. She was delighted to find that Rudolph, too, found merit in the novel. As she listened to him, Simone was fascinated by his astute observations. Engaged in lively banter, she suddenly remembered a particularly relevant passage. Again she experienced the eerie feeling that had at first possessed her as she read the words of Emma Bovary. It was a passage which Simone would not share, for it revealed the deepest wishes, not only of Emma Bovary, but of Simone Montpellier. Emma, too, pondered the vagaries of fate, and wondered how her life might have been different. She, too, envied her convent companions who "were living lives where the heart expands, the senses burgeoned out." And like Simone, Emma felt trapped, "her life . . . cold as a

garret . . . the silent spider . . . weaving its web in the
darkness in every corner of her heart.''

Rudolph's question broke her reverie. "Yes, I do enjoy
reading poetry, very much," she answered, almost too
quickly. She hoped that he had not noticed her preoccupation.

Although little passed Rudolph's scrutiny, it was not so
much her suddenly pensive mood that intrigued him, but
the insights of her obviously keen intelligence which had
gone before. He was still perplexed. The mystery of her
identity and the seeming contradictions she presented continued to plague him.

The two had passed a full hour together in this easy
manner when Rudolph stood and asked Simone to please
excuse him. He told her he had enjoyed their conversation,
but was now obliged to work on some naval charts. He
moved slowly toward his desk, and before seating himself
removed his jacket and loosened the top buttons of his silk
shirt. Almost instantly, he became engrossed in his work.

Simone sat near the fire, a blanket across her legs. She
resumed reading *Madame Bovary*, but found that she could
not concentrate on the words before her. She lay the book
facedown in her lap, and glanced across the room to where
Rudolph sat immersed in his work. The soft lantern light
gilded his profile as he bent in concentration. She thought
how pleasant was this scene—she at the fireside, he at his
desk. An interloper viewing them out of context would
judge it a perfect picture of domestic harmony. The true
picture, however, was so different. She had learned that any
harmony depended on her molding herself to his whims.
Simone knew that this rare moment was but a hateful
illusion. But she had had so few truly special moments in
her life that this one now took on an irresistible life of its
own. She felt that she was in a drama and must act out her
part. Compelled, she rose and walked to Rudolph, who
continued his work as if totally unaware of her presence.
She could not go against the script. Hesitantly she extended
her hand and gently stroked his golden hair. Surprisingly,
he too seemed caught up in the silent drama. He turned and
looked up into her eyes. Standing, he took her in his arms,
and kissing her tenderly, he led her to the bed. In a moment
he had disrobed her, and as he reached for his own buttons,
her hand closed over his. Unfalteringly, Simone undressed

him. Like two children they explored the wonder of their
bodies. At last stopping her hands with his, he raised them
to his lips and kissed each finger. Then cradling her,
Rudolph placed her on the bed. Reclining beside her, his
lips sought to possess each inch of her flesh. Feverishly he
sought the core of her passion. As his lips began to bring her
to fulfillment, Rudolph murmured, more to himself than to
her, "Someday, Simone, you will do this for me." A
moment later Simone tensed, the pleasure becoming almost
unbearable. "Come to me, Rudolph," she cried. "Fill me.
Fill me."

~ *Chapter 10* ~

Simone lay dozing, wrapped in a cocoon of well-being. As
her mind swam up from the depths of sleep toward full
consciousness, her first sensation was of being joyously
alive. Reflexively, her hand stretched out toward Rudolph,
but encountered only the bare bedsheet. Coming fully
awake, she opened her eyes. It was morning; he was gone.
Abruptly, she sat upright and faced the vacant spot where
he had slept only a short time before. Almost immediately
she felt lonely, empty. How curious that she should feel this
way. As she tried to analyze these new emotions, her mind
became a maze of images. How tender he had been with
her. And, as if the thought had become the deed, her body
began to glow with remembrances of their lovemaking.

Simone was startled by a sudden knock at the door.
Hurriedly, she pulled the covers to her shoulders. It was a
strangely sullen Yuri who entered with her breakfast tray.
Instantly detecting his uncharacteristic remoteness, Simone

queried if something were the matter. He answered unconvincingly that all was well. Pressing him further, she inquired as to the whereabouts of Captain Balenkov. Reluctantly, sensing that she would not be put off, the yeoman responded cryptically, "The captain is on the bridge, yet he is not really there, mademoiselle. He is in that dark place where only he ventures, and where no one dares to follow. He seems to have traveled more deeply than ever into those somber recesses. Never have I seen him so. I sometimes fear that he will never escape." As he stood regarding her, Simone fancied that she read censure in his large, liquid eyes. Was Yuri blaming *her* for Rudolph's depression? Did Rudolph hate her so much that even their happiness in lovemaking could so anger him? What kind of man was he? Only last night he had seemed so different. But Simone's silent questions went unanswered.

Diamonds coruscated in the troughs of the sun-kissed waves of the sea. The sea—she had been his most constant mistress; yet today she mocked him in her effulgence.

Within his mind, confusion reigned. He who prided himself on his quick rationality, whose very command depended on the incisiveness of his thoughts, now found himself totally at the mercy of unfathomable emotions. The desperate anger which filled him was more than a mere facet of his volatile personality. He refused to accept it as an integral part of himself. He sought to unmask its source. Yet when he attempted the savage unveiling, the only revelation was an image of medusan tresses, an overripe mouth and eyes—wild dark pools that seemed to ridicule his impotent rage.

Driven beyond his own will, Rudolph stood hypnotized by the grotesque image. The specter suddenly softened, and he beheld, not the lurid gypsy, but the warm and beautiful girl who had lain in his arms last night. As he watched in fascination, her body became a gentle haven as she beckoned him to enter her outstretched arms. Drawn toward her, he felt his dissolving anger crystallize into fear—a fear he could neither accept nor ignore. He would not surrender; he could not.

As the days slowly passed, Rudolph did not return. Through the porthole Simone sometimes heard his terse

remarks to his crew, informing her that he had not forsaken
his daily routine. And once she thought she heard his
familiar footsteps outside the cabin door. They lingered but
a moment and then retreated.

She longed to interrogate Yuri further, but sensed that he
would feel any revelation a betrayal of his captain, and
more, that such a discussion would be painful. The moonlit
nights echoed with her unspoken questions. Where did he
sleep? What was he doing? What was he thinking? If
Simone had hated Rudolph's anger, she hated this indifference more. She slept little, and when she did, it was a fitful
slumber. The large bed swallowed her, its emptiness derid-
ing her loneliness. In the mornings she often found herself
clutching a single pillow close to her body.

The days were lonelier than ever for Simone. Books were
her companions. She saw Yuri only at her mealtimes, and a
strained silence grew between them. Despondent and preoccupied, he no longer found time for her Russian lessons,
and she was forced to depend upon her own linguistic skills
to further her knowledge of this difficult language.

Lately, the weather had become as volatile as the perplexing Russian; the capricious sea changed her moods
without warning. One day Simone looked out to see ominous thunderclouds crowding the horizon. Even from within the small cabin she could smell the moisture clinging to
the overburdened atmosphere. The lowering sky burst with
momentary life as silent lightning traced jagged paths across
the heavens. The tiny chamber seemed more a prison than
ever. Gladly would Simone have surrendered herself to the
warring elements to avoid the growing oppressiveness. She
paced the room frantically, as if the atmosphere had infused
her with some strange, new energy. As the walls pushed in
around her, her darting mind refused to settle on anything.
Several attempts to read ended in futility. The monotonous
shipboard fare was now unendurable, and staring at her
untouched supper tray, she realized that she had consumed
almost nothing the entire day.

Finally, the enervating day passed imperceptibly into a
night that promised little relief. In fact, the day proved only
a precursor to the nocturnal violence which was to follow.
In desperation, Simone sought the comforts of the bed,
though certain that sleep would elude her. For a while she
remained unnaturally still, only the occasional illumination

of the distant lightning assailing her senses. Mesmerized by the eerie patterns of cold white light playing upon the cabin's ceiling, she fell into an uneasy sleep.

The late-risen moon lay secreted behind the rumbling turbulence of the angry clouds. She lay tossing on the bed where she had thrown herself long hours before . . .

Simone paced the deck of the ship, her white veil and filmy dress whipped by the wind. Try as she might, she could remember nothing of the origins of this mysterious voyage—nor of its destination. All at once, the gentle rocking of the great vessel turned into angry, twisting gyrations. The young girl clutched convulsively at the wooden railing, trying to steady herself. Methodically, she attempted to recall why she had never been taught to swim. Water rushed across the sides of the ship, drenching her pale, gauzy gown so that it clung intimately to her body. Vainly she attempted to shield her eyes, now burning with the salty residue of the sea's lusty assault. She could not stand upright much longer, and if she fell . . . As her wet skin prickled from the cold, biting wind, she became suddenly aware of an almost sultry heat fanning her body. Looking up, she beheld the sails, great sheets of flame that billowed in the icy gale, propelling the ghosty bark relentlessly across the sea. Transfixed, she watched in horror as the hungry flames raced down the towering mast to kiss the hem of her gown. The dancing conflagration encircled her; the wicked tongues of fire were like vigil lights in some demonic ritual. She must flee. She would not be the fire's vestal sacrifice. Yet she shunned the only avenue of escape, the watery eternity that lay beyond the rail.

Without warning, the world erupted in volcanic fury. She heard the violent explosion and watched as fragments of the ship rode up into the teeming air. She watched the fiery, aerial display almost abstractedly before realizing that she, too, had taken flight. For a while she floated freely like a new-formed constellation of the night sky. However, her wistful flight could not last. Suddenly, she began to plummet downward toward the writhing waves. Her shrill cry followed her plunging body and ended with her watery envelopment. The sea covered her face. She tried frantically to keep the fatal

*liquid from flooding her eyes, her mouth. Through a
watery film she glimpsed the now cloudless sky where a
solitary gull winged its lonely path among the stars.*

Simone bolted upright, on the verge of hysteria. She
could hold back the tears no longer. They came slowly at
first, then became great wracking sobs which shook her
small frame.

Suddenly she was alone no longer. Strong arms surrounded her. She rested her head against a broad, firm
chest. As her sobs slowly became soft whimpers, she felt the
gentle stroking of her hair. Tilting her head upward, she
beheld a familiar face. Was it his face, or a glowing
apparition which she saw? It can't be him. He hates me. We
have not shared the cabin for days. Soft lips planted a
tender kiss upon her forehead. Her eyes, still misted with
tears, sought to focus more clearly. It *was* his face, his
handsome face, the clear blue eyes, the golden hair tumbling across his brow. His sensuous mouth opened slightly,
soothing her as one would a child.

"Ru . . . Rudolph?" Simone faltered.

"Yes, Simone."

"It is you. I thought you were a part of my dream. It was
a horrible dream, Rudolph. The ship was ablaze . . . I was
drowning . . . I . . . I . . . "

"It is over, little one, try to sleep again."

"Will . . . will you stay with me, Rudolph?"

His eyes seemed to mist as he answered almost inaudibly,
"Yes."

As they lay back on the bed, Simone cradled in his arms,
each remained quiet, immersed in thought. The solitude
was broken at last by Rudolph's soft monotone, "St.
Petersburg is a very beautiful city. Though it is quite
different from New Orleans, you will like it, Simone. My
family has a residence there, but our ancestral estates are
near Moscow. You will, of course, live at my home.
Although it is smaller than my uncle's manor, it is quite
lovely there in the spring and early summer."

Simone jerked to attention, "Rudolph, what do you
mean, live at your home? You must send me back to New
Orleans at once. Surely there will be ships leaving St.
Petersburg."

"Must, ma petite? Surely you know that you are now

mine; just as my family's estates and the ancient *yarlyk* will one day be in my possession."

Her body frozen in anger, Simone tried to discern his features in the dark. "So these are your plans, Captain Balenkov! So that is how you see me—as your concubine! Oh no, m'sieur, you have had the advantage here, because I've had no choice. But when the ship docks it will be different. I am not your possession. I am no one's possession!"

In the sudden flash of lightning Simone saw that his position on the bed had not changed. He listened to her tirade with equanimity. Laughing, he reached out his hand and cupped her quivering chin. "This is what I like best—gypsy fire!"

As if to punctuate his taunting words, a bolt of lightning tore across the sky, and thunder echoed in its jagged wake. Simone would not be patronized. Incensed beyond bearing, she sought to wound. Her angry words flew forth, "How I hate you . . . you . . . you . . . you vile demon! That you must possess women I can understand—you could not evoke love. There is no heart within that cold breast." She flew at him and beat on his chest in a frenzy. "There is nothing here . . . nothing here!"

At her words, Rudolph's handsome face had become a chalklike mask, the eyes drained of all color. With fiendish strength he grabbed her wrists as they continued to rain their futile blows.

Outside, the sky and the sea, which for hours had gathered their forces for some final assault, began the furious attack. Rain in huge droplets fell fast and ever faster, as the heavens sought to drown the ocean in a torrent of its own life's blood. As a single shaft of lightning cast its white fire upon his demon's face, Simone knew her words had unleashed the terrible forces within Rudolph, as surely as the fury of sky and sea had been liberated.

He flung her violently onto the yielding cushions and straddled her flailing form, ripping her silken garment from top to bottom.

He mounted her as some wild beast would his ready mate. In a moment of freakish illumination she caught the flash of his white teeth. His face loomed above her impotence. Falling upon her, he bit into her lips, cutting their softness. As she tasted the rivulet of blood which his bestial

attack had wrought, she wished him dead. No part of her
body was sacred. He raked his tormenting mouth down the
column of her throat to find her breasts. At these temples of
love he tortured her with his urgent lips. As he supped on
her rigid nipples, a hand pried open her slender legs, and
began to tease and punish her intimately. Her mind attempted to disassociate itself from the violation of her body.
She would not think! A lancing pain split her being assun-
der, as she convulsed wildly beneath him. His pounding
body fought desperately with itself to achieve fulfillment.
Under his brutal thrusts, Simone's ragged sobs became
animal screams as the storm raged about them.

~ *Chapter 11* ~

Simone was cold, remote—he had taken everything from
her. All that remained was death; that might bring her
peace. Since the storm, she had kept him at a distance. She
must never again allow some brighter aspect of his complex
nature to mask from her the inner devil which possessed
him. She must not permit him to ensnare her with a
semblance of human warmth which could ultimately destroy
her. She could survive his possession of her body, but
enslavement of her spirit would, she knew, be fatal.
Daphnelike, her violation had rendered her immobile,
unfeeling. She had become rooted in an unnatural solitude
which grew daily.

Rudolph had met her indifference with equal coldness.
Their lovemaking, when it occurred, was passionless. He
came quickly over her unfeeling, unmoving body. He no
longer kissed her.

Simone's only solace was Yuri, who tried awkwardly to comfort her, though the reason for her depression remained unspoken between them. The food became more and more colorless and tasteless. She no longer read. Most often Yuri came upon her sitting before the open porthole staring at the blank, unending sea.

Thus he found her one evening. The pallid cast of her once lustrous skin wrung his heart. He could not stand to see her like this. Empathetic by nature, he had been touched by her vulnerability from the first. He knew that his captain was responsible, but his usual loyalties had been replaced by his growing affection for this beautiful young girl. Knowing Rudolph Balenkov to be driven by uncontrollable demons, Yuri hoped that his kindness might in some way atone for his captain's sin.

"Come, Simone, I have a surprise for you. Look, it is a cloak. The night is so beautiful—a calm sea and a full moon. It will do you good to leave this cabin at last. No one will see us; we will stay in the shadows." Yuri spoke rapidly as he pulled her up from her chair, wrapping her in the thick cloak and tucking her long hair inside a woolen cap. Taking her hand, he led her like an unprotesting child down the long corridor and up wooden stairs to a sheltered deck.

As if by magic, Simone bloomed. She breathed deeply of the salt air. Held in the shadows at first by the cautious Yuri, Simone soon ventured forward into the beckoning moonlight.

Her soft laugh of pure delight thrilled Yuri. How proud he felt to have worked this change in her. How beautiful she was. How could anyone hurt her? Surely Rudolph would not have denied her this moment.

Removing the rough seaman's cap, Simone walked closer to the rail. Released from its confinement, her long hair tumbled around her shoulders and teased her face in the soft breeze. As she lifted her face to the lambent moon, its silvery light threw her exquisite profile into relief against the velvet sky. Watching her, the words of an English poem sprang spontaneously to Yuri's lips.

I

She walks in Beauty, like the night
Of cloudless climes and starry skies;

And all that's best of dark and bright
Meet in her aspect and her eyes:
Thus mellowed to that tender light
Which Heaven to gaudy day denies.

II

One shade the more, one ray the less,
Had half impaired that nameless grace
Which waves in every raven tress,
Or softly lightens o'er her face;
Where . . .

Totally entranced by the nocturnal beauty before her, Simone failed to hear Yuri's whispered recital. It went unheeded by she who had inspired it. But there was one who marked every syllable. Gradually, Yuri became aware of a menacing presence. The words died in his throat.

The tall figure loomed up out of the darkness, the evening breeze rippling the folds of his cape. Yuri's sudden intake of breath caused Simone to turn abruptly in the direction of his frozen gaze. Rudolph Nikolaivich Balenkov stood there like some avenging god. Coming forward anxiously, Yuri stammered in the deathly silence, "Captain, I . . . I . . ."

Without warning, Rudolph's open palm crashed savagely against Yuri's face, knocking him from his feet. Simone cried out and dropped quickly to the deck, cradling her fallen companion.

"So, gypsy bitch, you grow cold in my bed, even as you cavort with this stripling." Yanking her up, he kissed her crudely and carried her to the cabin. Kicking the door open with a booted foot, he threw her unceremoniously onto the bed. After he stalked from the room, she heard the key turn in the lock.

Yuri lay sprawled on the deck where he had fallen. Slowly, silent tears made a path down his immobile face. For the first time in his life he hated his captain.

Simone remained paralysed where he had thrown her on the bed. She stared absently at the ceiling. She had not known she could hate anyone so much. How could Rudolph hurt Yuri? Yuri, who so loved the captain, who was so loyal. She could understand his hatred for her, but Yuri! No! And how stupid Rudolph was to think them lovers.

Yuri . . . her only friend . . . sweet, beautiful Yuri. If only Rudolph had some of Yuri's sensitivity, his kindness, his warmth . . .

Simone was startled by a movement at the door. Surely he would not come to the cabin now. Had he not had enough revenge for one night? She quickly turned to her side and feigned sleep.

Rudolph staggered into the room. He was drunk with wine and hatred. Again he had been betrayed by a woman. And worse, because of a woman, he had been betrayed by the one he trusted most. He undressed, leaving his clothes in a heap upon the floor. Naked, he crawled into bed, pulling the covers from around Simone. The masses of her dark hair were flung across the pillow, inviting Rudolph to grasp their silkiness. As he jerked her head toward him, her tears remained dammed behind her tightly closed eyes. Repulsed, she recoiled from his touch, as his wine-laden breath choked her. He grasped her head between his hands, the thumbs pressing her temples. At last the salty tears escaped her lids. Staring into his face, she was inescapably drawn into the vortex of his hypnotic gaze. In defense, she closed her eyes once more, lest she be lost forever in the depths of his soul. Unexpectedly, his hands released her. The pressure on her temples ceasing, she opened her eyes. His face was no longer visible above her. The sound of his heavy breathing astonished her. Raising herself on one elbow, she looked down to see his sleeping form beside her. The wine had claimed him, but there could be little solace in this momentary reprieve.

Simone awakened in the morning unrefreshed. Rudolph lay beside her, still in a deep sleep. She sensed that the hour was late; he should have been up long ago. An abrupt knock resounded sharply at the door. Rudolph groaned; Simone slid deeper under the covers. Again the knock came.

"Come in," bellowed Rudolph.

The cabin door opened slowly, revealing a reluctant Yuri bearing the morning's repast. Avoiding his captain's eyes, Yuri set the tray upon a table, and asked without inflection, "Does the captain desire his bath?"

Agitated and still tired, Rudolph arose, his body gleaming proudly in the morning light.

"No bath, Yuri . . . and no breakfast! Bring some wine
. . . now!"

Without comment, Yuri left the room. He returned
shortly with a large decanter of spirits.

"Is there anaything else you wish, Captain Balenkov?"

Requiring nothing further, Rudolph dismissed the yeoman with a wave of his hand.

Simone peered out covertly from her vantage point in the
bed. She watched as Rudolph walked to his armoire and
carelessly donned a velvet robe. He sprawled listlessly in
the high-backed chair, the decanter and glass stationed
conveniently at his side. As he continued to stare vacantly
into space, he lifted the crystal to his lips and sipped
absently.

Was this to be another dimension of *toska*? Simone
pondered in trepidation. Timidly, she crawled from the
bed, and hugging the edges of the room, she made her way
to the bath. Splashing cool water on her face, Simone
wondered what the unpredictable Russian might do next.
She returned cautiously to the bedchamber and hesitantly
began to eat her breakfast. Her meager actions went
unnoticed by the silent man, as he continued to drink.
Intimidated by his malignant presence, Simone self-
consciously sought out the bed once again, clutching a book
in her hand.

As the day stretched on, and Rudolph remained closeted
within his quarters, his duties neglected, Simone could only
assume that Yuri made excuses for his captain's absence.
She surmised that illness was the explanation which the
yeoman gave. Indeed, it was some strange malady which
affected him.

Several days passed in this weird fashion, Rudolph neither bathed nor shaved. He did not return to the bridge. He
ate little, but drank liberally. He neither spoke to her nor
touched her. The nights he spent in his chair. This new
behavior was more frightening than ever. The old solitude
had been preferable to this eerie presence. Was she to live
forever with this madman?

On the fourth morning of this strange existence, Simone
awoke to find Rudolph gone. As she entered the bath, the
smell of his bay rum soap lingered in the humid air. His
lather cup was in evidence. The unholy siege had ended, to

her immense relief. Her observations were interrupted by
Yuri's knock. He came in carrying her breakfast tray, and
left only to return bearing hot water for her bath. The two
young people, who had enjoyed a growing friendship, were
now awkward in each other's presence. She thanked him
politely; he smiled tentatively and left.

After breakfast, Simone sank gratefully into the steaming
water, content to let the welcome heat soothe the stiffness
from her taut muscles. She yielded herself totally to the
water's relaxing warmth.

Ever so slowly, the door of the cabin opened. Vladimir
Shenkerenko stood at the portal. Knowing the captain to be
on the bridge, and having set Yuri at some trivial task, he
felt secure in entering the room. In spite of his efforts, he
had discovered nothing concrete, and St. Petersburg, their
destination, would soon be reached. Yuri had been close-
mouthed, and only some nebulous talk among the lower
crew had lent credence to his suspicions. Cautiously, he
surveyed the quarters searching . . . searching . . . A faint
splash from the adjoining room caught his attention. He
was instantly alert, like a mastiff momentarily at bay. Then,
surreptitiously, he moved to the open door. None of his
suppositions had prepared him for this revelation.

Her back was toward him, only the black curls piled atop
her head showing above the high-backed tub. But her
incredible face looked out from the small shaving mirror
which faced the door, a perfect oval captured inside the
square frame. He was transfixed—a weird reversal of
Perseus's stratagem, as if her reflected image, rather than
directed glance, had rendered him to stone. Reviving, he
moved slightly, and was rewarded by a more encompassing
portrait. Her subtle reflection in the glass was perfectly
framed by the gilt edges of the mirror. She looked like
someone in a Rubens painting—a female at her toilette. Yet
that artist would have found her wanting—so small, so
delicate, were her proportions. She was more a Botticellian
maiden, risen from the primeval waters, though the dark
locks and dusky skin marred this illusion. It seemed sacrile-
gious that he should behold this Sybaritic tableau. But he
smiled at his violation, and began to grow warm as he
watched her tiny hands encircle her high breasts. His eyes
narrowed and his breathing quickened. With a conscious
effort, he regained control and pulled himself away from

the seductive vision. This time that accursed Balenkov has gone too far, he thought in triumph. This scandalous state of affairs was surely enough to discredit him in spite of his princely title and standing with the tsar. By god, it was an intolerable breach of conduct. The higher-ups would not hear it from him. But there was one they could not easily ignore.

BOOK II
St. Petersburg —Moscow

*"His heart was formed for softness
   —warped to wrong,
Betrayed too early, and beguiled
   too long, . . ."*

George Gordon, Lord Byron

~ *Chapter 1* ~

Peter the First of Russia was a complex man with a great many passions. Not the least of those was his driving ambition to build a great Russian capital where for centuries before there had been nothing but the scattered homes of Finnish fishermen and farmers. If Peter the Great had waged war against the Swedes for his royally designated site, he fought no less of a battle with the natural elements. For St. Petersburg was literally raised from the depths of swamps and marshes. Thus, in a few short years he converted a wetland in enemy territory to a city in the grandest European tradition. No mean feat even for the tsar of all the Russias.

For the city that was eventually, and without exaggeration, to be likened to Paris, St. Petersburg had a humble yet thoroughly militaristic origin. It began as a fortress—a fortress well placed against the Swedes who controlled nearby Finland.

On May 16, 1703, Peter cut two pieces of turf from the ground with his bayonet. A casket containing relics of St. Andrew and gold coins was ceremoniously buried, and the pieces of turf laid crosswise over them. To mark the consecration, Peter placed a stone upon the mound and blessed it with holy water. *Sankt Peterburkh* he called it. Characteristically looking to the west, Peter used the Dutch rather than the Russian nomenclature for the city that was to honor his patron saint.

After a decisive victory at Poltava in 1709, Peter wrote, *By God's blessing and the bravery of my troops, I have just obtained a complete and unexpected victory without much effusion of blood . . . P.S. Thank God the foundations of Petersburg are firmly laid!*

From this day to the ultimate realization of the city, all of Russia would be bent to the task of building on these foundations. The royal family and the court were moved from Moscow. Heavy taxes were instituted nationwide, and forty-thousand workmen a year were conscripted from the provinces. Every nobleman owning thirty families of serfs was required to build, at his own expense, a residence in the new city. If the nobleman owned five hundred families, the residence must be of stone. The site and style of these homes were prescribed by a central authority. Building in stone outside of St. Petersburg was strictly forbidden, to insure that all stonemasons and the materials of their trade could be utilized nowhere but in the emerging city. St. Petersburg was to be a city of stone. Early on, Peter had realized that wooden structures were easy prey to the ravages of fire and flood. In 1705, Peter himself was nearly drowned in a flash flood. Shortly after, a decree was issued to the effect that no one might enter the city without bearing a stone; those riding in carriages or carts must bring several. Peter's city would stand.

Simone rubbed the delicate flesh under her chin as she sat with Yuri in the small caique. The coarse fabric of her jacket irritated her skin. To the casual observer, she looked no different from the other seamen who had earlier disembarked from the ship, which had been in port since early afternoon. Simone had peered anxiously out of the porthole for hours at the impressive stone edifices which began almost at the water's edge. The red ball of the sun had sunk out of sight behind the tall buildings, and the moon had risen above the gently lapping water before a silent Yuri had come to fetch her from the cabin. The ship, too, was uncharacteristically quiet, she had thought, as they passed down the long wooden corridor to the deck. Most of the ship's company had departed shortly after the vessel docked, and it now stood deserted except for a small skeleton crew. Her mind had raced briefly with thoughts of escape now that only the preoccupied Yuri seemed to stand between herself and freedom. But even as the beating of her heart pulsed faster in her temples, she knew such a course to be madness. Where should a lone girl go in a foreign port with no money and only some borrowed seaman's togs to clothe her? She had sighed deeply to steady her breathing, and followed the yeoman to the small boat which lay below, secreted in the shadow of the larger vessel.

Despite her situation, Simone could not help but feel a certain restrained elation as she lowered herself into the small boat—the long voyage had finally ended. It was with some pride that she congratulated herself on having made the tedious journey without the physically compromising *mal de mer*. I am a good sailor, she quipped to herself. And as she once again surveyed her rough garb, she knew that she had resurrected at least a parcel of the truth. But still Simone chastised herself for her ridiculous naiveté. "Sailor, indeed!" she scoffed. "A prisoner is what I am . . . his prisoner!" Her dark eyes narrowed as her mind reviewed Rudolph's sarcastic words that night of the storm: "Surely you know that you are now mine."

His! I would rather be dead than his. She thought a moment about her silent words, then resisted the thought. No, not dead. I won't give him the sweet satisfaction. He would probably rejoice at my death. No, I'll stay alive and somehow I'll make him rue the day he ever set eyes on me, ever touched me! She smiled wryly, and tasted for the first time in her life the sweet elusive ambrosia of revenge.

A movement above drew her attention to the ship's railing, where Rudolph's frowning face had appeared out of the darkness. Involuntarily, she drew in her breath and shrank farther into the shadows. She watched as he swung himself easily over the side and descended the rope ladder, the play of his strong leg muscles clearly revealed under the moon's silvery caress. As he dropped into the smaller vessel, his sudden movement agitated the water and caused small waves to bite the sides of the caique. Simone steadied herself in the rocking craft, looking up as Rudolph turned toward where she sat. His usually bronze face was washed pale by the moon skirting through dark wisps of phantom clouds. Was it the naked light that made his visage go all white? Or was it some dark unreadable emotion that manifested itself in an unnatural pallor? Simone realized that as long as she lived, she would never unravel the secrets of this man's unfathomable soul. As they slipped easily along the narrow channel, the oar dipping evenly into the water, Simone took in the stolid black shapes that rose abruptly from the water's edge. She noted the many

cupolas, their crosses thrusting resolutely upward against
the gathering darkness. These rising domes offered the only
relief from the horizontal expanse of the sleeping city.

Simone had also noticed the arching silhouettes of
bridges which spanned the calm waters of the canal from
bank to bank. As they sailed under one of the vaulting
structures, Simone reflexively lowered her head beneath the
pleated canopy of the small vessel. But the caique glided on
smoothly, making an unimpaired exit from under the
sweeping arc. When the boat emerged, the panorama
resolved itself into an altered symmetry. Whereas before
the buildings had been a great unbroken chain of stark
rigidity, the scenery now was laced with boulevards of trees
and sculptured shrubs. Simone guessed from this enlivened
view that they had entered a residential area. At once her
heart beat faster at the prospect of nearing Rudolph's
home. Would he be a different man in his own territory?
Would she in reality be treated as a virtual prisoner? The
ugly thought of a demonic Rudolph chaining her to an iron
bed invaded her mind. His dark face contorted in a wild
laugh as the hideous whip descended. Realizing the absurdi-
ty of this image, she sought to consider her situation more
realistically. Surely he would not be that barbaric.

After a time, the two men drew the craft expertly to a
small dock in front of a large building. The growing
darkness all but obscured the huge bulk of the stone edifice
rising magnificently before them. Simone mounted the
granite steps behind Rudolph, trying in vain to discern
details in the teasing light of the moon, which now hid, now
winked momentarily from behind a concealing cloud. This
was no doubt the family residence of which Rudolph had
spoken. She felt so awkward arriving thusly at such an
imposing mansion. Who would be here to greet Prince
Balenkov on his return? Would she be expected to continue
the ruse of her seaman's disguise? Just for once, she wished
she knew what was expected of her. Never did he communicate to her his unwritten rules, which she seemed ever to be
transgressing.

The huge wooden door swung abruptly inward at their
approach. Rudolph strode forward into the foyer, Yuri and
Simone trailing in his wake. Unlike the night-shrouded
facade, the elegant interior of the Balenkov residence stood
awash in light. Candles glittered in profusion from gold

sconces on the walls and from gold and crystal chandeliers
suspended from the high, carved ceilings. The sheer opulence of this room went beyond mere display. The floor was
of black and white marble tiles, laid in a complex geometri-
cal pattern, overlaid in places with rich oriental carpets. The
walls were carved panels of bleached oak with intricately
molded cornices. A splended staircase dominated the
space. It wound upward; its frozen motion was overseen by
the age-darkened portraits of Balenkovs which marked its
spiral path. Antiquity, this aura of an unbroken line of
wealth and position, had been distilled through centuries to
a fine patina, settling on this house and its possessor.

The tall servant, who had greeted Rudolph immediately
upon his entrance, totally ignored the young sailor standing
idly behind his master. Although the older man showed the
customary reserve, his delight at seeing the returning prince
was obvious. The formality of the moment was shattered as
Rudolph stepped forward and embraced the man, "Feodor,
my old friend, it is good to see you again."

"The household rejoices with your return, my prince.
You look well as always. Welcome home."

"Thank you, Feodor. It is good to see Russia again."

Feodor had effectively assembled the house staff, and in
almost military precision each bowed or curtsied as their
master moved before them. Simone noted disdainfully the
blushes and shy looks on some of the younger female faces,
and the proud and polite greetings of the others. She could
understand this little performance, this rapport between
master and servant. Was he not a prince? Did he not exude
power and command respect? Had he not at times made
even her feel in some way special? She hated herself for the
times that she had been such easy prey for his predatory
instincts. And yet, she sensed that the fondness that these
simple people felt for their master was no charade.

But she was certain that she had seen a dark side of his
nature, a glimpse of the twisted soul which surely remained
hidden from others. The intensely handsome face, the
perfect body, the indomitable will—this sensual assault had
often proved too powerful in the past. But wiser now, she
would not allow his fatal magnetism to draw her to him.

As if he had read her thoughts, he stood before her, his
face unyielding. Without warning, he jerked the tight
knitted cap from her head, releasing the thick black braids

to tumble down across her back. The fire in her dark eyes
matched in degree the steely coldness of his. She was glad
that the only witnesses to his abusive gesture were Yuri,
Feodor, and the single remaining maid, a young girl who
now stared at her.

"Marya, Simone is to have the White Room. See to her
needs," instructed Rudolph slowly in French. The young
girl had been selected by Feodor on hearing from Rudolph
that a servant was required who had some knowledge of
French. When Rudolph turned again to his discussion with
the manservant, Simone realized that she and the startled
Marya had been summarily dismissed. For a moment she
stared in anger and disbelief at his broad back.

"Mademoiselle," intoned the girl, catching her attention.
"*S'il vous plaît*," she said, pointing toward the staircase.
Resignedly, Simone turned and followed the young woman.

A strange depression descended upon Simone; her legs
seemed leaden, almost unable to cope with the wide stairs.
She barely noticed the richly brocaded walls of the second
floor hallway or that Marya had paused before the third
door on the right. As Simone drew near the threshold,
Marya opened the door to allow her entrance.

The White Room evoked an immediate reaction in the
apathetic girl. Simone was enchanted, beguiled. Whiteness
abounded. A whiteness with a subtle iridescence of pink
rouging its purity. It was like crawling into a giant seashell
—a pearly exterior hiding the blush of a spiraling core.

The intimate room was an opalescent jewel box. The
sheerest snowy silk tenting the ceiling and shirred against
pale pink walls. Drawn to the petite hand-painted vanity,
she avoided her own reflection in the oval mirror, fearing
that her disheveled appearance would spoil the illusion. She
concentrated instead on the exquisite feminine appointments arrayed before her. Who had last used the delicate
mother-of-pearl comb? Whose locks had grown glossy
beneath the silver-handled brush? What woman had
scented her white bosom with the heady fragrance escaping
from the crystal vial? She strode to an armoire. Diaphanous
sleeping garments hung within. Unconsciously, a hatred for
the perfect creature who had inhabited this bower grew
within Simone, marring her pleasure in these beautiful
surroundings.

A light knock at the door signaled Marya's return with

hot water. The girl indicated in stilted French that Simone
was to feel free to select a night shift from the armoire, and
to avail herself of anything else she wished. With that, she
departed, leaving Simone to her toilette. After sponging
herself with the steaming water, Simone walked to the
vanity and contemplated her image. The seaman's garb
discarded, she did not now feel such an intruder in this
luxurious boudoir. She picked up the brush and idly stroked
her raven tresses as she smiled at her own reflection.
Remembering the flagon of perfume, she touched the
flowery essence to her throat and wrists. Suddenly she
paused, a spiteful look stealing across her face. Continuing
to stare ahead, she deliberately poured the perfume into her
palm and splashed it lavishly upon her breasts and abdomen.

Scorning the content of the armoire, she slipped her
naked body between the pink satin sheets and allowed
herself to luxuriate in their smooth coolness. She lay upon
her back, and drawing one leg upward, she caressed the
satiny surface with the sole of her foot, rhythmically tracing
a circular path in the rosy fabric. How marvelous it was to
surrender to one's hedonistic impulses, to forget everything
in the rapture of the senses.

⁓ *Chapter 2* ⁓

It was early afternoon when Simone awakened from the
most refreshing sleep she had experienced since first she
had encountered the quixotic Russian. The room, which
had appeared so magical by gaslight, retained its buoyant
charm even in the strong light pouring in through the open

window. Simone sat up slowly and stretched with a lazy feline motion.

She was donning a silken wrapper when a soft knock sounded on the door. Simone half expected to see Yuri, but, of course, it was now Marya who entered with a light repast.

"Bonjour, mademoiselle," she offered in her strangely accented French. "I trust you slept well. Prince Rudolph ordered that you were not to be disturbed."

"Bonjour, Marya. Yes, I slept very well, indeed. Oh, that looks delicious. I am ravenous."

As Simone devoured the *piroshki*, small envelopes of crusty yeast pastry filled with a savory mixture of meat and rice, Marya reflected on a Russian saying that a good appetite assists the struggles of the soul.

The splendid joys of her leisurely hours, however, were not to remain. For once again Simone began to analyze her dubious position in Rudolph's home. What was she to do? Was she even to venture from this seductive prison? However, she was not able to ponder thusly for long, because Marya once again entered the room, this time bearing several brightly beribboned boxes. The young girl placed the parcels upon a chaise. She smiled broadly, saying, "*Pour vous, mademoiselle.*"

"*Pour moi?*" questioned Simone.

"*Oui, oui,*" answered the girl. "And Prince Rudolph instructed me to request that you be ready to depart for Moscow by seven o'clock this evening. I will return at six to help you dress."

Simone eyed the attractive packages from across the room. Curiosity overcame her, and she walked to where they lay.

She opened the smallest one first, to find a selection of lacy silk lingerie. Now she was becoming anxious to discover what treasures lay hidden in the larger packages. Her efforts were rewarded as she opened successive boxes revealing an elegant traveling outfit of buff colored silk foulard. The skirt was fronted with kilt pleats blending into a back bustle and skirt of overlapping flounces. The apron overskirt was edged in a coffee colored yak lace. The bodice, fashioned in the Josephine style, sported half-flowing sleeves with reversed cuffs. A cashmere mantle completed the spring suit. The final box was the most intriguing of all, its revealing shape proclaiming that within lay that dearest of feminine appurtenances, a new hat! Simone squealed in delight as she removed the bonnet from its tissue wrappings. It was of natural leghorn with a brim rolled coquettishly upward on one side, and crowned decorously with curling brown and cream ostrich plumes. She could hardly wait for six o'clock.

Simone sat poised in a straight-backed chair, a French novel by C. G. Dupré lying opened in her lap. She rose and placed the book facedown on the desk, and walked to the cheval mirror to once again assess her appearance. Never before had she worn such finery. She held the mother-of-pearl and silver mirror so as to view her head from all angles. She was amazed at the skillful way in which Marya's fingers had coaxed her heavy locks into the latest Parisian upsweep. And the charming hat—it was as though it had been designed especially for her, the way it flirted with her oval face and small head.

A sharp knock at the door broke her reverie. "*Entrez*," she called out, expecting Marya. Rudolph entered the room, his imposing image appearing suddenly in the glass. Startled, Simone turned quickly to face him. He had forsaken his uniform for civilian attire, but looked no less commanding. He wore a fitted waistcoat of brown linen over mustard trousers. In spite of his aura of power, he looked boyishly handsome and well scrubbed. His hair was a golden mane, and fell sensuously across his high brow. Its loose waves captured the fire of the gaslights. The lemon fragrance of his bath filled the room like some incense at nature's own altar. The gray-blue eyes presented the only coolness in the total aspect of this bright god. It was a wickedness that he looked the fulfillment of her every girlish fancy.

Behind his air of nonchalance, Rudolph was taken aback by Simone's transformation. The elegant clothes, the upswept hair, had turned his street urchin into a princess. Gone was the wild gypsy, the girl-boy sailor; in her place was this beautiful woman. Rudolph looked more closely at the tiny face no longer framed by the mass of black hair. Older, he thought somehow she looked older. Who was this woman? Rudolph knew it was a question which might never be answered.

As the carriage moved rapidly along the wide streets, Simone concentrated on the sights and sounds of St. Petersburg. They drove along a wide avenue which ran parallel to the water. She noticed a ship disgorging a group of passengers. She deduced from the exotic cargo of parrots, macaws, and other exotic flora and fauna, that these rather gloomy and bemused people were, like herself, first time visitors to Russia. She had little time to speculate further on their origin, or as to why they had come, before the speeding carriage propelled her toward and past other equally engaging tableaux.

Simone noted a few Russians peasants on the quay. And unlike the morose-looking foreigners, they seemed quite jovial. They appeared rather charming in their sheepskin coats, worn to ward off the chill of the May evenings. It was the physical appearance of Russian men, especially the tradesmen, which most fascinated Simone. How different they looked from Rudolph, or Yuri, for that matter. They gave the impression of holy men, representatives of some mysterious religion, with their flowing beards and colorful long-skirted caftans.

The phaeton turned onto a broad boulevard, and Simone marveled at the huge expanse of space—St. Petersburg was overwhelming in its grandeur. They plunged into the thick traffic. Did no one in St. Petersburg walk? The huge thoroughfare was filled with every sort of conveyance, hurtling along at a brisk pace.

"*Huzza yukh, yukh*! Come my pretty pigeons, use thy strong legs," cried the *izvaztchik* to his horses as they plummeted past the slower phaeton. The *budochniks* in their hexagonal booths hardly noticed the exessive speed of the carts careening past. Cries of "*Zhivaye, zhivaye*. Faster, faster," were heard everywhere, as impatient passengers urged their drivers to even greater velocities. It was only when the rare pedestrian was injured that the policemen ran from their watch boxes. Then it was that they claimed the offending vehicle as their booty and threatened the hapless driver with the Siberian wasteland.

Simone, who had been sitting forward on her seat, now reclined deeper into the leather upholstery of the carriage.

Resting her head easily on the high-cushioned back, she gazed out into the dusky evening. How the silent, unmoving sky contrasted with the almost frenzied activity of the city streets. The gray-pink horizon was smudged with circular and spiral shapes—cupolas and domes of greens and blues, quietly offering their star-strewn surfaces to the approaching night.

Simone listened as Rudolph gave detailed instructions to Yuri for the servants who had followed them to the railroad station. How grateful she was for Yuri's competent language instruction. She would, she realized, have felt even more disoriented in this alien Slavic world, had she not first mastered its language. His voice trailed off as he moved down the track to the second of the three Balenkov coaches.

Simone gave in to the lethargy which had begun to claim her. She almost fell onto the plump cream-colored cushions of the long tufted banquette. The interior of the coach was a blur of ecru satin and twinkling crystal and brass. She closed her eyes against the fading northern light, which was strangely amplified in the glittering, shimmering enclosure. Immediately, an image of Rudolph as he had appeared in the carriage plagued her. He had sat across from her. Though she had sought to ignore his brooding expression, again and again her eyes were drawn from the passing scenery to meet his silent scrutiny.

Rudolph . . . Rudolph. Why did he have the power to upset her so? She imagined him again. How well these surroundings suited him. He was really quite an elegant man despite the complete disregard he had for the more ostentatious social graces. His bearing, his clothes, everything bespoke a man in total control. It was so easy for him. Yet Simone realized there were times, those dark periods, when the control vanished, and an almost unholy fury was unleashed. He was *not* a simple man.

Again her mind returned to Rudolph's face in the carriage; she pondered over the cool intensity of his regard. What had he been thinking, planning? He had said not one word to her since the night he had found her with Yuri. She wondered where he was now. In the adjoining car? The *sleeping* car?

As the words came to her, she realized that for the first time in a long time they would probably share the same bed.

The high collar of the traveling dress felt suddenly constraining. Unconscious of her actions, Simone fumbled with the topmost button of the fitted bodice, and idly her hand slipped inside to massage the warm flesh above one breast. Some subtle change in the room's atmosphere told her that she was no longer alone. She opened her eyes to see him standing over her. He was a frozen colossus looming above her; the only evidence of life was a slightly convulsive movement of the muscles in the square jaw.

His coldness continued even through an elaborate meal served lavishly by attendants bearing course after course piled on silver trays. Rudolph ate methodically, but Simone only toyed with her servings, moving the food across the crested porcelain.

As Simone sat staring at the rich dessert, *kulitch*, a cylindrical cake filled with raisins and almonds, she knew she could bear this enervating silence no longer.

"Rudolph, the clothes which you gave me are so lovely. Thank you very much. You are too kind."

The man across the table looked up, *"De rien.* It was nothing."

Defeated by his apparent indifference, Simone refused to maintain such a pretense at civility. She rose unexcused from the table, and seated herself on the banquette which ran below the windows of the elegant coach. She peered pensively out into the darkness at nothing. Her gaze went beyond the bright reflection of the room's glittering interior to the black void that she knew to be the Russian countryside. Why am I here? she thought. Why did he not allow me to return to New Orleans as I wished? The riddle of her life with this man had no solution. Exhausted by the tensions of the day, Simone gladly relinquished herself to the soothing rhythmic sounds and the gentle rocking of the great black beast which pulled her along its relentless course. She nestled comfortably within its belly and for a time was freed.

He had watched her as she moved from the table, allowing her snowy linen napkin to fall behind her. She had fallen quickly to sleep, huddled childishly into the generous cushions. Now he could eye her openly. Sipping his cognac, he went to stand by the sleeping girl. He stared at the relaxed features, her lightly fluttering eyelashes dark upon pale olive skin, her full mouth slightly parted. She made a sudden movement, slipping a palm under her cheek. Deftly, he lowered himself to the divan so that he could observe her profiled face more closely.

If not for the special bond between himself and Alexis, he would never have seen New Orleans—he would never have encountered her. He had delivered Alexis's reply to the tsarevich yesterday, and though he was not privy to the content of their correspondence, he surmised that it concerned Alexander's growing dismay over his father's longterm liaison with the woman Catherine Dolgourky. And *this* woman, he thought, looking at Simone. Why had he not rid himself of her in St. Petersburg?—sent her home as she wished? She could only be an added complication in his life.

He was tired, he realized, and he knew he needed sleep. He lifted Simone in his arms and carried her through the rear door of the compartment. As they passed through the breezeway between the cars, she stirred against his chest. He hushed her with a light kiss upon her murmuring lips. Gaining the sleeping coach, he placed her gently upon the large bed. Quickly he disrobed, scarcely allowing his eyes to leave her face. Easing his naked body on the bed, he began undressing her with soft, gentle motions. Once his hands had drawn the heavy outer garments away from the fragile body, he began the intricate task of freeing the full breasts from the tight corselet. This accomplished, he finished with her cambric petticoat and lace-trimmed pantaloons. After he completed her release, he stared at her for a long time. Whatever else she was, she was a seductive sylph. Every peak, every curve and hollow begged to be kissed, suckled, fingered. As always, the perfection of her body called forth the familiar response in his own. He had to content himself, however poorly, with a purely visual taking of her. Though he burned for the contact of flesh upon flesh, still would he deny himself. He did not question why he felt this immolation to be necessary, he knew only that she would remain chaste this night. When finally he did touch her, it was to simply caress her tenderly, press her to him . . . and sleep.

~ Chapter 3 ~

The procession of carriages bumped along the dusty road which led southwest from Moscow. The chill of early morning was dissipating now as the sun climbed higher in the sky. But it was not yet summer, and the day promised to remain pleasantly cool. Simone, who was traveling in the lead carriage, watched as the flatlands surrounding Moscow gave way to gently rolling plains.

The beauty of the landscape blurred before her as she began to recall the early morning hours when she had first awakened. She had opened her eyes to stare blankly upward at a white vaulted ceiling. A single brass chandelier, massive in size, hung from the room's center, and Simone could remember absently counting its tall, frosted globes. The walls of the compartment were of a dark green like a cool, thick forest. Gazing about the chamber, she noted that the sparse furnishings were of heavy polished mahogany, and that the only seating was provided by two regency chairs in black leather. A lush oriental carpet sprouted from the mahogany floor—a profusion of green and burnished gold and orange. And like towering trees, the thick wooden posts of the enormous bed grew toward the ceiling.

She remembered rising to her elbows, the covers falling from her to reveal naked breasts. She could not recall undressing or going to the bedchamber. A vague impression of being carried through a noisy, windy space teased at the edges of her consciousness. Who had undressed her? Marya? Another of the girls? Rudolph? Somehow she knew it had been he. But why had he not taken her? Obviously, even her body no longer attracted him. She looked across the carriage to where he sat. He was staring out at the passing fields where a number of peasants bent over the rich black earth. Why was she here? What did he want of her?

The land! After so many months at sea, how he longed to feel the fecund soil of Mother Russia running through his fingers. Unbidden, a scene from his childhood intruded. He was very young. It was the summer before his father had gone away. His Uncle Gregor's family had arrived for supper; he, Rudolph, had come in late from a day spent with the farm workers.

"Here is our little *kulak* now." He could still hear his mother's gay voice and see his father's indulgent smile.

"Oh, Katerina, he looks like a common field peasant." That was his Aunt Natasha's disdainful rejoinder.

Mimka had come in then to fetch him to his bath, his cousin trailing after.

"Me too, Mimka. Me too," cried his cousin.

"Nyet!" The ugly sound of the word from his aunt rang down the corridor, as poor Mimka pulled him reluctantly toward his bath. He could still see his cousin standing in the threshold, his small face looking bruised and hurt.

How strange that he should remember something so inconsequential. And why think of it after so many years? When had he last seen Pavel? How far apart they had grown since that late summer day, and how ironic that the thing which they both valued so deeply should be the instrument of their unfortunate estrangement. The cost of inheriting the cherished *yarlyk* would indeed be high.

"You are right, Rudolph. Your countryside is beautiful," ventured Simone.

"I am pleased that you like it, Simone, since it is now your home," he rejoined, his words tinged with sarcasm.

Simone, totally exasperated with his perversity, resolved she would not give him another chance to repulse her efforts at amiability. Her eyes blazed as she turned pointedly away from his cool appraisal. As she looked unseeing out of the window, she vowed to herself: Think what you will, Rudolph Balenkov; this will not be my home, and I will not be your whore.

He had seen the rebellion in her eyes. And as always her

futile attempt at defiance had the power to distract and
amuse him. His deep laughter reverberated mockingly
inside the coach, and resounded in the still country air.

The barouche turned abruptly down a narrow road. The
trees seemed thicker, somehow closer together. Along the
side of the lane, small bright spots of color appeared, early
spring wildflowers and downy thistles. This dense lushness
continued for but a short distance when suddenly the
countryside erupted into a large golden meadow broken
only by a placid lake. Simone was totally unprepared for
this unexpected idyll. As she leaned forward, she was
further rewarded by the sight of large white geese skimming
gracefully across the water. Her eyes widened in astonishment as she realized that it was not geese which she spied.

"Swans!" she exclaimed quietly. Simone had never before seen swans, and the absolute purity and solemnity of
the scene touched her strangely. Her soft cry had not gone
unnoticed by Rudolph, who had been watching closely the
play of expressions across her face. As he contemplated her
childlike animation, a single tear ran glistening down her
cheek. He knew not why, but he turned quickly from her
emotion.

From time to time, Simone caught a glimpse of a high
peaked roof through the spaces between the tallest trees. At
first, she had not been sure of what she saw, since in color
and texture it matched the bolls of the trees. But as the trees
gave way to low shrubs and bushes, she was able to view
more closely all of the imposing dacha. It was an enormous
rambling structure, three stories in height, solid, constructed of the native wood. The huge frame was fashioned
entirely of the roughhewn logs, while the roof and gables
were of overlapping shingles of the same rustic material. Its
most delightful aspect, however, was an abundance of
intricately carved wooden fretwork, which decorated the
roofline and each sash and sill. The color overall was the
silver-brown of weathered birch, gaily enlivened with
charming carvings of lions and angels.

It was Rudolph's house. It spoke more accurately of the
man than did the urbane elegance of the St. Petersburg
townhouse. It was big and sturdy, and there were no
contrivances here. Even the charming fretwork was entirely
essential. There was a completeness in it, and it heralded

something of man's basic need to be honest with himself. It embodied the primordial bonding of man with the earth and the necessary regeneration of life and living in accordance with the sacred mysteries of nature.

The three carriages pulled before the country manor. Simone's momentary pleasure in the majestic structure was immediately replaced by anxiety. As the barouche halted, Rudolph bounded to the ground and moved toward the other carriages. Simone sat unmoving on the seat, not knowing if she should alight. As she sat bewildered, Yuri appeared and offered his hand to help her down. Before she could thank him for his kindness, Rudolph's voice intruded. "Yuri, see to the horses!" Again she was left alone, and watched Rudolph mount the steps of his home and disappear inside. It was Marya this time who rescued the stranded Simone. "Come, mademoiselle, we go inside."

As she stepped inside the large foyer, it was to see Rudolph in the embrace of a short, rotund woman. It was obvious that Rudolph was special to her.

"Rudya, Rudya, why did you not send word you were coming, you bad boy? Mimka would have had your favorite *smettanick* ready for you. But let me see how you look," she continued, holding him at arm's length. "Oh so thin, my little Rudya. You have not been eating aboard that ship. They cannot cook like your Mimka, uh? But no matter, I will soon have you fattened up again. We will have baked fish and plenty of *kasha, da?*"

Simone could not believe her eyes. This barrage of scoldings and endearments had produced a most remarkable transformation in the impassive Rudolph. He appeared boyish and abashed. Was this the same cynical man with whom she had spent the last few months?

The woman once again caught her attention. She was certainly of the peasant class, but something about her told Simone that this woman held a position in Rudolph's household that was unchallenged. And the woman herself —there was less here of the common plebeian than one would at first suspect. There was a dignity and a nobility in her, and it was certain that Rudolph Nikolaivich Balenkov loved her.

"Ach, my Rudya," she continued. "I almost forgot to tell you. You see I am getting old. My memory is not so good. Your Grandmother Josephine has come from Paris. She is with your Uncle Dimitri and will be overjoyed to see you. You must send Peter with a message."

"Baba Mimka, you will never be old, and I know you only forget what you do not wish to remember. But I am most glad to hear that Grand-mère is in Russia. It has been a long time."

"You know your Baba Mimka too well, Rudya. But tell me, where is my little Yuri? He is with you, *da?*"

"He is tending to the animals," Rudolph replied simply. "He will be along, Baba Mimka."

"Oh, I cannot wait to see how he is grown. But I fear he is as thin as . . . But Rudya, who is this beautiful little flower?" she exclaimed, having at last caught sight of the lone girl standing just inside the door. She walked toward Simone, all the while scolding Rudolph. "You are rude, Prince Balenkov, has not your Mimka taught you better? You will not introduce us?"

"This is Simone, Mimka. She will be our guest. Marya will also be staying, as Simone speaks French."

Mimka eyed the dark-haired girl more closely, allowing no aspect of her to go unnoticed. Finally she spoke, "I knew you were not Russian . . . no one in Russia has hair such as yours. But poor Mimka, she speaks no French . . ."

Simone smiled warmly at her and earnestly wished that she could let this kind old woman know that she understood and spoke Russian. Indeed, that her own dear grandson had been her tutor. But Simone knew that this fact would have to remain a secret, at least for a time. In some strange way, she still felt that it was her only real advantage over the arrogant Russian.

Simone did not fully understand her own next action. Maybe it was that this simple woman had been the only person who had made her feel truly welcome. But what she did seemed the only thing to do—so natural, so right. The young girl moved forward and placed her arms around the peasant woman, embracing her gently. It was a language that both women understood clearly. After the tender moment had passed, Mimka clapped for Marya. She hurried the two young women up the stairs, promising hot water for a bath before lunch.

When she returned downstairs, Mimka did not see Rudolph. She proceeded to the kitchen to give the orders for lunch. Through the open window she observed Rudolph

and Yuri near the stables. Rudolph's favorite wolfhound sat
at his master's feet, its sharp muzzle pointed upward, the
pink tongue lolling from between the powerful jaws. His
golden brown eyes were closed in pleasure, as the man
scratched him lightly behind the small ears lying neatly
against the long head. As Rudolph stood, the great animal
began to jump and spring at him, begging for more attention. Rudolph laughed huskily as the canine bounded
upward and pushed insistent paws against his broad chest.
Playfully, Rudolph pushed the beast from him and sprinted
toward the house. But his speed was no match for the loping
strides of the borzoi, who threw all his weight against the
back of the retreating man and managed to knock him to
the ground. His victory was celebrated by a wet kiss which
he administered to Rudolph's laughing face with his great
pink tongue.

Such a little boy, Mimka thought smiling. Idly, her
attention shifted to her grandson. He was standing some
paces away from Rudolph, grooming Torjok. She noticed
how he had looked furtively in Rudolph's direction from
time to time. It was as though he was frightened to go near
him. Mimka frowned deeply. So this was why he had not
come in yet to greet her. Something was wrong between her
two boys. She would find out what lay between them. She
would speak with Yuri before this day was over.

The room in which Simone found herself was utterly
enchanting. It was a unique combination of the delicate and
the rustic. Though almost spartan in its severity, the
incredibly fine handwork of the crocheted coverlet, and the
vases full of fresh wildflowers relieved its stark simplicity.
So this was to be her home. Under other circumstances, she
thought, it could have been a peaceful haven. She stepped
to the window to see if she might catch a glimpse of the lake
which they had passed. To her delight, the window opened
onto a balcony. As she moved to the wooden railing, the
sounds of laughter and a dog's barking caused her to look
downward. From around the side of the house, Rudolph
ran, a large white dog bounding at his heels. As she
watched, the dog caught up with him, and man and beast
tumbled to the ground. They were a wild spectacle of
flailing arms and legs, pouncing paws, and silky mane.
Rudolph could not stop laughing, and the great beast
seemed to revel in his master's good humor. The man

sprang up and ran beneath her balcony, his face turned toward the dog, who once again took up the pursuit. Rudolph's deep blue eyes were merry, and his fair hair was tousled by the breeze. She continued to stare after them as they ran on down the gentle slope toward the lake, which lay like a great mirror in the noonday sun.

The image of Rudolph wrestling with the dog merged with the earlier one of him in Mimka's embrace. Simone decided not to attempt to understand these troubling contradictions, but to quietly savor the moments and secretly file away the memory of them. She knew they might help her some day to understand, perhaps even forgive, the man who had taken her as his prisoner.

~ *Chapter 4* ~

Rudolph sat at the large table in the kitchen eating breakfast and looking over the accounts. Mikhail Yesenin would be going over the estate records with him shortly, and he must familiarize himself with the details. It was good to have a man like Yuri's uncle managing his local holdings, since he was so often away for long periods.

Nearby, Mimka hovered about the *pleeta*. She had shooed the kitchen maids on to other tasks, and was attending to his breakfast herself. As she refilled his mug with steaming coffee. he paused momentarily over the ledger. She saw her chance.

"I must speak with you, Rudya. I am an old woman; but I am not a fool. It is about Yuri. I don't know what has passed between you. Yuri will say nothing, but I see the sadness in his eyes. Has he not served you well, Rudya?"

"He has been most exemplary in his duties," Rudolph said tonelessly, not looking at her.

"Still I do not understand. I know that Yuri is sometimes too sensitive, but there is a strength in him. He will be a good man to have at your back someday. You have been like a brother to him, but I can see his heart is broken. And I see, too, that you are unhappy over this thing which has come between you. Whatever, my Rudya, do not let it grow."

When she finished speaking, she touched his shoulder gently. She would say no more, she would allow time and the deep bond between them to heal the breach. She moved back to the long stove. She must send Marya upstairs to see after the girl's breakfast. As she worked, she could not help but review her earlier scene with Yuri. He had been so passive, so distant. And when she mentioned Simone, Yuri became even more withdrawn. Mimka's intuition told her that whatever had passed between Rudolph and Yuri somehow involved this beautiful young woman. And who was this sweet child? What was she to Rudya? She turned to look back at him. He had not moved, but had remained staring vacantly ahead.

Simone was awake and dressed when Marya came into the room. The ornate traveling suit seemed out of place here, but she had nothing else to wear. Later she would have Marya speak to Mimka about finding her some more suitable and comfortable clothing, something like Marya herself wore.

Mimka greeted Simone warmly as she entered the huge kitchen, seating her at the table and setting before her a hearty breakfast of soft-boiled eggs and a basket filled with various breads and rolls. Accompanying this was quantities of strong hot coffee. It was this last which most pleased Simone, who reveled in the rich aroma. It was the first she had had coffee since her abduction from New Orleans. As she sipped the dark brew, she looked about her. The kitchen was cavernous; pots and pans and utensils of every description hung from hooks on the forward wall. The most impressive feature, however, was the stove, a monolithic structure which ran the entire length of one wall. The top was of a dull iron, but the front was a bright expanse of white tiles which glinted cleanly in the morning light.

Mimka approached the table with a pot of honey and

butter. "*Bien*, Mimka," said Simone warmly, indicating the bounty of delicious food before her.

"*Yeshte na zdorovie*," replied the woman cheerfully, patting the girl's shoulder and hoping that her answer of "Please eat and have good health" had been somehow understood.

A young servant boy came in then, his speech and manner indicating that some type of emergency had arisen which only Mimka could solve. Good-naturedly, Mimka scolded him, but allowed herself to be drawn from her kitchen.

Left alone, Simone began once again to ponder her dubious position in Rudolph's household. What was she to do? Where was she to go? And where was he anyway? How dare he insist on imprisoning her and not give her the orders of the day? she thought sarcastically. Rebelliously, she rose and passed through the back door out into the yard toward the stables. The beauty of the late spring day subtly overcame her bitterness and anger. Suddenly, the large wolfhound, which yesterday she had seen with Rudolph, sprang up from its place by the stables and bounded toward her. He slowed as he neared her, coming to sit at her feet, his handsome face tilted back to receive her attention. She laughed at his obvious manipulations, and succumbed to his charming ploy. Reaching down, she vigorously ruffled the silky hair behind his ears.

Yuri, who was coming from the stable, gaped at the pair in astonishment. "Simone, I can't believe what I am seeing! Baktu lets no stranger near the stables, and allows no one to touch him . . . except Rudolph. He is devoted to Rudolph. But I can see he has made a new friend."

"Have I gained a new friend, only to have lost another?" she asked, looking at him in earnest.

Her words affected the young man deeply. When he spoke his voice trembled. "Simone . . . the other night . . . I'm sorry."

"Hush, Yuri, it was not your fault. Let's not speak of it, please."

"But, Simone, there is something I must say. I do love you, Simone, but not like . . ."

"Oh, Yuri, my dearest, my best friend. I know that." She walked closer to him and took his hand.

From a distance, Rudolph, approaching on horseback,

saw the pair. Slowing his steed to a canter, he neared them
unnoticed. How like children they appeared, he thought
. . . so innocent, so young. Perhaps he had been wrong,
unfair? What harm could come from their simple friendship?

Yuri heard the horse's approach as Rudolph rode up.
When Rudolph dismounted, the boy turned, shielding
Simone with his body. Although his frame trembled with
tension, his eyes were uncharacteristically defiant.

Rudolph stood facing them, casually, legs apart, the
riding crop held loosely in his hand. "Mimka tells me that
your mother is asking after you, Yuri. You may go tomorrow. Leave early and spend the day. And take Simone with
you. She should see more of our countryside." He tossed
the reins to Yuri and sauntered easily toward the house.
The pair looked in amazement at his retreating back.

As he walked, his face drained of its color, and his gray
eyes looked ahead at nothing. His whole face had become a
rigid mask. He gained the house, pausing just inside the
threshold. The knuckles of his hands whitened as he
clutched at the riding crop. Savagely he jerked them
downward, and it snapped.

Simone had enjoyed exploring the large house that
afternoon. To her delight, the dacha was well equipped with
an extensive library. If nothing else, books would help to fill
the many lonely hours she knew lay ahead.

She opened one of the volumes that she had brought to
her room. Idly, she thumbed the leaves of a history of
Russia, its leather spine stamped grandly in gold with the
letters RNB. Despite her efforts at distraction, her mind
wandered back to the early afternoon. What had the scene
at the stables meant? Had being home changed Rudolph,
mellowed him? Or was it simply that he no longer cared
with whom she spent her time?

A knock on the door interrupted Simone's fretful musings. Marya entered, her arms piled high with clothing.

"See what Mimka has sent you, mademoiselle. These
belonged to her daughter, Nadia. She hopes that you will be
pleased with them. I am afraid that they will be too large,
but I am clever with the needle and can alter them easily."

"Oh, Marya, they are lovely. What beautiful handiwork!"

They were simple peasant clothes, but finely made, and Simone felt that wearing them would certainly do much in helping to end her feelings of isolation. Marya held up one of the garments, a white dress of nubby flaxen cloth. The yoke and cuffs were embellished with charming folk designs executed in heavy threads of red and purple.

Marya was indeed expert with needle and thread, and it was but a short time before Simone gazed at her reflection in the mirror. The creamy white of the simple garment finely complemented her dark beauty.

"It is perfect, Marya. I must thank Mimka for her kindness." Continuing to admire her reflection, Simone queried, "Do I look Russian?"

"No, mademoiselle, you will never look Russian," laughed Marya, "but you look very beautiful."

They moved to the small vanity, where Marya began to brush Simone's lustrous hair. As she ran the brush through her mistress's dark locks, Marya's face suddenly brightened, "Mademoiselle Simone, let me make you look Russian . . . just a little." Separating Simone's hair into wide sections, the servant girl plaited it intricately after the fashion of Ukrainian women, twisting and pinning until she had worked her magic on the glossy hair. Simone looked at herself in amazement, "You are wonderful, Marya. And I do look Russian . . . *un peu*."

Marya, still glowing from Simone's warm compliment, answered a soft knock at the door. A very young maid entered, her eyes constantly straying to Simone, even as she delivered her message to the impatient Marya. Simone strained to hear the whispered Russian; though she could not catch every word, she knew the message concerned herself and was not simply a summons for Marya. As the girl departed, casting one last curious glance at their foreign visitor, Marya announced, "Prince Balenkov requires your presence at supper tonight. Dinner will be served in a half hour."

Simone's spirits, which had risen with her novel toilette, plummeted precipitously as she paused before the wide staircase which led downward to where Rudolph waited. She felt torn. More than anything she hated his indifference, and yet, now that he had summoned her to his table, she dreaded the prospect of his company.

Her palm skimmed the wooden railing as she reluctantly

descended. How he had the power to manipulate her emotions! Only a moment ago she had been almost gay, but now . . . Her heart beat rapidly, and she could feel a slow trickle of perspiration between her breasts. She felt doomed to some bizarre sentence. Her executioner awaited, the verdict rendered. But the nature of her crime—that remained a mystery.

The dining room was dark except for the eerie light of myriad flickering candles. He sat at the far end of a long polished table, the slender tapers perfectly reflected within the depths of its shiny surface. The weird illumination reflected upward, lighting Rudolph's features from below. He was dressed in black, and only his shirt front and the projecting planes of his cheeks and brow were touched by the light. He was a dark specter. Only the high bones of his face captured the glow of the flame, while the hollows and recesses were shrouded in sharp ugly shadows. His eyes, usually only unreadable, were now swallowed altogether in black hollows—bottomless, unfathomable. She only knew that he had marked her entrance when he nodded for her to be seated. He sat unmoving, imperious in the large chair, his broad shoulders resting leisurely against its high back. Between the chair's twisted finials, his large head loomed, casting a sinister shadow against the pallid wall. It was an inky silhouette resembling some grotesque gargoyle perched on high.

Rudolph nodded again, and immediately a manservant stepped from a shadowed corner. The meal was interminable; course after course was paraded in a solemn procession by the ubiquitous manservant. Even his footsteps, as he trod from table to buffet and back, were muffled in the thick carpet. The clink of a silver knife against a porcelain plate, or a crystal goblet against the table seemed only to intensify the deathly silence. Rudolph seemed entirely absorbed in his food, devouring the endless servings with slow precision. She, on the other hand, had no appetite for the rich food, and could only pick nervously at the portions before her. The unbearable silence became a roaring in her ears. It was an intolerable punishment. Simone thought she would scream if she had to remain a moment longer in the great chamber. And when Rudolph excused her politely with a wave of his hand, she almost ran from the room. When she reached the stairs, she did run, anger and humiliation driving her like twin demons. She was breathless by the time she had gained her darkened room, and almost immediately a wave of nausea overwhelmed her. Running desperately toward the chamber pot, Simone helplessly rent her sickness from her heaving body. She poured water from the pitcher into a small glass and into the porcelain bowl on her dresser. Methodically she bathed her flushed face, then sipped slowly at the cool liquid. But her momentary control deserted her, and the crushing memory of that hideous meal and what it portended for the future overtook her. Blindly she groped for the bed. First they were only small droplets stinging the corners of her eyes, but soon her body was wracked by great uncontrollable sobs, as she pressed her face deeper into the pillows and wailed out her frustration and loneliness. She couldn't remember when the weeping had ceased and the sweet bliss of merciful sleep had overtaken her. But suddenly she was awake, alert, and she felt curiously refreshed —calm descending upon her. She became aware of the door to her room quietly opening. She looked up. It was Rudolph.

He stood etched in the doorway, the light from the gaslit corridor outlining his tall frame. It seemed an eternity before he moved into the room and closed the door silently behind him. When he came to the edge of the bed, he looked down at Simone, but his face was oddly devoid of all expression. She lay paralysed on the bed, watching as he began to loosen the cravat at his throat. Then without warning he pulled and tore at his elegant dark suit, and it seemed only a moment until he stood naked before her. The moonlight which filtered into the room cast the perfect body in a silver hue, caressing every angle, every hollow. He was a silvered Adonis, pure of line and form. She felt a lazy warmth flood her body, and shamefully she realized how eager she was for what she knew must come. She closed her eyes, and soon she felt the pressure of his body on the bed. He touched her bottom lip with a single finger, and brushed it lightly. Lowering his head to hers, he ran his tongue over her opened mouth and quickly slipped it between her teeth. Her arms went around his neck and she buried her fingers in the thick hair at his nape. He broke the kiss and raised himself over her. She could feel his gaze in the dark, boring into her, searching for something that was hidden from them both. Rudolph began to pull the pins from her hair, and kissed each braid as it tumbled to her breasts.

Somehow she knew he was smiling as he ran his fingers through the loose plaits, completely freeing the thick black masses. As his breathing quickened, he took her face between his broad palms and began to slip his tongue inside one ear. He murmured something incomprehensible as he moved to her pulsing neck. He kept up the ritual kissing of her pliant body until no portion had gone untouched by his searching tongue and mouth. It was a passionate odyssey which had begun with his kneeling adoringly at her feet, kissing the small toes and slim ankles. He could not stop the feverish orgy and Simone lay wild on the bed, responding openly to his searing passion.

Oh, God, she wanted him so much. It was such ecstasy to surrender, to welcome his piercing maleness into the deep well of her womanhood.

He grabbed her wrists and jerked them above her head, causing her body to arch upward. She cried out his name as he fell upon her. He bit into the soft flesh of her neck, and Simone winced more in pleasure than in pain. She twined her arms about his hard body, hungrily pressing him to her burning flesh. He moved to the ripe breasts and Simone cupped them, willingly offering their sweetness to his open mouth. There was no hurt anymore, no anger, no fear between them, only the pure passion of their driving bodies.

Pulling him to her, she sought to take his weight full upon her smaller frame, as if the very mass of him could crush the sweet poison of his lovemaking from her treacherous body. But the riptide of desire swept her beyond all shame, and her wantonness was complete. "Yes," she breathed, her hips moving against his heaving thighs. "Oh yes . . ."

When she had freely opened herself to him, he entered her with a pleading desperation, a longing that seemed to reveal an emotional deprivation as much as a physical need. Hungrily, he had plunged deeper ever deeper into her velvet softness. And when the explosion came, he felt it more acutely in his head than in the core of his manhood.

They were quiet now, stilled with the warm fulfillment of their desire. At last Rudolph broke the silence. "I will have your things moved to my room tomorrow, Simone."

"Please, Rudolph, I love this room. It is good to have a place of my own."

"Very well, you may stay here if it pleases you, but you will sleep with me, Simone."

Again they lapsed into silence, each thinking their own thoughts. Simone began to reflect on her strange relationship with this enigmatic man. There was so little that they truly shared, but she was filled with a simple contentment in knowing that, at least, this intense physical bonding was a joy to both.

When Rudolph spoke again, his words revealed very little of what he had been thinking, but they were immensely pleasing to Simone. "We shall soon go to Moscow, Simone. I want you to see it. We will buy you clothes and anything else that you need."

"Oh, that would be lovely, Rudolph. I should like very much to see the city," said Simone eagerly. "When shall we go?"

"There will be time enough when I return from my Uncle Dimitri's, ma petite," Rudolph replied almost indulgently.

"Rudolph, may I get some paints when we are in Moscow? I used to love to paint when I was younger. Your beautiful countryside and its people have made me want to do so again."

Rudolph smiled. He was pleased with Simone's interest in the land, the land he loved above all else. "Yes, Simone, of course you may. You may have whatever you like." Kissing her lightly on her forehead, he turned and blew out the lamp.

~ *Chapter 5* ~

Simone awoke early and prepared for her outing with Yuri. Marya had evidently worked last evening on the other garments, and they lay neatly on a chair. She selected the simplest one, and plaited her hair, tying a babushka about her head as she had seen the other girls do.

Marya came in to collect the breakfast tray. "I see you are ready, mademoiselle. That is good. Yuri is impatient to be off."

"Tell Yuri that I shall be down shortly," replied Simone, turning toward the mirror. Looking at her image, Simone mused that if the softer colors of her garment could suddenly take on a more brilliant hue, it would be the New Orleans gypsy who smiled wryly from the glass. Remembering the gay abandon of that girl, Simone firmly resolved to have a good time this day.

As she moved downstairs, toward the kitchen, Simone overheard two servant girls gossiping furtively in the shadows. Because of their provincial dialect and their hushed tones, Simone did not quite understand the full import of their chatter, but the name Ilse was said repeatedly. The sound of their silly giggling followed her into the kitchen. As Marya had said, Yuri was waiting impatiently.

"Oh, you are here at last, Simone," exclaimed Yuri, rising from the table where he had been sharing coffee with his grandmother. "Let us be off."

"Please, Yuri, I must thank your grandmother for the lovely clothes she has given me."

111

She turned then to Mimka and thanked her profusely in halting Russian. Yuri looked at her quizzically. Had he not taught her better use of the language than her poorly phrased expressions indicated?

Mimka rose and embraced Simone warmly, her face revealing her pleasure. She spoke to Yuri, who relayed the message to Simone in French.

"Mimka is so pleased that you like the dresses. She says you make a beautiful Russian girl. She is delighted that you are learning our language."

Simone smiled at the woman in appreciation for her kind words, and would have continued their little conversation, had not Yuri interrupted.

Walking outside Simone complained, "I realize you are anxious to see your family, Yuri, but you were rude to hurry me away from your grandmother."

Yuri looked away and apologized nervously, "I am sorry, Simone. I did not mean to be impolite to you or my grandmother. But my mother expects us before lunch and my home is some distance away."

Strangely, his words seemed almost rehearsed, and her hopes for a pleasant day were somewhat dampened. She stopped in midstep. Instinctively, Simone felt that in her next question lay the answer to the boy's strained behavior. "Yuri, who is Ilse?"

Yuri froze at her words, but said only, "Why do you ask?"

Moving to where he stood, Simone continued, "I heard some servant girls talking. They mentioned the name Ilse several times. I had the impression their gossip somehow involved me."

He turned to face her, knowing she would not be satisfied with less than the truth. "She is Countess Ilse Ivanova Durenchev, the betrothed of Prince Rudolph Nikolaivich Balenkov." Softening his manner he hurried on, "Simone, I . . . Ilse and her father Count Durenchev are to arrive here within the hour. We must go."

"Oh," was all she said, but Yuri knew, as he looked at her small, white face, that his words had affected her cruelly. Yuri turned his full attention to the hitching of the horses. Suddenly, Simone's hand was on his arm. When she spoke, he hardly recognized her voice, "No,

Yuri, we will not go. I would see this Countess Ilse Durenchev."

"No, Simone, we must not stay. I dare not linger or the lateness of my departure will be an obvious disobedience. Do you understand?"

"Yes, I would not wish to be the cause of any more trouble for you. But you must go without me, if necessary, for I am determined to see her." Relenting a bit at his dilemma, she went on, "Oh, please, Yuri, do this one thing for me." Seeing the stricken look on her face, Yuri yielded. "Very well, Simone, but we must not be seen. And we must leave as soon as they are inside."

As he spoke the words, the sound of an approaching carriage was heard. Yuri grabbed Simone's hand and they scurried to the front of the house, concealing themselves behind the thick shrubbery. Almost immediately, an impressive landau pulled up before the dacha. Stepping down smartly from his perch, the uniformed footman opened the carriage door, and a rather short, bespectacled man emerged. He held out his hand to assist someone from the coach. An incredibly tall woman stepped down, her thin form unfolding gracefully from the carriage's padded interior. She was taller than what was considered to be fashionable, but her slim body and graceful movements distracted one from the excessive height. Her flaxen hair piled high beneath an elaborate bonnet seemed to blend evenly into her pale, almost translucent skin. She was dressed elegantly in a blue silk gown which matched exactly the color of her eyes. They were large light-blue orbs, astonishingly clear, and they were the only concession to roundness in an entirely angular face. Her face was flawless, the white skin stretched tautly over the high bones of her cheeks. The mouth was wide, though thin lipped, and it added to the hauteur of the arrogant planes of her face. But her most impressive feature was her delicate hands, their long tapering fingers seeming to hold the world and everything in it at bay. She was beautiful, but it was a beauty born of timelessness and ice; in it there was no part of life's warming tide.

Rudolph stepped from the house, greeted the small man, and kissed the woman's extended hand. She placed her arm within his, and the party moved inside.

Yuri took hold of Simone's arm and pulled her up, "Come, Simone, my mother is waiting."

For a time they rode in silence, Simone's mind seething with images of the fair beauty who was everything that she was not. But soon a more hateful vision came flooding into her consciousness—his hands, his mouth, his tongue raking her fevered flesh, bringing her to fulfillment. And her own shameless, unbridled lust. How could she be such an untamed wanton? Yes, she had become his whore. She was worse than he. At least he had never indicated that she was anything but the means to an end. But oh, how she hated him, his using of her. It was all so perfect for him. The prince could have his princess and keep his whore as well. She vowed to renew her efforts to escape.

Yuri broke into her troubled thoughts. "I think you will like my family, Simone. There are my parents, my sisters Natalie and Anna, and my baby brother, Step. Do you come from a large family?"

Simone hesitated for only a moment, then spoke softly. "I do not know, Yuri. I was taken as an infant to the Ursuline convent in New Orleans. I know nothing of my family."

"I am sorry, Simone, I did not know," said Yuri, regretting that he had chosen the wrong subject to pull her from her forlorn reverie.

"Of course, you did not, *mon ami*. There is no need to apologize. It is difficult for me to talk of it, but it is something which I must face. I shall never know who I truly am. But, come, tell me more of your family. I am most anxious to meet them."

The Yesenin family was of the *kulak* class. Unlike most Russian peasants who lived on the fringes of subsistence, the *kulaks* were peasants who, because of good fortune or industry, or a combination of these factors, had risen above their fellows. Because of their economically elevated position, the *kulaks* were often despised by their peers. Indeed, the word *kulak* meant "fist"—an unscrupulous fist grabbing at monetary gain whatever the costs. However, many were simply good, hard-working people who had used their natural aptitudes and ripe opportunities to the fullest extent. Such a people were the Yesenins.

Ludmila Yesenin no longer had to labor in the fields, and Ilia Yesenin could afford to employ other peasants to work on his land. The Yesenin children, however, were still expected to rise early each morning and labor painstakingly until the evening hours at their father's side. Such had been the life of Yesenin children for generations.

The Yesenin house was simply a smaller, cruder version of the Balenkov dacha. And it was from this simple abode that Simone now saw Yuri's mother emerge. She was a sturdy woman, who bore the weathered face and hands of the Russian peasantry. Ludmila smiled broadly as they walked to meet her at the door. She held a platter covered in snowy linen. Upon it lay *hleb ee sol*, a freshly baked loaf, and a small silver dish mounded with salt. *"Dobro pojalovat,"* she spoke—"Welcome, with good will." She bowed low from the waist. Simone cut a slice from the crusty bread, dipped it into the salt, and ate it, as Yuri had instructed. It was a lovely ceremony, she thought, passed down through the ages by people who, though they might have nothing more to offer than bread and salt, did so generously and with grace.

The ritual salutation complete, Yuri's mother threw her arms about her son and kissed him soundly on both cheeks. She spoke quickly, asking question after question, beginning another before the last could have a proper answer. Simone could catch little of the rapid exchange, much of it in the local dialect, but a grasp of language was not necessary to comprehend that Yuri's mother doted on him.

Although Simone was somewhat shy at first, it was not long before she found herself on the kitchen floor enjoying the precocious antics of little Step. As Ludmila prepared lunch, her joyful inquisition of her son continued. She listened attentively, as Yuri spoke interestingly of his voyage to the United States. This private moment between the Russian mother and her son had a special poignancy. How rare it was for such a pair to find the time to share intimate joys away from the mundane immediacy of their lives. Ludmila was almost totally absorbed in her various domestic duties, and Yuri had an existence far removed from the life of the *mir*.

The day passed pleasantly. Simone had insisted on help-

ing Yuri's mother with the evening meal, and the two were
still stirring at the pots when the rest of the Yesenin family
returned from the fields. The house instantly became a whir
of excited greetings, and Yuri was overwhelmed with hugs
and kisses from his father and two sisters. Simone gazed
longingly at the charming tableau, and once again she
reflected on the beauty of being a part of a loving family. Of
all the things she had missed in life, it was for this that she
most yearned.

Yuri, somewhat embarrassed by his family's effusiveness,
was glad to draw the attention away from himself to their
guest.

Simone liked Yuri's father immediately. He bore the
simple dignity of a man who had bound his destiny to
the black soil of Russia. Anna, the oldest of the children,
was gregarious like her mother, while Natalie, two years
younger than Yuri, was like him, shy and sensitive.
Both girls were obviously impressed with Simone's exotic
beauty, and exclaimed over her in their rich metaphoric
speech.

Yuri noted that during the day with his mother, and now
with the others, Simone took no pains to hide her limited
fluency in their language. He did not quite understand her
motives for keeping this ability a secret from Rudolph and
his household, but whatever her reasons, he would respect
them.

The only distressing moment for Simone came during
dinner, when Ilia asked about Prince Balenkov. It
was obvious that Rudolph was something of a legendary
figure to these simple people, and that they were in awe
of Yuri's closeness to him. Simone was greatly relieved
when Yuri tactfully avoided any direct references to his
captain, and only talked in generalities about the voyage.

After the dinner dishes had been removed from the table
by Anna and Natalie, Yuri's father called for the balalaika.
Simone looked quizzically at Yuri, but his only reply was a
simple "You will see."

It was but a moment before her curiosity was delightfully
satisfied, as the haunting strains of what sounded like a
mandolin filled the room. For what seemed like
hours, Simone whirled across the floor and sang with

the Yesenin family, laughingly accepting their polite compliments on her adroitness at learning the folk songs and
dances.

But at last, the hour grown late, they had to leave.
Reluctantly, Simone bid the happy family good evening and
thanked them for their many kindnesses. They replied that
they hoped she would return often.

The night was gorgeous, ablaze with stars. As they drove
along contentedly, Simone turned to her companion,
"Yuri, this has been one of the happiest days of my life.
Thank you!"

"Seeing you so happy pleases me, Simone. And you must
know you thoroughly enchanted my family. Hopefully, we
can return again soon."

"And the music, Yuri. I love your Russian music. But
why are all the songs so sweetly melancholy?"

"It is the long winter, Simone. You have yet to experience
a Russian winter. You must do so before you understand
the Russian soul. But it is spring, the best of the year.
Let me teach you a happy lyric." Soon the chill of the May
night was warmed by the lilting voices of the two young
people.

It was late when she mounted the stairs and entered her
room. Simone undressed quickly, the happy adventures of
the afternoon and evening still pleasantly lingering in her
mind. But she was tired, and sleep came immediately.
Suddenly she was awakened from her peaceful slumber by a
violent noise. It was the sound of her door being flung
wildly open and banging against the wall. She started
up. The room was dark, but she could make out the towering figure in the gloom. His angry voice was loud in the
quiet.

"Did I not tell you, you would sleep in my room?"

Disoriented only momentarily, Simone countered
viciously, "When will you learn that you do not own
me, Rudolph Balenkov? And besides," she spat, "I
thought your taste in women had become more refined of
late."

Too angry to absorb the import of her last words, he
swept her savagely from the bed. "But I do own you,
Simone. And you will not forget it after this night."

He flung her ignominiously over his shoulder and carried

her down the long hallway, Simone beating her tiny fist upon his broad back. Through her angry tears, she was absurdly mesmerized by the play of his muscular calves, which were bared intermittently by his short silk robe. It was to this and similar meaningless details that her mind clung, as if they could in some way black out what was happening. In the slow trajectory of her flight from Rudolph's shoulder to the massive bed, she took in abstractly the splendor of a large gilt-framed oil painting and then a wondrous chandelier of elkhorn. But with the impact of her body against his bed, she was instantly alert. She bounded up from the deep recesses of the plush coverlet and struck. Her nails, raking across his cheek, left bloody paths in their wake. Slowly Rudolph ran his fingers over the proud flesh of his wound, and then he leaped. Simone was totally unprepared for his catlike prowess, as she was crushed against the flat of the bed by his heaving body. His breath came forth in hisses as he struggled to pin her down while unbinding the cord of his robe. When he had freed himself, he whipped up her cotton shift above her breasts. He entered her like some wild animal, and his fierce thrusting shaft burned into her soft flesh. She knew that she could not fight him. He was too strong, too willful. At last she lay still, his large body pounding unmercifully against her fragile frame. Her only salvation was to continue to disassociate her mind from this brutal rape. She looked about the room . . .

~ *Chapter 6* ~

When she woke the next morning he was gone, taking Yuri with him. She surmised that he had traveled to his uncle's estate as planned. Simone tried not to think of what had passed between them last night. It was too painful, too frightening. And if her body felt bruised and broken, her spirit, her mind, was even more hatefully defiled. She remembered that he had promised to take her to Moscow on his return. After last night, she was sure, he would forget his promise. What did she care! She hated him now, more than ever. She hoped he'd never return at all.

But as the days passed, her loneliness became as great an enemy as her princely tormentor. Marya was sweet, but her French was limited, and she was hardly a stimulating conversationalist. Mimka was always kind, but her many duties kept her busy, and besides, Simone was still reluctant to reveal her knowledge of the Russian language.

Simone once again turned to her faithful companions of the past to relieve her boredom. When the books which she had borrowed were exhausted she returned once again to Rudolph's library. There were many volumes on the history of Russia and its people. And as Simone wished to better understand this intriguing country, she selected those texts which were written in French or English, not trusting her limited Russian. The one exception was a replica of an ancient illustrated manuscript called the *Primary Chronicle*, which began: "These are the tales of bygone years . . . from whence arose the Russian land."

119

Although the library contained a French translation of
this fascinating tome, Simone thought it worthwhile to
struggle with the original. It related the story of the
beginnings of the Russian state from the time of Rurik to
the early thirteenth century. Rurik was a Varangian prince,
who, according to the legendary chronicle, was invited by
the Slavs in 862 "to rule and reign over us." The seeds
planted by Rurik and his brothers flowered in the tenth
century with the golden age of Kievan Rus, and thus began
the rise of Russian nationality, the Russian state, and
ultimately the imperial tsardom. This flowering of Kievan
Rus meant quite simply that the inhabitants of the land
began to think of themselves as distinctly Russian, sharing a
common language, law, and art. The capstone of their
cultural and political unification, however, lay beyond intrinsically Russian sources, it rested firmly in their conver-
sion to Christendom.

To truly appreciate the significance of this period, one
had to consider the deep spirit of optimism displayed by the
people, noble and peasant alike, for their future. There
existed a sense of unity and a sense of purpose. It was good
that such solidarity prevailed, because in the year 1206, an
event took place which was to forever alter the course of
Russian history. The Mongols began their treacherous
march from the steppes.

Simone was fascinated by this colorful story which
seemed to be as much myth as factual history. But the tale
ended with the beginning of the Mongol penetration. So she
turned to another text, and there was able to pick up the
thread of the narrative.

By 1237, Batu Khan, the grandson of Genghis, had in
effect captured all of Russia. Although the bright sun of
Russia had set, it would dawn again, but the nucleus of
power would shift to a new city-state, the eventual seat of
the Russian imperial dynasty—Moscow.

The Mongols in one sense were passive rulers, allowing
the people to follow their own customs and laws. The real
essence of domination by the Golden Horde over the
Russians lay in their ability to impose a relentless collection
of tribute. At first, Batu amassed his revenues through
direct taxation, sending his merciless emissaries straight to
all the principalities. In time, however, a new system of
extracting the tribute was allowed to develop in the Mon-

gols' centralized bureaucracy. The Mongols turned over the task of tax collecting to the Russian princes themselves. Each prince was first required to journey to the capital of the Golden Horde in Saray in order to obtain a *yarlyk*, or charter. The *yarlyk* was an extremely valuable document which invested the prince with supreme power in his territory, and designated him a viceroy of the khan himself. The princes soon realized that this political investiture gave them such dominance that they were able to demand sums from the people far in excess of that required by the khan. The enticing lure of vast monetary gain imbued in the princes such ruthlessness and avarice that frequently they fought each other in order to gain *yarlyks*.

It was perhaps a fatal miscalculation to allow the princes themselves to function within the Mongol administrative system. For after the Muscovy princes had grown so wealthy and strong, they became motivated by something beyond mundane priorities. They were infused with the desire to rule once again by right where they now ruled by permission, and to shape a formidable destiny for the people of their ancient land. Therefore, it came to pass that the great princes of Muscovy threw off the Mongol yoke, and one emerged as most powerful. The grand prince of the Muscovite duchy eventually became the tsar of all Russia.

Throughout her reading, there was constant mention of princes, boyars, grand dukes, and finally the tsar himself. Simone was becoming thoroughly confused as to how the Russian system of nobility had evolved, and how it compared with the more familiar class structures of Europe. It was not until she discovered a highly informative French volume that she began to gain some comprehensible answers to her questions. The surprising fact was that there appeared very little similarity at all between the European and Russian social hierarchies.

In Russia, one had to make a certain distinction between the nobility and aristocracy. The nobility or *dvorionstvo* were those who had received a hereditary rank due to services rendered the state within either the military or civil service. The aristocracy, on the other hand, consisted of the descendants of ancient families of illustrious name, who might or might not be titled. There was, however, one group which stood apart. These were the descendants of the Varangian sovereigns, the princes of Kiev and later Moscow, who retained their titles even after the centralization of power under the tsar. The Balenkovs, Simone learned, were one of some forty families who could trace their lineage in a direct line to Rurik himself.

There was something daunting in this knowledge of her captor's heritage. She closed the book absently and left the room. When she emerged into the yard some minutes later, Baktu joined her. With the big hound at her side, she wended her way toward the cool serenity of the forest. Even the tranquillity of that verdant wood, however, proved an inadequate distraction. Her mind stubbornly continued to review all that she had read.

What a ruthless lot they must have been, these princes, to survive that cruel past with their wealth and lands intact. As the product of such an inheritance, Rudolph's arrogance toward her was not, after all, surprising. Still, she could not accept his unbridled cruelty. It might be true that he was a Russian prince, the culmination of centuries of breeding, and she an orphan with no real past. But, was she not too a person, a unique individual? Perhaps Rudolph's peasants might accept his word as law, but she, Simone Montpellier, would not.

As she made her way toward the lake, Baktu suddenly growled, his hackles rising menacingly. She, too, had felt some subtle emanation which charged the once peaceful atmosphere in the glade. She grasped the borzoi's collar and sought the source of the strange disturbance.

Standing at a distance was the very tall figure of a man. He stood almost casually beside his horse, the fanning branches of the oaks casting concealing shadows over his features.

"Rudolph!" Simone cried in surprise.

A deep chuckle answered her spontaneous exclamation. As the man moved leisurely toward her, the sunlight touched his face, startling her. It was not he!

When he approached closer, she understood the nature of her error. He was tall like Rudolph, with the same elegance of form, the same perfect symmetry. But the coloring was all wrong. Where Rudolph was fair, the stranger was dark. He bore the same handsome but arrogant features—the straight nose, the square jaw, the wide sensuous mouth. Night-black hair tumbled loosely over his high brow and temples, but it was to the eyes that she was drawn. They were golden-brown, like liquid amber lit from within. This mysterious interloper was a doppelganger from an alternate universe, a strange mirror twin. It was Rudolph, but it was not.

"I'm sorry to have startled you," said the man with easy grace. "I paused along the way to rest my horse, and fell victim to the beauty of the glade."

As the man spoke, Baktu continued to growl threateningly. Simone pulled harder at his collar and apologized.

"Please forgive him, he is wary of strangers. Hush, Baktu," she reprimanded softly. "The gentleman means no harm."

The animal succumbed to her gentle scolding, but curled protectively about her feet, his alert eyes never leaving the dark man.

"Please, dear lady, I am not afraid. He only does that for which he was bred. Surely, *you* do not think me the wolf which he was born to hunt."

"Oh, no, m'sieur, of course not," Simone acquiesced, still mesmerized by the man's uncanny likeness to Rudolph.

She watched entranced as he stooped to pick a single blossom which grew scant inches from where the wolfhound lay.

"I trust that we shall meet again, mademoiselle," he murmured, as he placed the fragrant bloom in her hand. His yellow eyes locked with her own. She had entered such treacherous depths before, but then it had been shifting gray mists, not blinding feral flame, which barred her farther entry. A strange lassitude pervaded her senses, and if it had not been for Baktu's warning growl, she could not have said what might have happened. Dreamlike she watched the dark stranger as he walked away. He mounted the large gray stallion, and was gone.

The inane noises of the party swirled about Rudolph as he stood isolated from his uncle's guests. He glanced across the room to where Dimitri stood deep in conversation with his old friend, Valery Sokolov.

Dimitri Balenkov was the only son of Grand Duke Peter Stephanovich Balenkov and his first wife, Maria. It was his tragedy that his wife had died, leaving him no heirs. For reasons known only to himself, Dimitri chose never to marry again, but instead to allow the Balenkov succession to pass eventually to one of the sons of his much younger half brothers. The half brothers were twins. Nikolai and Gregor, born to his father's second wife, Lisaveta.

It fell to Dimitri, according to the Balenkov tradition, to select the most worthy, not necessarily the eldest male heir, as his successor. The symbolic investiture with the *yarlyk*, along with the realities of bearing the title grand duke, and presiding over the vast Balenkov holdings, required that this heir be a man of incomparable integrity and strength of will.

His uncle had aged, Rudolph reflected, but he still projected an inner strength which could not be diminished by time. Since he had been a child, Rudolph had been unable to think of the Balenkov lands without the simultaneous thought of Uncle Dimitri. In his young mind the two concepts were inextricably linked. Dimitri was the land —majestic, durable, eternal. To be a Balenkov, a man had to take unto himself the glorious earthwoman, the Russian soil. He had to ply her with the labor of his hands and infuse into her the seed of his genius. No man had ever served this mistress better than Dimitri Balenkov. It was hard to conceive of a world which no longer contained his uncle's ruddy, bearded face. Rudolph wanted more than anything to succeed to the honor of the *yarlyk*, yet some childlike part of him that lingered, wished that it might rest forever in Dimitri's capable hands.

As Rudolph stood deep in thought, a group of students who had traveled from Petersburg, one a distant cousin, approached him.

"Good evening, cousin," said the mischievous Anton, gaining the man's attention. "We have just been discussing Mikhailovsky's latest essay. Perhaps you are familiar with it."

Rudolph nodded his head in assent.

"Well then, Prince Balenkov," began one bespectacled youth, whose self-conscious mannerisms and style of dress marked him as a member of the intelligentsia, "I am sure you could not fail to agree with his masterful conception of all history as an endless struggle for individuality."

"Yes," asserted another of the young men, vying for

attention, "Mikhailovsky is certain that the coming golden age will thus be one of subjective anthropocentrism . . ."

Across the room, Sonia Beloselski sighed to the group of ladies in which she stood, "The romantic story in the month's *Nina* is simply inspiring."

"Really, dear, I thought it quite insipid," remarked the Countess Arapov, "but the new novel by Bratsky—ah, the man is a genius at portraying the more sensitive emotions! Have *you* read it, Ilse?"

The Countess Durenchev answered briefly in the negative, adding some banal observation which seemed to satisfy her companions, who went on blithely with their conversation. But Ilse had only mouthed the words mechanically, her eyes straying to Rudolph, surrounded by the impish Anton and his friends.

Rudolph stood next to his cousin, his legs slightly apart, his arms folded over his chest. He said nothing, but his face was a study in boredom and thinly veiled contempt. The students, on the other hand, were oblivious to his detachment, and were much involved in the conversation. One, whom she recognized as Paul Sokolov, was gesticulating wildly. Ilse excused herself, cutting off the Countess Arapov in midsentence. Her friends stared after her in surprise as she made her way toward her fiancé. She was too late; he was already speaking.

"There is merit in much of what Mikhailovsky writes, but the great masses of men, not a few of whom are the man's greatest advocates, understand little of the individuality of which he speaks. The golden age is impossible because men are sheep."

Ilse was just in time to hear Rudolph's words and heed their effect upon the young Sokolov. His face reddened, and it seemed he would speak. But for once he was at a loss for words. He turned abruptly and strode angrily away, almost colliding with Ilse as she reached Rudolph's side.

"Bonsoir, Countess Durenchev," said Anton, bowing, and the others echoed his greeting. "You have just missed a most stimulating conversation," he continued, barely able to suppress his mirth. "But I perceive that you wish to speak with my dear cousin. Come friends, let us find more champagne." With this, the group dissolved, leaving Rudolph and Ilse alone.

"Why do you let yourself be drawn into these ridiculous conversations?" Ilse began at once. "That Paul Sokolov is an insufferable fool, but his father is most influential and a close friend of Dimitri's. You have needlessly offended him. I have no doubt that that sly Anton deliberately provoked the whole incident simply for his own amusement . . ."

Rudolph's contemptuous voice interrupted her whispered tirade. "It is the ideas of fools which topple dynasties, Ilse. There is much in Russia that must be changed if we are to preserve that which is most valuable."

Ilse turned toward Rudolph, prepared to chastise him for his unconventional opinions, when she noticed that they were being observed. Dimitri and Josephine stood across the room looking in their direction. It would not do to have either of them see us quarrel, Ilse thought. She placed her arm within Rudolph's, and smiled broadly into his face. Once again Ilse glanced at Dimitri's handsome companion. It was difficult to believe that she was more than seventy years old.

Josephine Aimee Bonneville met Vassily Egonovich Semolenski at a time when a Russian prince and a French countess were not so inclined to develop a friendship, much less a great love affair. The two young people courted and married during the closing months of the Napoleonic Wars. Josephine left the gay city of lights to live in a country that promised little of the sophisticated life of her native Paris. But beautiful Josephine loved her Russian prince with a passion. And so she settled into the routine of enduring long harsh winters, and coping with the drab provincial atmosphere of the Russian countryside. For the first fifteen years of their marriage, Josephine was barren, and therefore, it was with the greatest expectation and joy that she and Vassily awaited the birth of their first child. Katerina was a beautiful baby whose only real flaw was that she was perhaps, loved too greatly. In 1847, when Katerina was seventeen years old, she wed Prince Nikolai Petrovich Balenkov. One year later she bore him a son—Rudolph Nikolaivich Balenkov.

As Josephine stood by Dimitri, the only evidence that the years had treated her unkindly was the deep graying of her lustrous dark-brown hair. She was a small woman whose erect posture and quick movements showed that her characteristic vitality had not diminished through the years. Her face was traced with but few of time's wretched markings. The few lines which had formed were those at the sides of Josephine's sparkling blue eyes, and these appeared only when she smiled and laughed, which she did quite often.

"You know, Dimitri, I don't understand why I cannot get any of the Balenkov men to visit me in Paris," Josephine bantered. "It isn't fair that I have to travel to Russia every time I want to see my grandson."

"Josephine, I am an old man, and the days of my traveling outside of Russia are past," returned Dimitri. "And as for Rudolph, you probably see him as often as I do. I wish your favored grandson would settle down and marry. I would like to see new Balenkov blood before I die."

"Oh, Dimitri, what is this preoccupation with age. You will live forever," the woman quipped. "But don't be so hard on Rudya. Beneath all of his recklessness is a fine man. He is a Balenkov, Dimitri."

As the two gazed once again toward where Rudolph and Ilse stood, into their view came yet another Balenkov. Pavel entered the large ballroom with his mother on his arm. He had the easy grace of a professional actor walking onto a stage. Approaching Josephine, he kissed her on both cheeks and warmly embraced his uncle.

As he stood smiling and speaking animatedly, Ilse closely watched his little performance. If only Rudolph had such grace, such style, her future would be assured. And yet Pavel seemed almost too perfect. Look how he doted on his uncle. And that wench of a mother! As she continued to stare from half-closed lids, Ilse decided that the dark one could be her undoing, and that she must be constantly vigilant against all who might interfere in her plans. She would not be cheated of her prize.

As if he had read her mind, Pavel broke away from Dimitri and Josephine, leaving his mother to converse further with them. Ilse stiffened as he walked toward Rudolph and her.

"How beautiful you are this evening, Ilse. The latest Parisian fashion becomes you. And you, my dear cousin, are looking well. None the worse, I see, for your arduous voyage. Your devotion to the tsarevich is most admirable. I for one could not endure the asceticism imposed by shipboard life."

"We all do what we must, Pavel," said Rudolph pointedly.

"Even when what we must is not what we ought," parried his cousin.

Rudolph looked at Pavel closely, this cryptic remark unsettling him. It was so long ago that he and his cousin had truly been friends. Was it their quest for their mutual heritage that had torn them apart? It was wrong to feel such animosity toward Pavel, thought Rudolph. Does he not have as valid a claim as I? And yet . . .

~ *Chapter 7* ~

Gently rocked in her arms, he smelled her freshness. Like green fields, she was sweet. His small dark head rested on one full breast as he pulled at the nipple hungrily. Golden eyes gazed into the simple pure face of the young peasant girl. Seeing her, he suddenly began to cry. Rocking him more fervently, she hushed the child with a soft lullaby.

> *"Don't cry my little one,*
> *I am here to stay*
> *Don't die my little one*
> *To the angels I will pray."*

As his desperate wails filled the darkened nursery, the door opened. It was she.

She was a small woman who seemed somewhat overburdened by the voluminous, heavy costume she wore. Even its color and texture, a deep magenta moire, seemed oppressive. She gave the distinct impression of an overplumed bird. The face was thin and hollow, and the only real life in her entire visage was in the eyes —dark, shiny spots of color. However, the controlled contours and austere features were relieved handsomely by a glorious crown of dark black hair, lifted elegantly upon her small head. But still, there was a dryness in her, as if all that was soft and relenting had been somehow hideously dissipated by an unknown tragedy.

Her skirts rustled menacingly as she glided across the carpeted floor. She stopped a few paces from the wet nurse, "Can you not keep him quiet, Olga? He will disturb the guests."

Her thin face loomed whitely in the darkness. It seemed to be suspended in space, her highly colored gown almost invisible against the thick shadows. She looked down dispassionately at the beautiful child. He reached out to touch her, but she was gone.

"Don't cry my little one
I am here to stay . . ."

His own cries awakened him. He sat up violently in bed, the covers falling limply from his nude form. His face was wet, his breathing ragged. He wiped his eyes with the back of his hand, and massaged the tight muscles at the back of his neck. The room was hot and close. He walked to the window and flung open the shutters. The moonlight gilded his damp body. Another night when he would find no rest. His reeling mind struggled to recall the nightmare, but the memory was gone. Only the feeling of despair lingered.

His thoughts wandered to the party. If those mindless fools could see him now, what interpretation would they give to his infirmity? The dandy of the drawing room was now a haunted creature.

The early part of his evening had gone well, he reflected. Once again his tactless cousin had given offense with his terse and condescending remarks. Rudolph, always arrogant and aloof, had demonstrated a total disregard for the social amenities. He laughed to himself. I, however, am the very epitome of social grace. How well I play their game. And Ilse, he smiled, she was so obviously disconcerted over her fiancé's behavior. Yet now the master tactician frowned. The calculating bitch could prove more of a problem than his guileless cousin.

But soon the well-played game would end in his total victory. He at last had something that would irrevocably discredit his cousin: this young girl, this *fille de joie!* Shenkerenko had proved valuable. He had certainly been correct about the girl. However, the odious upstart could prove a problem in the very near future. It was obvious that their final goals were not one. He, himself, would do nothing to besmirch the Balenkov name. Holding up his cousin's disgraceful actions to public censure was unthinkable. The knowledge of Rudolph's compromising conduct must be kept within the family. Even his own obsession with the *yarlyk* could not take precedence over his sense of honor and respect for the Balenkov name. In his own perverse way, Pavel Gregorovich Balenkov was noble.

The sounds of insects invaded the still air that was pregnant with the scent of growing things. But the two in the carriage were oblivious to the late spring day. Each was lost in thought.

Natasha Balenkov and her son rode toward their country estate in silence. She sat perched on the leather seat like an angry crow. Her corvine appearance owed much to the fact that after eight years she still wore widow's weeds for a husband she had never loved, and in fact, had barely tolerated. From time to time, she glanced at her handsome son. How like his father he was in appearance. His dark looks were the perfect antithesis to those of his fair cousin. It was strange how those two mirrored their sires. It was as if they had sprung from the heads of their fathers, and not from their mother's wombs.

When they arrived at the dacha, Pavel proceeded directly to the drawing room. He poured himself a glass of red wine.

"Pavel, I would have a word with you," asserted his mother, following him into the room.

Ignoring her presence, he slowly drained the wine and poured himself another, before turning to face her. He said nothing, but only stared at her contemptuously. Undaunted by his affectation of disinterest, she continued angrily, "I can only assume by your apathy and seeming nonchalance, that you have conceded your rightful inheritance to your arrogant cousin."

"But Mother, have I not all that I need. I am titled, my estates are vast. My father's portion of the Balenkov estates is no mere pittance. What more could I desire?" he replied caustically.

"You do not expect me to believe such nonsense, do you, Pavel? I do not doubt that you covet the *yarlyk,* and your uncle's title and estates. What I question are your tactics. If you could but make a splendid match, Dimitri would be influenced in your favor. Rudolph seems bent on toying with Ilse. Princess Tatiana Sokolov is obviously besotted with you, and her family is as old as ours. Her father and Dimitri have been lifelong friends. It would be perfect, so natural that you should wed her."

"Marriage is not in my immediate plans, my dear Mother. When I win the *yarlyk,* it will be because my uncle judges *me* more deserving than my cousin. You should not be surprised that I am not eager to wed. You and father hardly set an example."

No sooner had the words been spoken, than the unpleasant memories came flooding back.

He was only sixteen when his father died, and in those years there were few happy moments. His father spent little time at their estate, and when there, the boy rarely saw him. The few times they had shared had been good. But their fragile relationship had little time to develop. For though his mother did not love his father and quarreled continuously with him, she would share him with no one, not even their son. So his father had died, almost a stranger, attacked by a band of rebellious serfs. Pavel never looked into a peasant face without searching for some sign that here, at last, was his father's murderer.

"You did not understand your father and me. You know nothing of what passed between us!" Natasha hissed viciously at her son.

"How can one understand strangers?" he retorted sarcastically.

Natasha glared at him, her face livid, defying him to say more. He did not bait her further, but turned away and walked deliberately from the room.

Within a few moments, he was astride his gray mount,

galloping toward the village. The control he had displayed in his mother's presence was gone. The distasteful scene with Natasha had dredged up all the hatred and bitterness that lay buried within him. The steed flexed the muscular length of its powerful form, his silky mane flying behind him. His nostrils flared wildly as his hot, fast breath punctuated the forging thrusts of his body. The man tightened his grip on the beast, crouching lower on the saddle. Together they resembled some finely precisioned machine pushed to its structural limits.

After a time, the dark rider slowed, the image of a face appearing in his mind. Suddenly, he knew his destination. He knew where his wild ride would lead him.

Sophia Istrin knelt before the icon in her secluded one-room cottage, her body bowed in prayer. She had knelt in the same position for hours, something she did often. Her lips moved repeatedly, the words barely audible as she spoke her simple heart to the Virgin of Vladimir.

"Holy Mother, I come to you again. I have no earthly hope. I seek only your intercession for one who is without faith. He is dark with sin, but I will give him the light of your grace. He will cleave to my body and in our oneness, he will be purified again. He comes now, Mother, I feel it.

"Holy Mother, be one with me; Holy Mother, be one with me, Holy Mother, Holy Mother . . . I am the Mother."

The door opened. He stood silhouetted in the doorway, a black figure against the late afternoon sky. She lifted her head from prayer to turn toward him. He stood there studying her face, fragile, white, childlike, almost unformed. A nimbus of fine silver hair like a soft cloud surrounded her upturned face. Her large blue eyes were stark in their transparency, like vacant crystalline orbs. They sought his in the gloom.

Latching the door behind him, he walked toward her kneeling form. He took her small head between his hands and pushed at her temples with his thumbs. Sophia remained stoic under the subtle torture. A sudden cry was wrung from his throat, as he flung her from him. Slowly she rose from the floor, unfastening the cord which bound her light shift. She allowed the coarse garment to fall to the floor. She went to him where he stood near the oven, one hand pressed against its rough surface. Silently she faced him, offering the thick cord. He stared transfixed for a long moment, then clutched it deliberately.

Sophia closed her eyes, her hands held limply at her sides, her face tilted upward. Her moist lips parted in a smile as the rope slashed again and again across the delicate flesh of her small breasts and abdomen.

His whole face was wet, perspiration forming a fine veil over his features, large rivulets of moisture sliding from his heavy locks of hair. His breathing came in ragged gasps from his open mouth, and his tongue flicked compulsively across his full upper lip. Some part of himself viewed the scene from a great distance.

Finally, the moment for release had come. He fell upon her quickly, his manhood completing the violation which the cord had begun. Her eyes flew open; her lips moved in a silent chant. Suddenly, she felt him shudder upon her flesh, and then he was still. She felt his tears upon her breasts as she stroked his thick black hair. After a time he whispered, "Forgive me, Sophia, forgive me."

"You are forgiven, my dark child. By the power of the Holy Mother, you are cleansed."

~ *Chapter 8* ~

The long spring days seemed to drag by, and still Rudolph had not returned. Perhaps I shall be granted my wish, thought Simone. Perhaps he will not return at all. An image of Rudolph, arm in arm with the tall blonde came unbidden to her mind. He was, no doubt, with the beautiful Ilse Durenchev. If he married his countess, might he not set *her* free? Simone reasoned, send her home to New Orleans as she wished? Strangely, this prospect did not fill her with elation. Unconsciously, Simone decided not to examine her feelings further. She stooped and petted the head of her companion. Now Baktu followed her everywhere. It was ironic that she should feel so close to his hound, while the master himself remained so remote, so distant. She gave the dog's silky neck a final pat, and went to the kitchen. It was well past lunchtime, and she had eaten little for breakfast.

Mimka stood before the *pleeta*. Though she had numerous kitchen maids to do her bidding, it was obvious that she considered the preparation of meals her special province. Simone noted the large array of pots upon the long stovetop. Was Mimka expecting someone for dinner?

The woman did not hear her enter, and for a moment Simone stood staring at her broad back. How fond she had grown of this charming old peasant. She could understand Yuri's deep love for her . . . and Rudolph's. Why had she so foolishly kept from her the fact that she could speak Russian? Why did she continue to deprive herself of a more meaningful friendship with this dear woman? No sooner had the question come, than Simone resolved that Mimka would know of her Russian fluency.

"Is someone coming for supper tonight?" Simone inquired softly.

Mimka turned then, her surprise clearly registering on her wrinkled face.

"Yes, Mimka, I speak your language. Your grandson, Yuri, taught me well. I should not have kept my knowledge secret from you, but I have my reasons. Would you understand if I ask that you do not reveal this to Prince Balenkov?"

The look of wonder on the old woman's face was replaced by one of solemn affirmation. "If that is your wish, my child. But come, sit down. You must have something to eat and we will talk."

Mimka placed a *pirog* of cabbage, rice, and mushrooms before the girl. By the time she returned with a bowl of *kasha* and a large pitcher of cold milk, Simone had all but finished the crusty pie.

Filling Simone's *kasha* bowl with the milk, Mimka noted the girl's empty plate. "*Yeshte na zdorovie,*" she said happily. "I am glad to see you eating again. It is not good to be so skinny," joked Mimka, patting her own large stomach.

Simone laughed at the woman's good nature. Already, she was convinced her decision to divulge her little secret was the right one.

Mimka joined the girl at the table, pouring herself a large mug of coffee. In a most natural fashion, they spoke of the fineness of the weather, and the beauty of the Russian countryside. Without stopping to consider the propriety of her next words, Simone asked openly, "Mimka, what happened to Prince Balenkov's parents?"

Mimka shook her head woefully. "Such sadness, little one. When Prince Nikolai brought the beautiful Katerina here as a bride, it was a happy day. A year later, when a son was born, it seemed as if this happiness would always be. But six years later, Prince Nikolai decided that he must fight for his tsar against the Turks. I shall never forget the day he left. Princess Katerina cried like a poor babe; no one could comfort her. And when the news of his death came, it was as though she, too, had died. From that day she never took joy in anything—not even her son. The poor boy grieved over his father's death, but it was his mother who broke his little heart.

"Before, the mother and son would spend so many hours together, laughing over their games. She was so like a sweet, trusting child herself. Prince Nikolai treated her more like a babe than he did his little Rudya. I can still hear his deep voice, 'You must take care of your mamma while I am gone, Rudya. I know you are a big boy now, and your mother depends on you.'

"But when Prince Nikolai died, she was no longer his dear mamma, she no longer laughed, no longer played little games with her Rudya. She had gone to some other place, and she had left her son behind.

"At first Rudya only cried and asked, 'Where's Mamma? What's wrong with Mamma?' I used to hold him and tell him his mamma would get better, but I think we both knew, even then, it was not true. As he grew older, he no longer wept and no longer asked for her. Yet his beautiful blue eyes would go all dark and gray like the sky when the storms come, and I knew that he cried out inside for her. He became so serious, never joking, never laughing; I knew he could never understand why she did not want him, why he could not take his father's place.

"For many years Katerina lived on, but her soul was already with Nikolai. I watched Rudya's hurt turn to bitterness. Then he began to blame himself for her sickness, and I felt he hated her and himself for what had happened. I think he thought often of his father's words. I tried to tell him that the fault was not his, but he would not have me speak of it. It wrings my old heart to know he feels such guilt. It haunts his eyes even now."

"What happened after Katerina died?" questioned Simone, almost in a whisper. "Was he left entirely alone?"

"No, I was here for him. And there was, of course, his Uncle Dimitri and his father's twin brother, Gregor. Gregor had a son, who was but one month younger than Rudolph. And that is a tale in itself."

"A *tale*, Mimka?" queried Simone.

"Yes. As I have said, Nikolai and Gregor were twins, the sons of Prince Peter and his second wife, Lisaveta. They were exactly alike except that Nikolai was light, Gregor dark. And strange to tell, each brother had a son so like himself, that all thought the cousins to be twins also. Katerina's mother, Countess Josephine, once spoke to me of a demon star, called Agol by Arab shepherds. They watched in fear as its bright light disappeared every three days. Many years later, wise men discovered a dark twin star which sometimes hid his brighter brother from view. Countess Josephine said the young princes were like the strange double star."

The image of the dark stranger in the wood invaded Simone's consciousness as Mimka related the weird parable. Could it have been the cousin that she encountered? Why did he not tell her who he was?

Before Simone could question Mimka about the dark cousin, the sound of a carriage was heard. It was Rudolph; he had returned. Mimka rose to greet him as he entered the kitchen. He looked tired and drawn; he asked Mimka to send for Oleg, as he was in sore need of a bath. He looked at Simone then, his voice terse. "We will leave for Moscow in the morning. Be prepared for an early departure." With that he turned and left the room.

~ Chapter 9 ~

Moscow, toward which the elegant carriage of Prince Rudolph Nikolaivich Balenkov tended this bright summer morning, was a city of some seven hundred years. Young by European standards, it had attained importance in Russia only after the destruction of Kiev by the Tartars in the thirteenth century, and had risen to dominance as the Mongol power declined. In the fifteenth century, the Tartar yoke was finally broken; Muscovy under the rule of Grand

Prince Ivan III, emerged as the major force in Russia. By
the end of his reign in 1505, Ivan, who styled himself tsar of
all the Russias had succeeded in consolidating some 55,000
square miles, bringing all of the great Russian principalities
under his domain. Moscow remained the capital of Russia
until the beginning of the eighteenth century when Tsar
Peter the Great built St. Petersburg as a window on the
West. But if St. Petersburg had become the representative
of the philosophical and artistic sophistication of the ration-
al West, Moscow was still the bastion of the orthodoxy and
autocracy of the occult East. And in Russian minds and
hearts, Moscow remained the nexus of all the national and
religious sentiments which flowed inward from the far-flung
provinces of that vast empire. It was said that if St.
Petersburg was the intellect of Russia, Moscow was its
heart.

Simone peered out of the gently rocking calèche. It was
impossible not to compare Moscow with St. Petersburg. It
seemed only natural that she should prefer the more
European St. Petersburg, and yet there was something
intoxicating in the mysterious and brooding presence that
was Moscow. This city, Simone concluded, was more
profoundly Russian.

Inside the carriage there was a strained silence. Rudolph
was proving no more communicative this morning than he
had been on the previous evening. Thus, when he finally
spoke, he startled Simone, who was still engrossed in the
spectacle of the ancient walled city.

"There is something that draws us here," he spoke softly,
almost to himself. "It is like this for all Russians, noble or
peasant, educated or no. Moscow is the Holy Mother that
calls to her children."

A subtle change in the gait of the horses and the sounds
of increased traffic on the thoroughfare diverted Simone's
attention to her surroundings. The calèche passed through a
large vaulted gate. Simone was totally unprepared for the
almost vulgar panorama which assaulted her.

A merchants' bazaar unfolded before her—an unbelievable display of human activity and craft. Her senses were so
bewitched by the foreign sights and smells that it was
impossible for her to focus long on anything in particular.
The raucous tolling of bells caused her to look upward, yet

no clue to their insistent clanging could be found. The whole of the scene was textured with an earthy muskiness, which revolted and compelled her all at once.

"*Kitai gorod*, the basket city," explained Rudolph. "It is said that anything one desires can be found within its walls."

At the next gate, the scene changed again. They passed into a huge expanse, cobbled in sandstone. Red Square was almost entirely deserted. As if in answer to Simone's unspoken question, Rudolph commented, "The oppressive heat of the Moscow summer drives many of her residents to the countryside. In the winter she returns fully to life.

The Cathedral of St. Basil stood at the far end of the plaza, thrusting its colorful minarets into the cloudless sky. Designs of blue, yellow, and red were gilded bright by the summer sun. It was like a child's fairy tale castle grown to enormous size, thought Simone in delight.

As they approached the ancient inner city, they passed through the gothic-towered Spassky Gate, the gate of the Savior. The Kremlin, the symbolic seat of tsarist power, lay before them. Riding along the wide thoroughfare, Simone was dazzled by the magnificence of the large buildings which abounded within the red brick walls. In the distance, dominating the skyline, was a tall majestic structure whose bulbous golden spire crowned its circular walls. Simone knew, without asking Rudolph, that this was, indeed, the Tower of Ivan the Great. As they rode, domed cathedrals rippled by in a profusion of pure color and rotund form, amusing in their whimsical aspect. Simone was impressed by the sheer number of cupolas marked by crosses. So many churches! After a time they reached Borovitsky Hill, the site of four of the largest and oldest of the Kremlin cathedrals.

In stark contrast to the lively diversity of the basilicas was an austere structure, enormous in size and flawless in its symmetry. Its broad facade was mirrored profusely with glistening windows, regimented between white stone columns. Ornamental bas reliefs and graceful arches capped each aperture. The whole effect of the edifice was one of order, power, permanence. "The Grand Kremlin Palace," said Rudolph simply. "Once there were many more palaces within the Kremlin walls. But over the centuries, much has

changed. After the great fire of 1812, many of the aristocracy left Moscow, never to return. The Balenkov residence
has fortunately been spared."

So it was that Simone entered yet another Balenkov
mansion. Like the others, it bespoke the family's rich
heritage and princely position. It was beautiful; the abundance of decorative detail was overwhelming. The ripe
colors of melon and gold, green and blue cast the rooms in
an opulent lushness. Every arched portal and vaulted
ceiling was encrusted with swirling designs, so excessive that
the very atmosphere seemed overburdened, heavy. It was
an exotic Byzantine pavilion and unconsciously, Simone
sniffed the air for incense. It was lacking, but it was the only
element that was missing from this rich Eastern tabernacle.

The room which Simone had been given was similar in
design to the ones on the ground floor. Yet there was a
delicacy here which had been absent from those more
ornate lower chambers. She attributed this air of lightness
to the soft golden hue of the room. The walls and ceilings
were a floral fantasy, the stylized motifs entwined organical-
ly in an endless dance. Upon the planks of honeyed oak lay
runners of handsome oriental design. Muted stains of
colored light filtered through the leaded panes and lay in
pools upon the floor. It was as if nature herself had decided
to enhance this fanciful apartment.

It was not possible to spurn the spell of gaiety which this
room cast ever so subtly. The excitement which had begun
to seize her during the morning's carriage ride blended with
her natural buoyancy. In spite of her uncertain future, and
in spite of Rudolph Balenkov, Simone vowed fervently that
she would enjoy herself this summer's day in Moscow.
"Today I will forget everything but the moment," Simone
whispered. "I will lose myself in the magic of this city. I
shall take away only happy memories from Moscow."

A knock on the door signaled the arrival of Marya with a
luncheon tray.

"Prince Balenkov requests that you join him immediately
after you have eaten," announced the girl. "He awaits you
downstairs."

Simone looked blankly at the food, knowing she would
be unable to eat. Hastily, she retrieved the straw hat which
she had flung carelessly upon the bed. Moving to the room's
large mirror, she surveyed herself. The leghorn framed her

face delicately. Spontaneously, she reached with one hand and cocked the straw rolled brim coquettishly over one eye. She smiled at the slightly wicked effect. Now she was ready, and with a wholly unaffected eagerness, she glided from the room. Simone descended the stairs, halting in midstep as she glimpsed Rudolph in the foyer. He remained unaware of her presence, and he continued to read a journal which had apparently just arrived. His profile was presented to her, and she studied him with new objectivity. Almost sighing, she concluded he was the most handsome man she had ever seen. Yet, as he read, Simone saw that his face seemed somehow innocent, cleansed of all the anger and darkness which so often marred his countenance. He appeared as some artist's model, completely neutral, unemotional.

Prince Balenkov, she thought, I will not allow you to spoil this day. I shall be the grand lady squired by her adoring young husband for a day of shopping in the city. What if the reality were so horribly different from her girlish fantasy! He certainly looked the part. Today would be hers.

Suddenly, he became aware of her scrutiny. Walking forward to meet her, Rudolph spoke. "Well, are you ready to go shopping, Simone?"

"Oh yes, Rudolph, that would be lovely."

The calèche drew up to a small but exclusive shop in the *gostini dvor*—the merchant's court. Rudolph escorted Simone through the door, a silver bell tinkling at their entrance. Simone glanced around her at the maze of satin, silk, and lace. Her mind was filled with fantasies of what feminine delights lay secreted within the tissues of the rainbow-colored boxes. Almost immediately, a petite, elegant woman in her early fifties came forward to greet them. Her thick accent rang through the salon. "Prince Balenkov, you are naughty, indeed, depriving me of your charming company for so long."

Rudolph smiled lazily and lightly kissed her extended hand, "*Pardonnez-moi*, madame, it is my loss." Madelaine Mereaux however, scarcely heard Rudolph's comment; instead, she focused her attention on his beautiful companion. She turned to face him again, one arching eyebrow conveying her curiosity, "Madame Mereaux, may I present Simone. Like yourself, she is French."

The woman rushed to Simone's side, taking the girl's

hands into her own, and brushing her cheeks with light kisses. "Bonjour, *bienvenu*, ma petite. Please call me Madi—all of my friends do." To Rudolph, she exclaimed, "*Elle est très belle*, Prince Balenkov." Rudolph smiled, but made no comment.

"May I offer you a glass of sherry, Prince Balenkov?"

"Non, Madi, I have important matters that require my attention. I will leave Simone in your capable hands. You know best what a young woman desires. See that Simone has all that she needs for the summer." And almost as an afterthought Rudolph added, "She will, of course, require winter clothing as well, Madi." As he exited, both women stared after him.

A moment later, Madi turned to face Simone, "Now, *ma chère*, let us go about making you the most beautiful girl in Moscow." She clapped her hands and instantly a young girl entered. The trio proceeded to a small mirrored room. As Simone disrobed, Madame Mereaux questioned, "You are from Paris, non, Simone?"

"Non, Madi, from Nouvelle Orleans."

"Oh, I have always wanted to visit your charming city. I have heard that it is much like my own Paris."

"Oui, Madi, it is a beautiful city," Simone said wistfully. "And I miss it so."

Perceiving the sadness in the girl's voice, Madi realized that to probe further would be an indiscretion.

As the apprentice took Simone's measurements, Madi exclaimed over her. "Such a perfect figure, such a tiny waist."

Simone smiled at the woman's effusive compliments. But unaccountably, she thought of the Countess Durenchev. How many times had she come to this very place with Rudolph? Might not Madi even now be working on her wedding gown? Simone had not long to speculate, however, because swatches of fabric and the latest copies of *La Mode Illustrée* were now produced for her inspection.

Hours flew by as Simone and Madi selected materials and designs for her winter wardrobe. As they busied themselves over the books of patterns, a young *midinette* altered several of the couturière's sample garments for Simone. Another of Madame Mereaux's young girls brought box after box of French lingerie and other accessories for the young woman's approval. Finally, Simone rose from the

small floral loveseat, where she had been trying on endless
pairs of shoes. As she began to remove the silk kimono, so
that she might dress, Madi protested, "Non, non, we have
one more set of measurements to take, Simone."

"But Madi, I have selected far too much already."

"But this shall be a surprise, ma petite. You must wait
and see. I promise you will not be disappointed."

As the last of the packages which Simone would take with
her were being tied up in ribbons, Rudolph's black calèche
arrived.

"You will be pleased with the selections we have made,
Prince Balenkov," Madi greeted him. "Your Simone makes
my creations more divine than ever. And those that we shall
make for the winter shall be truly *magnifique*, designed
exclusively to complement her beauty. These last," she
continued, "will be ready in early October. Shall I have
them sent to your estate?"

"That will not be necessary, Madi. I will be in Moscow at
that time, and can call for them myself."

Simone had remained quiet during the ride home, still
dazzled by this foray into luxury. However, upon reaching
the residence, she turned to Rudolph, lightly touching his
arm. "Rudolph, I wish to thank you. Today was so wonderful. The clothes . . ."

"It is nothing, Simone. You should go to your room and
rest now. Tonight we shall dine out." As he watched the
footman help her down, he discovered to his surprise
that her obvious happiness had also given him great pleasure.

~ *Chapter 10* ~

Simone was awakened from a refreshing nap by Marya. It was already darkening outside, and the girl was lighting the gas lamps. The romantic aspect of the room added to the aura of fantasy which had pervaded the day, and was intensified by the quickening night.

Simone stretched fully into the plushness of the bedding. The lacy sleeping gown fresh from its tissue wrappings moved upon her body like a silken caress. She sighed deeply and closed her eyes. If it were sinful to feel so wickedly pampered, then she would just have to risk the temper of the gods.

"Mademoiselle, mademoiselle," Marya's insistent voice startled Simone. "*Pardonnez-moi*, but the hour grows late, and there is much to do. Prince Balenkov does not like to be kept waiting. I will bring up your bath water. Which of your lovely new dresses will you wear?"

"What a choice I must make, Marya. They are all so beautiful. I know . . . the lilac. It is like summer itself."

Finally, she sat before the mirror, Marya piling her dark hair high upon her head. As Simone looked at her reflection, she was amazed by the image of the sophisticated beauty who stared back at her. Was this glowing woman she? Truly the night was magic.

Rising from the bench, Simone stepped into the lavender dress which Marya held for her. As the girl fastened the last hook of the bodice, she moved back and exclaimed, "Oh mademoiselle, you are so beautiful!"

Turning to her reflection in the long mirror, Simone

assessed the gown's effect. The pale lilac of the grenadine
silk seemed almost iridescent against her slightly olive skin.
The tight bodice extending below the waist emphasized her
breasts, which rose full above the décolletage of the Valen-
ciennes lace bertha. The delicately tinted lace was repeated
in an overskirt cut to follow the lacy scallops, and dip
coquettishly into a demitrain.

Yes, tonight I am beautiful, thought Simone.

The confident young woman glided regally down the wide
stairway. Rudolph was nowhere to be seen. Surmising that
he was in the drawing room, she proceeded there. He was
seated, one booted leg sprawled leisurely before him. He
gazed intently into his wine glass.

"Rudolph . . ."

He stood abruptly and faced her. After a moment, he
spoke. "Madame Mereaux was right, Simone. You are
beautiful. More beautiful than ever."

"Thank you, Rudolph," Simone almost whispered, her
eyes cast downward.

"You need not thank me for speaking simple truth."

For an instant, Simone was bewildered by his quiet
seriousness. But the moment passed, and he walked toward
her and helped with her wrap. "Come, let us go, Simone.
We have some distance to travel."

They drove silently through the night under a canopy of
stars, the open carriage allowing the soft summer breezes to
cool them. When at last they arrived at a large wooden
structure, Simone noted but few other carriages drawn up
under the nearby trees. As Rudolph guided her to a private
entrance, the proprietor greeted him.

"Welcome, Your Highness. I am so happy that you will
be dining with us this evening."

"Thank you, Constantine. I always look forward to an
evening at the Black Boar."

"It is my pleasure, Prince Balenkov. Please follow me.
All is in readiness."

As they passed through a dimly lit narrow corridor,
Simone glimpsed a great hall. Paneled in rough, dark oak, it
was the most completely natural room that the young
woman had ever seen. Trophies of caribou, elk, and bear
hung from wooden plaques—a great gallery of fantastic
fauna, testimony of the ripe abundance of the Russian
wood. Large brass containers held boughs of evergreen,

and in spite of the season, the fireplace was ablaze. Commanding the entire hall was the massive black head of a great boar, its angry teeth knifing downward from its gaping mouth. Unbelievably, Simone felt the ambiance of winter in the air.

They continued on through the hallway, and Simone caught sight of an adjoining room whose ceiling was hung about with all manner of fowl and small game. And on long wooden tables stood glass enclosures in which swam fish, lobsters, and other crustaceans.

Finally, they reached a stairway and proceeded upward to a private chamber. The small room was golden with candlelight, and Simone noticed how the dark interplay of their shadows gave the retreat another dimension. The hunting theme which so dominated the lodge was repeated in the engravings which abounded on the paneled walls. A round wooden table with two straight chairs stood before open latticed windows; the night air teased the flames of the long tapers. Moving to a small sofa, the woman ran her fingers over its nubby upholstery. How well such fabric suited the rustic room. Nothing intruded upon the simple honesty of the chamber.

The genial proprietor took Simone's wrap and motioned the pair to be seated upon the divan. He clapped his large hands, and immediately two immaculately clad waiters appeared with chilled champagne and caviar.

"Enjoy your meal, Your Highness, mademoiselle," said the jovial Constantine, and bowing once from the waist, he was gone. The waiters, having set their bounty upon the small table in front of the sofa, followed behind.

Rudolph poured the French champagne into two goblets. Handing Simone one of the crystal glasses, he stared openly into her face. "Welcome to Moscow, Simone," he said, lifting his glass.

"Thank you, Rudolph," she said, acknowledging his salute, "your city is beautiful. I can fully understand why you love her so."

Rudolph smiled, and the blue of his eyes shone indigo in the candlelight. "Have some of the caviar. Constantine serves the very finest Russia has to offer."

Simone accepted the canapé glistening with the pale gray, pearllike beluga. Yet her gay mood had been subtly altered. It was not that she was melancholy, but rather she was reluctant to violate the strange calmness which pervaded this moment. The woman knew that this evenness, this peace, emanated more from Rudolph than from anything else. It was as though the two of them had come to terms with each other, at least for the space of this summer's night. So they sat, sipping the sparkling wine, neither trusting themselves to speak further.

A soft rap at the door heralded the reappearance of the waiters, bearing large trays of *zakuski*. Simone and Rudolph sampled the delicious appetizers, choosing from several patés, smoked salmon, *gribok*, or little mounds of cottage cheese capped with small tomato halves to look like mushrooms, and *zalevnaia*, or fish in aspic.

The first course, a simple consommé, was brought in to the pair now seated at the table. As Simone looked across at Rudolph, involuntarily, the thought of their last meal together intruded. But how different he looked this evening, she reassured herself. She watched entranced as a slight zephyr teased at his hair, rippling it golden in the candlelight. As if he felt her gaze upon him, he lifted his eyes to hers and smiled. She smiled also, and offered her glass for more champagne. The waiter served their plates generously from a rack of venison, and placed a small ramekin of mint jelly upon the table. Simone, despite the fact that she had had no lunch, was thankful that she had eaten sparingly of the hors d'oeuvres, when a second platter was brought in heaped with steamed lobster and brimming containers of drawn butter. As they ate, Simone could hear the faint strains of a haunting melody. What was it? She closed her lids slowly . . . gypsy violins! She wondered from whence the music came, but as it drifted into the small candlelit room, it became a part of the growing magic of the night.

Simone was sure she could not eat another morsel when dessert arrived. It was that best-loved of all Russian confections—*kissel*. This one combined fresh strawberries and raspberries and was served ice cold with thick clotted cream. The delicious concoction proved irresistible.

As they moved to the sofa, Rudolph handed Simone a large snifter of brandy. For a moment, he stood looking down into the deep amber liquid, swirling the heady contents around and around the sides of the crystal. Simone looked up, almost mesmerized by the eddying liquor in his glass. Then he turned abruptly and walked to a small desk almost hidden in the corner of the room. Opening a drawer, he retrieved a tiny package. It was beautifully wrapped in silk fabric and encircled in velvet ribbons. Walking to the divan he stood before Simone, and without speaking, he handed the gift to her. She looked at him in surprise.

"It is for you, Simone."

With a tentative hand Simone reached for the package. Carefully, she removed the ribbons and wrapping until a small polished ebony box revealed itself. Again she looked at Rudolph, who had now seated himself beside her.

"Open it," he pressed gently. "It is my promise to you that we shall see Moscow in the winter."

Slowly, Simone lifted the lid of the box and beheld an exquisite object—a tiny hand-painted Fabergé egg. It was soft blue in color, ornately decorated with seed pearls. Nestled within its glazed shell lay a snow scene; two people wrapped in furs, pulled gaily along in a troika. The horses were poised in motion, their long manes flowing, their tiny sleighbells seeming to jingle in the crisp winter air. The diminutive evergreens were laden with fresh-fallen snow. Gently she removed the delicate egg, caressing it within her palms. "Oh, Rudolph, this is beautiful," Simone whispered almost inaudibly. "Never have I seen anything so lovely. I . . . I . . . I don't know what to say. I . . ." Her eyes brimming with tears, she touched his shoulder and kissed him softly on his cheek.

As she pulled away, Rudolph looked into her upturned face. Gently he moved one finger across her cheek and brushed away a single tear. Then with both hands he held her face; lowering his head, he kissed her deeply but tenderly. Lifting his parted lips from hers, his eyes seemed to cloud as he stared, unseeing, at Simone. Brusquely, he arose. His back turned toward her, he said tonelessly, "Come, Simone, it is late; we must go." The mood had been broken.

Rising from the sofa, she replaced the egg carefully into its box. So numbed was she by his erratic behavior, that Simone allowed Rudolph to place her cape around her shoulders and lead her from the lodge.

As they neared their waiting carriage, a deep voice bellowed, "Rudolph, my old friend, so you have returned." The man and his wife approached the pair, who had halted at his greeting. "Welcome home, my boy. I trust your journey to America met with success."

"It is always good to return to Moscow," Rudolph answered dryly, in bare recognition of the man's presence.

The man took little note of Rudolph's curtness, so enthralled was he by the prince's companion.

Ignoring the couple's obvious desire to continue the interlude, Rudolph concluded, "If you will excuse us, the hour grows late. Good evening, Countess Kerensky, count."

As they moved away, the count and his wife stared after the retreating pair. Their anger at his blatant rudeness was exceeded only by their curiosity about the mysterious dark-haired woman.

When they reached the residence, Rudolph proceeded directly to the study, and Simone mounted the stairs to her room. As she closed the door firmly behind her, she pressed her back against its unyielding hardness. Her eyes closed, her head tilted back against the lacquered wood, she chastised herself unmercifully. How could I be such a fool. I am no princess . . . no grand lady . . . I am Simone Montpellier, the concubine of Rudolph Balenkov. How little he thinks of me, and he is right. I am nothing . . . nothing. Viciously, she removed the gown, disdainful of its fineness, its quality. Tearing at the masses of her hair, she released it from its elaborate coiffure. Looking directly into the mirror, she spat, "This is better, this is me."

Suddenly, the door swung open. Rudolph was standing in the threshold. He had removed his waistcoat, his shirt was unfastened, his hair was tousled, his gray eyes were glazed. He was drunk.

Simone watched him in the mirror as he slammed the door and walked unsteadily toward her. Without turning, she spoke harshly to his reflected image.

"So I am good enough for your bed, but not fit to introduce to your friends."

Stopping at her caustic words, he returned, "They were not my friends."

"They seemed to think they were," she retorted.

"And how shall I introduce you, mademoiselle? Do you have a name?"

"It is Montpellier. Simone Montpellier." She spoke the words deliberately as she turned at last to face him.

"Simone Montpellier," he repeated slowly. "And just who are you, Simone Montpellier?"

"You are not the first to ask that question," she replied, her voice sinking.

"That is no answer," he shouted, beginning to lose control.

"Are you afraid of gossip, Prince Balenkov?" she offered flippantly.

"I do as I please; I care nothing for the opinions of others," he said through clenched teeth.

"Not even that of your Uncle Dimitri . . . even Ilse's?"

His face was livid as he stood watching her.

She had gone too far, yet she must press further. Walking closer to him, Simone pleaded softly. "Let me go home, Rudolph, let me go home. There is no future for me here."

"Your future is what I decide it shall be," he whispered. "And as for *who you are,* Simone. You are mine, . . . all mine."

As if to confirm his edict, he crushed her to him, kissing her open mouth brutally. Simone struggled futilely. He was too strong, too driven. Yet she would not allow him an easy victory. She would fight, fight for her very soul. She would fight as she had that first time. Insensitive to her ineffective efforts to free herself, he carried her to the bed. Ripping off her chemise, he mounted her savagely. As his body pounded violently against hers, the tears slowly came. And when his angry lust had been sated, she was limp, defiled, wasted. She had lost, as she had lost each time before. She was his possession. He always knew it, and now she too understood it. As he lifted his wet body from hers, his icy blue eyes seemed to mock the tears which stained her face. Without looking at her again he left the room.

She lay very still, for how long, she could not guess. She did not want to think; she did not want to feel. Slowly, she rose from the bed, her body bruised and torn. She walked toward the basin of water, which stood on a chest in the corner of the room. As she cupped her hands to reach into the porcelain bowl, Simone stopped suddenly. Lying on the chest was a small box of paints and a cache of sable brushes. She picked up the white card. It was emblazoned with a single word: "Rudolph." The card fell from her trembling fingers, and tears rolled slowly down her face. Soon her whole body was wracked in a frenzy of hysterical weeping.

She had fought so long. She had fought so desperately. But she could no longer deny the simple naked truth: She loved him.

~ *Chapter 11* ~

Rudolph made no move to leave Moscow, and Simone became the abandoned victim of his indifference. Other than Marya, who brought her meals regularly to the room, Simone saw no one but an occasional servant in her wanderings about the large residence.

On the third day she could endure the tedium no longer, and directed Marya to see that a carriage be made available to her. Even the look of fearful reproach, which she read in Marya's face at her order, would not stay Simone's resolve. Whatever Rudolph might think, she had an existence apart from him, and would not be consigned to the role of his whore. Indeed, she would gladly risk provoking his vile temper for but one day of freedom in Moscow. After all, what could he do to her that he had not already done?

And so she plunged ahead with her bold venture. Donning one of Madi's stunning outfits, she looked more confident than in truth she was. She had no real itinerary; indeed, she was a complete stranger to the city. Yet, she knew she wanted to see more of the Kremlin, especially the fantastic cathedrals, which she had only spied on her way to the Balenkov residence.

She rang for Marya, who affirmed that the carriage had been brought round. The servant girl protested against her mistress's unorthodox plan to go about the city without her, but Simone was adamant, and descended the staircase alone. As the footman helped her into the small curricle, she gave the order to drive to Borovitsky Hill. The man accepted her authority without question, and, with a new sense of power, she settled into the leather cushions.

The coach halted before the Cathedral of the Assumption, the most important of Russian churches. Built in the early fourteenth century and rebuilt during the closing years of the fifteenth, this cathedral was considered the Russian counterpart of England's Westminster Abbey, the site of coronations, and the final resting place for the highest ecclesiastics.

Simone instructed the driver to wait, and mounted the white stone stairs. The exterior of the church was a progression of arches, almost severe in its insistence on the repetition of this simple form. But as Simone passed through the angel-flanked portal, a wealth of color and rich imagery besieged her. The wide expanse of vaulted ceiling was supported by numerous towering columns, each ringed with the colorful images of God's chosen. It was as if the glorious litany of the saints had come to life, Simone thought, contemplating the flattened two-dimensional figures posed piously above her. The glint of gold and precious stones was everywhere, accentuated by the light from hundreds of candles placed in large brass chandeliers. The church is ablaze with stars, Simone thought, glaring upward at the flickering tapers. And the angels are soaring . . .

As Simone gazed at the successive tiers of icons, she marveled at the ability of the faithful to pray despite this assault upon the senses. She moved to the center of the edifice and looked upward once again at the central dome. Now she understood why the first bishops, upon entering this temple, had proclaimed that they had seen heaven. For high above the jasper floor was a magnificent fresco of the Christ. He was not the sentimental Savior of Western art, but rather a stark, avenging God who judged men with calm dispassion.

Simone took refuge at a small side altar, kneeling before the icon of the Virgin of Vladimir. As she stared into the Madonna's abstract face, Simone realized how different she now was from the girl who had attended Mass each morning at the Ursuline convent. Had she forgotten how to pray? Indeed, would her prayers be acceptable? She bowed her head. She was a Magdalene. At this very thought she took solace. Had not Christ welcomed the prostitute back into his fold?

"Holy Mother," she prayed, "deliver me. I am weak. I know my love can never be sanctified. Help me to escape from my temptation."

As she uttered her desperate supplication, it came to her that she herself must be the instrument of her own salvation. She tried to envision a return to New Orleans and a haven with the Ursulines. But as she gazed again upon the icon, the Virgin's sorrowful visage dissolved, and *his* taunting face loomed above her. The still air had become oppressive, and Simone fought back the dizziness that threatened to overcome her. She struggled to her feet, and made her way outside. She descended the stairs, half-blinded by the sunlight, her eyes still adjusted to the gloom of the cathedral.

"Mademoiselle, we meet again."

She turned toward the familiar voice. It was the dark stranger. Her questioning gaze brought forth his next words, *"Pardonnez-moi,* Mademoiselle, allow me to properly introduce myself." This time he spoke in impeccable French. "I am Prince Pavel Gregorovich Balenkov." And upon seeing the dawning recognition in her face, he affirmed, "Oui, I am Rudolph's cousin."

"I am Simone Montpellier, Prince Balenkov." she returned.

"I am honored," he said, his golden eyes fixed upon hers, even as he bent to kiss her hand. "But forgive me, mademoiselle. I am ill-mannered to keep you standing in this dreadful heat. Have you had lunch? I know a wonderful Armenian restaurant not far from here. I insist that you dine with me." Not waiting for her acceptance, he walked to her carriage and told Sergius that he himself would see the lady home. Returning to her side, he led her to his elegant barouche.

The restaurant was, indeed, charming—Middle Eastern in flavor. The ceilings were draped with colorful printed swatches of cloth to give the rooms a tentlike effect. Each of the intimate dining areas was separated by beaded curtains. Most of the rooms were furnished with low circular tables and plump cushions where patrons sat to eat in the traditional manner. The floors and walls were covered with oriental carpets, and the sweet aroma of incense perfumed the air.

They were greeted by a short, full-figured woman dressed in a native costume. Their affable hostess smiled broadly, and embraced Pavel, babbling something to him in a dialect incomprehensible to Simone. The woman was obviously overjoyed to see Pavel, and whatever it was that she had told him pleased him enormously. He laughed heartily and allowed her to shepherd them to an intimate alcove. Pavel helped Simone arrange her voluminous skirts upon the low pillows, the proprietress chuckling over the silly encumbrances of civilization. Simone understood the point of her humor, and laughed with her. Madi's elegant creation was rendered ridiculous in the context of this more basic culture. Suddenly, she was entirely glad that she had come.

As he discussed the menu with the proprietress, Simone observed Pavel closely. How correct everyone was to say that they could be twins. Bone structure, proportion, bearing—in all but the coloring, they were physically identical. It was as if one viewed Rudolph through smoked glass.

When they were left alone, he turned his attention to her.

"I knew from our first encounter in the woods that you were French, Mademoiselle Simone. The bewitching delicacy of your dark beauty could only be Gallic."

"And I should have recognized you at once as a Balenkov."

He laughed, and said archly, "But you did."

She blushed at this reference to Rudolph and cast her eyes downward.

Realizing that he had perhaps made a tactical error, he deftly diverted the conversation. "What do you think of Moscow, mademoiselle?"

"I find it fascinating, but I fear it difficult for a foreigner to understand its many mysteries."

Smiling, he asserted, "It is only because Moscow is a woman that she is mysterious. Have you been in Russia long?" he continued, subtly probing.

"No, not so very long," she returned pensively.

"I hope that you will not soon deprive Russia of your charming company, and return to your native *France*." He spoke casually, but carefully watched her reaction to his words.

She hesitated but a moment. "I have no definite plans as yet," she parried, lowering her eyes to avoid his.

As he looked at her, he began to wonder. Could Vladimir have miscalculated in trusting the word of the sentry who had claimed to have seen her smuggled aboard? Nothing in her manner or conversation suggested that she was a helpless kidnap victim. And yet even the simple allusion to Rudolph had the power to disconcert her. Had she not spoken only in vague generalities? Had she not resisted his artful probing? No, he would not give it up!

The food arrived, a succulent lamb dish with olives and brown rice, and a salad of tomatoes and green peppers in olive oil. He watched her as she began to sample the exotic food. He would give his cousin credit. He had excellent taste; hers was a rare beauty.

Pavel hardly tasted the spicy dishes, so intent had he become on studying her. At their first meeting she had seemed a sylvan sprite, but today she appeared like a princess. Who was this woman? Even Shenkerenko admitted he had no clue.

Simone savored the delicious fare, comparing it favorably to her native Creole cuisine. She wondered to herself how she appeared to her companion. Who did he think she was? Did he guess at her true relationship to his cousin? Indeed, could Rudolph have told him of her? At this last thought, a deep blush stole into her cheeks. These speculations were futile. Why torture herself with unanswerable questions?

"The food is marvelous, Prince Balenkov. It was kind of you to suggest lunch."

"I am delighted that you approve. But please, call me Pavel, Simone."

As they sipped thick Turkish coffee, Pavel's eyes turned again to Simone's face. She was so different from any woman he had ever known. There was a natural grace about her, a warmth and spontaneity. Catlike, the pupils of his golden eyes dilated, and his breathing subtly quickened. He drained the last of the hot liquid from his cup. He must not lose sight of his primary goal.

"Prince . . . Pavel, I am afraid that I must go."

"You need not apologize, Simone. It is enough that you

consented to have lunch with me. Never have I had such an enchanting afternoon. Unfortunately I must return to my estate this evening. But surely we shall meet again."

As they drove toward the residence, it became obvious that like Rudolph, Pavel had a special feeling for this city. He pointed out various places of interest along the way, and charmed Simone with amusing anecdotes about Moscow and her inhabitants. She could not help but compare his easy manner to his cousin's sometimes aloof, sometimes violent temperament. She had erred—he was not like Rudolph at all.

Upon arriving at the residence, the driver stepped down and opened the door for Simone. Before she could alight, Pavel gently pressed her arm. "I hope we shall meet again, Simone. It has been a very special day for me. If I can ever be of any service to you, please do not hesitate to call upon me."

Simone smiled, "Thank you, Pavel, for your kindness. It has been a most enjoyable day for me also. Perhaps we shall meet again." With that, Simone stepped out of the carriage; as she watched the retreating coach, she contemplated his last words. Would Pavel be her unlikely savior?

As she closed the heavy door behind her, Rudolph emerged instantly from his study, a small glass of vodka in his hand. "Where have you been?" he raged.

"What difference does it make?" she said flatly. "It is obvious you have little interest in me or in what I do. Am I to be a prisoner? Is my room a cell?"

Rudolph gave her no answers, but demanded once again, "Where have you been, Simone?"

"The Cathedral of the Assumption," she replied sharply. She would say no more. For some unknown reason, she knew that Rudolph must not know of her encounter with Pavel. "If it pleases you, you could lock me in my room from now on."

"That will not be necessary," he said dryly, though his eyes were afire with emotion. "We shall leave for the dacha in the morning. Be ready for an early departure."

He strode arrogantly from the hall and out of the house.

Much later, as she lay sleepless in her bed, she heard him come up the stairs. She held her breath as he passed her room. She could tell by his faltering steps that he was drunk.

~ Chapter 12 ~

Contrary to what Pavel had told Simone, he did not leave Moscow that evening. He had received a note from Shenkerenko, who had demanded a meeting. It had been an ugly scene, the lieutenant pressuring him to go to the naval authorities. The parvenu was not satisfied with the money he had received, but was hungry for a captaincy. He had threatened to go to the officials himself. The stupid fool did not understand that it was not his intention that the authorities should know of his cousin's misconduct. This was not a concern for public scrutiny, but a family matter. Pavel decided without further deliberation that Lieutenant Commander Shenkerenko would have to be disposed of. He had served his purpose; he was no longer useful. Pavel walked to a desk, and withdrawing some paper, penned a hurried note. His options were narrowing. His plan to discredit Rudolph in his uncle's eyes must succeed. He had hoped to have more against his cousin, but this would have to suffice. However, it would be better if the sordid tale came not from his lips. Yet the bearer of the story should be credible and impossible to ignore. He thought for a moment, his long fingers playing idly with the silken tassel which dangled from the desk key. Of course, his *dear* mother. She was perfect for the role. No one was more suited than she to reveal her nephew's indiscretion.

He leaned back in his chair, a smile of satisfaction curving his wide mouth, his yellow eyes half-lidded. He gazed down once again at the envelope on which he had inscribed but a single name.

When he looked up, she was standing there, so close to him that he could reach out and touch her. Each time he had seen her she was different—dryad, princess, now siren, the long folds of her semitransparent gown rippling like water in the wind. She glowed pink, mauve, azure, maize . . . an ethereal being, a rainbow creature. Her dark hair was wild and curling about her perfect face, glistening with dew. She seemed a growing thing, alive and fertile, yet undulating, unrooted, free. She was all the elements of nature—earth, wind, fire, and water.

"Simone?" he mouthed, reaching out his hand to her, but of course, there was no one to answer his entreaty. She was gone.

Pavel half-rose from behind the desk, one splayed hand supporting his weight. Slowly, he stood and made his uncertain way to a small burled cabinet. He poured himself a generous glass of vodka from the carafe. As he swilled the burning liquid, the reality of Simone Montpellier overcame his fantastic vision. He began to carefully assess the part she would play in his well-staged drama.

He had gained the young girl's confidence. That was a master stroke. He felt he could manipulate her if necessary. He knew Simone would not reveal their acquaintance to Rudolph. And yet he could not feel fully comfortable with his machinations concerning her. She was more than beautiful, he sensed that. She had displayed humor, intelligence, spirit. He cursed his cousin; he cursed himself for the relentless destiny which he himself had fashioned.

Suddenly he laughed, a cruel, mocking sound. He had accepted his lot long ago.

The burly man stared at the note before him. There were few words, but they were clear in their meaning. He had not thought that the message would come so soon, but it was of no matter. He was always ready, and good at his work. He remembered their first meeting. As soon as he had seen that one, he had known his purpose there, known that this stranger would seek him out. And when he finally came to him, the dark man had been very generous, but insistent on complete secrecy. Well, he had picked the right man.

The man turned his glass up and raised the empty carafe

for the bar hag to see. He was one of those rare men who could drink to capacity and still seem totally sober. No, the brew never bothered him. His red-rimmed eyes focused again on the missive. How like the man was the note. The black swirling script, excessive in its strokes, deliberately controlled and yet . . . He crinkled the fine yellow parchment in his rough hand. Each man had to wrestle with his own devils.

Vladimir Shenkerenko finished with the last button of his coat and stood at attention before the blemished mirror. In his mind's eye he saw the captain's stripes upon his sleeves. Surely he would be suitably rewarded for his sense of duty. They could not deny him his own ship now. Donning his cap, he left the room. Tonight he would eat well.

He stepped out into the evening. It was unusually humid, and he ran a single finger around the constricting collar of his tight jacket. The restaurant was within easy walking distance, and if one used the short alleyway . . . He moved to the side of the hostel and entered the passage. Night clouds shrouded the high-risen moon and rendered the narrow corridor completely black. Yet Shenkerenko sauntered easily into it. He was a hungry man. He was still smiling smugly when the lethal blade cut a thin red line across his throat.

"You stupid boy, are you in love with that demented peasant?"

Pavel turned to face the angry woman. "Don't be a fool, Mother, you have made me incapable of that tender emotion."

"Is that why you do not court Princess Sokolov? You would do well to marry that one. Her father and Dimitri are as brothers."

"Princess Sokolov is your insipid choice, dear Mother, not mine. But you need not overburden yourself with the nature of my romantic interests. I can assure you that I have not sabotaged my ascendancy to the *yarlyk*." With these, his last words, he strolled from the room, leaving the frustrated woman wondering if, perhaps, she had not underestimated her son.

He whipped the horse into full stride, the gray beast straining as his master's thighs pressed deeper into his warm, moist flesh. The rider was unusually restless and agitated this night. And the man's wretched mother had done little to improve his vile mood.

How did she know of Sophia? he worried. He had been so incredibly discreet. Who else knew? He resolved to be more careful. As his animal penetrated the thick underbrush of the darkening wood, his mind returned to that matter of more urgent consequence. If only there were some way of knowing for sure if his orders had been carried out successfully, he agonized. This part of the game was new for him.

She was not aware of his presence. Her head was bowed in prayer as she knelt before the icon, the single taper illuminating her fine silver curls into a halo about her face. Finally she glanced upward, her gaze moving directly to Pavel's face as he stood over her, watching.

Violently she recoiled from his yellow stare. Thrusting her arms before her face, she shrank closer to the floor screaming in near hysteria, "Your eyes, Pavel—your eyes! What have you done? Oh, oh, the blood, the blood. You have spilled the Blood of the Lamb!"

He reached down and jerked her viciously upward, "Shut up, Sophia. Shut up, you are mad!" he shrieked.

"The Blood of the Lamb, the Blood of the Lamb," she intoned ceaselessly, locked into her spirit world, her eyes rolled back in her head.

"Damn you!" He flung her unresisting body across the room. Slamming into the rough wall, she crumpled to the floor; the trance was broken. She watched him in silence as he paced the tiny cottage, moving back and forth before the candle, plunging the world again and again into darkness. Finally he stopped; hesitating but a moment, he moved toward the door.

"You cannot go, Pavel," her voice rang surprisingly strong in the small room. She was standing, her long black shadow towering behind her. He turned, still silent, toward her voice. He did not move. She stepped from her shift and walked toward him, the cord in her hand, her shadow lengthening across the wooden floor. When she reached him, she spoke again. "You cannot go, Pavel. You are not clean. The Blood of the Lamb is upon you."

He looked closely at her face and thought how like clear glass her skin appeared. Queer he should think of such a thing now, at this moment. Dropping his gaze, he stared transfixed at the little hand which offered the cord to him. Slowly, he reached out and lightly touched the tips of her fingers with his own. She should have felt warm, but she was cold, so very cold. And almost osmotically, he seemed to drain the chill from her. He shivered convulsively. Suddenly, he desperately clutched at the rope, his face a grotesque mask, the yellowed eyes burning nakedly in the dark visage. He raised his arm, and at first the rope fell almost limply against her nude body. However, as he repeated the ritual, the intensity of his lashing increased. Her milky skin blushed as the cord curled hungrily about her thighs, her breasts. She opened her mouth slightly and moaned softly, her little pink tongue running across her lips, catlike.

He could not stop now, and soon he began to babble, his incoherent chant orchestrating the movement of his arm. "I had to do it . . . there was no other way . . . forgive me . . . please . . . I must . . . Oh, Rudolph . . . I'm sorry . . . the *yarlyk* . . . mine . . . all mine."

His heavy body dragged her to the floor. She waited for him, her head thrown back, but strangely, he did not enter her. He uttered a curse and lay still.

She looked into his face. She was no longer afraid. The candle had gone out, but the moon was risen. His eyes gleamed, reflecting the light, the pupils contracted to points to hold in the darkness.

~ *Chapter 13* ~

She watched him from beneath lowered lids as he gazed out of the carriage, watching the land roll by. She wished she could read his thoughts. He looked so lost somehow, so unhappy. He seemed suddenly vulnerable. Remembering Mimka's words, she had an impulse to move to a position beside him, to press the golden head to her breast. It was ridiculous, of course. This proud prince of Russia would scorn her pity, if he but knew of it; she scorned it herself. She was again forgetting all that he had done to her. She tried to assemble his many depredations in her mind—his brutal use of her, his arrogance. But unbidden came the thoughts of more tender moments—a gentle kiss, their pleasure together, the mornings when she woke cradled in his arms. She tried to concentrate on what the future held for her, to remember that at any moment he might marry Ilse. And what then for her? She must crystallize her plans; she must find help.

There were Yuri and Mimka, but she did not want to involve them in something that would impair their relationship with Rudolph. Rudolph and Yuri were close again. She could never jeopardize that friendship. She cared too much for the boy to force him to choose between them. Mimka would help her if she asked. The old woman had become fond of her, but there too, Simone sensed that Mimka feared the involvement between them would somehow bring Rudolph harm.

Her thoughts turned to Pavel. He had gallantly offered to help her in any way he could. But although she did not understand his relationship with Rudolph, she sensed something dark and complex. Yet, soon she might have no other choice than to trust Pavel.

It was early afternoon when they arrived. Mimka greeted them both in her special way. Simone realized how deep her affection for the old woman had become. She was the mother Simone had never had. She watched as Mimka again embraced Rudolph. He kissed her warmly and turned to Yuri, who had been waiting impatiently to welcome him back home. How was it that Rudolph could inspire such love in two good people, who were surely aware of his grievous faults? What a fool I am, she thought. Have I not done the very same? She turned her back on the happy scene, and mounted the stairs to her room.

At suppertime, Simone declined to come downstairs, sending a message that she was tired from the trip and feeling unwell. As they had many times in his youth, Rudolph and Mimka shared a simple supper at the kitchen table.

After they had eaten, Mimka spoke. "Rudolph, what of Simone?"

He looked at the old woman, reading the concern in her eyes, and knowing he could not completely avoid her gentle questioning.

"Please, Baba Mimka, do not worry yourself needlessly. Simone is my concern."

"But I do worry, my Rudya. I have grown fond of the girl, and I fear that this situation can bring you both nothing but pain."

He rose then from his chair and without looking at her, he said, "We will speak of this no more, Mimka." She watched him as he walked from the room. Now she realized that even he did not understand what he felt for the girl.

Perhaps Mimka was right, he thought as he ascended the stairs. The girl was, indeed, a serious complication. Possibly he should do what Simone had suggested and send her home to New Orleans? As he opened his door he was surprised to see her in his room. She was sitting propped up in the bed, a book in her hand. But when she heard him enter, she looked up and smiled.

He moved to sit by her side. He did not touch her at first, but only stared at the beautiful face, and marveled for the thousandth time at the way the lamplight caught fire in the masses of her hair. Slowly, he lifted his arm and ran his fingers deeply into the lustrous black curls. With a single finger he traced the curves of her tiny ear. Then he tilted her head back, so that the flickering light was captured in her dark eyes. He released her head gently and allowed it to fall onto the satin pillows. He bent his mouth over her thick lashes, and passed his lips across the feathery fringe. He laughed softly—how they teased his mouth. The question of why she had so suddenly softened toward him nagged briefly at the edges of his consciousness, but she twined her arms about his neck and pulled him down to her. His last coherent thought was that he would not free her just yet; there was plenty of time for that later.

Weeks passed. On the surface, there was perfect tranquillity. Yuri thought Rudolph happier than he had ever seen him, and Mimka agreed that he did indeed seem happier than he had been since his father's death. But in her heart she feared for him; he would be hurt again.

There came early one morning a message from Dimitri, requesting that Rudolph join him and Josephine at the Moscow residence. As Rudolph read the missive, he knew he could not decline. Indeed, he realized he had spent too little time with his grandmother. And yet, there was much to do on the estate. His trip to America had interfered with the smooth operation of his properties. As he pondered his dilemma, her face came to him. He thought of how she had looked yesterday in the simple peasant dress, sitting barefoot, the sketch pad in her lap. She had insisted on accompanying him to the fields. He looked again at Dimitri's summons, folded it and placed it resignedly in his pocket.

He knocked at her door.

"Come in," she called.

When he entered, she was sitting by the window, working diligently at painting a colorful bouquet onto the center of a metal tray. As he bent over her shoulder to admire her handiwork, she explained, "It is for the fair. Do you like it?"

"Yes, ma petite. It is lovely," he answered, kissing the top of her head indulgently. He glanced out of the window, looking at nothing in particular. "Simone, I must leave you for a few days," he said simply.

She stopped her work then, and looked at him. "Leave, Rudolph? But where?"

He turned to her and smiled, "Not far, Simone. Only to my Uncle Dimitri's. I am afraid I have neglected my grandmother."

Casting down her lids, she whispered, "I shall miss you, Rudolph. How long will you be gone?"

"Only for a few days, ma petite."

"You will be back for the fair, then?" she said inquiringly.

"Yes, but if I should not, you may go with Yuri."

"Oh, thank you, Rudolph," she cried, rising and throwing her arms around his neck.

He held her to him, looking deeply into her face. "Simone . . ."

"Mademoiselle, Mademoiselle Simone," Marya entered the room without warning. "Here are the trays . . . Oh, *pardonnez-moi*," she stammered, the color suffusing her face.

Rudolph released Simone, and walked again to the window.

Simone went to the young girl and took the trays from her hands.

"*Merci*. It is kind of you to get these for me, Marya."

"*De rien,*" answered the girl, and bowing slightly, she left the room.

Simone looked back at Rudolph as he stared pensively out of the window. What had he wanted to say?

After breakfast, Simone and Mimka sat talking at the kitchen table. They chatted endlessly about the fair and the handiwork to be sold there.

Secretly, Simone was hoping that the money she would earn from her work would be at least a beginning. She would need money for her passage home.

She thought of how she had felt watching from her window as Rudolph departed for his uncle's. Could she ever bring herself to leave him now? Things were so good between them. It was so easy to do all that he wished, to be all that he wanted. Yet she knew that she had to face the undeniable truth that he could never love her, never marry her.

Simone gazed at the old woman, who now stood at the

pleeta. Oh, how she had always wanted to have a real mother, a father, to be a part of a family. She knew that even if she could remain with Rudolph, she still would not have that. Not even he could give her the identity she desperately wanted. Even love, if he could give it, could not resurrect her from nothingness. Yes, he should have his countess. There was a new fear now when she thought of the future, the possibility that he might, himself, ask her to go. She could bear anything, except hearing those words from his lips. If she were to preserve anything of her own identity, it must be she who makes the decision to leave. She would make her plans, even while she cherished the precious moments with him that were left to her; she would pray that when the time came, she would have the strength.

As Ilse looked at him from across the room, she became increasingly disturbed. It was not Rudolph she saw; this man was pleasant, almost affable. It certainly had been easier to manipulate the old Rudolph. True, he was nicer to her, but he was nicer to everyone. This bizarre metamorphosis was puzzling.

Pavel, too, was acutely aware of this change in his usually grim cousin. When he turned to look at Dimitri, he noticed that the old man was beaming, obviously delighted with Rudolph's performance. It mattered not, soon his cousin would be discredited forever before his uncle.

Pavel's eyes narrowed. Rudolph was clapping Paul Sokolov on the shoulder, and they were laughing. This was more than a performance. Why, Rudolph had always treated young Sokolov as beneath contempt, and now . . . He looked to where the frigid Ilse stood. She had not wrought this change; there was only one who could. So the fool had fallen in love with his whore. Perhaps, I shall have to do nothing more, he thought, smiling to himself. My stupid cousin may yet be his own undoing.

Ilse watched as Pavel made his way toward her.

"I must congratulate you, countess. Only love could have worked such wonders on my dour cousin."

"I fail to see why you are in such high spirits, Pavel. Just look at Dimitri. It looks as though he has found his heir. But please don't think me heartless, for I do think it somewhat unfair that the prodigal son should supplant you so easily. You, dear Pavel, who are always so engaging, go unappreciated."

"Do not worry about me, dear Ilse. Look to your own nest."

He left her still mulling over his last cryptic words. What did he know? The cause of Rudolph's sudden change in temperament? She must find out.

"Ilse, what has gotten into your Prince Rudolph?" said Sonia Beloselski as she joined the tall blonde woman. "I could never understand why you chose Rudolph, instead of that delightful Pavel. But tonight Rudolph is positively charming. Those eyes. They are so wickedly blue and . . . You are a lucky woman, Ilse. But you had better make your wedding plans or you are going to have competition."

"That is foolishness, Sonia," Ilse snapped. "It has been understood for some time that Rudolph and I would be wed."

"Forgive me, Ilse," the woman answered meekly. "I did not mean to offend you. It was just idle conversation."

As the embarrassed Sonia excused herself, Ilse thought, idle conversation, perhaps. But there might be some truth in it. She must be on guard. She would not see her careful plans go for naught.

"Well, dear," said Josephine, "I have always thought you the duplicate of your father, but tonight I see my little Katerina in you. That displeases you? Are you still so bitter then, Rudya? You wrong that gentle soul. She . . ."

"Please, Grandmamma, let us not speak of this."

"As you wish. It is only that I desire your happiness. But that is impossible if your heart is filled with anger. Non, I will speak no more of it tonight." Seeing the effect her words had had upon him, she sought to restore his humor. "You have made your uncle happy tonight, Rudya. And I thank you for coming. It has been a long time between my visits. I find it difficult to leave my home in Paris. You must come and visit me. Perhaps on your wedding trip . . . ?"

"Perhaps," he offered noncommittally.

"I should so like to visit you at your dacha before I return to France."

"That is not necessary, Grandmamma. You know how dull you find country life."

"It seems to agree with you, Rudya. And perhaps in my old age, I too, would find it amenable."

"You will never be old, Grandmamma."

She laughed. "You are gallant tonight, Rudolph. I have never seen you like this before."

"I do not understand, Grandmamma. I am no different than always."

"Ah, but that is not so. Is it, Tante Josephine?" said Pavel joining them.

~ *Chapter 14* ~

In view of her harsh, unrelenting clime and the turbulent nature of Russian history, it is no small wonder that her people looked forward to any occasion to celebrate. Feast-day, birthday, fair—all became sufficient reason for the populace to throw off their intrinsic melancholy and surrender to the merriment of the day's festivities.

The Harvest Fair was thus a time of great rejoicing. As the growing season in Russia was so short, there was much frenetic activity during the short spring and summer seasons. Every day of fair weather must be seized and utilized to the fullest, the peasants laboring in the fields from early morning to late evening. The harvest carnival marked the end of summer, the high point of the short span between the end of the growing season and the long, harsh winter of forced inactivity.

This year's carnival exploded into the late summer, bringing with it hawkers, players, and minstrels. It was often difficult however, to distinguish between the carnival visitor and carnival performer, so great was the revelry of all. And if the truth be known, it was in no small measure that the bawdiness of the crowds was attributed to the vast consumption of *kvass*, a bread-fermented ale.

Simone was amazed at the variety of crafts represented at the small fair. Each village in the district, it seemed, blossomed with its own particular talent. The crude wooden booths, which abounded, were unlikely storehouses of native beauty. The *kustari*, or craftsmen, of Sergeevsk were all represented with their gaily painted wooden toys. Simone was especially delighted with a sturdily carved peasant couple, their open mouths an invitation to small birds who would find a unique nesting place within their hollow heads. More refined, but no less charming, were exquisite lacquerwork boxes from Fedoskino, with their haunting fairy-tale scenes. But Russian artisans did not work solely in wood, and metal crafts were also in abundance. There were gold and silver filigree of the finest design, and little gold chains from Sinkovo. Simone was fascinated by the *nicello* work, which had been practiced in Moscow since the sixteenth century, its designs engraved in metal, the hollows filled with a special alloy.

At the end of the long promenade, Rudolph and Simone stopped suddenly. It came tumbling clumsily down the grassy hill—a large rotund mass of shiny brown fur, his many brass bells jingling merrily from his wide red collar. His completely ungraceful grand entrance was received with rounds of applause and squeals of laughter. When he had gained his balance, he rose to his hind feet and began a padded dance, his trainer pulling rhythmically and expertly on his long leash. He swayed his great hairy bulk from side to side, keeping some kind of primitive time to the beat of a small drum and the shrill toot of a horn. The musicians seemed to follow his ursine movements closely. The tiny dwarf watched from under the rim of an oversized hat, puffing earnestly on a bugle, while the drummer tapped his own feet to his rat-a-tat cadence.

Simone watched, her face aglow with delight and amazement. Never before had she seen such a spectacle. Rudolph chuckled huskily, more at Simone's enjoyment than at the antics of the burly animal. Squeezing her waist, he commented, "As you can see, Simone, we Russians are very fond of our bears."

Abruptly, Rudolph took Simone's hand and pulled her through a throng of street dancers.

Simone was bewildered as she stumbled after him. "Where are we going, Rudolph?" she cried, trying to be heard over the din.

"There," laughed Rudolph, pointing to a whirling structure which could be seen above the heads of the jostling crowd. Screaming and laughter could be heard from the brightly painted cars as they soared and dipped through the air.

"Oh no, Rudolph! I can't . . ."

"Of course, you can," he said, laughing at her childish fears. "We'll ride together."

The small car began to move slowly upward. Simone clutched at Rudolph, burrowing her head into his broad chest. Chuckling, he raised her lowered head and kissed her lightly on the nose. "Now, now, ma petite. It is not so bad," he taunted playfully. "Open your eyes. See—we are at the top," he teased.

Simone had just raised her lids when the churning machine plummeted them downward. Rudolph roared merrily at her frightened screams.

Rudolph was still laughing as he helped Simone to the ground. Still dizzy, she leaned against him gratefully till they reached the promenade. When she had regained her equilibrium, however, she pulled away.

"It's not funny, Rudolph Balenkov. I might have been ill!"

"Come, Simone, don't pout," he cajoled her. "I will buy you some lemonade and *kalachi.*"

"What are *kalachi?*" asked Simone, curious but not completely mollified.

"They are delicious little loaves of sweet bread, and will make you forget all about your wild ride."

When they had finished their refreshments, the two people walked toward a raised platform. It was outfitted for a puppet show with colorful makeshift curtains and a crudely sketched background. The wooden characters had just appeared when Rudolph stood behind Simone and whispered gently into her hair, "Forgive me?"

Simone nuzzled her back against his chest and smiled. "Of course," she said softly.

He then turned her to face him, ignoring the comedic performance before them. "A peace offering," he said, magically producing a small nosegay of pastel flowers. "I could not resist the crone's cry of *'Tsvety, tsvetochki!'* as she passed."

Simone took the delicate bouquet and brought it to her nose. She closed her eyes, inhaling the sweet fragrance. "Thank you, Rudolph. I'm glad you could not ignore the old woman. Both she and I are pleasantly rewarded," she quipped, her dark eyes flashing.

As the crowd dispersed, Rudolph and Simone caught sight of Yuri walking excitedly toward them.

"I have been looking for you, Simone. I have such good news. My sisters, Natalie and Anna, said that everyone wishes to buy your trays. They have never seen such flowers as you have painted. Gardenias and camellias are unknown in Russia."

"Oh, Yuri, I am so pleased. I was worried that they would not sell, and Marya was so kind to get the trays for me."

"Yuri, now that you are here, stay with Simone for a moment. I need to see Orlov Tobol about some horses I wish to purchase," interrupted Rudolph.

As Rudolph walked away, Yuri turned to Simone and asked, "Would you like a cup of *kvass?*"

"Oh yes, that sounds delicious. I have just had some lemonade, but already I am thirsty again. It must be the excitement."

Yuri had been gone but a moment when Simone's attention was drawn to a strange-looking man, who, like herself, stood apart from the bustling throng. He wore a wrinkled black caftan bounded tightly at the waist by a swatch of purple cloth. A long rope of brown beads hung loosely about his neck. Simone looked closely for a crucifix, but there was none. He held a brass-tipped wooden staff in his gnarled hand, and Simone could not decide if it were a concession to some infirmity, or symbolic of an ecclesiastical office. He certainly appeared a holy man. His eyes were so devoid of color, that for a moment she was sure he was blind. Yet the intensity of his gaze was so penetrating and so obviously focused on herself that she knew he could see. But see what? She turned to look behind her. Indeed, there was no one else who could be the object of his scrutiny.

When she turned to face him again he was ambling toward her slowly, the staff rising and falling before his booted feet. As he stood facing her, his eyes bored into her own. "Would you know your destiny? I would tell it." The portentous words clashed with the almost lyrical voice.

She stood rooted to the spot, transfixed by his glassy stare and musical intonations.

"You will not find peace, Alana, until the heart is opened. You will suffer much before you learn the secrets of your own soul. Do not be afraid of your life and its many journeys. You would know that what you are and what you will become are one." With these words he turned and walked away from her.

Simone was still staring after his retreating figure when Yuri hurried to her side.

"Simone, are you all right? I saw him with you. I'm sorry; please forgive me."

Simone did not look at the young boy, but asked almost inaudibly, "Yuri, who was that man?"

"He is one of the village *volkhvi,* a sorcerer. Oh, Simone, what did he tell you? Did he upset you?"

"No, Yuri, I am not upset," the girl answered quietly. "He told me nothing."

"Simone, I should have warned you. We Russians are a superstitious lot. And as for some of the villagers . . . well, it is the double faith they practice, *dvoeverie.* They believe these *volkhvi* as they do their priests."

The pair saw Rudolph's tall figure approaching. Quickly Simone turned to her companion, "Please, Yuri, speak nothing of this to Rudolph." The boy nodded in agreement.

"That Tobol is a difficult man to bargain with. Yuri, he will deliver several horses to the dacha before dark. You are to meet him at the stable."

"Yes, Prince Balenkov. I will go there immediately. Au revoir, Simone. I hope all your trays will be sold before the day is done."

"Merci beaucoup, *mon ami,"* Simone said, smiling.

As the night's shadows palled the carnival activities, Simone and Rudolph made their way to their open carriage. Rudolph looked at her closely as he lifted her into the droshky. Somehow, she had been more subdued since he had returned from his meeting with Tobol. It was nothing he could name, but she was more restrained, thoughtful; her laughter seemed somehow forced. Was she still angry with him about the foolish ride? No, that was ridiculous. She was simply tired. It had been a long day.

Simone was silent as they drove along. She should not let the peculiar incident trouble her so. What had he called her . . . Alana? That was a Spanish name. Had he mistaken her for someone else? He had said something about journeys. Well, wasn't that what all fortune-tellers said? And yet, Yuri had not called him that. A sorcerer . . . the word sent a shiver through her small frame.

"Surely you are not cold, ma petite," said Rudolph putting his arm around her. "There will be time enough for that. The Russian winter will soon be upon us."

"No, Rudolph," she said, feigning a smile, "I am not cold." Her thoughts went inexorably back to the old man's strange words. Open her heart, he had said. Had she not already opened her heart? Opened it only to be hurt eventually? That proved his prophecy was not for her. She was a fool to worry over his words. She must try, as she had vowed, not to think of her destiny, at least not now. She looked at Rudolph's handsome profile, and leaning against his shoulder, sighed deeply.

~ Chapter 15 ~

The rooftops of Moscow were iced with the first snow of the season, and still the large fluffy flakes continued to fall. The streets were thronged with carriages. It seemed that the city's inhabitants had come out in force to greet the Russian winter. Moscow wore the white patina like a bride.

The hoofs of the perfectly matched pair sank easily into the soft glistening powder. The fantastic panorama which greeted Simone as they entered Red Square was like nothing she had ever seen before. It was a circus of human activity. How very different it looked from the first time she had entered the broad promenade. Now it was a bustling, open-air marketplace—rowdy, brawling. Wealthy noblemen in sable-trimmed caftans milled easily with peasants in leather coats lined in sheep's wool. And everywhere gaily decorated sleighs and troikas competed with scurrying pedestrians. Hawkers of everything from silks to cabbages greeted old customers as friends.

Long-lost relatives embraced, kissed, and cried, swearing never to lose each other again. The square was full of pungent smells, raucous noises, bizarre sights; Simone loved all of it.

Saint Basil's was more like a fairy-tale castle than ever, the brilliant white of the snow reflecting the pure colors and gilt of its onion domes. The tolling of bells enlivened the crisp early morning air.

"It is wonderful," exclaimed Simone. "Thank you for keeping your promise, Rudolph."

"This is the Moscow I wanted you to see. This is *Mat Russkaya.*"

As the calèche passed through the Iberian Gate, Simone spied the little Chapel of the Iberian Virgin, nestled between the twin arches.

"Oh, Rudolph," she cried. "Please, let us stop here. I would like to see the chapel. I have read of it. Please."

Rudolph smiled, "Simone, Madi is expecting us. She can be very temperamental. If you wish to see a chapel, I promise that you will see one before the day's end."

The silver bell rang brightly as they entered the shop. A woman was leaving, her footman loaded down with packages. Rudolph gallantly held the door, and the dowager rewarded him with her most brilliant smile.

Madi greeted them effusively, bringing steaming cups of lemon-spiced tea from the samovar. They talked pleasantly for a time about the fine weather and the coming holiday season. Finally, Madi said, "You must excuse us a moment, Prince Balenkov." She motioned to Simone, "Come, a little surprise."

Simone followed the French woman into the dressing room. As Madi drew the damask drape behind her, she instructed the young woman to disrobe, and before exiting, she left Simone with one final admonition. "Ma petite, when you are finished undressing, you must close your eyes

and not open them until I tell you. This you must promise
Madi. I have a special surprise of my very own for you. I
will return with Colette and we shall dress you. You must
not peek, *n'est-ce pas?*"

Simone laughed, "I promise, Madi. Although I must
admit you have stirred my curiosity, and the temptation to
steal a look will be very, very great."

"Simone, please!" the couturière pleaded.

"I promise, Madi. I was only teasing you."

"*Bien*, ma petite," said Madame Mereaux, hurriedly
leaving the room.

Soon Simone stood in the center of the tiny dressing room
clothed only in her silken chemise and pantalettes. She was
delirious with excitement and anticipation. What delicious
creation had Madi designed for her? She pressed her lids
tightly and prayed that she could keep her promise.

Simone did not have to wait long, for Madi, accompanied
by Colette, quickly returned. And immediately the young
woman began obeying Madi's commands to "step into this,
raise your arms higher, stand straighter." She could feel the
softness of the lightweight fabric—some kind of wool, she
imagined. And more glorious, she could feel the luxury of
fur kissing her throat and wrists.

"Now, ma petite, open your beautiful eyes, and see what
Madi has fashioned just for you!"

Simone opened her lids slowly, almost afraid to see
herself in the cheval, now that her adornment was complete. But when she viewed her striking image, she could
only whisper, "Oh, Madi."

It was of dove gray wool, incredibly soft and thickly piled;
the long basquine fitted tightly at the waist and fell in
graceful folds over the simple skirt.

Simone strolled regally into the salon and stopped before
the settee. Slowly she turned round, one arm cocked
jauntily to display one fur muff.

"Did I not say your Simone and Madi's creations would
prove the perfect match?" questioned Madame Mereaux
brightly, as she entered the room.

But Rudolph had not heard the designer. He was totally
absorbed in the Tartar princess who stood before him.
Enchanted, he rose to his feet. He raised her hand to his
lips, and kissed the tips of her fingers as they peeped out
from the lush depths of the muff. His blue eyes sparkled,

and he smiled happily into her upturned face. He did not
speak to her, but she valued the look that she read in his
eyes more than a thousand idle compliments. He was proud
of her, she felt sure of this. At least physically she was not a
disappointment to Prince Rudolph Nikolaivich Balenkov.

As they pulled away from Madame Mereux's, laden with
a mélange of brightly wrapped packages and boxes, Rudolph instructed his driver to proceed to Ivan Tower. When
they had reached the tall structure, Simone noticed a nest of
tiny chapels, their cupolas rising like bright wooden eggs.
The coach stopped before one of these small churches, and
Rudolph stepped out, offering his hand to Simone.

"I said that you would see a chapel today, and I shall keep
my pledge, Simone."

As she stood before the beautiful building, Rudolph
began to speak softly, his gaze on the small church. "This is
the Balenkov private chapel—our *chasovnya*. The Chapel
of Archangel Michael . . . the patron saint of princes in
battle."

Simone was not sure, but his last words seemed somehow
bitter. His profile was unreadable, and as she looked at him,
the frosted air was wisping from his slightly parted lips. She
suddenly felt very chilled. He looked at her.

"I'm sorry, Simone. It is cold. Let us go inside." Placing
his arm around her waist, he escorted her up the small flight
of snowy steps and into the chapel.

It was exquisite. There were the same elements which she
had encountered in the Cathedral of the Assumption, the
same richness and ornamentation. But here there was less
profusion of detail, and more attention to spatial integrity.
She felt a tranquillity here which was totally lacking in the
larger structure. The floors were of black and white stone,
laid to form a diamond pattern. The walls were ivory
colored, climbing to vaulted ceiling on which were painted
the traditional floral motifs of Muscovy architecture. Huge
golden chandeliers depended from the ceiling, their curving
arms echoing the flowering vines above. The most elaborate
fixture, however, was the oconostasis, the decorative grill
which separated the faithful from the deeper mysteries of
the Mass. Its predominant color was a ripe melon, and the
numerous icons upon its broad surface were embroidered
about with organic forms, intricately carved of gilded wood.

Rudolph led Simone to a smaller side altar. Within this alcove was a mosaic of the Archangel Michael, his Byzantine image set into the surface of the wall. His visage seemed remarkably placid, despite the avenging sword held high above his head. She knelt before the image, and unselfconsciously, she folded her hands in prayer.

Rudolph noted how natural she appeared kneeling there before the icon. He remembered another woman kneeling in that same place, praying for her dead husband hour upon hour. How lonely those years had been for him. Once again he looked down at the girl's face. He could find no sadness there, only a kind of peace. He wondered what she really felt. How little he knew of her, and in dawning surprise, he realized that he yearned to know more. Slowly he knelt beside her.

~ Chapter 16 ~

"Ilse, you've hardly touched your meal. Is something wrong?" questioned Louisette Kerensky.

"Oh, Louisette, I deplore this dreary restaurant," retorted the haughty young woman. "And the service . . ."

"I'm so sorry, Ilse, I thought you really enjoyed this restaurant. I certainly would have chosen another."

"It doesn't matter. There does not seem to be a restaurateur in all of Moscow who understands fine cuisine."

"I know . . . yet, the Black Boar is still wonderful. We were there but a few months ago on the eve of our departure for the Crimea. In fact, if I'm not mistaken, your Rudolph was there that night. He seemed so preoccupied that evening, that he was hardly civil.''

Ilse had not really been listening to her friend, but with the mention of Rudolph's name she turned sharply to the woman. "Rudolph? Rudolph at the Black Boar? I don't recall . . .''

"Oh, I'm sure it was he. He was in such a hurry, he did not even introduce us to his companion.''

"His companion?''

"Yes, isn't his grandmother, the Countess Semolenski, visiting? I'm almost certain the girl was French. She certainly wasn't Russian. Sergei and I assumed she was a cousin.'' As Louisette spoke, Ilse's body went rigid, and her hand clutched tightly about her wine glass. "Sergei thought she was so beautiful,'' the woman continued. "I guess she was, in an exotic way. Ilse, does Rudolph have a French cousin visiting him?''

With that, Ilse abruptly rose. "Louisette, we must go. I can't tolerate this restaurant a moment longer.''

Ilse Durenchev paced wildly about the drawing room, her mind racing. How dare he! Who does he think he is, prince or no? And who was this woman? She halted, bracing herself against the high back of the settee. I must know. Nothing can upset my plans.

Suddenly the doors of the room opened. "Ilse, my pet, so here you are. I've been looking for you.'' She turned, her face almost deathly white with fury. "What is it? I have never seen you so agitated, my daughter.''

Count Ivan Durenchev obviously adored his only child, and chose to see none of her faults. But the cool beauty was far from serene; there was a hardness in the young woman. Perhaps this fatal flaw in her character was a result of Ilse's inability to accept the impotency of her father's personality. He cared little for power and position, and was content merely to live a pleasant life surrounded by his many friends. His *raison d'être* was to see his grandchildren.

But to Ilse, his boyar blood, though as ancient as any in Russia, was a dilution of her Varangian heritage. She had never forgiven her dead mother, whose family was descended from Rurik, for marrying beneath her. That she,

Ilse Durenchev, could not have been conceived apart from
this union never occurred to her. She dreamed only of
infusing her attenuated blood with new strength. And for
this purpose she had chosen her instrument—Rudolph
Nikolaivich Balenkov. Behind her sophisticated civility lay a
fierceness, a hunger. She was a savage Viking maiden
enshrouded in the trappings of a Russian aristocrat.

"It seems to me that Louisette Kerensky knows more
about Rudolph Balenkov than I," she announced.

"What do you mean, Ilse?" her father queried.

"I mean, dear Father, that your future son-in-law has
been squiring some French whore around Russia."

"Ilse!"

"And I mean to find out what is going on," she continued.

"Ilse, please. Don't do anything you'll regret later. Let
me speak to the boy. I'm sure it's some mistake. Besides,
you shouldn't take the word of Countess Kerensky. Everyone knows she's a notorious gossip."

"You fool, this is no idle gossip," she hissed. "And, don't
you dare go to Rudolph *or* Dimitri. I'll handle this in my
own way."

Snow, the constant Russian snow, fell in thick white
clouds. Simone sat close to the Dutch-tiled oven, the birch
logs crackling cheerfully in the grate. The stark pure light
which filtered through the double windows adequately
illuminated her drawing paper, but there was no warmth in
it. She sat closer to the comforting fire. Her hand moved to
draw the angle of the jaw more sharply. Holding the tablet
away from her, she examined her latest modification. No,
that wasn't right! Frustrated, she crumpled the white page
in her hand and threw it upon the floor. It fell impotently
among her other futile attempts at capturing the likeness of
Rudolph Balenkov. How many sketches had she made? Too
many to count. And always there was something wrong
—the shape of the eyes, the line of the nose, the curve of
that full sensuous mouth. Some had even resembled his
dark cousin more than he. Perhaps she was trying too hard.
She moved from her chair and tossed the bare tablet upon
the cushions of her bed. Just as she reached the windows
Simone saw a carriage approaching the dacha. She had seen

that elegant landau once before. Instinctively, she knew
who the passenger would be before she alighted. The icy
patterns that frosted the glass could not obscure the identity
of the visitor. She watched as Ilse Durenchev stepped from
the coach and disappeared from view. Simone passed
stealthily out of her room and onto the second floor landing.
She remained carefully in the shadows. She could not see,
but she could hear. She listened as the door was opened.

"Where is Prince Balenkov?" the woman demanded.

"He is not here, countess," Mimka replied flatly. "Is
there something I can do for you?"

"When do you expect his return?"

"I do not know. He did not say."

"I see. Well, I shall wait for him in his study."

"But countess, no one goes into the prince's study."

"I am not just *anyone*. Get out of my way, old woman."

Simone was shocked by Ilse's manner with Mimka. How
could Rudolph have chosen such a woman for a wife? She
remembered her first glimpse of the countess. She had
noted immediately the cool aloofness of the woman, but
had thought perhaps an inner warmth lay hidden beneath
the arctic beauty. Now she knew that body and spirit were
one.

Ilse prowled the study, searching for some clue to the
mystery of Rudolph's strange behavior. She stalked to his
desk. Perhaps a letter. But to her consternation, all the
drawers were locked. Looking up, her cold eyes once again
surveyed the room, but there was nothing, nothing. Frustrated, she moved to sit in the large leather chair which
stood before a slowly dying fire. He must have been here
scant hours ago, she thought, noting the still-glowing embers and the half-emptied wineglass on the table beside her.
Absently, she lifted the thick volume which lay facedown by
the crystal goblet, *Romantic Poetry of the Nineteenth Century*, she read. Intrigued, she turned the book over to the
selection which he had been reading.

The Girl of Cadiz

1

Oh never talk again to me
Of northern climes and British ladies;

It has not been your lot to see,
  Like me, the lovely Girl of Cadiz.
Although her eyes be not of blue,
  Nor fair her locks, like English lasses,
How far its own expressive hue
  The languid azure eye surpasses!

Prometheus-like from heaven she stole
  The fire that through those silken lashes
In darkest glances seems to roll,
  From eyes that cannot hide their
flashes:
And as along her bosom steal
  In lengthened flow her raven tresses,
You'd swear each clustering lock could feel,
  And curled to give her neck caresses.

Our English maids are long to woo,
  And frigid even in possession;
And if their charms be fair to view,
  Their lips are slow at love's confession;
But, born beneath a brighter sun,
  For love ordained the Spanish maid is,
And who—when fondly, fairly won—
  Enchants you like the Girl of Cadiz?

The Spanish maid . . .

It was worse than she could have imagined. The fool was
in love!

~ *Chapter 17* ~

The intense bitterness of the cold gray Russian winter usually conjured up long periods of loneliness and deep melancholy. But the season had proved unusually exhilarating for Simone.

She pulled her fur-lined boots up over the legs of the woolen trousers. She was excited at the prospect of visiting the Balenkov lodge on this December day. Rudolph had emphasized the need to dress warmly, as they would be riding in an open sleigh and might be late returning to the dacha; she had prevailed upon Yuri to lend her a pair of pants and a thick jacket.

She fastened the last hook, and remained sitting on the edge of the bed. She smiled as she thought of how good things had been between them these last few months. Now the battle was within herself; she didn't want to leave him. Yet the time would come when she had no choice. She thought of her small cache of gold coins. She had not done badly at the Harvest Fair, but the money from the sale of the flowered trays would hardly finance a trip to New Orleans. She would have to seek help somewhere else. She had not seen Pavel since that day in Moscow, and had long since abandoned the idea that he could be of assistance. But if not he, who?

She hurried downstairs to where Rudolph waited. As she stepped out into the brisk day, an enchanting sight greeted her—a small sleigh built to hold only two passengers. Lacquered a dark cobalt blue, the edges of the troika were banded in ribbons of deep crimson. And everywhere wonderful fantasy creatures prowled or flew across the shiny wooden surface. There were fat curving lions—bright yellow felines whose comical faces seemed more canine than anything else. There were wild birds with rainbow-hued wingspreads soaring and dipping deftly among swirling, entangling vines. This mythological menagerie was hitched to three large beasts whose great heads rose and fell in anticipation of the journey, and whose hot breath iced in the air.

After Rudolph had helped Simone into the open sled, he placed a large lunch basket behind their seat. With a short, shrill whistle and a slapping of the leather reins, they were off.

As the sleigh raced along over the snow-blanketed fields, the long flaxen manes of the prancing horses flew in the wind. The powdery snow sprayed upward in a fine mist as the silver runners traced a path across the gently rolling hills. A few light flakes drifted down from the soft gray sky to settle in the branches of the tall evergreens, their boughs already heavily laden. The merry sleighbells and the soft soughing of the wind in the pines were the only sounds in the great white world. Simone snuggled against Rudolph, and pulled the thick red fox throw up to her glowing pink cheeks. She thought of the scene in the egg. How like the little Fabergé couple they were on this day.

Finally, they reached the lodge. It was much larger than Simone had imagined, almost the size of the dacha itself. It was fashioned entirely of the wood of poplar trees, and in design and feeling it was reminiscent of the wonderful country restaurant where she and Rudolph had dined. All of the rooms were large, and appeared even more spacious because of the paucity of furnishings. Each sleeping chamber bore a great posted bed, spread with lustrous, thick pelts.

Soon a roaring fire blazed in the massive hearth of the Great Room. Simone had reclined upon the soft black expanse of a bear rug, and now she sipped steaming coffee laced with a sweet liqueur. Propped up on her elbows, she alternately raised and lowered her slim calves and repeatedly burrowed her toes into the carpet's furry depths. She turned her head and stared into the fire, watching the orange tongues of flame lick hungrily at the thick logs. Rudolph joined her on the rug, sitting in front of her, his muscular legs stretched out before him.

"What a shame to have killed such a magnificent animal," murmured Simone, stroking the long fur.

"You are too sentimental, ma petite. The beast was a match for the hunter."

"But surely the creature should have been left alone to wander his own wild paths. It does not seem fair that he should die in a battle not of his choosing."

"Life is rarely fair, Simone, but in this case I think you might judge the man justified. The bear was quite dangerous. He terrified some of the village children and I . . ."

"*You* killed the bear, Rudolph?"

"Yes, but it was nearly I who was killed. He was a clever devil and I was only seventeen."

Simone was silent, picturing an adolescent Rudolph pitting himself against the enraged beast.

"Despite this contest, Simone, I told you that we Russians are very fond of bears," he continued. "Legend has it that the bear was once a man who unfortunately was befriended by no one in his village. He became so lonely that he decided to live in the woods with the animals. As the years passed, the man became so like the beasts with whom he lived, that his very form began to change. He grew large and his body darkened with thick fur. He was a man no longer, but the great bear who now guarded the forest against men. Everyone feared him. So it became man's task to make peace with the great animal. The bear was captured, trained to dance and wrestle, and taught once again to live among men.

"So you see, Simone, the Russian fascination with bears is just our way of trying to restore the lost harmony among all of the creatures of the earth."

Simone had sat very quietly while Rudolph related his tale. When he had finished, she looked at him teasingly and exclaimed, "Why Rudolph Balenkov, that is a perfectly marvelous story, and you told it beautifully. You can be poetic when it suits you." She almost laughed aloud at the look on Rudolph's handsome face, so abashed was he to hear himself described so.

"Are you hungry?" he said rather abruptly. "Baba Mimka packed us some food."

"I am famished!" Simone confessed, graciously allowing him to change the subject. "Let us see what she has sent."

Rudolph retrieved the basket, and Simone made a performance of revealing its contents. Ceremoniously she removed thick black bread, cheese, butter, wild honey, dried fruits, and nuts. They laughed, declaring that there was surely enough for ten.

When they had partaken generously of the cornucopia of food which Mimka had provided, they lay very still before the friendly fire. Simone rested easily in Rudolph's arms. There was no need for words now, and whatever unspoken language passed between them, they both seemed to understand it.

After a time Rudolph rose, gently easing Simone's warm body from his. She regarded him sleepily, and was barely aware that he had left the room. When he returned with a large box, she was stretching lazily before the fire. He held out his hand to her.

"Something arrived from Madame Mereaux's this morning," he said, smiling as she stood. "It seemed quite suitable that you should have it today." He removed the lid of the large box and withdrew a length of beautiful dark sable. He placed the hooded cape about her shoulders and pulled the imprisoned masses of her hair from beneath its weight. He rubbed its own black silkiness between his fingers.

"How well this suits you, Simone. It is the exact shade of your hair." His eyes were liquid blue as they locked with hers, and she sensed in them some strange emotion which she did not fully comprehend. When she finally spoke, she did so self-consciously, her dark head lowered beneath his gaze.

"Rudolph, how can I thank you," she said quietly, stroking the soft fur.

Lifting her face to his, he whispered, "Don't say anything Simone." As he lowered his open mouth to her parted lips, they sank to the rug.

When he finally lifted his face, he knelt by her side for a moment and looked at the waves of her thick hair rippling wildly about her head. He gently fingered the collar of her blouse, then slowly loosened it from her shoulders. Carefully, he pulled one by one, the tiny pink ribbons that fastened her lacy chemise. Moving his hands to the tight trousers, he slid them from her long limbs. His breathing quickened when he saw that she wore nothing under the woolen breeches. Her body lay sensuously in the dark fur, the light of the fire bathing it in a pink luster. Only the rigid nipples of her perfect breasts and the soft mound of hair between her thighs remained dark and unrouged by the glow of the flames. He pulled her to him and held her, tightly pressing the length of her body to his own. She twined her arms about him, her face buried in his strong shoulder as he whispered her name over and over again into her hair. He released her slightly, and she fell back onto the fur. He kissed her full mouth, and when he had moved his lips and tongue from her arching breasts, he lowered his head and tasted further of her sweetness. As she could bear the teasing of his hungry mouth no longer, she pulled at his golden head, bringing it to her lips once more. She ran her tiny pink tongue over his mouth, breathing in little gasps, pleading for him to enter her.

"Rudolph," she murmured, "my golden bear, my wild beast, come to me. Tonight the bear shall win."

He drew himself up and gazed at her intently. She was so ripe with passion. He bent down and softly bit into her lower lip. "Yes, Simone, yes," he cried, as he plunged the full length of his burning shaft so deeply into her that he seemed consumed in her very being.

Again and again he took her, their passion finding no limits; his body begged her to understand what he had no words to speak. And though she did not fully comprehend, there came no thoughts of the future to mar the perfect rapture of this night.

When they finally fell asleep, naked under the spreading sable cape, it was early morning.

Simone awakened to find herself in one of the large bedchambers. Rudolph was sitting at the edge of the bed looking at her.

"Well, I'm glad you are finally awake, Simone. I was getting lonesome."

She sat up, stretching languorously. "Rudolph, I feel wonderful. What time is it?"

"I'm afraid you've missed breakfast and lunch, little kitten."

"What? But it's still dark."

"Dark, yes, but it is the afternoon. You forget that we get little sunshine in the winter."

"Should we not be getting back? Mimka will be worried."

Rudolph laughed, "Mimka has worried about me before. Today we will go nowhere. We are snowed in, my little one."

For two blissful days they became children, laughing, playing games, teasing each other. They were innocent, natural, totally freed of all the complications that had kept them from truly exploring each other as people. They found a purity in their snow prison that had never existed before. It wasn't anything that they said or did, rather it was the simple experiencing of each other. In this primitive environment, far from the urgencies of his heritage, he could lose himself; here, she needed no identity other than the one she discovered in his arms.

When they were able to leave, Rudolph wrapped Simone in her sable and carried her to the troika. As they pulled away from the chalet, Simone rested her head on Rudolph's shoulder. She vowed desperately that he would not see her cry.

~ *Chapter 18* ~

". . . and I said to dear Sergei, she must be one of Prince Balenkov's French cousins. Such a beautiful creature, you know, and so terribly chic. Her gown, I'm sure, was Parisian. I told Sergei, I certainly don't blame Josephine for not wanting to make the long trip alone! Is she here now? I should love to meet her. And as I've said, we were not introduced. Prince Rudolph was in such a frightful hurry that night."

As the insipid woman babbled on, Josephine's bright blue

eyes narrowed, and her keen mind began to review all of the seemingly innocent events that had transpired since her recent return to Russia. Rudolph had seemed so different of late, and he was reluctant for her to visit him at his dacha . . . His insistence that she not go was so carefully veiled in deference to her inability to enjoy provincial life, that she had thought nothing of it at the time. She had only reveled in the wondrous change in her Rudya, but now . . . Unbidden, a sense of foreboding crept into her soul. She would see for herself. Like it or not, she would go to his country estate. And she would go this day.

The two women embraced warmly. Josephine had liked Mimka since the day her beloved Katerina went to live at the Balenkov estate. And now they had a common bond which drew them closer, their love for Rudolph. Though Josephine spoke halting Russian, liberally flavored with her Parisian accent, she and Mimka had little trouble communicating. The Russian woman seated the countess in the parlor, bringing coffee and *medoviya prianiki*, "honey cookies."

Mimka apologized again that Rudolph was away for the day, and had left no word of what time he might return. Josephine replied that it was just as well that the boy was not there, since she preferred to speak to the one who perhaps knew him best, Mimka herself. Without hesitation, she questioned the woman directly.

"Mimka, surely you have noted the change in our Rudya. At his uncle's party the other night, he was so charming, so enchanting, a . . . a *chevalier*. I know it seems silly of me, but I find this uncharacteristic behavior troubling. Is there something you can tell me?"

The Russian woman looked down; she was evasive. She was torn between her loyalty to Rudolph and her conception of what was best for him. She longed to confide in his grandmother. Perhaps, Josephine might persuade him to do what was right. She was about to capitulate to the countess's determined promptings, when Simone entered the room.

The girl at first had been oblivious to the fact that the parlor was occupied. Still wrapped in her matinee, she wandered into the room. She had been ill that morning, and had not been able to eat her breakfast. Though weak and still feeling slightly nauseous, she had hoped that moving about the house might somehow revive her. She was about to retrieve a novel which she had left open on one of the tables, when she suddenly realized that she was not alone.

Although the girl was slightly pale, and her hair was bound loosely in thick braids, the French countess knew immediately that this was the *cousin* about whom Louisette Kerensky had spoken. The meddling woman had been absolutely correct on two points: the girl, indeed, looked French, and she was beautiful.

"Bonjour, mademoiselle, you are, indeed, as beautiful as I was told."

Simone's startled glance passed from Josephine to Mimka. The peasant woman rose slowly to leave the room. As she moved toward the door, she lightly touched the young girl's shoulder. Simone's gaze returned to Josephine.

"Won't you join me, *s'il vous plaît?*" invited Josephine. She poured the girl a cup of coffee and patted the settee, indicating that she should sit beside her.

"I am Josephine Bonneville Semolenski, Rudolph's maternal grandmother, and you are . . . ?"

"Simone Montpellier, madame," she replied quietly.

"Then you are French, like myself."

"But I am from New Orleans, madame," offered Simone.

"Nouvelle Orleans, a delightful city, I have heard," the woman said brightly.

They fell silent for a moment, sipping at the hot coffee, each thinking her own thoughts. Never had Simone felt so ill at ease, so compromised. What could she say to this elegant woman, Rudolph's grandmother? She knew she would be unable to lie.

Josephine's mind was racing. From New Orleans . . . could she have followed Rudya? They must have met there. She was obviously living here; the relationship was surely illicit. What was the boy thinking of, to have the girl in his home? Finally the countess spoke.

"Mademoiselle Montpellier, I am an old woman, and age gives one certain prerogatives. I shall dispense with the social formalities and come to the point. What are you doing here in my grandson's home?"

Josephine did not know what she expected from the girl, but she was totally unprepared for her response.

Simone looked up, her eyes brimming with tears, her

once pale cheeks deeply flushed. She looked, Josephine thought, like a child who had been scolded unjustly. "I . . . I can tell you nothing, madame," she sobbed. And excusing herself hastily, she fled from the room.

Josephine was so astonished that she could only stare after the girl's retreating form. When she recovered, she went in search of Mimka.

Simone still lay on the bed where she had thrown herself after the scene in the parlor. The fire was crackling in the oven, however, and a light coverlet had been thrown over her. Marya, she thought. Slowly the door opened.

"Ah, mademoiselle, you are awake at last," said Marya. The servant girl approached the bed, an envelope in her hand. "The Countess Semolenski asked me to give this to you when you were alone," she said quietly.

"Thank you, Marya," Simone whispered, taking the proffered letter from the girl.

The door closed. With trembling fingers she reluctantly slid the folded parchment from the envelope. The script was small and precise. She read:

My Dear Mademoiselle Simone,
The manner of your coming to my grandson's estate is still unclear to me. Because you seem unable to discuss it, I have chosen this manner to relate my feelings.
From all indications, you seem a person of refinement, and must surely realize the unsuitability of the present situation for both yourself and Rudolph. Perhaps, however, you are not cognizant of the threat you pose to Prince Balenkov's future happiness. Should your presence in this household become common knowledge, I fear the ensuing scandal could only result in a grave tragedy. For you see, Mademoiselle Montpellier, it is solely in the power of Rudolph's uncle, Grand Duke Dimitri Balenkov, to invest his chosen heir with the symbolic yarlyk, and bestow the title of Grand Duke and with it, the bulk of the hereditary estates. And while my grandson is clearly his uncle's favorite, and eminently suited to bear this honor, I have no doubt that any serious scandal would force the grand duke to look elsewhere for his successor.
After having spoken to Mimka, I am convinced that

*you will want to do what is best for Rudolph, and
will accept my help in arranging a swift return to
your country. No expense will be spared for your comfort.*

*If you would but give your reply to Marya, she will
see that I receive it personally. I am most hopeful of a
favorable response from you.*

                              I remain,
                 Countess Vassily Egonovich Semolenski

When Simone had finished reading, tears were coursing
down her cheeks. Here at last was her means of *délivrance.*
It had come from a most unlikely quarter. So she would be
returning home at last to her beloved New Orleans. She
threw herself upon the soft cushions and wept uncontrolla-
bly.

Late that night when Rudolph returned to his room, he
found Simone looking tired and wan.

"Ma petite, what is the matter? Are you ill?" He sat
beside her on the bed, stroking the tendrils of wispy hair
from her forehead.

She reached for his hand and brought it to her lips,
kissing the palm tenderly. "It is nothing, mon cher. I must
have caught a slight chill on our return from the lodge."

He looked at her closely. "Simone, are you sure? You
seem so pale. Perhaps I should delay my trip to St.
Petersburg . . ."

"Oh no, you must go," she said almost too quickly. "I am
sure I will be feeling better by morning."

"But I will be gone for several days . . ."

"Rudolph, you know Mimka will take care of me. Please
go, and don't worry about me. I can see that your trip is
important."

How insidiously clever was the Fates' plan for her
—Rudolph's journey to St. Petersburg timed so perfectly
with his grandmother's appearance. Yes, she would go
quickly while he was away.

Rudolph moved about the room, packing the things he
would need for his trip. From the bed, Simone watched
him, realizing that their time together was at an end. He
looked up suddenly, feeling her glance upon him.

"What is it, Simone? Why have you been staring at me
so?"

"I enjoy watching you, Rudolph. I want to remember how you look."

He moved to the bed laughing. "I won't be gone that long, little one. I promise I shall return on Christmas day. And what a Christmas Mimka has planned for us! She wants you to experience a real Russian holiday. She is planning to decorate the dacha as she did when I was a boy. It . . . Simone, what is it; why are you crying? Have I made you homesick? Forgive me, my angel."

"Hold me, Rudolph," Simone whispered, reaching out to him.

"Yes, Simone, yes."

He cradled her in his arms, and they lay back, watching the fire's glow. Slowly, Simone raised her hand to turn his face toward hers. As she looked into the warm blue of his eyes, she whispered, "Make love to me, Rudolph."

He lowered his head kissing her passionately. Her hunger matched his own. In the end, the physical sensation came only as a blinding light which fused their separate beings into one.

Simone stood at the window. She watched as he entered the waiting carriage. She knew this was the last time she would ever see him. But there was no turning back; the letter to his grandmother had already been dispatched.

She would go back to New Orleans. She would do what, in truth, was best for him. Her thoughts returned to the countess. How much she must love her grandson. Simone could not hate the woman, and yet she knew it would be best if they did not see each other again.

Her hand shook as she held the small white envelope and its contents to the flame of the candle. The girl did, indeed, love him. She would do everything within her power to see that the young woman had all that she needed. She would make the necessary arrangements immediately. Marya would accompany the girl as far as Odessa. She had promised the servant a position in France. She knew Rudolph would no longer accept her in her service. Josephine tossed the charred remains of the letter into the oven.

~ *Chapter 19* ~

"I have most distressing news, Mother," Pavel announced, feigning a deep concern as he poured himself a drink.

Natasha had been surprised to see him walk into the drawing room. It was rare that her son sought her out. Rarer still that he should confide in her. "What is it, Pavel?" she asked, her voice registering a wary interest.

"My dear cousin Rudolph, it seems, has less regard for propriety than I had first imagined. I could almost forgive him for his boorish nature, if his indiscretions did not threaten to irrevocably malign the Balenkov name."

"Pavel, I refuse to listen to this rhetoric. Come to the point."

"Forgive me, dear Mother, I did not mean to keep you in suspense. I have ascertained from a most reliable source that your nephew has, shall we say . . . a mistress living at his dacha. Of course, the poor girl initially had no choice in the matter. For you see, Mother, my dear cousin kidnapped the wench in New Orleans and smuggled her aboard his ship, a Royal Naval vessel."

As her son related his story, suitably punctuated with his characteristic dramatic flair, Natasha Balenkov scarcely breathed. Was it possible that Rudolph could be so stupid? Could her Pavel be so fortunate as to gain the *yarlyk* so easily?

He went on. "You realize, my dear Mother, that Uncle Dimitri must know of this. As head of the Balenkov family, he must deal with this detestable matter. Yet I cannot bring myself to be the bearer of such sad tidings. It would pain me

so to hurt my uncle in any way. And, of course," he added
dryly, "there is always a certain abhorrence which accrues
to the messenger of misfortune."

"Yes, I quite see your point," she concurred, her thin lips
curling in an ugly smile. "I shall go to Dimitri," she said,
easily assuming her role in his little scenario.

Even now, his mother was preparing to go to Dimitri.
The *yarlyk* would soon be his. It was accomplished. In a
way, he was being born again, he told himself, free from the
shadow of his accursed cousin. Rudolph would be as dead
to his uncle; he was sure of that. Death again, he must not
think of death. It was the new nightmare that plagued him
over and over again in his dreams. He would see himself
sitting in a quiet place. A beautiful place with fountains and
flowers and bright birds singing among the gently moving
boughs of the trees. But he was sad, sad. He sat in deep
shadow, the tears coursing slowly but ceaselessly down his
face. In the beginning, he was always puzzled. He wanted to
scream to himself, why are you crying? Why? But he knew.
He knew Pavel was dead, shut away in the dark earth. But
who then was crying? Who?

He shook his dark head against the vision, raking his
fingers through the thick masses of his hair. He had but one
more small task to complete before he would know absolute
contentment. Pulling a heavy, fur-lined cape from his
armoire, he suddenly felt a certain wretched repugnance for
what he had done. He could taste it like bitter bile rising to
choke him. He leaned heavily against the cabinet. He hated
the role which his destiny had forced him to play. He hated
the lies, the manipulations. He hated the vile alliance with
his contemptible mother, and yes, most of all, he hated that
Rudolph Balenkov was his victim.

"Damn." He hated his own weakness. "Enjoy your
glorious victory, you fool!" he cursed himself. He threw the
heavy garment about his broad shoulders savagely, and tore
down the stairs into the bitter cold of the late afternoon.

Unbelievably, she was not on her knees, prostrate before
the icon, when he entered. She turned to look at him as he
loomed in the threshold, a black pyramid of billowing fabric
and fur, the snow swirling in small drifts about his booted
feet. He walked but a few paces into her hut. He stopped,
his arms folded, his long legs spread wide, his head tilted up

so that his golden eyes, downcast, appeared as twin crescent moons in the dark visage.

"Pavel," the silver-haired girl spoke, her voice tremulous. "Something is wrong."

"Wrong? No, Sophia, on the contrary, everything is perfect. I am perfect, Sophia."

"No, Pavel, no one is perfect. All men have the stains of sin upon their souls. Only the Lamb is perfect. And the Mother."

"I am strong, Sophia. I don't need anyone. Damn the Lamb, and damn the Mother. And damn you, Sophia."

"No, Pavel!" she screamed. "You are not clean! The blood is upon you. You are damned, damned!" she shrieked. She launched herself at his body, her fingers like talons in his flesh.

"Let go of me, Sophia!" he demanded hysterically. "I am through with you . . . your madness . . . your insanity. Here, take this for your Holy Mother." He threw a bag of gold coins upon the floor; the shining pieces scattered over the dull boards. He broke her hold and walked toward the door.

"My Pavel, you are sinful. You are black with sin once again." She wailed, ignoring his offering. "Come to me, come to the Mother. I will cleanse you, purify you. Come. Come . . ." She flung herself at his legs, her thin arms impeding his exit with abnormal strength.

He flung his head back violently. His darkening face twisted grotesquely, the purple veins of his neck unnaturally distended with his quickening pulse. The large mouth opened wide, the lips stretched thin across the chalk white of his teeth. It came. At first it was only the spewing of a horrible hissing sound, wet, serpentine. Then it crescendoed into a deafening bellow, a scream for all eternity —echoing, echoing . . . A shriek, pitifully hollow, mutilating the deathly stillness of the night. And in that sickening cry he seemed to have retched some hideous being trapped within his bowels.

Wildly, he lashed out, his booted foot making a horrible sound against her flesh. He looked back only once. She was crawling toward him, her vacant eyes fixed upon his face, her lips chanting inaudibly. He found his steed in the gathering gloom. He was gone.

* * *

As he moved from his hiding place, the peasant ignored the babbling creature upon the floor. Swiftly he gathered the gold coins, and placed them in the leather pouch. He should attempt to aid the "saint," but he was in haste to get away. He had never seen so much money.

Sophia made her piteous way toward the village. Her hands grasping, grasping in a desperate attempt to drag her body along. The church beckoned, the Church of St. Gabriel, the patron of childbearing. Painfully she pushed her knee beneath her broken body and thrust herself forward, a trail of blood marking her agonizing progress through the snow.

~ *Chapter 20* ~

The bells were tolling in the village, and the sonorous tones reached Simone as she struggled with paper and pen. So much to say and so little time! She looked up. In the lamplight she could see her beautiful clothes hanging in the armoire. She would not need them in New Orleans. She rose and made her way toward the open cabinet. The shadowy mass which hung beside the dresses invited her touch. The sable. As she caressed its softness, a kaleidoscope of images assaulted her memory. A sob caught at her throat. She closed the double doors, pressing her forehead against the unyielding wood. *Don't think,* she told herself. *Don't think!*

These simple words had been her constant companions, the magic charm which got her through the lonely days since he had gone. Each time she'd felt her mind slipping back to the image of his golden head disappearing into the depths of the phaeton—disappearing forever from her life—she repeated the chant. When despair and grief welled within her at the sight of his chair, his hound, his Baba Mimka, when she stood at the door of his room, her hand on the cool porcelain knob and fought to stay within the safety of the corridor, the echo in her heart was, *I shall die,* but the silent words on her lips were, *Don't think!*

She would take only memories with her and nothing else. And still she fought the intrusion of those bittersweet memories. She would leave behind all else, everything that had meant so much to her—her growing filial affection for Mimka, the beautiful friendship with Yuri, and Rudolph . . . *Mon Dieu! Help me!*

As she looked about her room, she suddenly knew that there was one object, one token, one part of Rudolph she would not leave behind, would not surrender. She moved to her small vanity table and opened one of the tiny drawers. It was there, safe, protected, enclosed in the diminutive ebony box. She withdrew the case and slowly opened the shiny lid. The egg—her beautiful Fabergé egg. Rudolph's gift, his promise.

She ran a single finger over its delicate pale-blue surface, touching each tiny seed pearl. She then allowed the finger to intrude upon the snowy world within. The smiling couple were suspended in time. How safe they were, untouched, invulnerable to life's twisted ironies. She thought of the day that she and Rudolph had ridden to the lodge. How free they had been then, how totally beyond anything or anyone who could hurt them. How stupid, how naive she had been to think that they were as that enchanted pair in the wonderful egg. She looked at it again, but now the colors seemed so faded, so blurred. Even the tiny figures seemed to melt into dark smudges.

Cry, she thought, cry . . . cry for yourself, Simone. Weep for the girl who is no one. Weep for the woman who dared to love a prince. Cry, Simone, cry.

A soft rap sounded at the door—Marya.

"Are you packed, mademoiselle? It will soon be time," the girl whispered.

"I won't be long, Marya. I promise," Simone answered, returning to the desk as the girl slipped quietly from the room.

When she had finished her letter to Mimka and Yuri, she hesitated. If only she could leave a note for Rudolph. If only she could tell him all that was in her heart. But that was foolish, he would never understand. What a proud man he was! How he hated to lose that which was his. And she was his, as the land was his, as this house was his, as Baktu . . . She was his possession. Yet would he hate her so bitterly? Would he not realize that, in truth, she was the one possession to which he had no real claim? Why had he never understood this? Would he understand it now? She knew he would not.

She could delay no longer. She must be ready when the carriage came. He had said he would return on Christmas day. And if he should arrive early . . . ? She must be gone before Mimka, Yuri, and the servants returned from Midnight Mass. But still, she must leave him something, some token of the time they had shared. Then it came to her. She ran to the desk and withdrew the white sheet of paper. Though she had tried so hard, still it was not right, but it was the best she had done. She closed the drawer.

Hurriedly, she moved down the darkened hallway. When she reached his room, she halted. How hateful a closed door looks, she thought; how much it said. Slowly she reached and turned the knob in her palm. It was cold against her skin.

Upon entering she was startled to see how bright it was. The moonlight washed the chamber in silver. She stood for a moment looking about the room—his room. Everything in it was so like the man who dwelled there. It was strong and masculine, yet in its few appointments, one could discern a certain sensitivity, a warmth.

She glided to the center of the chamber and lingered there for a moment, as if in that position she could mystically absorb all that he was, all that was his essence. She spied his desk and walked to it. As she ran her palm over its polished surface, an image of him seated in the chair came to her. His golden head was bent in concentration as his great hand scrawled notations in that bold, oversized script. Turning, she sought his dressing chest. She lifted his brush from the silver tray and pulled free one of the golden strands trapped within its dark bristles.

The double doors to his armoire opened easily. Immediately she was filled with the heady scent of him—clean, fresh, yet completely sensual. Reaching within, she brought a sleeve of one of his jackets to her face. She rubbed the soft cashmere against her wet cheek. The garment fell from her hand.

Slowly, she moved to stand by his bed, their bed. She closed her eyes. He was kissing her, loving her, his beautiful mouth bringing her to fulfillment, his bronzed body transporting her beyond passion. Higher, higher, ever higher. Her eyes flew open. For an instant she had the strange compulsion to lie on that bed once more, to feel its softness under her, to feel him upon her. No! She turned back to the desk, and placing the sketch upon it, moved to leave his room.

She stepped into the passageway and closed the door resolutely behind her. She was not alone.

"Yuri, you startled me!" she said hoarsely. "Why are you not at Mass?"

"I could not let you go without saying good-bye."

"How did you . . . ?"

"So it *is* true. Oh, Simone, I know in my mind that what you do is right, but my heart tells me it is wrong," he said miserably. "I will miss you, Simone."

"I will miss you too, Yuri. You are my dearest friend . . . Oh, no tears, Yuri. I cannot bear it if you cry." She embraced the boy, her own eyes wet once again.

"Mademoiselle, you must hurry . . . the carriage . . . Oh!" Marya stopped, seeing them together.

Simone stepped back from Yuri's arms. "I will follow in a moment, Marya," she said, dismissing the girl.

"I've left a letter in my room for you and Mimka. You may read it when I am gone, Yuri," she whispered.

"And I have something for you, Simone. A little piece of Russia," he said, handing her a small leather-bound book. "When you read it, in the years to come, perhaps you will think of . . . your dearest friend." Awkwardly he bent forward and kissed her lightly upon the lips. Then he was gone.

From the shadows, Josephine saw the last of the baggage placed into the sledge. She watched as the young woman and Marya climbed in. As the covered sleigh pulled away into the night, she began to reassure herself that she had done the right thing. She knew that her grandson would be angry at first, but soon he would understand and be grateful. And yet, she thought, a worried look crossing her still-youthful face, have I presumed too much? But it was too late for self-recrimination. She had done what she thought was best.

She instructed her driver to pull closer to the house. As she stepped from the carriage an ominous peal of thunder resounded across the valley. She looked up to see dark clouds swallow the full moon. She shivered. It was foolish to worry, she told herself. Boris was an experienced driver.

Rudolph heard the single clap split the stillness of the night. The sleigh lurched as the horses reared upward at the threatening blast. Huge wet snowflakes cascaded wildly from the overburdened sky.

Rudolph wrapped the folds of his cape tightly about him, cursing the weather. The events of the last few hours flashed in his mind. He had been so anxious to return to his dacha tonight, Christmas Eve. It was to be a special surprise for Simone.

He was tired when the St. Petersburg train finally arrived at the Moscow station. The last of his baggage had been loaded onto his sled when the messenger intercepted him. It was a summons from Dimitri. He was to proceed immediately to his uncle's estate. Rudolph frowned.

Why the urgency? Had they not planned to spend Christmas night together? Why must he go to him tonight? He thought of his warm dacha, alight with candles and redolent of evergreen. They would all be there—Mimka, Yuri . . . Simone. He had hoped they might attend the Midnight Mass as he had as a boy. He remembered sitting in the dark church with his parents, the altar aglow with candles. And best of all, to ride home in the gay troika, gliding through the snow, bells ringing, to be greeted with Mimka's special cakes and cups of spicy tea served around the samovar. Strange, he hadn't thought of his early childhood in many years.

His fingers went to the velvet box beneath his cape—her Christmas present. He smiled as he thought of her childlike delight in the things that he gave her. Yes, tonight was to be for Simone. For a single instant he considered instructing his driver to turn and go to his dacha first. Surely whatever Uncle Dimitri wanted could wait a few more hours. But no, he knew the man too well. It was something very important. But what? Rudolph looked again into the dark rolling clouds.

The sledge pulled up before the imposing manor. As always, Rudolph felt a sense of pride in the Balenkov heritage. The house was more than a beautiful stone edifice, it represented all that was the Balenkovs.

As he mounted the marble steps, the doors opened before him. He was anxiously awaited. Something *was* wrong. His uncle's old manservant informed him that he was to proceed directly to the study.

He traversed the long colonnaded hallways, his steps resounding on the polished parquet floor. The familiar passageway seemed somehow haunted tonight.

He rapped lightly. There was no answer. Slowly, he opened the double doors. Dimitri stood at the window, his back to Rudolph, leaning upon the casement as if for support. For the first time, Rudolph noticed that his uncle seemed truly old, that the years bore heavily upon him.

"Uncle Dimitri, it is Rudolph," he said, closing the doors behind him.

Slowly, Dimitri turned. His face was livid, yet controlled, except for the eyes, which were feverishly glossy.

"I came as soon as I could, Uncle Dimitri," offered Rudolph, approaching nearer. "What is it? Are you ill?"

"Your concern is touching, Rudolph, but is misplaced, and comes too late. It is quite amazing, that one who professes to love and honor the Balenkov name, could have so callously brought discredit to it."

Rudolph's body went rigid, but he said nothing. His uncle continued. "How could I have been so stupid? Everyone seemed to know Rudolph Balenkov better than I. My mistake, Rudolph, was in loving you too much, and loving Pavel too little. For you see, Rudolph, it was you that I wanted to bear the *yarlyk,* inherit the full estates, and give heirs to the Balenkov family. But now you have betrayed my trust, and it is to Pavel that I must turn."

"Betrayed your trust, Uncle Dimitri?" The young man spoke for the first time. "How have I done this? Of what am I accused?"

At what seemed like Rudolph's feigned innocence, Dimitri's face reddened, his body quivering in rage. "In God's name, how dare you attempt to keep up this blasphemous charade with me!" he bellowed. "Did you think that you could keep your whore hidden from me forever?

"I did not in the past object to your lusty appetite, but this is too much. A whore ensconced on the Balenkov estates! Damn you boy, I gave you more credit! Yet for this indiscretion, I could have forgiven you. But to have kidnapped the wench, and kept her on board a Royal Naval vessel . . ."

Rudolph, who had listened to this tirade, was at first startled, then curious, and now angry.

"And from whom did you hear this, Uncle Dimitri?" queried Rudolph, struggling for control.

"So you do not deny that it is true?" the old man snapped.

"I do not deny or affirm it. I will say only that my actions have been misconstrued."

"I would like to believe that none of this is true," said Dimitri shaking his head wearily, "But you have said nothing to vindicate yourself."

Rudolph walked closer to his uncle. He could not bear to see him so shaken. "Uncle, I am sorry if I have hurt you, for I have loved you no less than I have loved the Balenkov heritage. If the *yarlyk* must go to Pavel, then it must, for I will discuss this matter no further." He reached for the old man, and kissed him tenderly on the cheek. "Merry Christmas, Uncle Dimitri," he said. And with that he turned and left the room.

As Dimitri watched the tall erect figure of his nephew disappear, tears came slowly to his eyes. Something irretrievable was gone. It was a crushing bitterness for his declining years.

~ *Chapter 21* ~

The silent dacha loomed in the darkness. They are all still at the church, thought Rudolph, as he entered the cold kitchen. Vaguely he wondered why there were no Christmas candles to welcome him. Had everyone gone to the Midnight Mass? Had Simone?

As he made his way through the empty house, he saw the glow of the gaslights streaming from the parlor. No, she had not gone with the others. Perhaps she had guessed that he would return tonight. He smiled to himself; she was waiting for him.

He opened the door in anticipation. "Grandmamma, what are you doing here?"

She was sitting before the dying fire. She rose and turned to him. He noticed the strained look on her face. So she knew about his visit to Dimitri. She walked toward him.

"Welcome home, my Rudya. You look tired," she said, brushing a lock of hair from his forehead.

As he stared into her troubled face, he sensed that something more was wrong. His blue eyes frosted; he was suddenly on guard. "Why are you here, Grandmother?" When his curt question went unanswered, he turned instinctively and strode toward the stairs.

Quickly, the woman followed, her insistent voice halting his wild ascent. "She is not there, Rudya."

He froze on the step, and looked down. His face was ashen, his fists clenched tightly at his sides. The gray eyes were almost transparent in their hardness. His look was cruel, impersonal. She had heard that he could be like this, but never before had she experienced his wrath. Shaken by his extreme reaction, she pleaded. "Rudya, don't you see? I had to send her away. How could you have been such a fool to keep her here in your own home, to flaunt her in Moscow society!" she exclaimed defensively. "You could have been discreet, kept her in an apartment in Moscow or Petersburg. Oh yes, I haven't lived these many years in Paris only to be ignorant of such matters."

As she looked at him, she realized that her words had had no perceptible effect. He appeared like an avenging colossus, unmoved, unrelenting, without mercy. But she could not stop. "Don't you see, you risk your inheritance for this girl. What if your Uncle Dimitri had found out?"

At this final appeal, she strained in the darkness to see his eyes. But his aspect did not change, only his lips moved. "Dimitri knows."

The words seemed to free him from his immobility. He turned abruptly and continued up the steps. She listened as he mounted the last of the stairs, his boots echoing angrily in the silent house. So Dimitri knew. Oh, Rudya, I have failed you once again. I should have come to you after my dear Katerina died, she thought in anguish. You needed me then. Now it is too late. No one can help you.

He was a Balenkov. Men of his type had graced her own family. But in the Russian temperament, such depth of feeling was more dangerous than usual, and tended toward melancholy. *Toska*, they called it. She could see it was useless to try and reason with him. She would leave him alone for a time to struggle in his own hell with his own demons.

Rudolph moved purposefully toward Simone's room. He paused a moment before the door, his hand tightly clutching the knob. Quickly he turned it and entered. He lit the gaslight, banishing the unfriendly darkness. The tiled oven was still warm to the touch and—how could he have missed it at first—the sweet smell of her perfume hung in the air. She must have left only a short time ago.

The light revealed most of her clothes still hanging in the armoire. Slowly, he moved to touch her things, his hand lingering on the fur of the sable, its softness and luster recalling her luxuriant hair. Painfully, he remembered the night before the fire. He drew away, closing the door. But the aching loneliness of the moment turned rapidly to anger.

How dare she leave him! Had he not told her that her future was his to decide? He closed the door of her room heavily behind him.

In the kitchen, Mimka stared at the letter which Yuri had read for her. Tears were streaming down her face. Poor little bird, what would happen to her now? In her heart she knew this was best for Rudolph, but the pain of never seeing her little Simone again was something almost too hard to bear. She had come to think of the girl as the daughter she had lost. And poor Yuri, he was heart-broken.

So deep was she in thought, that she did not hear him enter. But at his voice, she looked up quickly, the sorrow etched into her face. "Do you cry for her, old woman?" he demanded. "Did you not know of my grandmother's plans for her?"

"Oh, Rudya, I did not think that this would happen. See, this is all I have from her." Reaching for the proffered letter, Rudolph's eyes moved eagerly over the words.

My dearest Mimka and Yuri,

How does one say good-bye to the only family she has ever known? It is the most difficult task I have yet to do. I cannot begin to thank you for your understanding and generosity. It has greatly warmed my months in your country, and many were the hours when I felt the bitter coldness and loneliness of my Russian days.

Dear Yuri, you have been all that a brother could be—confidant, protector, and teacher. And Mimka, the acceptance and gentleness with which you embraced me have enabled me to experience the love which only a mother can give. Though I know that I shall never see either of you again, I shall carry the memory of your kindness to me always in my heart.

Yes, Mimka and Yuri, thank you for the most precious gift of all—your love.

Simone

So, she had gone willingly, Rudolph reflected, as he stared at her words. The fact that she had had time to compose the letter proved it. For how long had she and his grandmother planned this? What a fool he had been to think that she had come to accept his will, and that she was content to live in Russia.

He looked again at the words addressed to Mimka and Yuri. They were in Russian! Never had she indicated in any way that she understood his language. Like all women, she was so very clever at games of deceit. And he had thought that he had begun to make her happy! Obviously he had been mistaken. She had played him for a fool.

It was to Mimka and Yuri that she had offered her affection and appreciation. Did not his gifts to her remain behind to mock him? He glanced up to see Josephine standing in the doorway.

"Rudya, please do not vent your anger on Mimka," she pleaded. "She was unaware of the girl's leaving. I sent all in the household to Mass. Only Marya knew of our plans."

He looked at her, his contempt obvious. "What right have you to come into my home and involve yourself in my affairs? This matter did not concern you. This is my home, my land. I decide who goes and who stays. You have presumed too much, woman. Where is she?"

Josephine was stung by the cruel words. Never had he spoken to her with anything but respect and affection. "Rudolph, do you not understand that I did what was best for you . . . and for the girl. There could have been no future, no happiness for her here. You ask by what right I have acted—by the right of love!"

Rudolph was unmoved by this declaration. "I repeat, Grandmother, where is she?"

"That I will not tell you. But she is safe and well provided for. Marya will remain with her for a while. It is useless to look for her. Leave it alone. Perhaps in time, Dimitri will soften."

"With or without your help, I will find Simone." He spoke, her words having had no effect upon him. "And it will be I who decides when she leaves."

With this, he turned his back on the two women, and left, making his way to his room.

It was like Simone's room had been—dark. The fire had not been lit. The single lantern illuminated the room with a soft light. He rubbed his arms briskly; he was chilled. He moved to place several logs within the grate when he saw it. The wood fell dully to the floor. He walked toward it, arrested by his own image staring up at him from his desk.

He reached down and picked up the sketch. It was he, and yet . . . There was a softness about the eyes and a gentleness about the wide mouth. This was not the Rudolph Balenkov that stared back at him from his mirror. Was this how she saw him, or how she wished him to be? Her Christmas present to him, he thought. No, her farewell gift.

He tossed it contemptuously back upon the desk. He retraced his steps to the bed, where he had carelessly thrown his jacket. The velvet box had slipped from his jacket. Slowly he opened the lid; the emeralds, like green flame, sparkled in the lamplight. He removed the necklace from the case. The jewels, like fire and ice, burned into his flesh.

Her image taunted him; he saw the gleaming emerald and diamond offering encircling the creamy column of her throat. He snapped the box closed and walked deliberately back to her room. He placed the velvet case upon the dressing table among her things. He would order that nothing be changed here. He would find her and bring her back. And when he was finished with her, it would be he who sent her from him.

Once again he opened the box and stared at the shimmering gems. *"Joyeux Noël,* Simone," he whispered.

～ Chapter 22 ～

The bells sounded more like death knells than Christmas chimes, Simone thought as they passed from village to village. But she could not allow herself to be unduly morose. The journey she faced would be difficult enough without dwelling on her tragedy.

Rudolph's grandmother was a woman of her word. Simone had been provided with all that she would need for her arduous trip back to New Orleans. Her itinerary was cruelly stark in its simplicity. For the first time, her life lay well mapped out before her, she thought ruefully. By sleigh to Orel, by train to Odessa, by ship via Constantinople to New Orleans. Thus the salvation of Prince Rudolph Nikolaivich Balenkov.

She would travel southward, not westward, as was customary. Ice-locked St. Petersburg made passage to the North Atlantic impossible at this time of the year.

"Won't you have something to eat, mademoiselle?" said Marya, interrupting her thoughts. "See, I have packed a basket from the kitchen. Here are some of Mimka's special Christmas cakes, *tvarojniki.*"

"No, thank you, Marya. I don't think I could eat anything just now." At the mention of her name, the image of dear Mimka standing before her *pleeta* came vividly to Simone's mind. This was how she would always remember her.

The slim volume which Yuri had given her lay in her lap. She had read the title, nothing more. The small piece of Russia would have to wait, decided Simone. Wait until that

time when she could think of this land that had been her
brief home, and not so painfully remember Rudolph.
Rudolph . . . he was never long from the focus of her
thoughts. What would he think when he returned tomorrow? He would be so angry. She prayed that this wild
venture would not be in vain. But what choice was there for
her? If she should be the cause of his undoing, he would
truly hate her then. Anything was better than that.

Still, she could not envision the future. When she tried,
there was simply a void. Overcome with emotion and
fatigue, Simone dozed.

Outside the covered sledge, the driver urged the horses
on toward Orel. He had been loath to go out this night
—Christmas Eve and the promise of bad weather—but one
did not question the Countess Semolenski. Even as he
thought this, the wind heightened and the snowfall increased measurably. Boris struggled fiercely with the reins,
and cursed the shrieking gusts as they obliterated the tolling
bells which would direct his passage.

Boris flinched. His hand moved to his cheek, where the
hard ice crystal had cut into his rough skin. The small
wound did not bleed for long, as the bitter cold caused the
gash to crust over almost immediately. He knew, as he
moved the great bulk of his body from side to side, that his
worst fear had come to pass—the snowstorm was a *burran*.

Simone looked out at the swirling masses of snow. From
time to time a particularly strong gust blew a few flakes
down the long tunnel of the protective covering into the
recesses of the sleigh. She shivered reflexively. She wasn't
actually cold, as she sat wrapped in layer upon layer of
protective clothing under the fur throws. She would never
understand why Russian sledges were not completely enclosed.

It had been different of course, to drive with Rudolph on
a cold but clear day with his protective arm about her. She
stopped herself. She must not think of the past. She glanced
forward to where the driver sat completely exposed to the
elements. How was he able to go on in this raging hurricane
of snow and ice?

There was a hypnotic quality about the billowing white
curtain that seemed to hang just before the open sleigh, and
she dozed again. She was on the verge of deep sleep when
she felt herself tumbling sideways, Marya's body crashing

into hers. The servant girl's startled cry rang sharply above the din of the storm. The horses could be felt bucking and pulling; the troika was being dragged through the snow.

Fully awake now, Simone crawled to the front of the disabled vehicle. As she moved carefully forward, the horses seemed gradually to lose energy. Finally they stopped. As she emerged from the recesses of the interior, she saw that Boris was gone. Marya came after her, her frenzied words whipped away by the wind. As the servant girl sank to her knees, crossing herself repeatedly, Simone realized that she was hysterical. Pulling Marya roughly to her feet, Simone shook her in desperation, and shouted into her contorted face, "Hush, Marya! Stay with the horses and jangle the bells. I will go back a ways, and search for Boris. If I can hear the bells I will be able to find my way back to you."

Some semblance of reason seemed to penetrate the girl's mind. Slowly Marya grasped the leather strappings and began to ring the bells.

"Good, Marya, good," said Simone encouragingly, as she padded off into the deep drifts.

Visibility was extremely poor. She could barely make out the trees. It was impossible to tell if they were still on the road. Boris was nowhere to be seen, but surely he could not be far off. He must have fallen asleep, as she had, and allowed the horses to stray. She glanced behind her; she could still see the dark outline of the sledge and hear the bells. *Très bien.* Marya was at least following her instructions.

She looked ahead once more, shielding her eyes against the stinging crystals, and calling the driver's name as loudly as she could. "Boris! Boris!" she shrilled. There was no answer.

Off to the left was a dark patch in the snow, and she trudged awkwardly toward it. He lay still, his body an inconspicuous mound. She knelt beside him and frantically began to free his head from the deathly white powder. She removed her glove and tried to feel his breath upon her palm. It was futile. She could feel nothing but the icy blast of the wind. Simone attempted to lift him partially into her lap. As she did so, his head fell at a sickening angle. Simone choked on her own scream. It was obvious that the driver's neck was broken. Boris was dead.

Simone was immobilized—numb. But it was a numbness brought not by the piercing cold, it was the numbness of disbelief, fear, despair. The driver was dead. Marya would be of no help. She could see that their only hope of salvation rested solely upon her shoulders. Yet she felt so helpless. If only it were not so unbearably cold. If only the snow would stop falling, even for a few minutes. If only the wind would stop its unceasing wail so she could think.

Knowing that she could do nothing more for Boris, she methodically removed his coats. Avoiding his gruesome face, she whispered, "Thank you, Boris. You may save us with these."

Simone made her tedious way back to the overturned troika. Marya was still ringing the bells, her arm rising and falling, her haunted eyes staring at nothing.

"Come, Marya," pleaded Simone wearily. "We must right the sleigh. Boris can help us no more."

She drew Marya to the side of the sledge and loudly commanded her to push. The unwieldy mass refused to yield. Marya began to sob, "We will die, Simone! We will die!"

"Stop it, Marya," Simone demanded fiercely. "You must stop this! We will die only if you do not help me. Now push, push!"

As Simone strained against the unmoving bulk, she began to muse that perhaps it would be better if they were to die. It would be so easy, just to lie down in the white drifts and sleep . . . sleep. But no, what was she thinking! She had endured too much to die stupidly in the snow along some obscure road in the Russian countryside.

"Push harder, Marya!" she screamed.

As they pressed harder, the body of the troika slowly began to move. Finally it was upright! Totally exhausted by the effort, and barely able to stand against the fury of the storm, Simone leaned against the vehicle and sighed. Now what? she thought.

The pair crawled into the protective depths of the sleigh. They huddled closely together in an effort to warm themselves.

"Marya," Simone said after a time, "surely you have been this way before. We could not be far from the road. Is there a village nearby?"

Marya, who seemed now to have found some well of

courage, replied, hope rekindling in her face, "We have been gone for some hours. Orel cannot be far, and there are many villages along the way. We must move forward and listen for the bells. They will guide us."

"And perhaps," said Simone, her confidence somewhat restored by Marya's recovery, "we can get a new *izvoztchik* to drive the sledge. We must get to the train as soon as possible. You remain here in the back, I will drive. But talk to me, I must not fall asleep."

They made their way through the snowstorm. Close behind her, Marya talked, often lapsing into fervent prayers to the Holy Virgin. Simone lifted the collar of Boris's coat over her face so that only her eyes were exposed. Her body heat, however, was no match for the bitter cold which stole, layer by layer, through the protective clothing. But after a while she seemed no longer to feel the invading chill. She was somehow isolated from all about her; Marya's murmurings no longer penetrated her consciousness.

The horses plodded on through the tempest; the ground beneath them seemed to be solid. They must be on the road. Simone's benumbed mind clung to this one thought, as she stared blankly in front of her. The whirling particles of white were no longer articulated, but merged into a shimmering blue haze, in which strange moving lights seemed to dance. She watched with sightless gaze as they executed their strange pirouettes.

She woke with a jolt that precipitated her headlong into a snowdrift. The soft powder closed over her. She struggled to a standing position, sputtering and shaking the snow from her garments. The horses were pawing wildly at the crusty snow, and Marya had resumed her hysterical wailing.

Simone had tried so desperately, but she had fallen under the storm's lethal spell. She walked to the troika, which once again lay on its side. To her horror, she saw that the central shaft was broken. It would go no farther this night. Simone collapsed against the shattered vehicle. She longed for a place of warmth and comfort. She thought of Rudolph and the bed with the fur coverlet. How easy it would be to lie down in the soft snow and dream of his protective arms encircling her.

~ *Chapter 23* ~

For days the pack had been away from the den, and still there had been no food. Nature could be cruel even to those creatures who were at one with her designs. The lead animal suddenly halted the slow trek through the lessening storm. He raised his gray muzzle, frosted with his breath, and sniffed the moving air—*blood!* The golden eyes lit with the certainty that prey was near. The others now reacted to the scent. They hastened their pace through the falling snow.

The young woman had rested wearily against the crippled sleigh for only a moment. She could not allow this snowy Circe to seduce her into surrendering to her fatal charms. She looked up into the lightening sky. The snow still fell, but the wind had dropped. She must act; she must do. Time was so important. At any moment, the storm might intensify.

"Marya," Simone cried, "we must unhitch the horses and ride to a village."

One of the animals had been badly injured by the splintering shaft. Poor beast, Simone thought. She could do no more for him than she had been able to do for Boris. The other two animals were in good condition, but worked against her clumsy efforts to free them. As Simone steadied them, Marya wrestled with the harnesses, the cheery jingle of the bells ringing out in ironic counterpoint to their grim situation.

The uncanny music suddenly ceased. Marya's hands fell

to her side. Simone glanced up quickly from her position by one of the drays. She started. The face of her companion was a study in abject terror. Her mouth gaped, but no sound came forth. And her bulging eyes seemed so terrified that Simone hesitated to look behind her. She turned slowly and beheld the awful vision which had claimed the servant girl. She marked the approach of several black shapes, loping gracefully across the white plain.

What was it? What were they, to cause such stark fear in Marya? Even as she watched, their pace quickened. And as they moved closer, Simone's expression changed from perplexity to dawning horror. *Wolves!*

Acting quickly, she retrieved her reticule from the sledge and grabbed Marya's hand, pulling the girl away from the frenzied horses.

"Come, Marya, they are still some distance away! We must run into the forest!"

The paralyzed girl refused, at first, to move, but as she saw Simone's retreating form, she ran after her. Simone glanced back and noted that the wolf pack was almost upon the rearing horses, who tried in vain to run with the broken sled. She could only hope that the wolves would be diverted by the poor encumbered beasts. She shut her ears to their wild neighing; throwing off Boris's impeding coat, she pressed on, oblivious to all but survival.

Finally, her lungs bursting, she stopped just within the first line of trees, and looked back to see Marya a few paces behind. The snow had once again begun to fall heavily, and the scene around the abandoned troika was mercifully shrouded from her sight. In the nearer landscape her eyes focused on a lone form silhouetted against the snow. It did not move, and at first, she thought it some permanent feature of the terrain. Suddenly, it was alive—the yellow eyes aglow with an inner fire. She could not move, locked in the hypnotic golden gaze.

Marya's piercing scream shattered the spell. She had caught sight of the solitary hunter. Simone watched abstractedly as Marya plunged into the darkness of the woods.

And still Simone did not move, but turned instead to stare at the wolf, who, incredibly, had not altered his position. This renegade had come for her. Simone seemed to feel the keen lupine intelligence behind the predator's penetrating gaze. Without warning, he lowered his head, and turning, padded silently away toward where his fellows feasted.

Simone knew that some judgment had been passed, and she had not been found wanting. Comforted by this unnatural reprieve, she turned deliberately toward where Marya had disappeared. She plodded on in search of her companion, calling her name.

Once again, Simone looked up into the sky through the canopy of pines. It seemed paler now, as if some feeble light were trying to filter through the heavy clouds. She had no idea what time it was. It seemed she had existed forever in this mad white world. Her search for Marya had been futile. Perhaps the girl had made it safely to a village. Yet, in the abating wind, she heard no bells. Had she been walking in circles? She would have to pay closer attention to the landscape. Suddenly, the position of every tree, the shape of every snowdrift became of vital importance.

She looked about her, trying to orient herself. A strange light seemed to seep into the landscape from nowhere in particular. The heavens, the hills, the frozen streams, all were painted with a leaden brush. Simone longed for even a small patch of color to relieve the monotony of her surroundings. She lifted her head, trying to catch some sound; there was only the moaning of the wind, which still blew in icy blasts.

She was cold, so desperately cold. Hours and hours in the merciless elements had defeated the warm clothing. Her feet and hands were beginning to lose feeling. She began to walk again. All the trees looked the same. Hadn't she seen that broken branch before, angling downward, crushed by the weight of snow upon its fragile limb? Was that not the same white mound which she had passed . . . when, when? A minute ago, an hour? Oh, God, it was useless, useless.

The earth was a cold orb of ice and snow, and she was its solitary inhabitant, doomed to trudge its endless paths forever. Why go on when it was the same everywhere? No warmth, no welcome . . . no Rudolph.

She tried to think of his face, see his warm blue eyes, the wide giving mouth, the golden hair . . . but she could not summon his image. She began to cry tears of hopelessness and despair that crystallized immediately upon her frozen cheeks. She trudged onward, as if her mind had given her legs an instruction which it now lacked the energy to rescind.

The wind seemed to haunt the woods, whiffing an eerie lament, as its icy breath frosted the tops of the pines. Simone shivered. She was cold, so intolerably cold. She had lost all sensation in her hands and feet. At first her extremities had been merely deathly cold, painfully riddled with icy needles. But now, *nothing.* It was strange how she knew she was walking, yet she could not really feel it. She slowly flexed her fingers in the gloves, watching the motions with bizarre detachment. It was all so unnatural. To comprehend with her intellect the reality of mobility, but to have no sensory perception of it. She was grateful that her mind, at least, remained unfrozen in this glacial cosmos. She ambled on. She marked the towering trees, their snow encrusted boughs, their ice capped cones. A bit of bark exposed here, a bit there. She moved now without thinking, positioning one tiny foot before the other into the deep consuming drifts. Nothing else would she demand of her body . . . one foot before the other. She knew she had raised her arm to touch her muffled face, but it too was gone, lost to the icy world.

A small tree appeared in her path. It stood, a single perfect evergreen, against the blinding whiteness. Virgin green needles pierced the alabaster icing. The reluctant sun, still cold in its morning ascent, faintly burnished the feathering of the tree with pink, blue, gold—tiny crystal prisms sparkling and shimmering in the wind.

Simone was captivated by the sight. Of course, it was Christmas! Look at the ornaments, she thought, as she reached one tiny gloved hand toward the cones, which glimmered in their frosty sheaths. See all the pretty baubles. She laughed. How had she forgotten Christmas? Sister Agnes always had such clever surprises for the girls. Perhaps it would be a doll. A doll with shiny button eyes and hair of yellow yarn . . .

Beyond the tree was a clearing. As she ventured into the open expanse, Simone stopped abruptly. Before her, several yards away, was a human form kneeling in the snowy carpet, its back to Simone. For a moment the young woman stared blankly, her eyes trying to focus. She mouthed a single silent word. *Marya!*

At first, Simone trudged through the deep drifts, her progress across the frozen plain excruciatingly slow. But as she drew closer to the figure, her legs began to fight the thick mounds with renewed energy. Tearing through the icy weight, pressing, pushing, faster, faster.

"Marya, Marya, my friend!" she cried hysterically. "I am here. See, it is Simone. I have found you at last." Simone ran, forgetting all else—the cold, the numbness, the exhaustion. Her mind was riveted to a single goal. She must reach her companion; together they would find the village. The memory of her encounter with the wolf was suddenly stark in her mind. She had been spared; it was not yet her time to die.

As she reached Marya, Simone flung herself at the girl, embracing her tightly. "Oh, Marya, see, your prayers have been answered. God is good, Marya. God is . . ."

Suddenly, she recoiled from the stiff form which she had held closely to her breast. The girl had not moved. The lips had not spoken a greeting. Insanely, Simone memorized the frozen countenance. The pale eyes were visionless spaces, the mouth a thin white line poised forever in some pathetic supplication. Simone lowered her gaze to the small hands; the rigid little fingers pinched catatonically at the brown beads. Ironically, the rosary was all that moved, swaying hideously in the intermittent icy gusts.

Simone eased herself from her knees. As from a far distance her mind watched the frozen form topple slowly, slowly into the hungry snow. She ran, on, and on, and on, her deranged screams echoing and re-echoing in the cruel meadow.

~ *Chapter 24* ~

The young girl struggled to pull herself to an unsteady consciousness. But wave after wave of blackness rolled over her mind, washing all semblance of awareness against a shore of nonbeing. She slept.

"She sleeps still," whispered a soft voice.

A bizarre stream of visitors paraded before her, old faces lined with the labor of many years, young faces with round questioning eyes. Was she dead? Did these curious strangers come to mourn her?

"Another blanket, she shivers." The same sweet voice came. Then the voice had a face, a round gentle image of a woman.

"Mimka?"

"Pyotr, she speaks. There, there, little one. You are safe. Mimka? That is your name, yes? Here, Nina, bring us a bowl of *kasha*. She is awake. Can you hold this, my pretty? No, I see you are too weak. That's right, Nina, prop her up against the *pleeta*. Do not worry, little one, Yeta will feed you."

As the women coaxed the hearty cereal into the girl's mouth, she continued, "You poor angel, it is a wonder that you live. So cold, so frightened you were. We thought we would lose you. And how you wept, little one. Never have I seen so many tears. It hurt my heart to see you cry so. Pyotr said you were probably wandering about in the snow for hours. But it is no matter. You are here with Yeta. She will take care of you."

In spite of the warm *kasha,* in spite of the glowing oven, in spite of the woman's reassurances, the girl was ice. Her gelid bones were like cold iron inside her flesh. She slipped again into unconsciousness, thinking only of the unbearable cold.

When she woke, the woman who called herself Yeta brought more of the *kasha.*

"Ah, I can see you look better. Yeta's *kasha* has had its effect, but you must have more. *Yeshte na zdorovie.*

"Yes, you may hold the bowl yourself. Good, good. If you eat all of this, I shall see that you have some *s'chee.* The grain is good for you, but you must have the soup also. The meat and cabbage will make you strong, my pigeon. And you look so pale, such a white little face beneath all that beautiful black hair."

As the girl ate, she became fully aware of her surroundings for the first time. It was a simple peasant hut, small, compact, rude. Yet it was a place of warmth and friendship, a home where the members of the large family gathered to share meals, relate folk tales, and sing their melancholy songs. Where the family experienced joy and sorrow, and ultimately rested from a day in the field. It was a place of begetting, a place of living and loving, and yes, a place of dying.

Everyone seemed happy despite their obvious hardships —all of them. Grandfather, grandmother, sons, daughters, husbands, and wives, children . . . dogs. She had seen such a home before, had known such a family. Yet it all happened so long ago, and its brighter memory was locked deeply within the dark recesses of her mind.

A week passed, and she improved physically, though she still felt unnaturally cold. Her mental state, however, had not improved. She remained disoriented and unresponsive.

One day as she sat by the fire with Yeta brushing her heavy locks, Pyotr approached her, smiling.

"You are looking better, my child; you will soon be able to travel. You must tell us your name and where you live, so that we may return you to your estate. Your family must be searching for you."

The young woman looked at him blankly. The old man's comments had penetrated the pleasant fog in which she dwelt. To her puzzlement, she realized she could not answer

him. She did not know where her home was, and more
frighteningly came the realization that she was unaware of
her own identity. Who was she? As she looked into the
expectant faces about her, tears of fear and frustration
sprang to her eyes. She whispered hoarsely, "I don't know.
I don't know."

At her words, they looked at each other in consternation.
The weather had cleared somewhat; they would have to
make inquiries in the district. Perhaps in her reticule was a
clue. At her grandfather's command, Nina hastily retrieved
the young woman's purse, which she had been clutching
desperately when she was found.

Pyotr handed the velvet pouch to the girl, who took it
woodenly. It meant nothing to her. She looked to him as if
for permission to open it. At his nod, she withdrew its
contents. They gasped at the sight of so many golden coins.
The book that she removed bore a brief inscription in
French—*Never forget, Yuri*. Next, wrapped tightly in a
heavy woolen sock, was a small ebony box. The girl opened
it slowly. All looked wonderingly at the fabulous object
thus revealed.

She gazed into the egg, and a fleeting shadow of recognition passed briefly across her features. But then it was gone.
She sat immobile, her face vacant. Gently Pyotr removed
the bag from her lap. Reaching into its silken depths he
removed an envelope, which contained several tickets. The
bright pieces of paper seemed to catch the young woman's
attention. She brightened. Pyotr handed the tickets to her.

In her hand she held two pair of railroad tickets. One pair
was marked Orel–Kiev, the other Kiev–Odessa. In a smaller envelope was a ticket for passage on a ship departing
Odessa for New Orleans. The ticket was made out in the
name of Simone Montpellier. She now had a name and a
destination.

BOOK III
Constantinople

*"Know ye the land where the cypress and myrtle
    Are emblems of deeds that are done in
        their clime?
Where the rage of the vulture, the love of the turtle,
    Now melt into sorrow, now madden to crime?
Know ye the land of the cedar and vine,
Where the flowers ever blossom, the beams ever shine;
Where the light wings of Zephyr, oppressed with perfume,
Wax faint o'er the gardens of Gul in her bloom;
Where the citron and olive are fairest of fruit,
And the voice of the nightingale never is mute;
Where the tints of the earth, and the hues of the sky,
In colour though varied, in beauty may vie,
And the purple of Ocean is deepest in dye;
Where the virgins are soft as the roses they twine,
And all save the spirit of man is divine—
'Tis the clime of the East—'tis the land of the Sun—
Can he smile on such deeds as his children have done?
Oh! wild as the accents of lovers' farewell
Are the hearts which they bear, and the tales which they tell."*

George Gordon, Lord Byron

~ *Chapter 1* ~

The train pulled slowly into the station. The large sign near the tracks read ODESSA.

Simone rose gingerly from her seat. She felt stiff from her long journey. A warm bath would certainly feel wonderful. As she gazed at her reticule and the small suitcase of clothes she had purchased in Kiev, Simone smiled wryly to herself. How little she owned in this world. At least she traveled in first class accommodations. Was she, perhaps, wealthy? The peasants had mentioned her *estate*. They had said her family would be searching for her. But what estate, what family? Why did the French language seem more natural to her than her *native* Russian? She seemed to struggle with the harsh sounds. Montpellier, that certainly wasn't a Russian name, but if she wasn't Russian, what was she doing here? Still she remembered nothing of her life, and the only clue to her identity was the name which stared up at her from the ticket to New Orleans.

Why was her ultimate destination that faraway city? Was it her home? Who waited for her there? She knew she should try to find answers to these questions. She should have some plan of action. Yet the pounding in her head each time she tried to wrestle with the mystery of her life, stopped her. And the cold, the cold which she could not seem to dispel no matter how much clothing she wore. She should have attempted to seek help—go to the local authorities as Pyotr had urged—but something deep within her held her back. As she stood on the station platform, she lightly massaged her temples. Her headache seemed to have become more intense. She remembered that she had eaten very little. Perhaps she would feel better after a hot meal.

She searched for a carriage. She must go to the office of the shipping company today. She had lost so much time. The boat would sail day after tomorrow, and she must confirm her passage and secure lodging for the night.

As she walked toward the street, the crowds jostled her. She hailed a carriage, and asked the driver to take her to the offices of the Mediterranean Lines. As the man helped her into the coach, his practiced eye evaluated her appearance.

The painful ordeal of the past weeks had not marred Simone's incredible beauty. Perhaps she was thinner, but her body still was soft and sensuous, a woman's body. Her hair had not lost its luster, and although the eyes did not sparkle with their usual wit and intelligence, they were yet lovely. Beyond these physical realities, the driver perceived her distracted air. She looked like a foreigner, and her accented Russian confirmed this. She appeared to be a woman of breeding, and yet she traveled alone. No Parisian or Russian waiting maid accompanied her. The only luggage she carried was a single baggage case and a small reticule. The risks would be minimal, he concluded.

Simone emerged from the shipping office and entered the waiting carriage. She gave the driver the address of the hotel recommended by the clerk. Oblivious to the passing scenery, Simone sat deep in introspection as she rode in the carriage. If she had hoped to gain some information about who she was, she had been disappointed. She had not even ventured to ask the polite young man at the desk anything beyond the departure time of the ship, and where she might obtain suitable lodging. Indeed, Simone concluded woefully, such questions as she would like to have asked, would certainly have seemed peculiar. She was trapped. She faced the cruel dilemma of not knowing, and fearing to ask, lest she appear some madwoman. Perhaps aboard ship . . .

Before entering the hotel, she made arrangements for the driver to call for her, and deliver her to the ship morning after next. As he helped her from the coach, he smiled into her face. In her haste to mount the stairs, she failed to note the speculative gleam in his rapacious eyes.

After her arduous journey by rail, Simone was glad of the short respite before she must board her ship for the long voyage to America. The hotel provided excellent accommodations, and she was grateful for the gold coins in her purse. As she prepared for a second good night's rest in the comfortable bed, she noted that her mind seemed somewhat less befogged. Yet she could not focus on her strange circumstances without inviting the blinding pain in her head, and the thought of going to the authorities seemed no less threatening than before.

But tomorrow she would board the ship for New Orleans. She dreamed of a pleasant voyage. They would be heading southward. She would be warm again. And when she reached New Orleans . . . ?

The rough hand tightened over her face, and the dirty cloth gagged her. That odor . . . It was so . . .

Her body rocked back and forth on the floor of the carriage. From the haze that shrouded her mind she caught fragments of a conversation.

"Dark and beautiful . . . bidding will go high . . ."

Always the pieces of the conversation were punctuated with coarse laughter, almost obscene. She slid again into the mist. Her last conscious effort was to once again clutch the velvet bag between her bound hands.

The bright lights flashed on and off in her mind. Was she still dreaming? She felt so tired, unable to think. Slowly she opened her eyes. The erratic flashing came again. She knew the lights were real, not part of some wild nightmare.

The coach was moving at a brisk pace, passing row after row of dimly lit buildings. Dark, light, dark, light. Where were they taking her? Why? Why? She prayed for the sickly sweetness of the drugged slumber. Being awake, thinking, questioning—it was all too painful. She again struggled with the tight cords that held her wrists and ankles. Useless. Arching her head back, she renewed her effort to work the ugly sash from her mouth. She only succeeded in irritating the tender skin of her face and neck. They were good, very good at their nasty work, she thought.

Suddenly, the careening vehicle stopped. She held her breath. Within seconds, the door flew open, and they dragged her from the carriage floor. Looking up into the strange faces, Simone was more angry than afraid. Despite her recent travail, her resilient spirit had not been crushed. On some deep level she recognized that this new threat was one that might be resisted. Her enemy was man, not the implacable forces of nature. She would fight.

As they moved her quickly into a building, she began to writhe and twist violently in their grasp. It was immensely satisfying when she felt the heel of her dainty boot connect with one of her captor's ribs. His foul curse sounded in the dark as he allowed her legs to fall to the floor.

The other man continued to hold her tightly beneath her arms until the door was closed and locked. This completed, she was cast unceremoniously onto a pile of dirty cushions.

"This one is a little she-devil," chuckled the dark, heavy man, rubbing his side. "I pity the poor soul who buys her, though I do admire a woman with spirit." His accent was thick. He was not Russian.

"And she's a real beauty," replied his companion. "I would like to be the man to tame her," he continued, kneeling to lift Simone's face up to the light. "I would think her master might be grateful for my services."

"Don't be a fool, Leo, Shikory would not be pleased if the merchandise were in any way damaged."

"Ah, but who's to say the wench has not been tupped long ago. Such a one as she must surely have experienced a man's lust."

"Shikory has his ways, my friend. That son-of-a-dog would know. And I, for one, am loath to taste his wrath."

The Russian shrugged his shoulders almost indifferently at the Turk's comments.

"It is little use to fight, my beautiful lady," said the foreign man, seeing the look of hatred and disgust upon her face. "Things are not so bad as they seem. Soon you will live in a fine palace, and have all that you wish. You may even come to be grateful to my friend, Leo, and to your servant, Vahid," he went on, bowing from the waist at his last words. He watched her carefully as he unbound her hands and feet, and loosened the gag from her mouth.

When Simone attempted to rise, she almost fell because of the numbness in her extremities where the ropes had cut.

The Russian laughed coarsely. "Let us see what she has in that velvet bag which she clutches so tightly," he said, moving menacingly toward her.

"No!" she screamed, startling the men with the fierceness of her cry.

"It is no use, my lady, you might as well give Leo the purse. I'm afraid he will take it anyway."

But Simone was not so easily dissuaded. She looked around desperately for a place to run. Before she could move, they were upon her. She fought wildly, sinking her teeth into the hand that sought to part her from her only connection with her past. The Russian cried out in pain, but tore the pouch from her grasp, as his companion piniioned her arms behind her.

The one she had wounded soon forgot his anguish in his discovery of the gold coins. "Vahid, come quickly. You must see this," he said, almost reverently. His captive was forgotten, as the Turk gladly released her to join his compatriot. Together they marveled over the unexpected booty.

Instantly, Simone retrieved her reticule where it had fallen. She searched for a means of escape, but the dim lamplight revealed no windows in the tiny room. She had seen them lock the single door.

"I do not like this, Leo," the dark man protested. "She must be very wealthy in spite of her unconventional traveling arrangements. Her disappearance will be investigated. Shikory would not like that."

"What does it matter? With this we can disappear if necessary. It is more than we can ever hope to make in a year working for Shikory. He need never see these coins. He will be so excited over her rare beauty, he will think of nothing but the price he will get for her. He will care little about where she came from. Where is that bag? We must see what other treasures she is hiding."

At his words Simone crouched in the corner, clutching the bag to her breast. From her attitude it was clear that she would not surrender the pouch without a struggle.

"No, Leo, let her have it. We cannot risk injuring her. Shikory would have our necks if he but knew that we withheld the gold. Yet I would dare it, and share the prize rather than have him suspect that his new flower is one of high birth, and could see him on the gallows. But we can take no more chances. Time grows short; she must be prepared for the voyage. There must be nothing unusual in her delivery, or suspicion will be aroused."

"Come, mademoiselle, surely you must see that your cooperation must benefit us all. If our master should suspect that you are the noblewoman we believe you to be, he would kill you, and your body would never be found. Keep your bag, if you must, but take care that you do nothing to draw suspicion to yourself."

Simone thought quickly. Perhaps, by acquiescing to the man's demands, she might gain time. She still had her reticule and the ticket inside. She might yet escape. She nodded.

"That is better," said the dark man, a wide smile creasing his swarthy face. "My friend and I will leave you for a moment. You must be wearing only this when we return," he said, producing a simple shift. "Please, my lady, do not disappoint me. I do not think Leo would tolerate any more stubbornness. I might not be able to hold him in check," he said, indicating his leering companion.

As the door closed, Simone recalled the Turk's words. Was she in fact a noblewoman? Would her disappearance cause grave repercussions? She knew the men, especially Vahid, were concerned. Obviously, human life was cheap to this man, Shikory. Hastily she withdrew the ebony box and removed the fragile egg. Within its delicate beauty lay the secret to her identity. But this innocent object could also mean danger, possibly death for her. Quickly, she ripped the lining of her velvet reticule, and slipped the egg, swaddled only in the woolen sock, into the casing. Then she removed her clothes, trying not to think of what humiliation might yet come. She donned the simple garment. It was clean but ill-fitting, and threatened to slide from her shoulders. She was concentrating on the careful folding of her discarded garments when the men reentered.

The Russian had walked in first, moving to stand at Simone's back. Vahid, the Turk, stood in front of her, smiling. As she continued to smooth the folds of the clothing, she kept her head bent, afraid of what her face might betray. It happened quickly, as it had before. The hand at her throat, the rag pressed to her nose and mouth. The sweet odor, then darkness.

From somewhere far away she felt the tug on her arm as he opened the drawstring bag and looked within.

"Only a book," he snarled, "and a boat ticket. Have your way, Vahid, she can keep her precious purse. There is nothing valuable here."

* * *

The floor was cold and hard, the soiled blanket which had been carelessly thrown over her scantily clad body was hardly warm or comforting. From her position far in the corner, Simone surveyed her crude accommodations. The dark, dark hole smelled sour, like rotting grain. It was a storage room of some sort, dirty, filled with large wooden barrels.

She had lost all sense of time since her kidnapping. Was it day or night? This last query was soon answered, however, as the door of the cramped room opened, allowing a pale stream of moonlight to bathe her dark lair.

She had refused from the beginning to really look at her abductors, to see them as people; she concentrated only on the impersonality of their worn garments and shoes. It was as if she knew that by avoiding their faces, she could maintain some kind of detachment, a detachment which could somehow save her fragile sanity.

As he walked over to her, she listened closely to his heavy step, and focused her attention on his dirty brown shoes. His callused hand pulled at her shoulder, drawing her up to a sitting position. The blanket fell limply to her waist. The chill in the damp room caused the nipples of her breasts to rise beneath the thin gauze of her shift. She would not look at his face. Roughly she was swooped into his massive arms, her body intimately pressed against the hardness of his chest. She fought a wave of nausea as the odor of perspiration and stale *kvass* overcame her. She bit fiercely at the folds of the cloth which bound her mouth. She would not be sick, she told herself. She closed her eyes tightly as she swayed within his arms. After a short distance, they entered a small office adjacent to one of the warehouses. Simone somehow knew that her imprisonment in Odessa was drawing to an end. She had gleaned from some nebulous conversation that she was to be transported by boat to Constantinople. To be sold as a slave!

Simone could not bring herself to digest this last thought, so abhorrent, so barbaric was it to her. She had tried to fight them, but escape was impossible. Escape was impossible? She frowned. Had she not fought desperately but futilely for her precious freedom once before? When? Where? Against whom? Her head pounded, and the deathly penetrating chill, which had consumed her for weeks, again overtook her. She felt entombed, enclosed within some hideous vault, cold, cold. Would she never again be warm? Mercifully, the deep sleep came once again. She surrendered almost peacefully to it this time. Slowly the large hand removed the cloth from her nostrils and parted lips.

Again she sailed on a sea of semiconsciousness. Rising and falling. Rising and falling. She could remember waking briefly and being fed some tasteless gruel. Then the awful mush rose to her throat, followed by violent heaving. Someone had pressed a cool rag against her forehead as she fought the spasms, which wracked her body until her throat was raw and the sides of her body ached. She heard the sounds of voices, female voices, intermittently penetrating the fog. But they seemed so distant, so far off. When she tried to rise from her pallet, she sank helplessly back, weak, sore, ill. There was only one relief for her pitiful misery. She slept.

~ *Chapter 2* ~

He sat looking at his animated friend. Jalal never grew tired of Razid's fantastic stories. He was the most thoroughly entertaining person he had ever met. If a man would lose all, he would yet be rich if he had but one friend. Razid was Jalal's friend.

"I'm afraid you have not heard a single word I've spoken."

"Oh but I have, Razid. I am forever enchanted by your tales. Of course, to be enchanted and to be a believer . . . Well, that is two different things." The dark man laughed as he brought the cup to his lips.

Jalal was an incredibly handsome man. Although he was what many considered to be beyond the prime years of his manhood, at forty-one, he still wore the unlined, serene face of his youth. His dark almond eyes were almost black, and seemed to have a life of their own. It was said that when the *qadi* Jalal sat in his court to render judgment, one could look into his eyes and know the verdict before he spoke. His skin was honeyed, the mouth full, the nose aquiline, and his thick mustache curved around the beautiful white teeth when he smiled. The only mark of his age was the slight graying at the temples of his dark brown hair. He was taller than most Turkish men, and slimmer. And if there were one other feature that distinguished the *qadi,* it was his remarkable hands with long tapering fingers, the veins showing above the tawny skin. Delicate yet strong. Like the man, they were a contradiction.

"But Jalal, you must go with me. I have heard that there is a rare jewel to be offered tonight, and I would see her. Come, Jalal, admit it, the prospect intrigues you."

"Perhaps, Razid. But surely, it is not the sort of place for men in our position," he said mildly. "Have you not said, many times, my friend, that a *qadi* must set an example for the people to follow? The old ways die hard, and their spell is most seductive. But if we are ever to westernize, to pull our country into the modern world . . ."

"Oh come, come, Jalal, we will only go to . . . observe. It is harmless, and exceedingly enjoyable. You have grown serious of late; besides, you will be quite surprised at the number of high ranking officials you will discover among the bidders."

"Very well, Razid, you have piqued my curiosity, and I see you will not rest until I have given my promise. I will come."

As he bade his friend good-bye until that evening, Jalal wondered why he had let himself be so easily swayed. Why not admit it? He wanted to go. What had Razid said . . . that the prospect intrigued him? That was not quite true. It *excited* him.

Simone lay stretched out on a marble table; a silk cushion rested under her head. She still felt the effects of the drug. Although she was fully aware of her surroundings, a total lethargy possessed her. She had no will; she did not care what happened to her. Her mind had slipped into a healing place where there were no questions.

The Turkish women had attended her for the last three hours. She had been bathed in hot, steamy water, her skin rubbed to a pink luster, and, incredibly, all of her body hair had been removed with a rich white cream. She was then misted with a cool spray of water, her muscles massaged with a light oil, and her pulse points scented with a heady floral fragrance.

She lay very still now, staring vacantly at the stone ceiling, and the cornices that were heavily adorned with intricate carvings. Irresistibly, her mind began to find strange shapes in the swirling designs. Oddly, she remembered the child's games she had played. *Find something pretty in the clouds. A peacock with a fanning tail! A camel! A dromedary, one hump, a Bactrian, two.*

The soft voices of the women floated over her nude body. A strange tongue, like none she had ever heard. Arabic? She looked at the woman's hands as the tips of her fingers brushed over the small open pot of reddish paste. Next the dye was kneaded into the palms of Simone's hands and the soles of her feet. Then the fingers began to delicately massage the henna into the aureoles of her breasts. Instantly the nipples grew taut.

One of the older women took Simone's hands into her own, and gently pulled the girl to a sitting position. A young attendant, with very dark eyes, presented a golden tray of combs and brushes for the woman's selection. The hairdresser scrutinized the array for a moment, and then removed a large, heavy brush. She turned to Simone once again, and removed the cotton turban which bound her head. Quickly, she ran her deft fingers through the black hair, allowing the air to dry the damp locks. When the woman was satisfied, she began to pull the stiff boar bristles carefully through the masses of the girl's hair, until it shimmered in the glow of the oil lamps. Then she lifted the hair around Simone's temples, and drew it back from her small face, plaiting it into one thick braid. She allowed the plait to fall loosely onto the soft waves which danced about the girl's shoulders.

The hairdresser then tilted Simone's head backward so that the brightness of the light fell full upon her face. The dark-eyed attendant presented yet another tray, laden with pots of rouge and kohl and silky white powder in a crystal jar. But the older woman waved the girl away. This one's face had no need for the cosmetic palette; her pure beauty required no enhancement. The perfect face would go untouched, unadorned this night.

As Simone was allowed to lie back on the cool surface, a large man entered the room. His flesh was ample but firm, and he towered over the tittering women who retreated to the periphery of the room at his approach. The large head was completely shaven, and he had no eyebrows, which gave his face a queer, naked look. Brightly hued pantaloons, adorned about the waist with a silken sash, were his only garment. Twin serpent bracelets encircled thickly muscled arms, which he held folded over the smooth expanse of his chest.

The man came to where Simone reclined, and stood looking down at her. Strangely, she felt no fear, only a detached fascination for the genielike creature. She watched as his comical face split into a wide grin, and his huge hands reached out to explore every inch of her, in a manner at once intimate and impersonal. Finally his hands sought her softly rounded belly, and here they lingered, rubbing, prodding. Suddenly his giant's head was thrown back, and the wide grin exploded into deep throaty laughter that echoed in the marble chamber. He spoke to the women in rapid Arabic as he patted Simone's abdomen. Their shrill giggles followed him from the hall.

Simone was bemused by this strange performance. She barely noticed when a transparent teal-blue caftan was slipped onto her body. But she smiled once, dreamily, when the silken cord of her reticule was returned to her arm.

There was no moon. The courtyard was very dark, with only one small torchlight at the entrance of a deserted looking building.

"Your informant must have erred, Razid, or, perhaps you have the wrong place," declared Jalal, a hint of relief in his voice.

His friend only laughed and pulled him to the doorway. Three times the heavy brass ring sounded against the dark wood. Nothing happened. Two more knocks. The portal swung slowly inward.

Jalal followed Razid into a small hallway. It was darker here than the night itself. A wizened old man in flowing garments and a turban materialized with a candle, and led the visitors to a room where they donned caftans and silken masks. These last were simply bright sashes with eyeholes cut into the soft fabric. Razid secured his own and turned to help his less experienced companion.

"Really, Razid, this is all just a bit theatrical," Jalal said, his normally deep voice dropping to a low murmur. He chuckled ruefully, realizing that he had whispered in response to the carefully calculated atmosphere.

Jalal walked a few paces ahead of Razid, brushing aside the heavy tapestry curtain which barred his entrance into the main chamber. As the voluminous drape whipped behind him, the man's dark eyes narrowed behind the silken mask, and his nostrils flared at the pungent odor of incense.

The whole of the great room was carefully decorated, carefully contrived to assault the senses, to cause the mind to be inundated in a glorious wave of sensuality. Jalal was totally unprepared for this hedonistic onslaught, very disturbed by his reaction to it. He suddenly became cognizant of his quickened breathing and the slight flushing of his face. He was cool, yet he could feel a thin film of perspiration glaze his tawny skin. The temples throbbed, and unbelievably, there was a tightening of his groin. By Allah, the room was a sensual woman, a teasing, taunting courtesan who played games with the mind as well as the body. And standing in her threshold, Jalal the *qadi,* had succumbed . . . He was making love to her.

All of his life, Jalal had fought a battle within himself; he had waged a war against his triune nature, against the accursed trinity of his own being. Sometimes Jalal, the perfect rationalist was the victor—libertarian, intellectual Westerner. At other times, Jalal, the strict Muslim triumphed—superstitious, rigid, conservative. But tonight Jalal, the man of passion, the sensualist, the ultimate pagan would win.

Jalal turned to Razid. His friend wore a broad smile. For once, he had not overembellished on a story. And Jalal could understand why. Words were poor tools with which to describe this place. It touched all the senses, and had to be experienced directly.

The immense room was circular, vaulted with a tremendous dome painted to mimic the nighttime sky, and open to the heavens at its zenith. On this cloudy night, it appeared as if the stars were falling over a precipice into some central void; on a clear night, he guessed, it must be difficult to distinguish the thin line between nature and art, so cleverly had the zodiac been depicted. Beneath the painted heavens was a small marble pavilion, its rosy dome fleeced with wispy clouds and winging, pale-gray doves. It was a temple of Aphrodite, replete with slim Ionic columns, and with lavender, diaphanous fabrics floating airily in panels between the slender supports. Hanging from delicate shimmering chains were golden chandeliers whose flickering oil lamps bathed the room in a pink glow. Tall brass jars and round lacquered pots offered flowering trees and lush verdant ferns. The natural scent of rose and jasmine blended with the rich musky aroma of incense rising in blue serpentine trails from small brass urns. And from somewhere came the faint hint of opium teasing the nostrils.

They had stepped out onto a bridge which was one of many that spanned a moat of crystal water fed at intervals by sparkling fountains. These were surrounded at their bases with flotillas of lavender hyacinths. Crossing the bridge, they left the colonnaded waterway, and descended marble stairs to the large arena. Upon the cold marble floors ran long tongues of deep crimson, magnificent oriental carpets ablaze with a menagerie of colorful fantasy creatures. Upon closer observation, it could be seen that their playful gymnastics were less than innocent. Stretched languorously upon one of these luxurious rugs was a living beast, who seemed to have risen quite naturally from the red expanse beneath him. His great paws set in front of him, sphinxlike, his beautiful body a texture of soft butter swirled artfully with black ribbons. The tail flexed occasionally, but the massive head never moved. The slim ebony lines of the painted face were executed perfectly, giving the creature a wonderfully oriental countenance. The large slants of warm amber peered inscrutably ahead—a great Confucian feline.

A dark-skinned youth, naked to the waist, came up to them; Razid whispered something to him as he placed several gold coins into the boy's hand. They were escorted to a place very near the elaborate pavilion, and motioned to soft cushions around a low table.

"Mali is a good boy. We are very late. I marvel that he was able to save us this choice position."

"Perhaps, the gold was an inspiration," Jalal laughed. "But my friend, this place . . . There are no words."

"You have yet to see the most wondrous of its treasures. I pray we have not missed the best of Abdul Hasseim's offerings. But I am sure he has saved the most precious for last, as is his custom."

Jalal looked about him. It was even as Razid had said. The filmy masks concealed little, and he recognized many senior government officials at the near tables. "Are we in the bidding section?" he asked suddenly.

"Why yes. It is, of course, the best vantage point," Razid replied. "And it is not incumbent that one participate in the transactions," he continued, going on to explain the bidding procedure.

As Razid spoke, the sweet reedy voice of a flute ran out over the din of the assemblage, followed by the deep bass note of the *darbuka*. A troupe of boy dancers, *chengi*, wove their way onto the center of the floor. Dressed as girls, they were expert at their ancient art, moving suggestively and tossing their long black ringlets as they clicked their wooden sticks in time to the music.

A tray of food arrived, borne by a veiled girl with flashing eyes, her hips swaying to the beat of the dance. She placed the offering upon the low table within easy reach of the two men. Razid took a piece of warm, unleavened bread, expertly splitting its crusty edges. He filled the pocket with thin slices of young lamb and fried eggplant, lacing the contents with tangy yoghurt. He placed his creation upon a small brass platter, along with spiced black olives and chilled *dolma*. "Eat, my friend," he said, passing the plate to Jalal.

Immediately, Mali appeared with a small pitcher of red wine, filling their cups. Razid smiled roguishly as he lifted his tumbler in a silent toast to his friend. Scarcely had they finished the refreshments, when the lamps about the room were dimmed, except for those near the pavilion. "Ah," breathed Razid, "now you will see why Abdul has become justly famous."

Over one of the marble bridges came a strange procession. All in the large hall turned to watch, as two huge black eunuchs, their eyes shining eerily in the darkened room, escorted a pair of small cloaked and hooded figures toward the dais. Their journey seemed interminable, and the atmosphere of strained expectancy became palpable, as the shrouded pair moved into the lamplight. Simultaneously, the eunuchs moved, tearing the concealing garments from their charges. Identical females, startling in their twin blonde beauty, stood revealed.

Like the others, Jalal was at first astonished by the display. They were indeed lovely, and the double oddity of their blondeness and their twinship was an added piquancy. But they did not stir him. There was a blankness in the porcelain faces and china blue eyes. They made him feel unnaturally cold; their foreign paleness and delicacy held him at bay. They seemed two-dimensional, as if there were nothing beyond the perfectly molded facade—no warmth, no fire . . . no intellect.

He could never understand mindless passion. It was always the complete woman, her personality and spirit, which he took to his bed. It was the substance as well as the form he entered. Perhaps that is why he had at first balked at Razid's suggestion to come tonight. True, he had long ago acknowledged his passionate nature. But unbridled lust was another matter. He knew that his ultimate sensual satisfaction could only be achieved if he could kiss the soul as well as the mouth. He felt somehow betrayed, as if this place which had seduced him so cunningly had left its promise unfulfilled.

He seemed to be an anomaly. As he listened to the husky murmurings of the gathering, he overheard several lusty remarks regarding the interesting possibilities presented by the two blonde women. He knew that many of his contemporaries were here tonight to bid, not to partake of a simple intrigue. Yet, he could understand their needs.

Within the strict code of conduct of Moslem life, there had been from the beginning the accepted, nay, expected, practice of polygamy. Yet, the observance was more religious and biological than sensual in nature. But within the confines of the harem, the natural passions could grow, develop. So when the urbane Moslem began to forsake some of the trappings of his world that marked him as a primitive, and began to look to the West, a sensual void appeared. Thus, they came to places such as this.

Razid smiled broadly at him from across the table, and many rose for the bidding room as the girls were led away. Jalal leaned toward Razid. He was going to suggest they leave, as he was beginning to regret again his decision to come.

The music began. It was played on the classical *Osmanli* instruments: the *kemancheh,* the *kanun,* the lute, and the *ney*. The lilting music told a simple story of love and passion, strangely at odds with the bizarre presentation which had gone before. Insidiously, the lyrical instruments wove their irresistible spell, the haunting melody recalling emotions long abandoned. They spoke of an unbearable yearning, even while they hinted at the promise of fulfillment. As the music wove its seductive tale, the lavender veils of the pavilion began to flutter as if some stray sprite had been captured within the delicate temple. All eyes watched intently as a form rose slowly upward into the enclosure. The small head, haloed with the dark outline of masses of hair, appeared first. The straight shoulders gave way to the slim body. The silhouette emerged as some forbidden statue whose unearthly beauty, too perfect to behold, lay hidden behind the billowing folds of the silk.

By some unknown device, or perhaps by some mystical intervention, the sheer curtains parted—the goddess stood revealed. Her skin was creamy against the teal caftan, the raven hair, like the night, framed the perfect oval of her face. Arching brows, like tiny wings, hovered over the thickly fringed eyes. The small nose, slightly upturned, the full pouting mouth, the slender column of the neck—no sculptor could have created such a work! One of the black eunuchs appeared suddenly at her side and lightly touched one milky shoulder. The caftan fell.

There was a slight gasp. The audience had been tantalized with all that had gone before. Now it seemed as if they were not prepared for the absolute revelation of this woman. Indeed, her beauty seemed too sacred to behold, as if the vision of her was too much—the senses reeled, the body burned. She turned almost mechanically to display every angle, every curve. Her breasts rose high, firm. The narrow waist gave way to rounded hips, and the small naked mound of hairless skin between her beautiful thighs seemed innocent, vulnerable.

For just the briefest instant, Jalal thought it was Maryan come back to him; his first impulse was to go to her and veil her from the eyes of these strangers. But immediately he knew his mistake, and he simply sat upon the cushion drinking of her like a man at a well in the desert.

"Is she not the most exquisite creature you have ever

seen?" whispered Razid at his side. "Mustafa will bid highly for that one. It is rumored that his . . . *collection* . . . is the finest."

Jalal went rigid. The thought of the Mufti Mustafa with this girl, who so reminded him of his beloved, was an abomination. A thousand hateful images followed one another in rapid succession through his mind. "We shall see!" he muttered beneath his breath, startling Razid with the intensity of his words.

The gauzy curtain closed once again, and slowly, slowly the perfect form disappeared. Instantly, excited murmuring erupted. The Mufti Mustafa was the first to gain his feet. The second was the Qadi Jalal, begging directions to the bidding room from his astounded friend.

When Jalal returned to the table, he said nothing. Mali had brought coffee, and left a plate of *helve,* and *baklava* upon its gleaming surface. Jalal seated himself and sipped thoughtfully from his cup.

His friend's brooding attitude silenced the usually garrulous Razid, and he occupied himself with sampling the delectable sweets. After a time, a turbaned manservant appeared at the table. Bowing low, he informed Jalal that his presence was requested by the master himself.

He arrived to find Mustafa already within, an ugly scowl upon his coarse features.

"Excellencies," Abdul began, "it seems that many desire our perfect jewel. But yours have been the most generous offers. Since the figures were so nearly identical, it is customary to invite you both to resubmit your bids." He handed each a small piece of paper and a pen.

Mustafa regarded Jalal coldly, a contemptuous sneer on his swinish face. Quickly he scribbled an amount, and tossed the folded paper upon the desk. Jalal did not hesitate. He penned an absurdly high figure onto the small parchment square and handed it to the waiting man.

"I thank Your Excellencies," said Abdul unctuously. "You will be informed shortly of success . . . or failure," he continued, bowing the pair from his office.

When Jalal returned to seat himself next to his friend, he was still strangely withdrawn. Never had Razid seen him so. But if the man had wished to probe Jalal's aberrant behavior with oblique queries, he did not have the opportunity, for one of the tall turbaned attendants of the bidding room

had entered the hall. To whom would he deliver Hasseim's
note indicating the successful bidder? Mustafa's small beady
eyes fell upon Jalal, but the man did not return his gaze.
Rather, he stared intently at the male servant walking in his
direction. When he received the folded slip of paper, Jalal
could hear his rival's whispered curses as he and his retinue
filed angrily from the room.

Jalal made his way toward Abdul Hasseim's private
chamber. He refused to allow himself to think of what all
this would mean. He moved almost woodenly across the
hall and into the small office. As he entered, Abdul
Hasseim rose to greet him, kissing Jalal soundly on each
cheek; his heavy perfume was almost overwhelming.

"My dear Jalal, I am most honored at your esteemed
presence in my humble establishment," exclaimed the
heavy man, his bejeweled hands punctuating the effusive
salutation.

"Thank you, Abdul Hasseim. Your gracious hospitality
likewise does me honor."

The man looked at Jalal's thinly masked face, his stubby
fingers pulling at his dark beard. "I was most surprised to
see your final offer. Never has one bid so high. But then,
never has there been such a prize as this one."

Jalal did not speak, but only continued to look at the
overripe man, whose single earring winked beneath his gold
turban.

"I am sure you wish to see your little treasure once again,
before she is sent to your home tomorrow," Abdul volun-
teered.

"No, thank you, Abdul. That is unnecessary," Jalal said
blandly as he placed his draft for payment upon the man's
desk.

As the man reached hastily for Jalal's note, he said
smiling, "Thank you again, my exalted friend. May you
spend many evenings of pleasure with your beautiful dove."

Jalal bowed stiffly at the man's last comment, and then
was gone.

Jalal lay awake upon the cushions, nude between the
silken sheets. His mind would give him no rest, saturated as
it was with the images from tonight. How had this happened? He remembered the magnificent marble hall, a
slave market carefully calculated to cast the participants

back into a former age, an age from which his country was slowly beginning to free herself. And he, had he not been a proponent all these years of this push toward modernization? What had happened to him? He was forced to admit it. Emotionally, the old ties bound him as surely to the ancient ways as they had his ancestors. It was distasteful, but it must be faced. He had felt at home in that primitive environment—more alive.

But what of the morrow? How would he feel in the light of day? And what was he to do with this girl? True, her presence in his home would be questioned by none. But he did not feel comfortable with the situation. By Allah, she was now his concubine. Keeping a slave was a practice he had viewed disdainfully. And yet he knew in his heart, he would not change one moment of this night.

~ Chapter 3 ~

Simone lay upon the cushions. She drifted between unconsciousness and awareness; the drug was finally loosening its hold on her mind. She became marginally aware that her surroundings had changed once again. She still wore the transparent caftan, and her precious reticule had been returned to her. Her eyelids flickered open, but she did not alter her position on the divan. She peered down the length of her body, noting the filmy blue garment and the silvery slippers. Their pointed toes winked at her above the hem of her robe as they caught the light of the oil lamp. She was cold despite the heat, which reached her from a nearby brazier.

Where was she? She tried to remember. The boat?

No . . . no . . . Not the boat. The carriage? She had gotten
into the carriage. The men . . . the hand over her face . . .
the sickly sweet smell, and then . . . Suddenly, her tortured
thoughts were interrupted by the sound of a door opening.
Quickly, she lowered her lids and feigned sleep. Through
her slitted eyes she perceived the figure of a man standing
over the cushioned divan on which she lay. He stood,
staring.

The minutes slipped by. Slowly, he moved quietly away.
She was alone once more. Who was this man? Should she
know him? Everything was so confusing. Her costume . . .
and he, too, had worn some strange Eastern attire. Her
head began to throb, a wave of nausea threatened to
overcome her. She fought down the bitter bile that rose in
her throat. Tears of weakness and frustration spilled from
her eyes. Mercifully, she slipped into unconsciousness.

It was late afternoon when Simone woke. She lay beneath
a thickly padded quilt. The winter sunlight filtered through
the high, latticed windows of the large room, falling upon
the bright carpets that lay everywhere. Charcoal still
burned in the ornate brass receptacle near her couch. Her
mind was brought to full focus by the voice of a woman not
far away. She knew two things—it was not a language with
which she was familiar, and the voice shrieked in anger . . .

"This act I do not understand, Jalal, you of all people.
And what am I to do with her . . . this girl, this heathen
woman?"

"Be still, Yamna. Hold your tongue. You need do
nothing. She is not your concern."

At this she ceased. Yamna knew she had gone too far.
Her brother's calm tone, she knew, masked his irritation.
Even though she had been reared in strict Moslem fashion,
she feared little. But she hesitated to push her brother past
certain limits, for his temper, though slow to rouse, could
be formidable. "You misunderstand me, Jalal. I think only
of you and your happiness. I want only what is best for you.
I know that you still mourn Maryan. And though I have
tried very hard to make your life more pleasant since my
return, I know, too, that it has not been enough. For this I
am sorry, my dearest brother. But this woman will not bring
you happiness," she concluded, lowering her head and
turning away, as if to hide tears.

Immediately, Jalal softened. He reached out, and turning

her toward him, he tilted the heart-shaped face upward, and planted a gentle kiss on the smooth brow. "Do not be sad, *habibee;* you have been all that a sister could. Do you not know that your tears tear at my heart?"

"Oh, Jalal, I love you, Jalal. I cannot bear it when you are angry with me," she cried, throwing her slim arms around his neck and kissing his cheeks.

Pulling her arms away, he looked deeply into her dark eyes. "Little sister, I worry for you. You think too much of me and not enough of yourself. You must marry again and bear children. A woman is not happy until she has borne a son."

"No, no, Jalal. Do not force me to marry again. I am happy here. I will never leave you."

"Hush, hush, little one. You know I will not force you to go. But you will feel differently one day; you will see. Now go to your duties and send Esma to me shortly."

Simone listened as the voices softened and then ceased. She sensed someone approaching the room. Sitting up, she pulled the coverlet about her defensively. She shrank farther into the soft cushions at her back. The man who entered the room was the same who had stood at her bed . . . when? Was it last night?

He stood just inside the doorway. So she was awake, but obviously frightened and confused. He spoke to her softly in Russian. "I trust that you have slept well. Esma will be here in a moment; she will attend to your needs."

Simone was startled by his speech. He spoke Russian, but that was plainly not his nationality. He moved closer to sit on the edge of the couch. He looked at her closely, and after a moment spoke again.

"I am Jalal, and this is my home. I hope that you will soon regard it as your own." He reached for her hand and questioned her. "What are you called, little one?"

He was amazed at the look of anguish which passed over her beautiful features. It was as if the simple question was too much for her. He had begun to fear that the fools had administered too much of the calming drug, when her face cleared and she whispered, "Simone. Simone . . . Mont . . . pel . . . lier."

"Vous êtes francaise!" he exclaimed in delight.

Her face brightened as if some wonderful secret had been revealed to her. "Oui! *Je suis francaise,"* she replied.

He smiled at her animation. Praise Allah, she would be all right. As Esma entered the room, he rose. "See that she is made comfortable." To Simone he said, "I shall return later, and we will talk." With that he left, Simone's eyes following him from the room.

Jalal, he had called himself. Who was this darkly handsome man? And what am I to him? He said this was to be my home. My home? Simone could not begin to answer these questions any more than the others which had flooded her confused mind. It was better that she just act without thinking, go through the paces. Don't question, don't consider, don't analyze.

She moved docilely as Esma wrapped a heavy cloak about her, and led her through a hallway, down two flights of stairs, and into an open courtyard. The shrubbery and grounds were dusted with the remnants of a light snowfall. Simone shivered. They entered a small domed building in a corner of the yard. Simone found herself in a marble anteroom. After disrobing and placing high wooden pattens on her feet, she was led to a larger bathing chamber. Water gushed from little copper spouts into the marble basins which lined the tiled walls. A young servant girl took a small brass bowl and poured hot water over Simone's body. As in a ritual, the washing would be carried out exactly three times. She was scrubbed with a coarse bag, the soles of her feet were scoured with rasps, and her hair washed with egg yolk. She was then led to the cooling room, where she was soothed by the play of a fountain rising and falling in its marble basin. After the washings were completed, she was dried and her body oiled expertly by the young servant girl. An exotic perfume concluded the ritual.

Simone had the incredible sensation of floating as she reclined upon the silken pillows. Was it the sweet liquid she had had with her dinner? *Nabidh,* Esma had called it. Sleep would come easily this night. As she drifted into a light slumber, she sensed a presence in the room. Lifting her heavy lids slightly, Simone beheld Jalal standing over her. In the darkness his expression was unreadable. His light fragrance filled the room, and Simone listened as his breathing mixed with the sounds of the night.

She opened her eyes wider, and saw that now he was smiling. Slowly he lowered his body to the divan. He moved to brush his hand against the silkiness of her hair. Lowering his face to hers, he kissed her lightly on her open mouth. He lifted his head and stared deeply into her eyes. He whispered something softly in Arabic, as he pressed his mouth again against her lips. This time he drank more deeply, and only for an instant did she struggle, then she surrendered to his passion. Her hands moved to his head and she caressed his dark hair. Even as she returned his kiss, he broke the embrace.

Gently Jalal drew back the sheet. The glow of the moon bathed her beautiful breasts in silver light. He ran the palms of his hands around the soft mounds, then he teased her nipples with his warm mouth, his tongue tracing delicate circles around the dark peaks.

Simone moaned softly, but her eyes flew suddenly open as she felt the warm oil run across her abdomen and into her navel. Expertly Jalal began to massage the balm into her skin. His mouth and tongue followed his hands upon her lower body. She arched her back with pleasure and tension. Abruptly he stopped, and Simone was rudely pulled from the edge of fulfillment. She opened her eyes and looked quizzically at him. His face was full of desire, yet there was something else, something which Simone could not understand.

He lowered his head again and began to lightly kiss her rounded belly. He seemed to be driven as his lips brushed feverishly against her warm skin. He murmured unintelligibly between his kisses. Simone was no longer aroused, but perplexed, confused. When at last he raised his head, he whispered, "Ma chère, you will bear a beautiful son."

Simone lay motionless. It seemed that many hours had passed since Jalal had left her, gently kissing her eyes and hushing her to sleep. But sleep had not come, and her mind fought once again with questions that had no answers. Yet all that had plagued her before, seemed to diminish in the stark reality that Simone Montpellier was with child. "A son," Jalal had said she would bear. And the father? Who was the father of this son? She must be married, yet deep within her she knew she was not. Did she at least love this man who had fathered her child? She knew she was capable of passion; certainly Jalal had proven that this was true. But love . . . Love was something more.

The questions spun round and round endlessly in her

brain, until her head throbbed. Finally exhausted, she resolved that for a time she would live only in the present. The past would be dead to her. And the future?

～ *Chapter 4* ～

The muezzin's cry floated over the city and reached Yamna as she lay unsleeping.

"*Allahu Akbar,* ha *ilaha illa* Allah; *Muhammad rasul* Allah. Come to prayer; come to salvation. Prayer is better than sleep."

Yamna rose reluctantly, and splashed her face, hands, and arms with water from a small copper bowl. She patted a few drops through her long, black hair. Next, she washed her feet up to the ankles. She covered her head and rolled out the small but intricately woven prayer rug in the direction of Mecca. She made her declaration of intention in which she stated that the morning *salat* would now be made, and specified the number of *rak'as,* or ritual movements, which she would perform. Standing on the carpet, Yamna raised her hands, palms up beside her head, and whispered, "*Allahu Akbar.*" This first utterance was most important, as it signified that she had severed herself from the secular world. She bowed and prostrated herself, reciting passages from the Koran. Then sitting, she recited the *shahada,* "There is no God but Allah; Muhammad is his prophet." Finally, she turned her head first right, then left, saying "Peace be with you in the mercy of God." These words were addressed to the angels which, according to Moslem belief, sat one on each shoulder to observe the sincerity of the one at prayer.

Yamna rose, and called for her servants. She had decided to go to the Buyuk Charski this day. She desired some new embroidered slippers, and perhaps even a jewel to add to her collection. She knew that Jalal did not approve of her going into the streets. For a man of the world, who prided himself on his progressive attitudes, he was a traditionalist where she was concerned. Jalal was truly Moslem in this respect.

Maysun and Tanya entered on silent feet, bearing her breakfast of goat's cheese, fruit, and unleavened bread spread thickly with fig preserves, accompanied by a delicious tea.

As she ate, her attendants readied her attire, removing the garments from the latticed wall niches and cupboards which lined one end of the apartment. They carefully untied the large kerchiefs in which the requested items had been stored, and draped them over the cushions of her bed for her approval.

Yamna rose from the floor and allowed Maysun to remove her sleeping garments. The early morning sunlight revealed that her body, though no longer that of a young maiden, had lost none of its exquisite proportions. Her breasts were full, but not pendulous, and were complemented by her softly rounded hips. Her waist was small and her abdomen flat, attesting to the fact that she had as yet borne no children. By Eastern standards, she was less than voluptuous, but her beauty was undeniable. Her blue-black hair, which fell in a straight line to her waist, framed a perfect heart-shaped face. Her features were flawless, and yet, an astute observer would have noticed a certain hardness in that visage. This quality was most evident in a certain coldness in her eyes, which did not thaw even when she laughed. However, this same observer might also note that the haughty features did soften and become truly beautiful in the presence of her brother.

Tanya held the waistband open, and Maysun assisted as Yamna slipped into the burgundy pantaloons. As the servants slid a fine gauze shift, lavishly embroidered, over her, she smiled inwardly, remembering her reflection in the fountain of the mosque when last she had worn these clothes. Yamna reveled in her beauty, though such vanity was unbecoming in a daughter of Islam.

Over the high-necked shift Maysun buttoned a wine-

colored velvet waistcoat with long sleeves which fell back
gracefully over the arms. Tanya held out a close-fitting,
ankle-length caftan of the same hue, embroidered heavily
at the borders with jet beading. A girdle of black silk held
the long robe in place. On her feet were set soft leather
socks, and over these, black leather slippers with upturned
toes. In deference to the weather, a loose fur-lined robe of
brocade was fetched. Atop her gleaming hair, Maysun
placed a tasseled cap, following this with the required veil.
Ironically, the thin fabric which Yamna had chosen was so
transparent as to tantalize rather than conceal, as was its
purpose. Strings of pearls fell provocatively across the sheer
veil. Yamna was ready to go out.

The Buyuk Charski, or Great Market of Constantinople,
had the largest collection of merchandise to be found
anywhere on earth. It was encompassed by an enormous
walled expanse, where a buyer could gain entrance at any
one of eighteen gates. There were over sixty streets within,
each bearing the name of its resident guild. Three to four
thousand separate shops, mosques, warehouses, work-
rooms, as well as trade schools, comprised this huge marketplace.

Yamna walked through the aisle of the kerchief makers
under the high vaulted ceiling, accompanied by her servants. As she approached a small stall, the proprietor who
sat upon a stone bench in front of his shop sighed deeply.
Well he knew the sister of the Qadi Jalal. She had been to
his shop many times before, and he knew that each item in
his array of goods would pass under her close scrutiny
before her selection was made. No scrap of cloth would go
untouched, its merit appraised as it passed through her slim
fingers. Silman knew that he would have the unpleasant
task of rearranging his stock after her departure. Thankfully, she was a good customer, and the disorder which she
caused was outweighed by the profit that could be expected.

On this day her purchases were many. She bought several
caftans and silken girdles, as well as quilts, napkins, and
towels for the household. Surprisingly, however, she lingered longest over the selection of a finely woven *hamman*
wrap from Damascus. These purchases made, she moved
through the streets, passing carpet sellers, coppersmiths,
and goldbeaters. Her eyes were assailed by a myriad of

colors, shapes, and textures which attested that Constantinople was, indeed, one of the world's great centers of trade. Through it all she proceeded, trailed by her entourage of servants. Her measured tread proclaimed that all this glittering spectacle, this culmination of toil and enterprise, had been placed here solely for her convenience.

She approached the *bedesten* with growing anticipation. It was here that she would find the finest silks and brocades, as well as gold and that which piqued her interest most, precious stones. Upon reaching the display of jewels, her eyes sparkled. She watched as their cold glittering edges caught the morning sunlight that streamed through the high windows. Yamna fingered one of the stones delicately, her eyes reflecting its smoldering fire. It was a large cabochon ruby. Unlike the other stones, whose faceted surfaces danced with an obvious brilliance, the cabochon emitted a subdued glow, its fire captured, controlled. She held the gem against the folds of her caftan. How beautifully it complemented her costume. But the figure quoted by the jeweler was far in excess of what Yamna had in her purse. Hastily, she sent a courier with a written request to withdraw from the family repository in the *bedesten* the necessary gold coin to cover the purchase.

As she was discussing with the merchant the possible settings for the newly acquired jewel, the wailing of the muezzin echoed through the din of the *charski*. It was the familiar call to all shopkeepers and customers, that it was time for the noonday prayer. The woman cursed silently. Allah did not defer to his faithful, not even to the arrogant Yamna.

One by one the shopkeepers drew down their doors, and their customers scurried toward the mosques. Yamna was thankful that the courier had not tarried too long, as the jeweler grew impatient. Hurriedly, the woman completed her transaction and dropped the jewel, hidden in a small silken pouch, into her purse.

The mosques of the Eastern world were patterned after the home of the great Prophet himself. They were great rectangular structures composed of a series of arched colonnades. Sensitive to climatic conditions and the social, educational, and economic needs of the people, these mosques were erected with more than religious considerations in mind. Within its arcaded porticoes one could find

religious scholars or *ulamas,* lecturing students, or see
reclining souls seeking a cool retreat away from the deafening din of the marketplaces. The spacious courtyard, the
central gathering place of the town, was usually filled with
milling people, or customers who had come to make
purchases from one of the small shops of the bazaar.
Routinely, veiled women entered the large square to fill
their jugs with water from the fountain, often the city's
primary supply of the precious liquid.

From the beginning, water was a major element in the
Islamic faith. Five times a day the believer made ablutions
before his ritual prayers. Thus, water became twice precious, both as a necessity of life for the desert dweller, and
as an integral part of his religious practice. It was given this
double association by the Prophet himself, who reputedly
said, "Prayer is like a stream of sweet water that flows past
the door of each one of you; into it he plunges five times a
day; do you think that anything remains of his uncleanness
after that?" And again, when asked to name the act of
highest value, Muhammad was quoted as replying, "To give
people water . . ."

The mosque was essentially a place of worship where
Moslems would enter upon hearing the ritual calls of the
muezzin, wailing atop the domed minaret. The faithful
would move through the courtyard, make their ablutions,
and then proceed to the sanctuary.

The sanctuary's solid rear wall, the *qilba,* held the sacred
niche, or *mihrab,* which indicated the direction of the
holiest of Moslem cities, Mecca. Near the *mihrab* was the
minber, or raised pulpit, from which the *imam* would
deliver his sermon on Friday, the principal day of worship
of the Islamic faith.

The mosque was usually an edifice of imposing size whose
simplicity of design and exquisite stylized decoration made
it a place of breathtaking beauty. The entire feeling of the
structure was one of openness, which was expressed in its
large courtyard and arcaded porticoes. The building was a
creative synthesis of marble, brick, stucco, and stone,
whose symmetrical arrangements offered dazzling images in
perspective. Carved reliefs of Syrian rosettes and swirling
Persian vine leaves adorned the repetitive archways. But
the highest artistic achievement was to be found in the
mihrab, usually a fanciful work of intricately carved

marble and lustrous, patterned tiles. It was to such a mosque that the sister of Jalal went on this day.

Yamna went through the ritual ablutions, hastily dipping her hand into the water from the fountain of the mosque. The sunlit courtyard held many of the faithful on their way to prayer, yet it seemed empty, so vast was the space enclosed. Yamna moved past stalls where religious objects were sold, and past the petition writer on his low stool. The scribe rose as she passed, joining in the general movement toward the sanctuary. She retrieved her prayer rug from a male servant as they entered the sacred area. Accompanied by her handmaidens, she proceeded to the concealed section, separated from the male congregation by a tightly woven latticework of teakwood.

Faultlessly, Yamna mouthed the holy words, but her thoughts were profane. She brooded over the intrusion of the infidel woman, even as she consoled herself with thoughts of how pleased Jalal would be with her gift.

~ *Chapter 5* ~

From the moment Jalal stepped from the great marble hall in which he had found her, two questions had come to plague him: Who was this beautiful woman to whom he was now master, and how had she come to the slave markets of Constantinople? After four days, the questions remained unanswered, and had grown in complexity.

At first, he had hoped that she was Russian. He knew that many of the peasant girls of the Caucasus came willingly, eager to trade their hard lot for the pampered life of the *haremlik*. If this were true for Simone, he would be in some measure absolved for his part in this barbarous transaction. But he was denied this balm. She was neither Russian, nor a peasant. She was French and a lady.

She could remember so little of her past, and it was unclear whether her amnesia was a result of her abduction or of something which had gone before. She knew only her name and that she was to have boarded a ship in Odessa to . . . And so the guilt remained with him. As the final participant in this savage business, was he not as culpable as the dishonorable rogues who had obliterated all that had been her life and had reduced her to the status of a slave? And yet . . . and yet he had saved her from such as Mustafa. Did this not count for something?

Kismet! His destiny and hers entwined without purpose or will. Yes, a useful concept. There was no choice, and again was he absolved. But, by Allah, he hated such a principle; it condemned all men to the role of victim. Persecutor or deliverer? Exploiter or savior—which was he? He could not answer. He knew only that he was glad she was his, his by whatever means, and worse, glad for the immolation of her memory, the severing of the ties that bound her to any but he.

Initially, Jalal could not avoid the comparison he had made between Simone and Maryan—the dark liquid eyes, the flawless creamy skin, the lustrous, thick black hair, the sensuous lines of the body. There was an uncanny physical similarity between this beautiful young woman and his beloved.

Maryan, his Maryan. To this day he could not think of her, or whisper her name, without feeling the terrible aching within his heart. Maryan, his very breath. How he had dared to question Allah when she had been taken from him, still a young bride.

Maryan was a cousin, who had often come to Jalal's home on special feasts and holidays. They loved each other from the moment their dark eyes met. Yet, Jalal could not see his lovely Maryan as he wished. He had to be satisfied with catching a glimpse of her dark little head as she was scurried off with the other women to the *haremlik*. How he had hated his Islamic faith in those early years, refusing to accept a system which required that men and women exist on different planes, segregated, isolated from each other.

However, Jalal's metaphysical confrontation with his religion mellowed as he grew into manhood, and it was ultimately assuaged when the two families agreed that Jalal and Maryan should be wed, when Maryan had passed her fifteenth year.

How wonderful had been the day when Maryan was led in procession to his home. And how his young heart beat wildly within him when he was finally escorted to the bridal chamber to the cry of "The groom is coming; the groom is coming!" Jalal could still envision his shy dove as she removed her veil, and they beheld each other face to face for the first time since the innocence of their childhood.

And if his wedding day had been wondrous, the day on which Maryan told of the coming birth of his child was even more perfect, more complete. How he had longed for a son—his son, his seed, given to him from the flesh of his beautiful wife, made from their precious love.

But it was not to be. When the epidemic raged within the city, he had been so cautious—the water was boiled, the food prepared carefully, the house guarded against all possible contamination. Yet, he had failed, failed to protect his Maryan and his son. And when she closed her beautiful dark eyes for the last time, pressing her small hands over the child within her womb, Jalal prayed that he, too, would die. But Allah was not so benevolent, for Jalal lived, lived with the awful sadness and loneliness, lived without his Maryan, without his son.

Jalal lowered his head and ran one of his beautiful hands across his forehead, as if trying to erase the pain which he had borne for so many years. And when he could think again, he realized with perfect clarity that the resemblance between Simone and Maryan was only superficial. Maryan had been a woman of her time, a woman content to play the role that was hers under Moslem law and tradition. And Simone . . . Simone was different. Although she appeared subdued, Jalal knew that it was because of the tragedies which she had so recently endured. This docility was not intrinsic, not part of Simone's true nature. Had he not glimpsed that nature on that first night, when he lay with her—the passion, the fire? He had been able momentarily to release that smoldering essence, and he knew that this vitality, this energy imbued more than her body. It was integral to her mind, her soul.

And if he were correct about this woman called Simone Montpellier, he suddenly realized with an undeniable joy that he would look forward to the dawning of each new day. She stirred him like no other since his beloved's death. She was in some way symbolic of the path he had chosen for himself and his country. That he had found her amidst a decadence which recalled the barbarities of his ancestry was a delicious irony.

He was intoxicated with her. But though he longed to possess her, he must not consummate his desire until the birth of the child. He had told her it would be a boy, and somehow he knew it would be so. Simone and her child would be safe; he would see to it. She would not be given over to the women. She was French, not Moslem; tradition did not apply where she was concerned. André Duval would attend her.

Not for the first time, he wondered about the child's father. What had he been to Simone? Husband, lover . . . ? But it did not matter. Simone could remember nothing of her former life. And in any case, the past was dead. He, Jalal, would be her future. She had given him a priceless gift. He realized that for the first time in over twenty years, the future was truly a place he longed to be.

As the days passed, Simone slowly began to regain her physical health and mental alertness. Still, she could not pierce the black curtain that shrouded her past. She could recall only vaguely a train ride, getting into a carriage to go to . . . a ship? Then the hand over her face, and . . . darkness. The next thing she remembered was awakening in this room. And then seeing his face . . .

Jalal had been very kind. Her every physical need had been provided for. She felt sheltered, protected. He did not seem to mind that her past was a blank. He told her that it did not matter, that it was her new life with him that was important, and the past could only be an encumbrance. Her new life with him . . . Who was this dark man, this exotic foreigner? The mystery that was Jalal was no less disturbing than the mystery of Simone Montpellier. When he spoke of her life, it was always in terms of his own. What was she to him? His mistress? His slave? She should hate him, hate what was happening to her. Instead, she thought of the warm, dark eyes looking down into her own, the soft lips kissing her eyelids, his gentle whispers like some trapped bird fluttering against her ear. And the expression which she beheld upon his face when he told her she would bear a beautiful son—it was like no other she had ever seen.

As her body and mind grew in strength, she dwelt more and more on the mystery of her past. There was nothing for her to do during the long days, and she continually pondered her situation. She was in a country totally alien to her. The great mystery was, what had she, a French woman, been doing so far from home? She could speak Russian. Had she lived in Russia? Had she a family somewhere? Would they meet the ship and wait in vain for her to disembark?

But she had been kidnapped and sold in an illicit slave market. She tried to better assess her own feelings regarding this degradation. She should feel something: horror, repulsion, indignation. But she was numb. She had a nagging feeling that she herself had sinned by omission, but she could not summon up the requisite moral outrage.

And this child she carried—why was she so sure she was not married? Who was the father? Did he love her? Did she love him? Did he even now search for her somewhere?

On a day like every other, Simone awoke late, ate the breakfast which Tanya served, and spent the afternoon sketching the street scenes which she glimpsed through the latticework of her window. Her room was in the women's quarters on the third floor of the large *konak*. Simone knew that the townhouse was extremely spacious, yet she had not been able to venture beyond the *haremlik* except for the regular visits to the *hamman* to bathe. These short journeys to the bathhouse always involved passing through the beautiful garden. She hoped that soon the weather would clear, and she would be allowed to paint among the trees. For now, she had to content herself with depicting the activities of the busy street below.

Today, her attention was drawn to a particular street vendor who had stationed himself outside her window. *"Igde, igde,"* he sang seductively. Simone watched the young man pour a thick syrup from the heavy cask which he bore on his sturdy shoulders. She observed that the liquid was extremely popular, and that most of the young vendor's customers were veiled women. She strained her eyes to see his face. There was something extremely earthy about the man, his primitive virility, especially when he moved, seemed somehow out of step with his urban surroundings. Simone concluded that he was not from the city, but probably from some outlying district or province. If only she could see him better. She longed to read the expression in his eyes, which she imaged to be black and full of mischief. Perhaps if she opened the lower shutters . . .

"My lady, what are you about?" questioned Tanya in distress as she entered the room. "The bottom shutters of the *haremlik* are never opened," she continued, as Simone turned from her efforts at unlatching the window.

Jalal had assigned Tanya to Simone, as she was from the Caucasus region in Russia, and thus, was the only person beside himself with whom Simone could communicate.

"Why?" asked Simone with a sigh.

"Because it is forbidden for men to gaze upon the women within the *haremlik*," answered the girl didactically.

Resignedly, Simone abandoned her sketch pad and sought the needlework which she had begun on the previous day.

Hours passed slowly. Jalal had traveled that day to Bursa, and had as yet not returned. Simone would miss talking with him this evening. She worked awhile on her embroidery, glad for the intricate patterns that occupied her mind. Sometime later, Simone looked up to see Tanya nodding over her work. It had grown late. She dismissed the girl and walked to the wooden lattice. To her shock, light flakes of whirling snow danced outside the window. Simone drew back involuntarily, a nameless dread descending. Unaccountably, the wintry scene had the power to totally unnerve her. She began to shake as she felt the cold steal into her flesh. Drawing her quilted caftan more tightly about her, she added more charcoal to the *mangal*. All to no avail. The icy fingers that gripped her body were more a product of her mind than a physical manifestation of the weather.

She repaired to her bed, burrowing under the heavy coverlets and trying in vain to still the tremors in her body. She was confused by her strange reaction to the peaceful winter scene beyond the window. But when she sought to analyse it further, she found she could not penetrate the

hazy blue curtain of terror that shrouded her memory.
Finally she slipped into an uneasy sleep.

*It began with the jingling of bells, tiny brass sleigh
bells ringing merrily in the frosty air, as the wonderful
sled flew effortlessly over the ground. She was safe and
warm, protected in the magic circle of his arms. The
snow came, lightly at first, the big fluffy flakes drifting
lazily down from the dove-gray sky. They melted like
kisses against her cheek.*

*The church bells tolled. Imperceptibly, the snowfall
intensified until the sky grew dark with churning particles that were like angry needles piercing her skin. She
was alone in the howling madness, no longer in the
sledge. She was trudging through great white drifts
which threatened to devour her.*

*A dark shape loomed against the white plain and grew
into the tall figure of a man. She moved anxiously
toward him, calling his name, her words stolen by the
wind. As she neared, he turned, his eyes penetrating the
blue haze. They were not the eyes of her beloved, but the
glowing yellow eyes of the wolf. She screamed.*

Esma and Tanya were still trying to calm the hysterical
girl when Jalal appeared. Pushing aside the two women, he
took Simone into his arms.

Yamna stood in the doorway, her dark eyes glaring. She
felt a sickening tightness grow within her breast. Her
breathing had become rapid little pants, and her flushed
olive skin dampened with a thin veil of perspiration. Her
long fingers clawed at the folds of her caftan as she watched
her brother comfort the girl whose body pressed intimately
against his chest. As Simone clung to the strong figure
whose comforting arms enfolded her in the darkness,
Yamna heard her muffled cry, "Rudolph, oh, Rudolph!
Hold me, hold me."

~ *Chapter 6* ~

As Yamna recited her morning prayers, her mind could not concentrate on the sacred words of the Koran. Rather, her focus was on the heathen bitch who had disturbed her sleep with her mad wailings. The infidel was possessed by vile demons. Surely Jalal must see that the situation was impossible. She would bring evil down upon his house. But the woman had bewitched him. He was like a madman as he ran into her room, soothing her as if she were a child. A child of the devil! She would not allow her brother to be ensnared by this wicked sorceress. He must be protected from her, and she, Yamna, would save him as she always had done. Then life would once again return to as before . . . just she and Jalal.

She would request a visit this morning, and give Jalal the gift. The token would confirm her love for him, and he could not fail to recognize her sincere concern regarding the effect of this intruder on their lives. She would make him see that this foreign woman did not belong, and must be sent away. The peace and happiness of the entire household was threatened. Already the servants had decided that the girl's beauty had attracted the baleful glance of the evil eye. The blue glass balls which could afford protection were much in evidence. An ostrich egg had been placed in the woman's chamber, but even this powerful charm had proven ineffective. Yes, Yamna thought, this was the correct approach. Jalal, as master, could not but act in the best interest of those under his protection. For the first time since the arrival of the heathen woman, Yamna felt in control. She smiled as she sent Maysun to Jalal with word that she wished to speak to him.

After a time, Jalal appeared, kind and polite as always, though somewhat preoccupied.

"Thank you, my dearest brother, for seeing me. I know that your time is very precious, but many days have passed since we spoke as brother and sister."

"Forgive me, my little one. It was not my intention to neglect you, but as you know my time has not been my own these many days."

"I know, my Jalal, and it troubles me to see you so tired, so unhappy. I cannot bear it when you do not allow me to share your pain, your sorrow."

"Yamna, please. You misunderstand. I am more at peace with myself these last days than I have been since the death of Maryan. You have nothing to share, dearest sister, but my happiness."

"Happiness, my brother? Is it happiness that drives contentment from this house and wakes us with its screaming in the night? How can you be at peace when your own servants walk in fear and dread of the foreign woman? Jalal, she is not Moslem; she cannot understand our ways. Her place is not here, not in your *haremlik*."

Jalal had listened attentively to his sister's words. When he finally spoke, Yamna began to smile inwardly at the success of her tactic. "You are correct, my dear sister, Simone does not belong in the *haremlik*. And you need worry no longer about the serenity of my household, for she will be removed today from the women's quarters." But Yamna's happiness was destroyed by his next words. "Simone will be given a room on the second floor, so there will be little need for you or any of the other women to come in contact with her. Only Tanya will accompany Simone. I hope that this will be satisfactory, little sister," he said, moving forward to plant a light kiss upon her forehead. "I must go now, dear Yamna. I have business in the city. Be well."

Yamna stared after her brother as he walked from the room. During his speech she had not moved, had not spoken one word to him. Her mind had been frozen by his incredible proclamation.

The second floor! The *selamlik*! But that was reserved as the men's quarters. Of course, the *konak* was huge, and

there were only Jalal and a few of the higher ranking men
servants on the second floor, but still . . . It was unthinkable! Truly her brother was possessed. She must plan carefully. This state of affairs could not be allowed to continue.

She walked to her divan where his gift lay. Slowly she
drew the *hamman* wrap to her lips and kissed its soft folds.

Although he respected his sister's opinion, Jalal's primary
concern in removing Simone from the *haremlik* was for the
girl herself. He reasoned that Simone might improve were
she to be placed in more familiar surroundings. Accordingly
he saw to it that two rooms on the second floor of the *konak*
were furnished in the European manner.

One spacious room was outfitted as a sitting-dining area
where they might dine and relax in the evenings. The room
adjoining his own was provided with a large bed, a chaise,
vanity, and other pieces appropriate to a lady's bedchamber. He planned to lay with her each evening until she slept,
and then to leave the door between their rooms ajar, so that
he might hear immediately if she stirred. Her nightmares
were frightening in their intensity. And though she remembered nothing of them, they left her pale and shaken in the
mornings. Jalal feared the effect that this might have on the
unborn child. And too, if she felt secure, the dreams might
stop; then she would no longer cry out for Rudolph.

Simone was delighted with her new quarters. She
bounced around on her bed like a child until the somewhat
staid Tanya dissolved into giggles. Not that she had been
physically uncomfortable in the *haremlik*, but somehow its
alien decor had seemed to immobilize her. Perhaps it had
been the austerity created by the room's lack of furniture,
and the closely latticed windows.

She knew that if she were to revive, she had to be
involved in her own life. Jalal had been so good to her,
attentive to her every want and need. Yet she could no
longer remain passive about her own existence. Perhaps in
these new surroundings, that were more intrinsically her
own, she could begin to restore some semblance of whole-
ness to her shattered life.

Now she had the freedom of most of the second floor,
including the library. Here she had found many volumes in
French—and magazines! She was part of the world again.

As she lay upon her chaise reading, Tanya entered. "I believe this is yours, my lady. It was stored in the wall niche when you came. I thought you might wish to have it in your new room."

Simone rose and reached out a tentative hand toward the black velvet bag. As she clasped it, a flood of images clashed through her mind in rapid juxtaposition.

"My lady!" cried the frightened Tanya, as she saw Simone sway against the small couch.

"It's nothing, Tanya," said Simone, clutching the high back for support. "I shall be all right. You may go now."

She sat down slowly. But when the girl had departed, she opened the pouch deliberately.

That afternoon, Jalal entered Simone's room to find her staring pensively at a small object. Quietly he moved to stand before her.

"*C'est belle*," Jalal spoke softly, as he discovered the delicate egg which she held.

"Oh, Jalal," Simone exclaimed, brightening, "I'm sorry, I did not hear you enter."

"I know, my dove. You were very far away—inside your tiny egg." Simone looked down, the expression on her face again becoming wistful. Slowly, Jalal withdrew the egg from her hand. "Does it have some special significance, Simone?"

"Yes . . . no. I really don't know, Jalal. I found it in the lining of my reticule. I feel that it is very important in some way, very precious to me. But I can't remember. I can't . . ." Her fingers moved to her temples.

Immediately concerned by her obvious distress, Jalal placed the egg gently into her palm and folded her fingers over its beaded surface. "Do not think of it now, my angel. It is no longer important. You will have many new things of equal beauty which will become precious to you. Let us lie together and rest now. Tonight we will have guests, my good friends, André Duval and his sister, Marie."

Simone was well pleased with the effect she had created. It had been a pleasure to set the table herself, creating a unique blend of East and West from the diverse elements provided. The tablecloth was of the finest silk, embroidered in gold thread. Plates of brass underlay fine English china, and beautiful Bakhmutyeu crystal from Russia captured the light of the candles. Simone rechecked the placement of the silverware, and pushed the Chippendale chairs into position. Everything must be perfect for Jalal's guests, she mused, as she returned to her room to dress.

She selected one of the beautiful caftans which Jalal had presented to her. She did not regret her lack of European clothing, but reveled in the loose filmy garments that hid her growing pregnancy. As Tanya brushed her thick black hair in long easy strokes, Simone's attention went to the Fabergé egg which sat upon her dressing table. She ought to put it away, she thought. Its serene beauty mocked her. She could not keep her eyes from it when she was in the room. It seemed to hold out some promise that went ever unfulfilled. Did it have any special significance, Jalal had asked. If only she herself knew the answer. He had said that it did not matter. But could she accept that?

Although Jalal had seen the egg, there were two other pieces of her torn life concealed within the velvet purse that she had not shown him. She felt guilty about not revealing all to him; he certainly deserved to know. Yet she knew that in unraveling the thread of her own life she would somehow hurt him. And it was more than protecting Jalal, this course which she had undertaken. It was a perverse form of self-preservation, a means of also saving herself from some unknown, painful reality. She would know the truth, and yet, she was frightened. But she had fervently committed herself to living—living the life of Simone Montpellier, whoever she might be. She could not renounce this oath, no matter how hurtful its fulfillment might be.

She knew now that New Orleans had been her destination. The ticket she had found within the reticule had told her this. Was New Orleans her home? Nouvelle Orleans, she repeated to herself, giving it the French pronunciation. Yes, it felt right somehow. But try as she might she could conjure up no images to go with the words.

And the tiny leather volume . . . *The Lay of the War-Ride of Igor.* An epic poem of some type. Although Simone had struggled with some of the Russian passages, the beautiful lyrical rhythms were not lost to her. As she recalled a particularly poignant fragment of the poem which she had memorized, she wondered if therein lay the mystery of her past.

It is the voice of Yaroslavna which is heard.
Since morning she sings like an unknown seagull.
Like a seagull I will fly along the River Danube.
I will dip my beaver-trimmed sleeve into the
*   River Kaiala.*
I will cleanse the bloody wounds of my prince,
*   on his mighty body.*

O wind, why do you my lord wind, blow so
*   fiercely?*
Why do you bring on your light wings
Kuman arrows against the warriors of my
*   beloved?*
Isn't it enough for you to blow under the
*   clouds, to loll the ships on the blue sea?*
*   over the feathergrass of the prairie?*

Simone mourned with Yaroslavna as she awaited the
return of her beloved prince, his fate in battle unknown.
And did she, Simone, also await someone, her *prince*? She
remembered the brief inscription penned inside the cover of
the small book: "Never forget, Yuri." Never forget, never
forget . . . what? And who was Yuri? Was it he she
awaited, longed for, loved? Was he the father of her
child?

Jalal entered, and took Tanya's place with the brush.
Simone smiled up at him from the mirror as he resumed the
long stroking rhythm.

How she touched him. With her hair pulled back from
her smooth forehead, she appeared very young and very
vulnerable. "You look beautiful as always, my dove," he
said, admiring the glossy locks as they sprang from beneath
the moving brush. "And you have created a magnificent
setting for dinner tonight," he complimented. "But I wonder if having guests will not overtax you. Perhaps I should
have waited . . ."

"Oh, no, Jalal. I feel well," she assured him. "I look
forward to meeting your friends."

"They will be delighted with you, my treasure. And it will
be good for you to have Marie as a companion. Like
yourself, she is French."

He abandoned the brush, and began to caress her hair
with his long fingers. "I want you to be happy here. It is the

thing I desire above all else," he murmured, as his eyes sought her own in the glass.

"I am happy, Jalal, truly. You have been wonderful to me," she said, dropping her gaze to the tiny egg on her vanity. "It is only . . ." she faltered.

"I understand, my angel. But you must not worry yourself so with what is hidden from you. Cherish the present and look forward with joy to the future. But come, our guests, will soon arrive and I have something to show you," he said, removing a mysterious leather bag from the folds of his caftan. "It is said that the markets of Constantinople have no equal. And it is so, for within their compass have I found the perfect pearl," he declared, his hand withdrawing from the pouch a large luminescent gem, his eyes full upon Simone's upturned face.

"Jalal, it is magnificent," she breathed, as the creamy droplet dangled before her on its golden chain.

He smiled, relishing her pleasure, as he clasped the fine chain about her neck. "But see, *habibee*, it is no match for the luster of your skin."

Her hand went to his as he fingered the pristine ornament where it lay within the hollow of her throat. He bent down and placed a lingering kiss against the glory of her hair.

"I must go now," he murmured. "Tanya will come for you when it is time."

"Simone Montpellier, *mes amis*, Mademoiselle Marie *et le docteur* André Duval."

Simone smiled, and extending her hand to André, received a light kiss upon her fingertips. When she turned to his sister, the young woman was pleasantly surprised by Marie's warm embrace and effusive greeting.

"Oh, Simone, I am so happy to meet you at last. It is absolutely selfish for Jalal to keep you for himself."

"And I am delighted to meet both of you. But Marie, please do not blame Jalal, I am afraid that it was entirely my fault."

"Forgiven," laughed Marie, as she pulled Simone to her side, and the two women proceeded to the sitting area.

"She is very beautiful, Jalal," said André, watching his friend, whose eyes had followed Simone. "I can fully understand your deep concern for her. Is she feeling better?"

"Yes, André. Her health seems fine, although I do want you to examine her soon. The bearing of children was Allah's exclusive gift to women, and men have little to do but wait. Yet I worry . . ."

"Jalal, please do not worry. She seems well and I will be with her through her delivery."

"Thank you, dear friend, but it is not that I fear for her physical health. Simone is still so disturbed that she has no memory of her past. It is like a spirit which haunts her."

André had never seen Jalal so concerned. His distress went far beyond a solicitous attitude, it sprang from a far deeper, more complex emotion. "Jalal, please listen to me. The human mind is a fantastic mystery. It is full of shadowy places that neither science nor philosophy has explored. Sometimes in my practice, I feel so helpless, however, I do not allow myself to be defeated by what I know to be conquerable. Do not despair, my friend. It will require time and understanding, but I know that Simone will be well. And Jalal, you are the one to help her."

As Jalal listened to André Duval's words, he looked closely at the kind boyish face, the sincere brown eyes, and he understood more fully his love for the younger man.

André Duval and his sister came to Constantinople as children. André was fifteen, Marie, four. They were the offspring of one of the most intelligent and sensitive men Jalal had ever known.

It was 1854, the beginning of the Crimean War, when *le docteur* Honoré Duval and his beautiful wife, Claudette, arrived in Turkey with their two children. Honoré Duval was possibly the most brilliant doctor to have ever graduated from the French Academy of Medicine in Paris. But he detested the elitist practice which he had inherited from his father. He felt that he had betrayed his medical potentialities, and that morally, he had betrayed himself. In essence, Honoré was a classic humanitarian. So when the tsar engineered a war against the Ottoman Empire, and conflict broke out between Russia and Turkey, Honoré left Paris with his small family and little more than his altruistic principles. If French soldiers could fight for the Turkish cause, he could at least attempt to save some of those lives.

In 1856, when the Treaty of Paris was signed, Honoré Duval, still the idealistic young surgeon, remained working in one of the state hospitals in Constantinople. He was to continue his noble work for fifteen years, until his death.

It had been five years since Honoré and Claudette had died in a tragic fire, and Jalal had not been surprised when the younger Duval decided to remain in Turkey to work at the same hospital as his beloved Pappa. But it was more than an emotional choice for the young man, Jalal knew. It had been dictated by the same professional and philosophical motives that had brought his father to Turkey. André Duval was his father's son.

And Marie . . . Jalal always smiled when he thought of her. Her delicate blonde beauty belied her forceful, pragmatic personality. And although she was totally exasperated by the male-dominated Moslem culture in which she found herself, Marie adored Turkey. In a perverse way, Constantinople gave Marie the freedom that Paris never could. Because she functioned outside the Islamic culture, her actions were to a great extent uncensurable, and . . .

"Jalal, I refuse to allow you to be Moslem tonight. Simone and I will not be relegated to the *haremlik* this evening. So if you two will please come and join us . . ."

Jalal chuckled deeply at the girl's taunting. "My deepest apologies, my dear Marie," said Jalal gallantly, as he and André moved to where the women sat.

After a pleasant interlude, the four sat down to a sumptuous meal of traditional Turkish food served by wide-eyed attendants, unused to such an exotic manner of dining. Over a first course of cold chicken in walnut sauce, they spoke of the unseasonable weather.

"I have never seen such a late snowfall in all the years I have lived in Turkey," commented Marie.

"It is unusual," said Jalal, "but not unprecedented. I remember a similar occurrence when I was young."

"And are you so old now, Jalal?" teased Marie. "You seem younger tonight than I ever remember. Do you not think so, André?"

"Yes, Marie, I believe you are right. If you have found some elixir, you must keep it secret, or you will put me and all other physicians out of work," he laughed.

"Seriously, my friend," André said in a lower tone, "you are feeling well? You have not asked to see me professionally in some months. Perhaps . . ."

"I am fine, André, fine. I have never been better," Jalal

assured him. "Do not look so skeptical, my friend. The pain has not reoccurred. It was nothing."

While the men had been speaking together, Marie regaled Simone with an amusing story involving one of the patients at the clinic. Simone laughed merrily, as much at Marie's effective mannerisms and mimicry as at the tale itself.

"Do not encourage her, Simone. My sister is quite the raconteur. She will involve you for hours with her little stories."

"I should enjoy that very much, indeed," Simone assured him.

"I will consider that an invitation to visit you, Simone," Marie warned her brightly.

The conversation was interrupted by the entree: *Imam bayildi,* braised eggplant with tomatoes and onions. According to legend, *Imam bayildi,* literally, the *Imam fainted,* received its name when a holy man swooned upon sampling it, so heavenly was the spicy dish. When talk resumed, it remained general and pleasant, touching upon the current political situations within Turkey and France, and upon the approach of *Ramadan,* the sacred month of the Moslem faith.

Dinner completed, they returned to the sitting area for coffee and *baklava.*

The men continued their discussion on Jalal's favorite topic, the trend toward modernization within his country. Simone and Marie repaired to the settee and chatted about the relative merits of European and Turkish clothing.

Marie confessed, "If it were not for dear André, I should run about constantly in the native costume. I insist upon caftan and pantaloons at the hospital. It is so much more sensible than all *this,* she said indicating her high-necked Parisian gown with its full bustle and train. "Dress is the one area in which the Moslem woman is freer than her European sister."

"You are right," agreed Simone. "I find the Eastern mode of dress very much to my liking. And, of course, it is most convenient now with . . ."

"With the baby coming," finished Marie matter-of-factly. "Jalal wishes André to be your doctor. My brother is a most competent physician. He will take good care of you and your child," she said warmly.

Simone smiled, "It is wonderful to have the two of you as friends. You will promise to visit me often, won't you?"

"I promise," laughed Marie, squeezing her hand. "And after the baby is born, you and I will have such fun. Constantinople is a marvelous city.

"What do you think of this Turkish coffee, Simone?" asked Marie, pouring herself another cup of the dark brew. "Do you not prefer it to the French? So thick and rich . . ."

"I am used to it, Marie. We often drink it very strong in New Orleans. Although, *café au lait* is very popular also.

"During the war coffee almost disappeared, and I think the people missed it more than . . . Oh!" Simone looked up to see all eyes upon her. Jalal stared intently, his dark eyes unreadable. Simone's hand went to her brow; her headache had returned.

"It is time we were going, Marie," said André, rising from his chair. "Simone needs her rest, and we must be at the hospital early tomorrow."

Thanking their host, the Duvals bid Simone adieu, and Jalal accompanied them to their carriage. Simone walked slowly down the hall to her room.

When Jalal entered, she was seated on the edge of the bed. He sat behind her and pulled her close, massaging her temples with his marvelous, sensitive fingers. She sighed and relaxed against his chest.

"Tonight was wonderful, Jalal. I am fond of Marie and André already. Everything was perfect. The food, the room . . ."

He turned her toward him, his brown liquid eyes searching her face. "You are remembering, Simone?"

She closed her eyes briefly, as if trying to summon her thoughts. "Only a little, Jalal. I lived in New Orleans, at least when I was younger . . . a few fragments . . . a building . . . a woman's face, a nun. I was on my way home, when . . . when . . ."

Jalal took her in his arms and held her fiercely against him, stroking her beautiful hair. He wanted her healthy and whole, but Allah forgive him, he dreaded her memories.

"Do not cry, my beloved, nothing can hurt you now. The past is dead. Your future and that of the child is with me."

Simone was silent, but her arms encircled his waist, and she buried her head against his chest.

Jalal said no more, but fear had crept into his heart.

~ Chapter 7 ~

Marie waltzed into the room in a bright caftan and pantaloons. A thin scarf covered her yellow curls and veiled her face below the bold green eyes.

Simone looked up from her book as the girl entered. "Marie, how wonderful; when I saw André this morning, he did not tell me you would come today."

"I wished to surprise you," laughed the girl.

The two women sat crosslegged on the bed, surrounded by plump cushions, talking as if they had known each other for many years.

"Oh, Simone, I can't wait until the baby is born. Constantinople is fabulous. But we won't confine ourselves to the city. We will go to some of the provinces, the rural areas can be positively charming. We will even cruise the Aegean. The Greek isles must be experienced to be believed."

"Marie, it all sounds marvelous. I'm glad we can be friends. Sometimes when Jalal is not here, I get so lonely."

"It's not surprising. You've been living like a woman of the *haremlik*. You must be delighted to at least have your own apartment."

"Marie, please understand, Jalal has been wonderful to me. And if I have been secluded, it's been my own doing. I have not been able to . . . able to . . ."

"Simone, you must know that our friendship requires no more than our mutual affection. You owe me nothing more."

Seeking to lighten the mood, Marie grasped her dangling veil and pulled it once more across her face. "How did you

269

recognize me so quickly when I arrived. Don't you find me a convincing woman of the harem?" she teased. "I might even have been the mysterious Yamna."

"Never," laughed Simone. "Not with those flashing emerald eyes. Yamna's eyes are nearly black, and they do not flash—they smolder."

"So you've met the invisible sister."

"Well, not exactly. But I've seen her. She is very lovely. I don't think she likes me," she added.

"Hah!" interjected Marie. "I have no doubt of that. The lady and I have not been introduced, but I know her by reputation.

"She was married, you know. She left her husband after seven years. Moslem law is quite liberal in this regard. Of course, it is much easier for the husband to initiate such a proceeding. He has only to say, *I divorce you!* three times and it is done. A woman must have such an option written into her marriage contract, or be rich enough in her own right to purchase her freedom. It is also necessary for a *qadi* to adjudge her case. As you can imagine, the whole affair was embarrassing for Jalal. But still, he welcomed her into his home, and apparently dotes on her. He has spoken of her often with affection, but I have never met her. But let us talk of something else. Where are those sketches you promised to show me?"

"Oh, Marie, they are really not very good."

"If there is one thing I detest more than ineffectual people, it is those with false modesty. So let me be the judge."

"All right, but I warned you," laughed Simone, as she rose from the bed and went to the sitting room.

When she returned, she handed her friend a very large sketch pad. Marie leafed through the portfolio, falling into an uncharacteristic silence. She paused at a drawing of a young Anatolian boy, and looked directly into Simone's eyes. When Marie spoke, her voice was filled with a tenderness in stark contrast to her usual flippancy.

"Simone, these are incredible. You have captured the soul of Constantinople and her people—such sensitivity. I have always known that I was in love with this city, and now you have helped to show me why. You have that rare gift of translating the intangible into a poignant visual image. *Merci beaucoup*, Simone."

Simone stared at the pretty blonde woman, whose face suddenly seemed younger, vulnerable. "Marie," she said softly, her eyes misting, "thank *you,* dear friend. Never has anyone spoken to me as you have. Though I can remember little of my life, I know in my heart that no one has ever valued me as I would wish. It seems to me that the most important aspects of people often go unnoticed. Is it not *what we become,* rather than *who* we are that is truly important?"

As Marie rose from the bed with the sketch pad, a loose sheet fell to the floor. When she reached to retrieve it, Simone's hands were already clutching at the sketch.

"What is it, Simone? Are you ill?" she asked, noting the girl's sudden pallor.

"No, Marie. It is nothing," Simone whispered unconvincingly.

"It is the drawing, isn't it? You did not wish me to see it?"

Simone lowered her head. "No, Marie, it is not that I didn't want *you* to see it. It is just that when I look at it . . ." Simone extended her hand, offering the picture to her friend.

Marie took the sketch and stared at it for a long time before she spoke. "Simone, he is beautiful," she murmured. "Who is he?"

"Oh, Marie, that is the problem. I don't know. I don't even remember sketching it. But I . . . I . . ."

Marie reached for Simone, her arms encircling the weeping girl. "Simone, dear Simone, it is best that you cry. Cry away the pain and the hurt. Cry, little friend, cry."

That evening, Simone lay restless in her bed, still haunted by the image of that face. Seeking a more comfortable position, she turned toward the door. Jalal stood in the threshold, staring at her.

"Jalal, you are home at last. I missed you at dinner," said Simone, sitting up as he moved to the edge of the bed and pressed her to him.

"And I've missed you, my little one," he whispered, showering her face with light kisses.

Simone sighed. It was so comforting to surrender to his arms. He was her anchor, her shield; the only thing in her life that need not be questioned or doubted. But it was more than this. Without uncertainty or shame, she knew that he was more than her champion and protector. He was a man, both worthy and desirable. His strength of spirit roused her body, even as it soothed the turmoil in her mind.

Simone reached for his handsome face, stilling his feverish movements so that she could open her mouth to his. As she felt his warm lips move to her breast, her mind reeled with an urgency she dared not express. Jalal, Jalal, how my body begs for you. Please, please don't make me wait. The thoughts echoed wildly in her brain. But though the words were unformed, her passion was not. She moaned heavily, her hands pressing against his dark head, forcing the wet mouth to suckle more deeply at her ripened nipple.

"Simone, no!" he cried, rising from the cushions, his back toward her as he moved to the center of the room.

Simone sat up. "Jalal, what have I done?"

When he turned, she saw that lines of tension marred his face, his eyes wore a look of pain, and his fists were clenched tightly at his sides.

"Oh, Jalal," she breathed, going to him and placing a hand upon his shoulder.

His body tensed under her touch. "Please Simone," he begged, moving away from her.

"What is wrong, Jalal? Have I made you angry?" Simone pleaded.

Turning to face her again, Jalal spoke, fighting for control. "Simone, don't you see that I want you, more than I have ever wanted anyone?"

"And I want *you*, dear Jalal."

"No!" he protested fiercely. "I will do nothing which might harm the child, or you."

She moved to embrace him, her small head pressing into his chest. Suddenly his arms were about her, crushing her to his hard body, his open mouth seeking her yielding lips. But at last he gently pushed her from him.

For a moment she looked up into his face, then slowly, her hands loosened the sash which bound his waist. Sinking to her knees, she pressed his inflamed body to her face.

He pushed her back gently and tilted her head up to meet his gaze. His voice was husky as he spoke. "My precious flower, you do not have to do *this* for me."

"I know, Jalal, but it is what I want to do."

As she drew him nearer, his last remnant of control was swept away, and he surrendered at last to her waiting lips.

"Oh Simone, my Simone . . ."

~ *Chapter 8* ~

Months passed; Simone grew heavy with child. Physically, she was stronger than she had been for many months. Although she had remembered nothing new about her past, she was beginning to accept the patterns of her new life with Jalal. It was he who was the true healing force; they drew closer each day.

Simone sat in the circle of lamplight, pulling the silk thread through the delicate gauze. She smiled as she looked down at the tiny garment. It would not be long. Through the open shutters came the wail of the crier. The new moon had risen; the holy month had begun.

Ramadan, the ninth month of the Moslem year was the most sacred in all of Islam. It was a curious blend of religious ritual and secular diversion. From sunrise to sunset, the believer maintained a highly disciplined posture, one of fasting and prayer. But a blast of cannon fire and the cry of the muezzin atop a lighted minaret heralded the beginning of fantastic entertainments which occurred at no other time of the year. The usually darkened and vacant streets of the city were filled with men—*hammals* and beggars milling with pashas and *bays*, freely moving in and out of crowded coffeehouses and the courtyards of palaces, their gates left open to all during the evening's festivities. At *Ramadan,* the joy of participation rendered all Moslems equal. And such joy . . .

Everywhere there were live theater performances, usually satirical in nature, the players giving exaggerated character imitations: the stupid peasant Turk, the cunning Jew, the simpleton Frank. There were the incomparable storytellers from Erzurum and the suggestive dancers of the Armenian *chengi*, who upon completion of their finger-snapping whirl-

ing, bent backward to have gold coins stuck to their
foreheads by the enthusiastic audience.

And the booths which lined the streets were a
kaleidoscope of the bizarre—exotic snake charmers,
scorpion-eating dervishes, sword swallowers, acrobats,
tumblers, and jugglers. But it was to the sheds of the
fortune-tellers that most of the revelers thronged. And each
group had their own infallible method of soothsaying.
There were those who gazed hypnotically into black ink,
cupped within the left palm of a young virgin boy; there
were the bag throwers, who read the scattered pieces of
shell, colored glass, small coins, and beans. It was perhaps a
jaded but happy mass that made its weary way home to
partake of the last meal, a rice pilaf, before the rigors of the
next day's fasting and prayer.

Simone found the concept quite fascinating, a strange
cycle of strict Lenten days and wild Carnival nights. In
deference to Jalal, she had offered to join in the ritual
fasting. But he would not hear of it; an expectant mother
must be constantly nourished, was his decree.

Simone felt her rounded abdomen as the child stirred. He
was as eager for the birth as she. *He*, she mused, a boy. A
son for Jalal. Yet she could not forget that Jalal was not this
baby's father. Who was? Would the child mirror his unknown sire? In the face of the son, might not the father's
image be discovered? She closed her eyes and leaned
against the cushion at her back. Deliberately, she summoned Jalal's form. She saw the taut muscular frame, the
dark sensitive eyes, the strong handsome face softened in a
tender smile. Her face relaxed, and her own lips curved in
response. She rose and summoned Tanya. It was time to
dress. Tonight would be special. The *karagoz* players would
perform in the courtyard.

As Simone sat next to Marie, she looked from beneath
half-closed lids to where Yamna was situated a few paces
from them. How unyielding in her aloofness was Jalal's
sister. Her manner had been so controlled, so restrained
when Jalal escorted Marie to where the women would view
tonight's performance. Yamna had acknowledged the
young French woman's presence with a stiff bow of her dark
head as Jalal introduced them. He had smiled through the
amenities, his deep voice sounding almost musical as he

spoke in his native language.

Simone turned now to gaze at him. How easy were his movements, how quick his glowing smile, and his hands . . . Those beautiful expressive hands, lightly resting upon Razid's shoulders, gesturing gracefully, as he conversed with André, and when they touched her, warm, intimate . . .

Marie, too, looked sideways at the figure on Simone's right. Yamna, like her brother, had inherited their father's good looks. She had the same large, dark, slightly uptilted eyes, consummately expressive, as were the eyes of all Turkish women. It was the sole benefit they derived from the enforced concealment of the veil.

Marie reflected on the brief introduction. What had Yamna's eyes revealed? Contempt, scorn, and yes, a certain envy. From the little Jalal had said about his sister, Marie had gleaned that she was quite intelligent, even something of a scholar. Surely such a woman must chafe at the Moslem yoke, even if she did not admit it fully to herself. If a questing, aggressive spirit is forced into a rigid mold, what sort of outlet does it find? Marie pondered.

Once again, Simone stole a glance at the sister who so radically contrasted with her gracious brother. Simone tried to understand Yamna's cold manner toward her. Was it only the natural reserve of a sheltered Muslim woman toward a foreigner? The accepted posture of a believer toward an infidel? No, decided Simone firmly. It was more.

Simone looked at her more boldly now. The woman was staring at where Jalal stood laughing at one of Razid's classic stories. She watched the woman closely. Yamna gazed almost transfixed, as if she could not withdraw from the image she beheld. There was an elegant serenity about her, a cool detachment that seemed to elevate her far above her surroundings. She was a painted vision, an exotic virgin—goddess, undefiled, perfect. As the woman sat unmoving, Simone realized that there was something which betrayed the dispassionate demeanor. It was the eyes; the dark liquid pools seemed to burn, to consume as they gazed upon her brother. What nameless thing had Simone seen in them? Quickly she pulled away. She felt suddenly chilled.

"What is it, Simone?" Marie said, a concerned look on her pretty face.

"It is nothing, Marie. I am fine."

"There is André," said Marie. "He is talking to that devilishly handsome Razid. I love to watch that man; he is so animated. I've seen him in passing, but have never really met him. André says he is most amusing, and more than a match for the infamous Marie Duval in the art of storytelling."

Simone laughed, "Razid has dined with us, and his tales are, indeed, engaging. Jalal maintains that Razid can turn the merest incident into a soul-stirring saga. Perhaps, we could arrange a meeting, a sort of contest between the two of you," joked Simone, catching her friend's lighthearted mood.

"Hmm, that is not the sort of arrangement I had in mind," said Marie wickedly. "No, I should fancy a more stimulating contest. Oh, how I should love to slip from behind this screen to enliven that conversation."

"Marie!"

"Oh, don't worry, Simone," Marie laughed softly. "I shall behave. You know I would never do anything to hurt Jalal. This is after all, in celebration of a Moslem feast, and it is only fitting that I act the proper Islamic woman. Besides," she added gaily, "tonight, I will be content to play out another fantasy. I shall be the observer, unobserved," she chuckled, as her bright green eyes fixed themselves on the scene beyond the lattice.

Within the courtyard a *karagoz* theater had been erected, a three-sided booth covered with a curtain imprinted with rose bushes. A large white cotton screen was stretched across the front. An oil lamp was lit within the structure, and the three-piece orchestra which sat before the stage began to play, signaling that the performance was about to begin. The flares in the garden were dimmed, and the guests seated themselves on the low benches which had been provided. A hush fell over the audience, as there appeared on the screen a writhing seven-headed serpent pitting its awesome strength against that of a burly wrestler.

Simone gasped in amazement as the combatants fought their way across the taut cotton fabric. It was hard to believe that the complex sinewy movements of both figures was controlled by a single puppet master.

"He is very good," breathed Marie at Simone's side. "I have never been privileged to attend the performance of a six-tasseled *karagoz* master."

"Six-tassels?" questioned Simone.

"Yes. If you look closely you will see them hanging from the screen. Seven is the highest number a master may be awarded. But there are few who attain that rank."

"I don't see how he could be better," asserted Simone. "The man must be equipped with four arms."

The epic battle ended with the human triumphant. It was succeeded by the appearance on the screen of two bearded men in brightly colored clothes and fantastic headpieces.

"These are the principal characters of *karagoz*," Marie explained.

"The one on the right is *Karagoz* himself, a common man, uneducated but clever; the other is *Hajivat*, a city dweller given to putting on airs."

Simone watched as the skillfully manipulated shadow puppets acted out several comical stories. Though she did not comprehend a word of what was said, an understanding of the language was not necessary to the enjoyment of the drama. The theme was universal, the comedy broad, the music delightful.

As the colored shadows of the small figures danced jauntily across the screen, the dark eyes of Yamna were veiled against the sparkling performance. Yet her mind was alive.

The heathen bitch grows heavy with child. Even from behind the lattice her shame defiles this holy night. And the blonde infidel—no better than the dark daughter of Iblis —coveting Razid. Like a street whore, she lusts after his seed. *Je comprends, je comprends*—I understand well the black venom which spills forth from your red mouths.

Slowly her eyes closed and from the darkness he came, his mouth opening like a flower to hers, his long delicate fingers like small butterflies moving against her warm flesh. Oh Jalal, Jalal . . .

When the performance came to an end, the puppet master emerged to much congratulations, and the puppets themselves were brought out and offered for sale. Made of oiled camel skin and brightly colored, they were over a foot tall, held together with waxed thread at the joints.

Simone watched as Jalal, who stood in conversation with the artful craftsman, was handed a beautiful equestrian figure. When he slipped behind the grill a moment later, he placed it in her hands as he bent down to whisper in her ear, "For the boy."

~ *Chapter 9* ~

Yamna sat idly running an ivory comb through her dark straight hair. She felt the emptiness of her room now more than ever. Jalal no longer found the time to spend a few hours each day with her. No, the harlot had seen to that. As she stared at her image in the mirror, a smile slowly crossed her face. It was so simple; why had she not thought of it before?

"But mistress, the master has said that I should not leave her unattended. Please send Maysun in my stead," Tanya begged.

"Watch your tongue, you forget your place; you also forget that I am mistress in this house. You will do as I say. Maysun is stupid and cannot handle the merchants as you do. You will go directly to the marketplace and secure the things I have requested. Yasar will accompany you. I will send word to Simone that you are doing my bidding. Of course, she will understand. Now go quickly."

Simone grew slightly anxious; Tanya was late. The afternoon prayer had already been heralded, and still the girl had not come for her. She looked forward to her visits to the *hamman*, especially now, in her eighth month. Where was Tanya? It was unlike the girl to be remiss in her duties. In fact, Simone often felt smothered by her excessive attentiveness. Of course, she knew that it was on Jalal's orders that the girl acted. Growing more impatient, Simone decided that it was foolish not to go to the *hamman* on her own. Jalal would be furious, but perhaps he needn't know.

Placing a loose caftan over her cotton shift, Simone proceeded down the hall. She moved slowly, waiting for her vision to adjust to the darkness of the corridor. When she reached the top of the stairwell she paused briefly.

Suddenly, strong hands pressed on her back. She was pushed forward, the violent action propelling her downward . . . downward. As she tumbled over and over, she struggled vainly for control. When she came to rest at the bottom of the stairs, the swirling kaleidoscope of images resolved itself into one dark specter on the landing above —a woman, totally concealed behind the shapeless fabric of a *yasmak*.

A sudden sharp pain split her bruised body. The spasm did not last long, but dissolved into a mindless void.

Simone was in pain, terrible pain. It throbbed through her battered body in time with the chanting of the midwife. "Allah, *akbar,* God is most great. There is no god but Allah . . ."

With increasing frequency, the harrowing pain would coalesce into a piercing spasm that caused her to cry out and grip convulsively at the sides of the birthing chair. The guilt-stricken Tanya hovered at her side, wiping the perspiration gently from Simone's bruised face.

"Push, my lady, push," she intoned softly in Russian.

The words caught Simone's attention, the phrase echoing in her mind. Yes, she thought, *Push, Marya, push.*

Suddenly, her mind was detached from the pain, and she seemed to float somewhere near the ceiling above the chaotic scene. A barrage of images inundated her mind.

Mother Superior smiled as Simone showed her the delicate stitches with which she had embellished the linen altarcloth. "Très bien, ma petite," she said.

"I will require the sleeping draught tonight," said Madame Felice. Simone moved through the narrow streets exhilarated by the crowds and the glittering parade.

Suddenly, his arms were around her. She felt his familiar lips upon her mouth, and she surrendered to his insistent passion. She opened her eyes to gaze into the azure depths of his, as the thick flakes of snow fell all about him.

A stab of sudden agony drew her relentlessly back to her tortured body.

"Rudolph, Rudolph!" she screamed, her cries melding with the shrill wailing of the infant. Giving in to mental and physical exhaustion, Simone lapsed gratefully into the comforting blackness.

The midwife directed as the umbilical cord was severed and the baby washed. Three sesame seeds were placed in the navel, and the baby was bound and swaddled, then dressed in a cotton smock and blue shawl. The women noted that although the child was a month early, he was large and well-formed, with little of the wrinkling and redness of the premature infant.

Esma carefully pinned the blue bead amulet with its red ribbon to the shoulder of the baby's smock. From that position it could ward off the baleful influences of the evil eye. Simone was placed on cushions, covered in rich shawls, and propped up with matching side pillows. Above the divan hung a Koran. From the book dangled an onion, cloves of garlic, and blue beads. It was common knowledge that mother and child were especially vulnerable to evil influences in the first few days after birth.

As the women were finishing their ministrations, the door was suddenly thrown open. Jalal had come, in response to the urgent summons of his manservant, Emen. His body held rigid, worry etched into his handsome features, he stood in the doorway. The women bowed to him as they filed from the room. His questions could wait; his only thought was for Simone, who lay unmoving on the bed.

Slowly he walked to the couch, his eyes taking in the traditional bottle of sherbet at the bedside. The red gauze was tied round the neck of the flask. *So it was a boy*. Coming to stand at the bed, Jalal looked tenderly downward on the sleeping pair, and stroked Simone's glossy hair. At this she murmured softly in her sleep and turned her face toward him. His eyes widened and his breath caught in his throat.

His exultation became blind fury as he abruptly stalked

from the chamber. He found it unnecessary to call for Esma, as she stood just outside the door, apparently awaiting him.

"Esma, what has happened here? The child is early, and Simone bears the marks of some violence."

"Master, do not upset yourself. The midwife says that the child is healthy, and your lady has suffered no apparent harm. The bruises which mar her beauty will soon fade."

"But what happened, Esma? And why was André Duval not summoned as I instructed?"

"There was no time, master. The child came quickly. We were fortunate to get the midwife."

"And the bruises?"

"She was found by Tanya at the base of the stairs. She must have lost her footing."

Jalal was about to instruct Esma to fetch Tanya, who had now become the object of his wrath. Had he not given orders that she remain with Simone at all times? But before the summons could be issued, Simone's voice called weakly from the room.

"Jalal."

Swiftly, he forgot everything and returned to her bedside. Simone, the child in her arms, watched his approach, and reached out her hand toward him. He took it in his, and sat at the edge of the cushions.

"You have done well, my flower. Your son is beautiful."

She clutched at his hand, and as if she had not heard his words, she muttered almost feverishly.

"At the top of the stairs . . . a woman . . . all in black. I saw her as I fell. What does it mean, Jalal? I am so frightened."

"Hush, my little one, you have been through much this day; all is well now. I am here."

Inwardly, he was perplexed and fearful. Had there, in truth, been someone on the stairs? Someone who wished her harm? He looked again at Simone; there was something more.

"My dearest, what still troubles you."

She paused. She seemed to be searching for the right words. Finally she spoke. It was almost a whisper.

"Jalal, I remember."

He said nothing. There was something of resignation in

his countenance, but beneath it she perceived a tender vulnerability. She went on with it, though she knew the words would hurt him. It had to be said. Her silence would form a greater wall between them than the truth ever could.

"His name is Rudolph . . ."

~ *Chapter 10* ~

Simone stood in her room looking down at the sleeping infant. He seemed so tiny nestled within the ornate cradle that had been Jalal's. The silver and mother-of-pearl inlay reflected back the early morning light of this mid-August day. At least it would be cool in the *hamman*.

She stroked the golden down that had begun to appear on the smooth skin of her son's head. At her gentle touch, he opened his bright blue eyes, his small pink mouth widening in a yawn. How glad she was for this child, this last link with him. She wished that he could see his son, this precious creation that bound them together as nothing else could. There were times when she yearned for him with the old desperation. But she was no longer a child, her experiences had matured her, and she had come to terms with the fact that their relationship could never be.

With the lifting of her amnesia had come the ironic realization that her real identity remained, as always, a mystery. But this did not seem as important as it once had. It was futile to rail against fate. She must make a life for herself and her son—Rudolph's son.

And Jalal . . . he was, she realized, the only honest thing in her life. All else had been a sham, a masquerade. How good he was to both her and the baby.

Tanya entered. It was time for the Fortieth Day Ceremony.

Simone, accompanied by the midwife and all the female members of the household, proceeded to the *hamman*. They passed into the cool room; the scent of aloe wood and the soft strains of music filled the air. Before they bathed, each of the women greeted Simone ritually, congratulating her on the baby's birth. Later, the midwife removed the child from its basket and unswaddled it. Wrapping it in a shawl, she took it to the bath for the prescribed Fortieth Day Ceremony.

The infant was washed and then lacquered with a duck's egg, which had been broken into a bowl. This was done in the belief that the child could thus be both accustomed to and protected from the watery element. Next, a gold piece was immersed in the flowing water and the *Fatiha* was recited. "In the name of God be Merciful, the Compassionate. Praise is to God the Lord of the Worlds, Master of the day of judgment. Thee do we worship and Thee do we ask for aid. Guide us to the straight path, the path of those to whom Thou has been gracious, not those who have been visited with wrath nor those who go astray."

As the midwife's words rang out in the marble chamber, Simone looked forward with anticipation to the evening. Tonight the child would be circumcised, and a small celebration would follow. And the night held another promise. The fortieth day marked the passing of the birth period; Jalal would now at last be free to come to her as a man. Simone's cheeks flushed at this prospect, which filled her with a growing desire.

She was drawn back to the moment however, when one of the servant girls placed in her hand a small silver bell, a gift for the newborn. One by one they followed, presenting amulets of protective prayers, blue beads, some with five holes representing the senses, and a bone teething ring. The last in line was Yamna. The woman, her face an unemotional mask, extended her token—a traditional silvered wolf's tooth. A shiver of fear passed through Simone. Was it the gift or the giver that disturbed her?

It was a late summer evening, but the hint of a cool breeze filled the garden. Nightingale voices filtered through the myrtle and vine, and the deep lavender sky was hung as some glorious harem's canopy over the night. The small party strolled leisurely among rows of citron, olive, and

cedar. An unusual spectacle of sheer delight evoked a burst
of laughter. Jalal had spared nothing to make this a magical
night; tortoises bearing small oil lamps on their backs
meandered languorously among the beds of rosebushes.

Simone and Marie stood chatting as they sampled the
delectable hors d'oeuvres which had been placed on a
nearby table.

"Simone, what a little angel your son is; not a tear from
him when André performed the circumcision. You and Jalal
must be so proud of him . . ."

As Marie continued animatedly, Simone reflected on the
ceremony and its significance. Although the operation was
secular in nature, it was the indispensable rite de passage
for all male members of Islam. And as it had become
apparent that the child was to be considered Jalal's son, it
was only natural that he should assume his father's faith.
The old Simone might have felt guilt that Rudolph's son and
hers would be reared in an alien belief. The woman she had
become accepted this as a simple matter of another time,
another place.

"Simone, you have not heard a single word I've said,"
Marie lightly bantered.

Joining them, André remarked playfully, "No, my dear
sister, I don't think she has. She seems so preoccupied. Do
you not think so, Jalal?"

His host did not reply, but gazed appraisingly at Simone,
who returned his look with a matching intensity. Jalal's
pulse raced as he beheld Simone's lush beauty. With the
birth of the child, she had ripened, had become more
sensual, almost Eastern in her aspect. Her look promised
that tonight complete fulfillment would be theirs.

Yamna stepped into the garden. For the occasion she had
donned her most elegant costume. The rich purple fabric of
her robe was heavily knotted with silver thread. Her only
jewel adornment was a circlet of perfectly matched diamonds which hung sensually across her high forehead. A
single stone dangled beneath the sharp widow's peak.

Aware that all attention was now focused upon her, she
loosened the thin veil of indigo which had concealed all but
the unfathomable pools of her dark eyes. Swiftly Jalal
moved to his sister's side and drew her forward.

"*Le docteur* Duval, *ma soeur*, Yamna. Marie, you, of
course, have met."

"Bonsoir, madame. *C'est mon plaisir*," said André.

Yamna smiled radiantly and greeted the couple. *"Bonsoir."*

Jalal was obviously proud that his sister could converse in French, a rare accomplishment in a Moslem woman. He had never denigrated Yamna's quick intelligence, and had in fact encouraged her education. The death of their parents had left her in his care; he had made one exception to her strict Moslem upbringing—Yamna was allowed to have a mind. And after her early divorce, she returned to Jalal's house as mistress, and assumed her former role as a willing student.

At the servant's announcement that dinner was ready, the party moved to a small *yali* in the middle of the garden. The gaily painted pavilion was illuminated with brass lanterns hung from coiling chains. The soft lights bathed the outdoor chamber in an almost ethereal glow. The sky was now velvet, and the night whispered forth her secret sounds.

As they seated themselves upon large colorful floor cushions, a tray of *dolma* was placed before them. This was followed by deep fried fillets of *kalkan*, a type of turbot possessing a unique flavor. Course after course was presented to them upon brass trays and in deep copper bowls: cups of *dugun corbasi*, wedding soup, so called because its intricate preparation meant that it was served on only the most special occasions; whole roasted lamb with spicy rice pilaf; a salad of *patlican yogurtlu*, eggplant and yoghurt. Finally the dessert tray arrived, overflowing with rich confections: *gullac*, *helve*, and *baklava*. Rich Turkish coffee completed the meal.

Throughout supper Yamna had been silent, but her mind was seething. This invitation had certainly pleased her. That her brother would include her with his foreign friends bespoke clearly that her importance was not diminished in his eyes. Yet this did not temper her hatred of the heathen woman and her bastard. Did Jalal mean to adopt the boy as his own son? Certainly the circumcision and this blasphemous celebration would indicate this. How could Allah not have been with her in the execution of her plan? She would not, could not, fail again.

Marie broke the stillness with a soft laugh. "I have heard that there is a Turkish saying that when a moment of silence falls during a meal, somewhere a girl is born. I'm afraid that if we remain silent much longer, your son, Simone, will have too many young maidens from which to choose."

"That would indeed be an embarrassment of riches," commented André as Jalal and Simone laughed appreciatively at Marie's jest.

As the last tray was cleared away, they sat replete in the lambent aura of the oil lamps. André noted the way in which Jalal looked tenderly down on Simone's radiant face. The import of that glance was not lost on the Frenchman.

"Come, Marie, it is time for us to go. Simone will be tired. Babies can be very demanding of new mothers."

Marie rose, hugging Simone affectionately. André promised that the next dinner party would be theirs.

In the semidarkness of her room, Simone bent over her sleeping son . . . and now Jalal's. As she fingered the nascent ringlets of gold which feathered his temples, she heard the door open. Jalal moved to stand at her side. His arms encircled her tiny waist, and her head rested against the firm surface of his chest.

"He is beautiful, isn't he, Jalal?"

"Yes, my precious one, like his mother."

For a moment longer they stood in silence, then Jalal spoke almost tentatively. "Simone, the time has come. You must name the boy. Have you given thought to this?"

"Yes, Jalal. I have selected one." She turned toward him then, her eyes intent on his bronzed face. "He shall be called Rudolph! Can you understand this, mon cher?"

He answered her with a gentle kiss, which spoke more eloquently than words. When he did speak it was tenderly but with conviction. "Simone, with tonight's ceremony, you have allowed me to share this son with you. You have also given him to the traditions of the Islamic faith. I very much desire that he should bear as his second title one of Moslem heritage, a hero's name, as is traditional. May I select that name?"

"No, for you see, I have selected that name as well." So as not to see the pain deepen on his face, she added quickly but sweetly, "It shall be Jalal."

She was rewarded by the metamorphosis that this simple statement wrought in his countenance. Beneath his luxuriant mustache, his even white teeth shone in a broad smile. But it was his eyes that revealed how deeply she had touched him. He bent his head to hers, his lips expressing his gratefulness in an indulgent kiss. She yielded herself to his embrace and she felt the rapid alteration of his mood, as ardor blossomed swiftly in the wake of gratitude.

They undressed each other with feverish, anxious hands, impatient for fulfillment. In the soft light of the chamber, their bodies were magnificent figures, Caravaggio images, light and dark planes of moving passion.

Sinking deeply into the cushions of her bed, they locked in a relentless embrace, their bodies fighting to become one—pressing, molding. They struggled to transcend the purely physical and unite their separate beings in the white heat of their yearning.

Simone thrust her body upward and moved rhythmically against the muscular column of Jalal's form. She felt drugged by the intensity of her own need, and he was charged with the urgencies of his own inflamed flesh. Never before had he experienced such an unbridled desire—an all encompassing lust coupled with an ennobling love.

Simone's breasts burned deeply into his heaving chest, the nipples torturing his warm, moist skin. Slowly, his hands moved lower against the flesh of her softly rounded body, pressing and lifting her nearer. He plunged deeply into the well of her womanhood, and was swallowed into her welcoming depths. She had accepted him willingly, lovingly.

They lay together in sweet exhaustion, and it was sometime before Jalal trusted his voice to intrude into the haven of the unspoken covenant which now existed between them.

"Simone, when my wife, Maryan, died, I felt that I could never love any woman again. I now realize that I misjudged my own emotions. I know now that I am still capable of loving. For you see, Simone, I love you as I have never loved anyone. You are my life. I could never be whole without you. Marry me, my precious one. Be my wife."

It was a few moments before Simone had the courage to look into his eyes; when she did, her own filled with tears.

"Jalal, I never believed that I could find happiness, peace. But I, too, was wrong. You have given me more than your love, you have given me to myself. Yes, beloved, I will become your wife."

As he bent to kiss her, the insistent cries of the baby broke the embrace. Simone laughed. "Forgive me, my love, but another claims my attention."

She retrieved Rudolph and returned with him to the bed, where she rested against the headboard, Jalal's protective arm encircling her. The baby's wails had ceased the moment his mother had lifted him into her arms. And now he lay upon her stomach, his small head bobbing as he tried to focus his blue-gray eyes—his father's eyes.

Slowly, Simone drew the infant to her breast; eagerly his cherubic mouth found the nipple, and he sucked hungrily, pulling at its firmness. Jalal moved closer and slowly lowered his head over the suckling child's. Deftly, he pressed his mouth next to the boy's, and momentarily, he, too, supped lovingly at the sweetness of Simone's milk. She whimpered in pleasure. Jalal stilled her cries with his lips, as the infant once more became the sole possessor of his mother's breast. The child at last satisfied, Simone returned him to his crib, where he settled immediately into a contented slumber.

When Simone returned, Jalal was standing at the side of the bed holding a small, embroidered pouch. Simone climbed into the bed among the cushions, knelt, and sat back upon her heels. Her hair tumbled over her naked shoulders, her eyes sparkled.

"You look like such a child, sitting that way," Jalal said, smiling.

"Am I your child?"

Lowering his lean body onto the bed, Jalal peered into Simone's upturned face and responded. "Yes, my dove, I now have two little ones to care for, to pamper . . . to love."

As he spoke, he opened the silken purse and idly fingered its contents. Simone's eyes followed his hand.

"Jalal, what is it?" she squealed.

Laughing heartily, he replied, "You are a child, and a very curious one, but I won't tantalize you any longer."

With these words, Jalal withdrew a small glittering object; pulling the child-woman's hand forward, he slipped a large yellow stone onto one slender finger. Its magnificence awed Simone, and her exclamation was barely audible. "Oh, Jalal, it is beautiful. I've never seen such a gem. What is it?"

"A very rare jewel, my sweetness, a canary diamond. I had it fashioned especially for you. It gives me great happiness that it pleases you so."

Simone looked into the tanned face of the man before her. His liquid eyes, which sometimes appeared so darkly mysterious, were now very readable; they clearly revealed his deep love for her. She pulled him to her and rained feather-light kisses upon his face. They made love again, and this time, though the intensity remained, there was less urgency. They could afford the simpler pleasures of love-making, secure in the knowledge that a lifetime of mutual exploration lay before them.

It was hours later. Jalal stood at the window; a cooling breeze carried the scent of flowering jasmine into the room. On the bed Simone lay curled in untroubled repose. The boy in the cradle slept on. All was peace. But Jalal could not sleep. An exaltation, that paradoxically had its origin in this tranquillity, welled inside him. This overpowering joy forced him to seek the openness of the garden below.

The waxing moon hung low in the sky, and the dawn ran in pink rivulets in the eastern sky. He walked leisurely among the trees, the delicious fragrance of the roses plying his senses. He breathed deeply. Never had he felt so happy, so free. He seemed more alive then, than he had ever been. His whole being sang with the sublime contentment of his soul. He could see more clearly, and feel more acutely. Never had the heavens seemed so bright or the smell of the blossoms so sweet. His awareness of everything was keener. He could see the scent of the myrtle and smell the sky colors. It was as though he had transcended this dimension and had escaped all the logical boundaries which chained man to earthly realities.

And Simone had done this for him. *His Simone*, the beautiful woman who had so recently and so readily caused his life to once again have meaning. Was she a sorceress, or simply the most intelligent, lovely, and enchanting woman in the world? Whatever the answer, he cared not. For the only significant truth was simple—she was his.

Behind the latticed window far above, another soul whose emotions would allow no rest, peered down at the lone figure in the garden. Always before it was he that had the power to soothe her. Instinctively, she was drawn to him. Quickly she donned the obscuring *yasmak*. It would conceal her from the eyes of any curious servants who might be about. She glided like a wraith down the stairs, and stole quietly into the courtyard.

"Jalal," she called to him as she approached along the flower-bordered path.

He turned. "Who is it?" he queried, trying to make out the dark form hidden within the shadow of a nearby olive tree.

"It is I, Jalal."

"Why are you about at this hour? Is something wrong?"

"I could not sleep."

"Come then, and walk with me, little sister." They walked awhile in silence, the rosy glow deepening and spreading toward the far horizon.

"For many years have I mourned the passing of my beloved Maryan," began Jalal. "And I have been a fool to have barred love from my heart. But no more. My days of loneliness have passed. I have found peace and happiness once again. I have found love, Yamna. I have found Simone."

As he spoke, they had paused along the path, and now in the growing light, Jalal looked closely at his sister. A small part of his mind registered surprise at seeing her in the dull black robes that she usually scorned. Her face mirrored the somber tone of the garment. Yet Jalal was too engrossed in his own emotions to fully comprehend the import of his sister's withdrawn demeanor. He continued as they walked, "This night I have asked Simone to become my wife." Now Jalal turned to her again, seeking some approval in her face, some sign that she understood and shared in his joy. But she stood like a graven Fury, the features chiseled in hard white stone. As he gazed in astonishment, the frozen lips at last opened to speak.

"Lonely, Jalal? How could you have been lonely? No peace? No happiness? I can't believe you are saying these hateful words to me. Have I not been with you? Have I not answered all of your needs? Have I not been all that you wanted in a woman? By Allah, Jalal, you have been more than a brother to me! Have I not forsaken all others for you? No other man would I allow to touch me—no man but you. Not even Hamid was allowed to come freely to our marriage bed. For you, Jalal, I have saved myself. And now you forsake me for that infidel woman, that vile prostitute!"

Jalal stared in disbelief at the shrieking harpy who had usurped the place of his beloved sister. Her words were, at first, incomprehensible to him. In spite of the morning

coolness, he began to perspire, and a wave of nausea
gripped him. When at last he spoke, his labored breathing
punctuated his words. "By all that is sacred, what have I
done? Am I to blame for this? How could you have so
misinterpreted a brother's affection for his only sister? I did
only what I thought best, but now I see that I have been
blind. Even when you were but a child, I yielded too readily
to you. This is an unholy madness, an unspeakable perversion! I am your brother. I can give you nothing but a
brother's love."

As if through a red haze, he watched her, the blood
pounding in his temples.

Clenching her fists she threw her vicious indictments at
him. "You are wrong, Jalal. You did love me! I know it. It is
that woman who has changed you. She has brought evil on
this house, she and her blue-eyed bastard. She has bewitched you! Why did she not die when I pushed her!"

At this last revelation, the warring emotions within his
breast tore him asunder. A searing pain ripped upward
through his arm and exploded violently in his chest. Yamna
watched in horror as he sank to the ground.

~ *Chapter 11* ~

A fleecy armada of lofty clouds drifted slowly along in the
blue dome of the sky. Through the small openings of the
woven lattice, the bright sunlight fell in long diamonds
across the marble floor. Above the shutters, an arching
arabesque of pure blue sky was clearly visible. The summer's breeze carried the bouquet of late-blooming flowers
and a vague promise of autumn. Beyond the window the
garden was strangely quiet. Only the intruding purling of a
lone peacock broke the peace.

André Duval stepped into the hallway. It was a moment

before he lifted his face. He looked all of his thirty-six years this morning—tired, drawn, and with an inestimable sadness in his soft brown eyes.

"It is not good, Simone," he said, going to her and taking her hand, "It is his heart. There have been warnings, but he seemed so well, so happy of late. I took him at his word that he was experiencing no problems. Perhaps I should have been more insistent and . . ." his voice broke.

"Oh, André, please, no guilt. Jalal would not have it so. But André, he must live; Jalal cannot be lost to us."

André could not answer Simone's pleas. His throat had tightened, and he could only look at the distraught young woman, a sad, almost vacant stare clouding his handsome face.

Marie came forward and placed her arm about Simone's trembling shoulders, gently hugging her.

His sister's strong presence seemed to restore André somewhat. Recovering himself, he said simply, "Jalal wishes to see you, Simone. Go to him."

"And me?" the voice had an edge of fear in it. Yamna stepped to face André. She was still clothed in the black *yasmak*, the queer attire hideously appropriate to the occasion.

André looked at her face. The lustrous skin seemed pasty now, and the dark eyes were glazed, somehow wild, out of control. He did not speak, but turned to Simone, his hollow silence answering Yamna more clearly than any words he might have said.

Simone entered the room; her small, bare feet padded silently across the cold floor. She pulled the folds of her flowing caftan more closely around her nude body. As she knelt beside the divan where Jalal lay, the deep blue of the thick fabric made a cascading pool about her. She brushed aside the heavy waves of her loose hair as she bent over the unmoving form. Oh God, she thought.

Jalal lay on the large couch, his head propped up, his body sunk deeply into the soft cushions. He was dressed in a magnificent brocaded robe which lay open to the waist. He appeared to be sleeping. A chalky pallor underlay his bronze skin, but his cheeks were flushed in a mockery of health. His lips were slightly parted, and his breath came in rasps which punctuated the slow rising and falling of his chest.

With a tentative hand she stroked the warm, moist brow.
He turned at her light touch, opening his eyes. He smiled
and kissed her palm.

"Oh, Jalal . . ." she could not finish, her words trapped
by the tears which had sprung to her eyes.

With great effort, Jalal reached out his hand to brush
away her sadness with his long delicate fingers. Those
wonderful hands, she thought, as she felt his gentle touch
upon her wet cheeks. Scant hours ago he had played upon
her body as the master musician plies his most beloved
instrument, sounding its every note, bringing forth the
sweetest music of which it is capable.

"Do not cry, my beloved, my life." Jalal spoke softly, his
voice weak and thin. "I cannot bear to see the salty waters
of pain flow across your beautiful face. I cannot allow
sorrow to rain from your bright eyes. You must not weep for
me, my Simone. For me, my precious one, you must always
smile, you must always laugh. The thought that I could do
anything that would bring you suffering hurts me beyond
understanding. No, my little one, even if I must die, you
must smile for Jalal. Smile."

Simone searched his handsome face; as her full lips slowly
spread into a gentle smile, Jalal touched the corners of her
mouth, and whispered, *"Très bien*, ma petite, *très bien.* I
am content. I praise Allah that he has made the last part of
my life the best. Be grateful for the precious time we have
had together. You are brave, my heart, braver than you
know. And I shall see that you and the boy are safe and well
provided for." He struggled to reach a parchment that lay
on a table near his couch. Simone, seeing his intention, took
up the document. "Read it when I am gone," Jalal said
simply. "André will explain." Then with a quiet urgency, "I
would see my son once more."

Simone kissed him lovingly on the wide smooth brow and
went quickly to the door. Esma waited with the others in
the passageway. The child lay in her arms, sucking quietly
on a small knob of marzipan. Without speaking, Simone
gathered the baby to her breast and returned to the bedside.
She crept onto the divan and nestled next to Jalal, placing
the softly cooing infant between them. Tenderly, he stroked
the lavish coils of her hair which lay upon his broad chest,
whispering to her softly in Arabic, as his fingers moved
through the soft waves. "I love you, Jalal," she murmured.

Suddenly, the gentle motion ceased. Simone looked up fearfully. His eyes were closed. The baby began to wail.

"But I don't understand why you must leave, Simone, Jalal has left you everything," said André.

"Don't you realize that all that was here for me is gone?" she answered almost without emotion.

"But where will you go?" interjected Marie.

"I shall return to New Orleans where it all began."

The words seemed to hang heavy in the air. *New Orleans, where it all began.* How long ago, how many memories past? Rudolph, Jalal, her son—the sired of Rudolph, whom she had borne to Jalal, the son who uniquely belonged to both men. And now, the uncertainty of the future. She felt numb, disoriented. It was as if some malevolent spirit sought to destroy her each time the thin thread of stability was woven into the yet muted and blurred tapestry of her life.

Oh Jalal, my sweetness, my . . . husband. Yes, he had been a husband to her, even without the spoken vows. He had completed her as no man ever had. Why, Jalal? Why are you gone?

Even as she thought of him the image of another was unconsciously resurrected—Rudolph! And what had Rudolph been to her? No, she would not answer this. She would return to New Orleans . . . home . . . the convent. She would build a new life for herself and her young son . . . her Rudolph.

"Simone," Marie said gently, touching her arm to draw her back. "We will miss you terribly. It is too much to lose Jalal, and now you also. You have a home with us for as long as you wish. And there is Rudolph, he is too young to make such a long voyage. Say you will stay, Simone."

"Dear friend, I shall miss you and André more than you could possibly know. But I must go. It is too painful for me here, and winter approaches. I must leave as soon as I can get passage," Simone said with finality.

Simone looked about the room. The European clothes, which she had obtained with Marie's help, and the baby's things lay deftly folded in the large trunk. Only a few objects remained to be carefully tucked away for the long voyage to New Orleans. The perfect pearl, the canary diamond, the charming *karagoz* puppet, and one beautiful embroidered caftan were all she would have to remind her of the happiest period of her life, the short span of months when she had found peace.

She could still hear Tanya's words and feel the cold hand on her shoulder, rousing her from dreamless sleep, "Come quickly, the master is ill!" Simple words which had sundered her tranquil world, and left her at the bottom of a dark chasm amidst the rubble of her hopes and dreams, the erratic past and uncertain future like twin precipices far above.

Rudolph awoke and began to cry. She lifted him from Jalal's cradle and unbuttoned her basque. Immediately he found the ripe nipple and began to suckle, making happy little sounds. How she envied him his uncomplicated existence. How she longed for a haven, someone to assume the burdens of her life. The baby opened his eyes. It always came as a shock. Those eyes—they were not the uncertain milky blue of an infant, but the clear blue-gray of his father's. Rudolph's eyes. Rudolph, oh Rudolph . . . No! He was dead to her. Lost to her with a greater finality than Jalal, whose spirit infused her, strengthened her for what lay ahead. He had said she was brave, and she must believe him, the wisest man she had ever known, and the kindest.

She must go on. She would take a little of the inheritance Jalal had left her, enough to see her through to her new life in New Orleans. She would devote herself to her son. She must see that Jalal's son had a place in this world.

Rudolph slept again, his golden head pressed close upon her breast, one tiny thumb between the pouting lips. She lay him in the crib and returned to her packing. She walked to the vanity, retrieving the slim leather volume and the small oval form wrapped securely in the silken scarf. Deliberately, she placed them in the trunk next to the equestrian puppet, and closed the lid firmly.

The woman stood at the window, gazing into the garden. Was it only hours before that she had walked by his side, felt the warmth of him, heard his strong voice ring through the gentle night, and then . . . She turned abruptly from the peaceful view. By Allah, she could not accept this, would not believe any of it—his cruel words, his denial of their love, his hatred. Oh, how that look in those dark eyes tore at her, and now his death. Oh my sweet, Jalal. No, I believe none of it, none of it.

As she stood in the center of her room, the bitter sorrow gradually transformed itself into a blind, ugly rage. "The heathen," she spat. "The black bitch and her vile bastard! No, none of this would have happened, had she not come to this house." As she continued to speak, her voice lowered, becoming almost guttural. "Die, thou unholy whore, but suffer first, suffer! And may the boy who suckles the poison from your venomous paps—die!" Her body shook with her terrible anger, and her eyes reddened in the white mask of her contorted face.

After a time she turned to the garment which lay ceremoniously upon her bed. The *hamman* wrap from Damascus. Jalal's gift. It was so beautiful, with the shimmering gold and silver threads shot through the lustrous black silk. How wonderful it felt to the touch. She dropped the *yasmak* to the floor. Slowly, artfully, she began to rub the gilded smoothness of the wrap over her nude body, pulling it against her rigid nipples, around her soft shoulders, across the smooth skin of her face, and between the growing warmth of her thighs. She closed her eyes. As she gave herself to this narcissistic orgy, she whispered and made deep throaty sounds. Once or twice a fragment of Arabic filtered through her breathy mutterings. She tensed suddenly; the black cloud of the caftan fell to the floor like some great wounded bird.

When the sweet rigidity eased from her body, she stooped and reached for the robe. Carefully, she placed it upon her body and knelt upon the prayer rug.

"Allahu Akbar. La ilaha illa Allah; *Muhammad rasul Aklah . . ."*

Simone sat in the small cabin, Rudolph cradled in her arms. In a few moments the ship would sail. She tried to keep her mind a comfortable blank. She had asked Marie and André not to come, but they had insisted. In the end, she was glad to have André's masculine presence to see that everything was placed safely on board, and Marie's loving voice to tell her that they would write each other, and someday visit.

She peered out of the porthole. It was another gorgeous day, her last in Constantinople. "Good-bye, Jalal," she whispered. "Good-bye, husband of my heart."

BOOK IV

*St. Petersburg
—Moscow*

*"My dwelling is the shadow of the Night,
Why doth thy magic torture me with light? . . ."*

*"It is an awful chaos—Light and Darkness—
And mind and dust—and passions and
    pure thoughts
Mixed and contending without end or order,— . . ."*

George Gordon, Lord Byron

~ Chapter 1 ~

It was the year of Our Lord 1872. Josephine Bonneville Semolenski sat before the roaring fire of Dimitri Balenkov's manor. This was the coldest January she could remember. Her body of seventy-three years could no longer endure the severity of Russian winters. She would have returned to France long ago, but for her grandson.

She had not seen him since that terrible confrontation on Christmas Eve, but had spoken to Mimka on several occasions. He was in St. Petersburg. Rumors of Dimitri's and Rudolph's estrangement were rife in the drawing rooms of Moscow, and it was speculated that his sojourn in St. Petersburg was due to his loss of favor in his uncle's eyes. His scandalous conduct in the capital only fanned more furiously the flames of gossip. Only she knew the real motivation behind Rudolph's mad flight to Petersburg.

Although her grandson, she knew, was deeply hurt by the loss of his inheritance, the object of his wild hegira from Moscow was Simone Montpellier. In that sense Josephine's scheme had succeeded. She had known he would go west to the capital, thinking that she planned to hide the girl in the city until the spring, when passage across the North Atlantic would again be possible.

Yet, she could not avoid a pang of guilt over the way she had tricked him by sending Simone south such a great distance, to traverse the more temperate Mediterranean. But she knew that her feelings of remorse and her grandson's temporary anguish would have been a small price to pay for what she had hoped would be his ultimate salvation. How could she have known that Dimitri had already discovered the illicit liaison? But no matter, the relationship with this woman was impossible for a Balenkov prince. And too, with the girl out of Russia, might not Dimitri yet soften? But still, something in his attitude disturbed her deeply. Had her grandson violated the family code of honor more perversely than she knew? She could only wonder, for Dimitri would not speak of what had passed between himself and his nephew. If only Dimitri would confide in her. She had never seen him look so old, so worn and haggard. He had worshipped Rudolph Balenkov and considered him a son. To have had to disinherit the boy was perhaps the deepest pain that the old man had endured in his long life. It was not that he cared so little for Pavel, she knew, it was rather that he had loved and respected Rudolph so much.

She had acted to save Rudolph and would do so again, though the consequences of her actions had been grave indeed. She crossed herself as she thought of the two lives that had been lost in the execution of her plan. When Boris had not returned, she had made inquiries. She had discovered, to her horror, that both he and Marya had died in the blizzard which had come up that night. For a time, she feared that Simone, too, had perished, but further investigation had revealed that the girl had been rescued by the peasants of a nearby village. She was informed that Simone had lain ill for a time, but had at last been driven to Orel. Beyond this she could discover nothing. The passenger list of the ship that had sailed from Odessa had disclosed no one by the name of Simone Montpellier; Josephine assumed that the girl might be traveling under another name. She had considered writing to the Ursuline convent in New Orleans, which she knew to be the girl's ultimate destination, but thought better of it. She had done what she had to, and now it was best that the matter remain closed.

As she gazed down at the slim crucifix of her rosary, she prayed that in time her grandson might forgive her, and come to realize that her actions were solely for his benefit.

Rudolph coughed as he poured a glass of vodka from the tall carafe at his table. He had been ill, and it showed in the thinness of his face, and the dark circles beneath the steel gray eyes. There was a hardness about the mouth and in the set of his jaw. A kind of desperation, no, vengeance,

burned in the hollows of his eyes. He was unkempt, his
well-tailored clothes hanging loose and wrinkled on the tall
gaunt frame; his beard had been allowed to grow untended.
Although he was leaner now, and the angles of his tall body
had become sharper, he was still a handsome man. That this
was so, was attested to by the fact that the tavern wench had
not taken her eyes from him since his entrance some hours
before.

He reached for the flask again, and refilled the small
tumbler. The clear liquor burned his throat as he swilled
down a full glass. He rocked back in the straight chair, his
booted leg sprawled before him, balancing the length of his
lean body. As he surveyed his surroundings, a humorless
smile crossed his unshaven face. The floor was damp and
reeked of spilled *kvass*. Several empty tables and chairs
littered the far corner of the room, while a few others were
occupied by men who had little purpose in life beyond their
cups. It was strange, but he had gotten used to the foul
smells and the icy dampness. He had even accustomed
himself to the coarse, unsociable company he now kept.

He allowed the chair to fall forward, and rested his arms
upon the table. Absently, he raked his fingers through the
dull gold waves of his long hair. "More vodka," he called.
The girl brought another carafe immediately. Her hair was
dark, almost black in the dim light. He hadn't noticed it
before, but it tumbled forward in loose waves obscuring her
face as she placed the container on the table.

"Anything else, sir?" She was smiling, a knowing woman's smile.

"No."

She left him, but turned to cast a provocative look over
one bare shoulder.

He refilled his glass, this time sloshing the contents
around before emptying it. He set the tumbler down with an
impotent thud. Spreading his hands upon the rough surface
of the table, he began to examine them with a certain
detachment. It was as if they were not his own—the
bronzed skin pulled across the long fingers, the thick veins
showing beneath the fine hairs. He looked then at his
palms; fine lines marbled the planes. He wondered absently
if a gypsy could foretell the future in the markings of a
man's hands. He laughed, a dry sound. A gypsy? And
where was the gypsy now? How many times had he asked

himself that question? Perhaps that was the answer—she had used her sorcery and had simply disappeared. Yes, disappeared. At least that was as good an explanation as any.

He had gone out very early that Christmas morning; he had ridden up and down every passable road between Moscow and Petersburg. No one could positively identify a sleigh carrying two women of Simone's and Marya's descriptions. This could, of course, have been attributable to the heavy Christmas Eve traffic. He had returned to his estate late Christmas morning half convinced that she had not yet set out for St. Petersburg, but was hidden somewhere on his estate. He had saddled a fresh horse and donned warmer clothing, but had refused Mimka's pleas that he stop to eat. The peasants in the several villages through which he rode could be of no help. How he had cursed his grandmother and Marya and . . . Simone. Most of all Simone. The ungrateful bitch. She had fooled him, they all had.

He dropped his gaze to his glass. She must be in St. Petersburg, she must. It was ridiculous, of course, to suppose that he would catch sight of her in the crowds that thronged the thoroughfares. But he looked, he always looked. He searched through every sector of the vast capital in his aimless wanderings to and from the small apartment he had rented. Yet the wanton had eluded him. But she would have to reveal herself soon. The spring thaw would mean the opening of the port, and he would intercept her as she boarded a ship, and . . . His eyes turned almost white as he thought of how he would surprise her. Of how much pleasure he would receive in foiling Josephine's little plan and after . . . It was strange, but there was a burning, a tightening in his groin as he thought of how he'd punish the gypsy whore.

His bottle was empty again, but this time his black thoughts had diverted him momentarily from his drinking. But she had noticed, and slowly the young woman sauntered to his table, and placed a flask of vodka in front of him. Her hand lingered but a moment about the thin neck of the bottle, her tiny fingers dropping, and gliding playfully across the table. He grabbed her wrist then, and the unexpected pressure of his large hand encircling her arm caused her to whimper. He looked up at her, the gloom

playing tricks upon his eyes. She was raven-haired, her long
thick tresses coiling wildly about her tawny face. The eyes
were dark and seemed to capture whatever feeble glow
there was in the room. Her breasts were full and ample,
waiting for a man's mouth. And when she suddenly
laughed, her red lips opening wide, he pulled her down to
him and whispered, "Gypsy, gypsy whore . . ."

He stood in a corner of the small room while she slowly
undressed, her eyes never leaving his face except to follow
his strong hands to the buttons of his breeches. Rudolph did
not remove his clothes, but as she stood at last naked before
him, he sprang at her, knocking her to the bed. He fell atop
her, pinning her cruelly down, his nails digging into the
tendons of her wrists, his knees pressing into her fleshy
thighs, his full weight driving her deep into the soiled
cushions.

She lay under him, struggling seductively, using each
move, each thrust to tease his already inflamed body. She
twisted to free herself, but only managed to cause her large
breasts to brush intimately against his warm chest. She
laughed, the vulgar sound filling the small, dark room.
"Hurt me," she hissed, "hurt me."

He looked into the dancing eyes, their fire taunting him to
do that for which she openly yearned, to push him beyond
the limits of his passion, to force him to fuse pain and
pleasure into one. He bent his head to the mocking face, his
rapid breathing seeming to increase her excitement. He
opened his mouth and raked his long tongue across her
face. It traveled impatiently over the small nose, lapping at
the eyelids, around the curves of her ears. No inch of flesh
within his reach was not touched, scorched, by the thrusting
snake that was his tongue. He traced his mouth down her
throat and found her large breast. He encircled one dusky
nipple with his cunning teeth, biting the soft flesh till tiny
red droplets blossomed about the rounded peak. She
moaned, her back arching upward, offering the sacrifice for
more of his sensual punishment.

He opened his mouth wider then, and it seemed as if he
would devour her, taking in as much as he could of the wet
rising mound. He lifted his head and sat, still straddling her
slim waist. Roughly he spread her legs and lifted them to his
broad shoulders. His hand sought the moist recesses, hid-

den beneath the soft swell of hair. He fingered her intimately until she begged, "More, more."

Deliberately, he pulled her bottom up to meet his engorged shaft. He entered her savagely, and worked her hips again and again to meet the urgency of his manhood, again and again . . . again . . .

He screamed, throwing her body from him, his face wet with perspiration, his body straining. He stood clutching at the back of a small chair with both hands. His head dropped forward, a tiny muscle in his cheek twitched nervously, and the veins in his neck stood distended with his coursing blood. He had not been able to . . . Damn her soul, damn her black gypsy soul.

When the summons came, Rudolph looked at himself in the bespeckled vanity mirror. He certainly did not look like one whom the tsar would call upon. Was this Prince Rudolph Balenkov? He rang for hot water to shave the now full beard. As he gazed at his reflection, his mind drifted to the long months he had spent in St. Petersburg. The months in which he had seen the melting of the frozen snow, and with it, his hopes of finding Simone. No, he had not found her; he had not been successful in preventing her from slipping away aboard a ship for New Orleans. How had she managed to trick him again? He and his hirelings had been so diligent in watching the port. But they had failed—all of them.

When he was finally dressed, he looked more like the old Prince Balenkov. As he left to keep his appointment with the tsar, he hoped that this royal imperative would not long delay his search. The late spring weather was now perfect for sailing the Atlantic. But in a matter of months the port would again be impregnable. He could not wait; Simone must be found. He would not rest until he had settled with her.

~ *Chapter 2* ~

He sat across from his daughter. Her silence had a way of intimidating him more than her frequent caustic remarks. His voice seemed somehow false as he spoke. "Have you yet heard from Rudolph?" gently probed Ivan Durenchev.

Her cold stare answered him, the icy blue of her eyes momentarily freezing his further efforts at conversation. Yet he felt it his parental duty to span the perilous chasm which she had so conveniently erected between them. It would be a small endeavor, but he would at least try to help his daughter in what seemed a most volatile situation.

He thought of the man who had provoked these present difficulties. Rudolph Balenkov was at least as perplexing as Ilse Durenchev. Why couldn't his daughter have selected some simpleminded noble of moderate fortune to be his son-in-law? Did it have to be the most complex, unsociable man in all of Russia? Hang his title anyway.

For some reason he knew the bond between Ilse and her prince had not been one of love, not even one of passion. As much as he loved his daughter, he knew her aloof and unapproachable manner did not invite affection. And the idea of the young Balenkov and his Ilse together in the marriage bed . . . He erased the thought.

Surely she had heard the numerous rumors that were running rampant in Moscow and St. Petersburg. How Rudolph had been severed from the prestigious Balenkov *yarlyk*. And how his crude conduct seemed only his way of antagonizing old Dimitri; it was his coarse vengeance against his uncle. Yet he knew that such a game was not at

all like Rudolph. He scoffed at the opinions of others. And
Ivan had to admit that Rudolph Balenkov was the most
unpretentious man he had ever known.

And what of his daughter? He knew Ilse. Rudolph
Balenkov with title and estates was far more attractive than
a Rudolph without them. Perhaps the matter had already
been settled. His lack of communication certainly attested
to that possibility. He sought to draw her out further on the
subject. "Though young Balenkov is reported to be discredited with his uncle, he is still a favorite with the Romanovs.
I hear he is engaged in a most important mission for our
tsar. Perhaps it is this commission which has prevented him
from seeing us."

"I doubt very seriously if our tsar is keeping Rudolph that
occupied, dear Father. But you can be assured, I will not
tolerate this much longer."

They lapsed once again into silence. Ivan concentrated on
the food before him. He realized his daughter was not going
to confide her feelings on the matter. It was pointless to
discuss it further.

Ilse cut viciously into her cake, and pushed the morsel
about on the fine china plate. She was more disconcerted by
Rudolph's inattention than she was willing to reveal. How
dare he treat her in this manner! A direct confrontation
would be greatly preferable to this utter indifference, she
decided. Oh, it was so humiliating to have to rely on
Moscow gossips for any news of him. It was as if the
understanding between her and Rudolph had never existed.
Did Rudolph no longer consider them betrothed? This was
the first time she had allowed the thought to fully develop in
her mind, and it was intolerable. Was she to permit
Rudolph and his inheritance to escape her?

But what of this rift with Dimitri? It was stupid. What
could have gone wrong? Had it something to do with the
French woman? She thought of her visit to his estate, and
the open book of poetry she had found in his study. *Love*
poetry. She had not been able to deny the facts then or
now. He was not the man she had thought him. He was a
weak fool.

Never one to readily abandon a carefully conceived
course of action, Ilse was realistic enough to explore
alternatives. As she sipped desultorily at her coffee, she

reviewed a party she had attended just last week. Pavel, as always, had been the darling of the salon. But she had noticed a subtle difference, a new aura about him. It was something in those uncanny eyes of his, at once more feral and more compelling. For the first time, she herself had experienced that magnetism which drew others to him. She had discounted it then, though it had disturbed her. But now her mind returned to it. Many times had it been commented that perhaps she had selected the wrong cousin to wed. Indeed, was Pavel Gregorovich the better choice? It was certainly worthy of consideration.

From across the table her father read the cold smile upon her face, and shuddered.

~ Chapter 3 ~

Why had he come? It was always the same. The same stale mixture of mindless gossip and effete philosophy. Once it had been amusing to manipulate these fools, to maneuver them like so many empty-headed puppets, to insult them so cleverly that they praised the witty turn of phrase and begged for more. But the game had palled long ago; there was no pleasure in it, only boredom, an unspeakable ennui.

"Try some of the *piraski*, Pavel," trilled Tatiana in her high birdlike voice. "They are your favorite, rice and mushrooms. I had our Masha make them especially for you." He forced himself to look at her, smiling into her vapid face as he took one of the crusty pies.

"You are so quiet today, Pavel," complained Paul.

"Come, amuse the ladies. Tell them that delightful anecdote about Countess Arapov's awkward little Katya's desire
to become a ballerina."

Why had he come here? he asked himself again as he
absently massaged the length of his right arm. Why give in
to Tatiana's suggestion that they picnic on his estate? And
then why come *here*? He gazed at the rapidly flowing water.
The stream was turgid, swollen now as it had been nineteen
years before.

"Later, Paul," he answered finally. "Mother is expecting
us at the house for tea. Take the carriage. Genghis is in need
of a workout," he continued, indicating the gray grazing
nearby. "I will pace him awhile, and join you shortly."

The dark man watched as the open coach disappeared
into the distance. Deftly, he massaged the throbbing muscles of his lower arm in a circular motion. For the fourth
time on this lazy afternoon, Pavel had consciously ignored
the quick sharp knifing that had shot from his shoulder to
his palm. Suddenly the intensity of the spasm brought his
brain to full focus. He winced as he gripped the wrist and
squeezed. Clenching his teeth, he stared in disbelief at the
paralytic limb. The cold naked stab caused his head to reel
backward, and his eyes shut tightly against the agony.
Slowly the tears ran in great drops from the outer corners of
the golden eyes. The convulsion had lasted but a moment,
as it had that very first time so many years ago. Had he been
four, five . . . ? He couldn't remember. But the pain, the
sweet pain. This, his mind had recorded accurately, precisely. Every nerve had imprinted the poignant sensation upon
the fabric of his memory, to cherish, to hold closely to him,
to bind him to the other. He looked down at the arm as the
ache subsided. Oh Rudolph, was it so long ago that you fell,
and *I* screamed, my cousin? Screamed as I felt the anguish
of that broken bone in my own accursed limb. How was it so
that your pain became as mine, even across the honeyed
fields that divided us?

Other scenes came back to haunt him. A game of hide
and seek with the Belhunin children. He and Rudolph
always *knew* where the other was secreted. Accused of
cheating, they'd made a silent pact not to find each other
after that.

And that other time . . . How old had they been then?
Six, perhaps. It had been the summer before Uncle Nikolai

had gone to the Crimea. He remembered a childish argument over some technicality in their war game. Rudolph had gone off to the fields, while he, Pavel, had run angrily down to the forbidden stream. He gazed into the tumid water before him. He saw it all again. The sun sparkling in the raging current as it tumbled over and against the dark protruding rocks, the daring game, his light agile feet dancing over the slippery stones, his sudden miscalculation . . .

He would have drowned had Rudolph not *known* of his plight, and come in time to pull him from the water, almost unconscious, the blood streaming from the place where his head had struck rock. They had been closer that day than at any other time. But shortly after, Uncle Nikolai had been killed in the war, and the visits stopped. Aunt Katerina never left her estate, and his mother refused to visit her sister-in-law while she remained "in that demented condition."

It was not until they attended the university that they saw each other with any regularity. But they could no longer be close. Outwardly friendly, they avoided contact, as if some subtle magnetism had reversed polarity, pushing them apart, making any intimacy impossible. But that mysterious link, that had been manifest in the early years of childhood, was not a thing easily obliterated. It lurked beneath the surface of their separate lives, defying exorcism.

I'm not like him, thought Pavel. He is a fool. A blind idealistic fool. His kind will bring ruin on *Mat Russkaya*.

Yet in their love of the Russian land, he admitted, they were one. Even his own mother, in her perversity, could not deny that Rudolph Balenkov cleaved to the great bosom of the earth-mother with as great a passion as did her own son.

In Pavel it was a purely metaphysical union, but in Rudolph it translated itself readily into the working of the soil with his own hands, bending with serfs among the furrows of the fields. Thus, while Pavel's *affaire de coeur* with the fecund land bore the markings of Platonic intellectualization, Rudolph's was intensely carnal.

And more . . . Pavel saw Rudolph as weak, corrupted by the eighteenth century Age of Reason, and by the vulgar bourgeois mentality of the nineteenth. His cousin worshipped at the altar of equality, and made individual freedom a god. Rudolph Balenkov, the gauche libertarian, would dilute the Balenkov strain, that heritage which had thrived in the ferocity of its Slavic breeding. That noble ancestry understood that their kind could survive only at the expense of others, others who were in truth, inferior. Always, there was the ruthless protection of the integrity of the land above all else. And he, Pavel, was the unvarnished Varangian. Not the one whose blood had been tainted with the effete European philosophy, encrusted with the impotent Gallic veneer. Not the one who saw serfs as worthy parts of the great system, holding inherent claims to that which was the natural fruit of their enterprise. No, their labor did not infuse proprietorship upon the soil. Cattle cannot own. Cattle *are* owned. How stupid of his cousin not to see this. Did not his greater perception of the realities of the grand scheme of things make him the natural bearer of the *yarlyk*?

As with the force of his thoughts, Pavel walked steadily downstream, his heavy boots leaving their deep imprint in the soft earth near the bank. Some distance from the rapids was a small inlet, a quiet pool formed by the great gnarled roots of an ancient oak. Here he stopped, attracted by the cool serenity of the tree-shaded pond. Adroitly, he moved down the mossy incline to the water's edge, kneeling to bathe his hot face in the refreshing pool. The interplay of light on the gentle ebbing and flowing in the shallow basin distorted his reflection. The bright sunlight made a burnished surface of his dark hair while the yellow eyes lay in shadow, tinted with the water's silvery hue. *Rudolph's face*!

"No!" he screamed, as his fist came down, smashing the heresy of the mirror. "No!" But the gesture was futile, the image reforming even as he lifted his hand to strike again, and again . . .

He clutched at his wrist. The glass, falling from his rigid hand, splintered into a hundred wicked slivers upon the damp floorboards. The excruciating wrack of pain had pierced his arm but a fleeting moment, and now Rudolph rubbed what was only a dull gnawing sensation in the limb.

~ Chapter 4 ~

It was spring of the year 1873. Rudolph tossed his uniform jacket upon the bed. He would not be needing it now. What answer might he have given Alexander had he known that a year would pass in the execution of his commission? He looked at his luggage, which stood near the door of the elegant room in his quarters in the Imperial Palace. Though his obsession with Simone had lain dormant these many months, it was now easily resurrected. He was once again his own man, and personal pursuits could be resumed.

He had returned only briefly to his estate, to insure that all was well. Mikhail Yesenin was a capable manager, and Rudolph appreciated the man's loyalty as well as his tremendous abilities. And Rudolph thought of Mikhail's nephew, Yuri. It would seem strange to travel without the boy this time. But the prince recognized that Yuri Yesenin was becoming a man now. He had long ago understood the boy's sensitivity and keen intellect. Aptitude such as his should not be wasted. When he had handed the young man those funds which would enable him to attend the university, Rudolph could barely look at Mimka, so intense was the gratefulness which shone on the old woman's face. She'd had tears in her eyes as she thanked him for his kindness. If there was nothing else in the whole of his life of which to be proud, Rudolph Balenkov would be proud of Yuri, and the role he had played in his development.

A knock sounded on the door. It was a servant announcing the arrival of his carriage. This time nothing would stop him; he would be on the open sea well before winter closed the port. How different it would feel to cross the ocean as a mere passenger, and not as the ship's captain.

The manservant carried out the luggage, glancing back once at the room's occupant, as he prepared to leave. Prince Balenkov always looked so grim and determined, but today there was something more intense in his manner. The prince's reputation as a man of honor was well known, yet somehow Karl was glad that on this day he had done nothing to provoke the tsar's royal guest.

The door of Dimitri Balenkov's study opened. A high ranking ecclesiastic stepped into the hall, turning back as he did so to have a final word with his host and good friend.

"I am sorry, my dear Dimitri, to have brought such an ugly tale to you. Little did I suspect when I ordered an investigation of this unfortunate incident, that it would lead me to your door. You know that I will do all in my power to keep this quiet, but I must warn you that this story is known to many of the peasants of the district. You can, I am sure, imagine how difficult it is to handle these uneducated, superstitious people. They are so like children. You understand there is no legal proof, but the peasant's story is unshakable.

"Seek me if I can be of further assistance," he said, as he embraced the old man. "Please do not bother to see me out; I know my way well."

With that, the bishop closed the door behind him, leaving the other man to his thoughts. As he proceeded down the long marble corridor, he thought about this whole sordid mess. Ironic how these mystics often did such damage. *St. Sophia* they called her, the peasants both male and female who sought her intercession on their behalf. If her parish priest had handled the situation better, had not been blinded by his own petty ambitions, and jealous of her influence over his parishioners, he might have salvaged the situation before it became a serious matter. But, the bishop supposed, even the best of prelates could not have long suppressed speculation on the outrageous circumstances of the girl's death. It was the fabric of legend: the bloody trail through the snow, the corpse lying prostrate before the altar when the priest came in for Mass, the aborted pregnancy. And the pressure from the peasants—they would not endure the violation of their *saint*.

The Virgin spare us from peasants who know too much and have dreams of angels who command they reveal the truth! The single witness had apparently lived with the knowledge of the grisly crime for well over a year, before his conscience overcame his fear of the authorities.

The bishop was truly sorry for Dimitri. First the mysterious estrangement from Prince Rudolph Balenkov, and now this repugnant affair with the other nephew. He feared for the old man's health. Alas, neither of them were young anymore, he sighed, as his carriage began the journey back to the patriarch's residence.

Dimitri stared unseeing out of the window which overlooked the formal gardens of his estate, but the beauty of the scene was lost upon him. He was weary and sick to his very soul. He tortured himself with questions which had no answers.

How could Pavel have been so stupid? Why pick such a one to satiate his lust? Why had fate placed the peasant at the scene to witness his nephew's crime? Pavel's manner with his serfs could hardly have inspired loyalty; now they had turned on him with a vengeance. Why, why, why? Horrified, he realized what he was thinking? My God, Pavel was a murderer! Did he really want this crime excused? Was such a beast fit to bear the *yarlyk*? With even crueler comprehension, he realized how little he knew his nephew. How could he have erred twice? But was not Rudolph's the lesser sin? He did not look forward to the impending confrontation with Pavel. But it was inevitable.

The black clouds hung in the sky, threatening to spit their fury as the cloaked figure urged his gray steed forward. He surmised that the ominous weather meant that he would spend the night at his uncle's palace. He smiled to himself, thinking that it was only fitting that he should become accustomed to the elegant residence. After all, it would soon be his. He was sure that his uncle had decided in his favor. It would be official; he would be Dimitri's heir. Why else would he be so urgently summoned by the old man?

As he rode on at a brisk pace, Pavel thought how he would relish seeing the expression on his mother's face when he told her of his imminent good fortune. And how he would savor the look on Rudolph's countenance. Of course, his stoic cousin would never reveal his true feelings. Indeed, grinned Pavel, he will probably congratulate me. How typical of Rudolph. So noble, so honorable. Believing himself the proper bearer of the *yarlyk*, yet resigned to my investiture. And what of his French tart? Even he had to admit that she was an enchanting creature. But to fall in love with such a piece! To jeopardize one's inheritance!

He knew his stupid cousin searched in vain for her in Petersburg, his spies had told him that. But who had helped her to escape? He had been unable to ferret out that secret. But, no matter. He, Pavel, had won. Dimitri had taken the bait, and the trap had sprung. It was all so easy, so clean. His timing had been perfect. No sooner had he and his mother returned from the Crimea, than Dimitri's message had arrived.

Pavel knocked crisply on the study door, but his uncle's expected invitation to enter was not forthcoming. Puzzled by the silence, Pavel turned the knob; as the door yielded, he walked in.

Dimitri sat behind his huge desk, looking up as his nephew entered. Undaunted by his uncle's lack of greeting, Pavel proceeded toward him. As he approached, Dimitri rose to meet him.

"Dear Uncle, you are looking well. Mother sends her greetings. We have both sorely missed your company these last few months."

The impact of his uncle's hand on his cheek totally shocked him. But this physical blow proved far less violent in effect than his uncle's words that followed. "I curse the day you were born. I curse the womb that bore you. Better it was that my brother died in his prime than to see that he had sired a wretched murderer."

Pavel stood unmoving, numb, incredulous. This was a mad dream. This was not how he had played the scene over and over in his mind. The dialogue was twisted, the plot perverted. Something had gone hideously wrong.

"Were not the whores of Moscow to your liking? Did you have to select one of your own peasants, and a demented girl at that, in which to spill your seed? Are you insane? What kind of monster deflowers a religious fanatic, then kills her and the child of his flesh in her belly? It makes me sick to think of that wretched creature crawling through the snow, trailing her life's blood to mark your despicable brutality for all to see.

"Never do I expect to see you again. Mark that you do not cross my path! The bishop is doing what he can to protect the Balenkov name. Pray, if you can, that the full knowledge of this affair dies with me."

As his uncle spoke, Pavel began to assimilate the full import of Dimitri's words. How had it come to this? He had dismissed the sordid incident long ago as trivial. Why had the bishop become involved in a peasant's death? Who could have seen him? Her cottage was so isolated, and he had always taken care that he came unobserved. Rapidly, he began to calculate how his position with his uncle might be salvaged. Surely there could be no concrete proof. The old man was malleable. Plant a seed of doubt . . .

"My dear Uncle, you are too upset. I fear for your health. I am deeply hurt that you would give credence to this preposterous tale. You must know that it cannot be true. But you are too overwrought to discuss it further now. In time, you will realize that I have been gravely maligned. Until then, however, I will abide by your wishes." With that, Pavel turned and strode confidently from the room.

Even after his nephew had moved out of his sight, Dimitri remained staring. Pavel's response had not been what he had expected. Could the boy be innocent after all? What real evidence was there? The word of a peasant? But no, his friend, the bishop, had been so sure. And there was something else. It was something he had never before articulated. Something indefinable in Pavel that all along made him favor Rudolph. He knew deep within himself that the story was, indeed, the truth.

The lightning flashed and the booming thunder drowned out all but his thoughts. The heavens pelted horse and rider with a merciless barrage of water. The man's black curls were pasted in thick ringlets about his face, his clothes plastered firmly against his hard body. He crouched low against his stallion; they melded as one against this elemental assault. This desperate ride acted as a release for the rider's raging emotions. Finally, he allowed the horse to slow to a more reasonable gait. His mind, too, stopped its wild racing and began to come to grips with all that had transpired. He realized that he had suffered a most serious setback, but refused to believe that he had forever forfeited his birthright. He must come up with a new plan, a permanent solution. He hated his cousin. How he hated him!

BOOK V

New Orleans

*"All lost—that softness died not—
    but it slept;
And o'er its slumber rose that strength
    which said,
'With nothing left to love, there's
    naught to dread!' . . . . . ."*

George Gordon, Lord Byron

~ Chapter 1 ~

"Jeremiah, can't you go any faster?" urged the young woman, raising her soft, ladylike voice in an attempt to be heard above the din of the streets.

"I'se doin' the bes' I can, Missy Y'vet," came the answer. "Yo knows dere's an ord'nance bout goin' too fas' in de streets. Ol' Jeremiah don' aim to have no trouble wif no Yankee soljers."

Yvette peered about nervously. The banquettes were infested with unsavory characters of all descriptions, bands of shiftless Negroes wandering aimlessly about, more often drunk as not; ill-bred Yankees, like vultures come to pick over the carcass of the South; poor whites looking for work in the city; and, that most scurrilous of all creatures, the turncoat Southerner, the scalawag.

Father and Etienne are right, she thought despondently. These outings are dangerous. Things are growing worse. Ironic that Reconstruction should be far more terrible for Louisiana than the war itself. The depredations of the Radical Republicans, who controlled the political machinery of the state, had become so odious that good citizens were convinced that there were no alternatives to open violence.

As the carriage passed a group of scruffy white youths, they began a ditty calculated to annoy a trio of filibustering politicians who stood nearby.

The other day in a swampy bog,
A serpent hit William Pitt Kellogg.

Who was poisoned, do you say?
The snake; it died that very day.

Yvette's mind shifted then to Simone. How different the young woman was, so changed, not at all the gay, ebullient girl she had remembered. A sedate, almost maudlin maturity seemed to replace the girlish sparkle. What had happened in the almost two years since she had been away, to have wrought such a reversal in her personality? And where had she been? Simone had given no clue, and Yvette dared not press her. She knew that her friend would confide in her when and if she felt the need. Besides, she had been so happy when Mother Angele had called her. And then to see Simone, dear Simone. Quite simply, nothing of the past mattered now. Simone was safe, alive.

And had they not all changed? Certainly, they could not be unaltered, unaffected by the tragedy of the past few years. Poor Maurice, killed in that stupid duel over cards. Mamma had never quite recovered; though Papa had often found fault in Maurice, he had been, after all, his only son and heir. And then there was the death of Grand-mère in the terrible yellow fever epidemic. She remembered how Simone had cried when she told her. The tears had run down her solemn face, and she knew the depth of feeling that Simone had had for her grand-mère. Yes, these last years had been very difficult ones in New Orleans.

The girl looked about the bare cell. Little had changed over the years. The aged and scarred floorboards, the stucco walls—were they ever really white? She moved to the crack above her cot, and tracing her finger over its jagged path, she noted that the fissure had traveled but slightly in the five years since her departure from the Ursuline convent.

Aimee Tabory, they had called her. Simone could still see the young girl with the incredibly large eyes, sitting with her arms wrapped around her legs in the bed next to hers. They would talk into the late hours of the night about nothing and about everything: about life and love, as only twelve-year-old girls could. *Life and love*? Simone laughed dryly, Oh, Aimee, *ma petite*, where are you now? How could we have been so foolish?

She stared blankly at the crib; its emptiness mirrored her

own. Every time she thought that life had done its worst, some new catastrophe came down upon her, as if to illustrate the folly of her thinking. The one thing in all her life that had been truly her own, was now lost to her. The yellow fever that had left her gaunt and weak had been too much for her little Rudolph. He had fought the disease with all the strength his tiny body could muster, but in the end, he had succumbed. She remembered how gentle Mother Superior had been when she told her of her son's death. She wished then that she could have returned to the delirium of her own illness, where reality did not have to be faced. Mother Angele had recounted how they had baptised the child, and buried him in the small convent graveyard. She remembered her first day out of bed. She had gone to the tiny grave, and placed a bouquet of flowers, fresh from the convent gardens, upon the small mound. She had thought of Jalal, buried so far away. Now, at least, he had the boy with him. She was the one left behind.

As her physical strength improved, she joined in the convent routine. Rising at daybreak, attending Mass, partaking of a light breakfast, she would leave early from the morning meal to place flowers upon the grave before going to her assigned tasks in the vegetable garden. She worked there until the noon Angelus. Then there was lunch and an afternoon of sewing in the room. Before the evening activities, she would often help Sister Terese with the washing and ironing of the altar cloths. Her day concluded with the evening meal in the community dining hall, prayers, and then sleep. She lived the life of a nun; no choices, no decisions, no idle time. Weeks passed and her routine never varied. Simone assumed that her life was to be one endless cycle of simple, unselfish acts—with the only commitment to God.

~ *Chapter 2* ~

It had been late winter when last he stood before the small residence. Now more than two years later, it was summer, and the tall man felt keenly the intense heat of the sultry New Orleans afternoon. The appearance of the house had not altered, he noted, as he strode up the steps, his eyes taking in the oddity of the black crucifix which hung above the heavy cypress door.

The door swept open before his clenched fist could sound upon the wood. The tall black youth had not changed with the intervening years; the colorful cotton headcloth which he wore was the same that the visitor remembered from that earlier time. Some of the scalp remained exposed and gave evidence that the head had been shaven. He wondered idly whether this was for ceremonial purposes, or as a mere concession to the heat. But it was not the rather benign appearance of the Negro that unnerved the man. As he stood in dark relief against the bright undulating waves of heat coming from the street, it was his singular impression that on this late afternoon his visit was entirely expected. The boy said nothing, but continued to stare with vacant eyes as he opened the door farther inward, so that the guest could enter.

Following the sticklike form through the semidarkness of the parlor, a sudden darkness enveloped him, and a scent, pregnant with the black earth, filled his nostrils. The next room was as it had been before. It was as if this chamber, with its subtle emanations, had the power to warp the perceptions of all who entered, and mold them to its own dark will. The focal point of this primitive energy was the woman who sat behind the heavily draped table.

"*Bienvenu*, Monsieur Balenkov," she spoke, her words only intensifying Rudolph's intuition that he had been expected, and more perversely, that his purpose there was known to her. Her next utterance confirmed this. "Why do you seek the girl here? Why do you come to me with the same questions?"

Rudolph could not answer her. Why had he come? He had supposed there was, after all, some connection between this woman and Simone. But on what he had based this, he could not remember. His light gray eyes closed slightly, as if to refocus his mind. He stared at the vision before him, her skin honeyed beneath the soft light of the tapers, and stretched in sharp angles across the fine bones. From under the heavy lids, her black eyes drank in every motion, every articulation of his lean body.

She knew. But how? Rudolph allowed the last remnant of reason to be finally sucked into the swirling eddy of her world, into her dimension. To offer rebuttal, to play devil's advocate, to be the knave in her compelling game—it was useless.

"So, Prince Balenkov," she intoned at last, "it is not enough that Madame Ninon foretold your destiny, now you desire that I also walk the dark, unseen paths with you. But that I cannot do. Yet I would cast the light of one candle upon the way.

"The gaslights of the Rue Royal still rape the darkness of the falling night. Seek not the shadows of other courts. Sup a third time, where twice you dined before. Tonight you will taste of the truth."

Rudolph stood in the circle of lamplight before the gate of wrought iron, his hand hesitating over the bell cord. The courtyard beyond was aglow with soft moonlight, and a gentle breeze stirred the growing things within. Might not the gypsy step from the shadows and beckon him forth? Damn her! He cursed the thrill of pleasure which this mental picture evoked, this vision born of memory and desire.

With a deliberate motion, he yanked the bell pull, and was rewarded by the heavy clanging which dispelled the image. There would be no need of explanations, he assured himself. Had not the Durands extended their hospitality of his last visit? It mattered not, he must be here. It was his destiny, he reflected wryly.

Presently, his summons was answered by a houseservant, who showed him inside. The Durands, who had just seated themselves at the table, were surprised and delighted with their guest, and insisted on his joining them. Rudolph politely accepted, as Armand called for another table setting. Seated to his host's left, he was introduced to Yvette's fiancé, Etienne Renaud, and with little preamble, was drawn into their conversation.

"Before you graced us with your presence, Prince Balenkov, Etienne and I were discussing the volatile political straits in which our poor city is so embroiled. I am afraid that the situation has deteriorated greatly since your last visit. In truth, la Nouvelle Orleans, the Queen of the Great River, the South's richest pearl, has lured the lowest of humanity to reap the spoils of victory. The war was but a prelude to this travesty which they call Reconstruction.

"Reconstruction," scoffed Armand, "It should more aptly be labeled *destruction*. Union soldiers insulting our women, vindictive radicals making a mockery of the law, carpetbaggers and scalawags like eaters of carrion feeding greedily on the misery of our people. And the poor illiterate Negroes, they have become the unwitting dupes of the lot, goaded into the most vile acts, and invested with political power which they are ill-equipped to handle. All of them have sinned, and the measure of those black deeds has reached outrageous proportions."

"Please, Armand," sighed Cecile, from across the table. "Perhaps the prince is not interested in our local problems."

"Nonsense, Cecile. I am sorry for all this man's talk at dinner, but these are extraordinary times." He continued speaking at length on the factional rivalries of the day and the measures that the White Leagues throughout the state were taking to reverse the disastrous policies that had driven Louisiana to the brink of chaos and anarchy.

Yvette, who had heard it all a thousand times before, closed her mind to his excited ramblings, and instead, concentrated on their royal visitor. She blushed as she

thought of what a fool she had made of herself that first
time. But she had been a child then. She looked at Etienne
beside her. Perhaps he did lack the virile sensuality of a
Rudolph Balenkov, but her Etienne was kind and gentle,
and he offered her what she wanted most—stability. Her
father's voice, raised in emotion, brought her back.

". . . race riots in Colfax, Coushatta, and in our own city.
It is civil war all over again."

She thought of how the last two years had changed her
father. He had become so intense, so involved—almost
fanatical. He had lost much of the joie de vivre of his Creole
heritage. She wondered if ever again he would be just her
own dear Papa.

Her mother, who could see that the three men would
go on in this vein for some time, leaned over and asked
her daughter, "Did you visit Simone today at the convent?"

Rudolph, who had only feigned interest in his host's
tirade, overheard Cecile's remark. His fingers gripped his
wineglass convulsively, almost snapping the slender stem.
His face had frozen into a rigid mask, except for a small
muscle that jumped in his smooth cheek. He scarcely
breathed that he might not miss Yvette's answer.

"Yes, I did Mamma. I am so glad she is with the
Ursulines, but I do worry for her. She looks so worn and
thin, so unhappy."

"And still she has given you no hint as to where she has
been for so long, or what happened that night she disappeared from our home?"

"No, Mamma, and I am afraid we shall never know."

~ *Chapter 3* ~

In no other endeavor was the rivalry between the American and Creole segments of New Orleans society more artistically manifested than in the construction of two of the most magnificent buildings ever erected.

The St. Charles Hotel opened its doors on Washington's birthday in 1837. The Gallier-inspired structure was to become the visible and lasting testimony to the good taste and refinement of the *American* Orleanians. Thereby, they forever banished their plebeian image, which the French had so inelegantly bestowed upon them. The St. Louis Hotel followed a year later becoming the *Creole* counterpart of the *American* edifice, its beauty attesting, the French believed, to their more patrician sensibilities. Although the St. Louis rapidly took its place as the center of the city's social life, the larger and more centrally located St. Charles would outlast its *Creole* rival by a century.

Upon its completion, the St. Charles was hailed as one of the architectural wonders of the New World. The New York politician, Oakey Hall, was quoted as saying: "Set the St. Charles down in St. Petersburg, and you would think it a palace; in Boston, and ten to one you would christen it a college; in London, and it would remind you of an exchange. In New Orleans, it is all three."

Fourteen Corinthian columns gave the facade the classic appearance of a Greco-Roman temple. Its glistening alabaster dome, crowned with an open turret, dominated the urban landscape. The enormous ballroom, the scene of many an elegant soirée, was reached by an imposing double flight of stairs. Even the draperies which graced the windows of the great parlors were unequaled anywhere.

He cursed as he nicked himself for the second time. The eyes that stared back at him from the shaving mirror were darkly unreadable. He wiped the last of the stinging lather from his jaw and walked to the open armoire. "This damnable climate!" he muttered, as he ran his fingers over the heavy garments which hung there. It was unreasonable to expect a man to wear civilized attire in this heat. Impatiently, he knotted the ascot tie about his throat and reached for the dark gray coat.

As Rudolph exited from the crowded lobby of the hotel a young *métis* boy, liveried in black silks, held open the door for the preoccupied guest. He stepped into one of the waiting hacks, and instructed the driver to the Rue Dauphine, and the convent of the Ursulines. As the carriage pulled away from the expansive St. Charles Hotel, Rudolph's mind was drawn back momentarily to a comment that Armand Durand had made last evening.

". . . and our beautiful St. Louis, like so much of our Creole life, has also succumbed to the vulgarities of the age. It is now the new state capital, a den of thieves and barbarians. Gone is the romance from our souls, I'm afraid Prince Balenkov. *N'est-ce pas?*"

Rudolph smiled as he recalled that morning when he had visited his dear friend, Alexis, in his suite at the St. Louis. Is it possible that it was only two years ago?

A neat Negro maid answered his knock. Giving his name, he requested that he might speak with the mother superior. The young girl bowed politely, leading him through a dimly lit corridor and into a cool drawing room. He sat stiffly in the high-backed chair, alone with his questions. Would this be the end of his quest? Was Simone here? What would he do if she would refuse to see him?

Mother Superior waited curiously for her unexpected visitor. She reflected on the name he had given Cassie —Rudolph Balenkov. What was it about that name which pulled at her memory? She rose as he entered, indicating that he sit in the chair before her desk. "Welcome, Monsieur Balenkov, I am Mother Angele Camile. How may I help you?"

"Thank you for seeing me, Mother Angele. It is my hope that you *will* be able to assist me. Do you have a young woman living here by the name of Simone Montpellier?"

As soon as he had spoken the words, Mother Angele realized why his name had seemed familiar. Was this the father of Simone's child?

"Yes, Simone is with us. Do you wish to see her?"

"That was my hope in coming here, Mother Angele."

"Very well, I will send her to you."

The young girl reached down and wrapped the hem of her skirt around the handles of the buckets which stood one on each side of her. It was awkward, but afforded some protection to her tender palms. The brimming pails seemed too heavy for her fragile form as she carried the containers methodically to the end of the row of thirsty young tomato plants. No sooner had she set them down, than Cassie scurried up to her.

"You has a visitor, Missy Simone. He sho' is fine lookin'," she said playfully.

Simone disregarded the girl's words. Cassie was well-known for her teasing manner. She wondered why Yvette had come back so soon. She had not been good company on the preceding day. This time, she promised herself, for her friend's sake, if not her own, she would try to be more companionable. As Cassie led her to the parlor door, Simone stopped abruptly. So it wasn't Yvette. They always visited in the flower garden. Hastily, she passed her handkerchief across her brow, and untying her dirt-smudged apron, handed it to the servant girl.

He stood at the window, looking out into the courtyard. She could not see his face, but she did not have to. She would recognize that tall form anywhere. She stood in the doorway, unable to move.

He turned absently. So quietly had she opened the door, that he had been unaware of her presence. He did not move, nor speak; her altered appearance had rendered him immobile. Yvette Durand was right—so thin, so sad . . . yet still beautiful. "Bonjour, Simone," he murmured as he walked toward her.

At his approach, Simone at last stirred. She backed away slightly, a hunted look appearing in her dark eyes. He saw it, and stopped a few paces in front of her. "Do I frighten you so, Simone? There was a time when you welcomed my touch." He watched as the wildness in her eyes slowly diminished, and a remnant of the old Simone appeared. "And in fact, my little gypsy, you burned for it."

The old spirit momentarily rekindled, she raised her hand as if to strike his face. He caught her wrist in midair and pulled her to him. "This is what I've missed," he laughed, "and that is why I'm taking you back with me."

"You are an egotistical fool, Rudolph Balenkov. I didn't come willingly the first time, and I won't now."

"And so I must kidnap you again, it seems," he said, his wide mouth curving into a smile as he held her tightly.

"I hate you!" The words were almost a sob.

He released her then, and stepped back, a puzzled frown marring his handsome features, his dark blue eyes graying as he analyzed the angry creature before him. Who was this haunted woman who confronted him? He had tasted her fury before, but this was something deeper. What had happened to her since they had parted? Whatever it was, it had devastated her. It went beyond the old antagonisms. "Simone," he whispered. "I . . ."

She looked up at him for a moment, the tears streaming from her eyes. And then she ran.

Mother Angele sat behind the polished desk, unable to concentrate on the ledger before her. Her thoughts went unbidden to the couple in the parlor. Her romantic soul had taken wing, and her imagination fancied a tender scene between the two young people. But then her practical mind asserted itself. There were so many unanswered questions surrounding Simone's mysterious disappearance, and now her return. What exactly had her life been in the intervening years? What role had this man played in it? Obviously, it was an integral one. She checked herself; this speculation was futile.

She rose, knowing that the bell for the Angelus would soon toll. Just as she opened her door, Simone flew blindly past, the sound of her passage echoing in the vacant hall. Instinctively, the nun looked back toward the parlor. He stood in the doorway, staring blankly, even after the hollow sounds of her footfalls had died. She watched as he turned and moved toward the front doors. Cassie awaited him at the portal; the heavy oaken door swung closed behind him.

* * *

The door of Simone's tiny room slowly opened inward. There having been no response to her light knock, Mother Superior stepped into the semidarkness of the small room. When Simone had not appeared at the evening meal, Mother Angele had become concerned. "Simone," she addressed the figure huddled on the cot. "Are you awake, my child?"

At the sound of the nun's gentle voice, Simone sat up. "Yes, Mother," she said softly.

"Are you feeling well? We missed you at the evening meal, and you were not at prayers. Is there something I can do for you?"

The sensitive tones of Mother Superior's voice broke down the girl's reserve. "Oh, Mother Angele, what am I to do? Why did he have to come back into my life?"

The nun sat beside her now, and held her gently as the pitiful sobs shook her thin frame. "I thought I would never see him again."

"Simone, who is this man?"

"He is someone I once cared for. We were together for a time in his country . . ." Facing the kind sister, Simone hesitated, then spoke the words deliberately. "Mother, he is the father of my child."

"It is all right, child. Cry if you must," she said, stroking the girl's long hair. After a time, the nun spoke again. "Simone, there is one who always hears us in our time of need. Come, let us pray to the Virgin. She will intercede for you." She drew the girl down to kneel on the hard floor beside her.

> *Remember O Most Blessed Virgin Mary,*
> *That never was it known,*
> *That anyone who fled to thy protection,*
> *Or sought thy intercession was left unaided . . .*

~ *Chapter 4* ~

August 5, 1727 was an important date in the history of the city of New Orleans. The Ursulines, the Gray Sisters, as they were known in their native France, arrived at five o'clock in the morning. They had come at the request of Jean Baptiste Le Moyne Sieur de Bienville, commandant of the struggling colony. He understood that if anyone could bring peace where there was disorder, hope where there was despair, light where there was darkness, it was the good Ursulines.

Their five-month voyage from Europe to the New World had been riddled with hardships from its beginning. Tempests, seasickness, pirates—none of these could deter the small band of nine nuns, two postulants, and one novice from their avowed mission.

Their remarkable achievements attest to the fact that John Baptiste Le Moyne had not erred in his judgment. Over the years, they established the first educational institute for girls, the first orphanage, the first free school, and the first retreat for ladies. They organized the first classes for Negro and Indian girls; they worked in the military hospital as medical aides. Over the years they sheltered and cared for the homeless and destitute.

The persecuted and the afflicted, the orphaned and the neglected, officials and citizens, all turned to the Ursulines as a haven of safety, peace, protection, and solace in whatever difficulty arose.

They gave a much-needed religious atmosphere, and a sense of dignity and respect to womanhood. In the stemming of the tide of debauchery, irreligion, depravity, and laxity in the home, in inculcating the principles of true Christian womanhood, the labors of the Ursulines will never be fully evaluated or realized.

Marie-Madelaine Hachard, a member of the original group of Gray Sisters who came that hot August morning, left an interesting and lively account of those early days. In writing to her father, perhaps she has best characterized the devotion with which the Ursulines met the challenge of the New World. She wrote: ". . . not one of us has ever repented of the sacrifice which she made of herself to God . . ."

"Prince Balenkov, I am sorry, but she will not see you," replied Mother Angele Camile, her tone sympathetic, but firm.

"I see."

"Come, take a walk with me in the garden. Everyone is resting at this time, and we can talk a little."

As they walked along the flower-bordered walks of the small garden, Mother Superior reflected on the beauty of the summer blossoms. Finally, the nun stopped, and bending, selected a particularly beautiful flower. As she brought the fragrant bloom to her nose, she spoke directly, but her eyes avoided her companion. "Are you aware that Simone Montpellier is not her real name?" Turning to face him, she realized from his expression that Simone's past was unknown to him. "She came to us as an infant," she continued, "one of the few survivors of a tragic fire on a passenger vessel which arrived from France. We must assume that her parents were among the casualties. Beyond this we know nothing." They began walking again, the man concentrating on the sister's words as she resumed her tale.

"Simone developed into a complex and intelligent child, completely aware of the limitations that her lack of identity imposed. Yet this realization could not subdue a natural vivacity; her charming personality compensated in many ways for her anonymity. When she turned fourteen, we lost her to the Durands, a prominent and well-respected Creole family. We were sorry to see her go, but we knew that she must make a life for herself; as companion to Madame Felice Durand, she became an important part of the family. We were distressed when we learned of her sudden disappearance two years ago. And though she has returned to us, the circumstances of her going remain a mystery."

They turned then, proceeding in a different direction, which led to a small grove of trees. As they moved into the cool shade of the intertwining branches, Rudolph noted several rows of plain white markers. The interplay of green and white was curiously soothing. At the far end, the symmetry was broken. The marker here was a cherub, whose base was encircled with freshly picked blossoms. It was there that Mother Angele hesitated, observing her companion as he glanced idly down at the anomalous stone and read the inscription.

> *Rudolph Jalal Montpellier*
> *Born: June 15, 1873*
> *Died: December 23, 1873*

He knelt on one knee, his fingers lightly tracing the graven letters. After a time, he turned and looked over his shoulder to where Mother Superior stood.

"Yes, Monsieur Balenkov, your son."

Rudolph lay stretched out upon the large hotel bed. His bronze body was propped up, dark against the cream satin pillows. The early morning sounds filtered into the open window, and still he had not slept.

Why had she not told him she was with child? Had she known? Where had she spent the months between Russia and New Orleans? And with whom? The nun could give no clue. Why did she avoid speaking of the child now? Was not the death of his son something which he should have known? And the strange middle name . . . ?

He rose, desperate for some physical activity to still his restless mind. He stood at the window, staring out at the city below. New Orleans was stirring from her brief slumber, the night's adventures blending almost imperceptibly into the daily routines of living. The dawn's pallid light touched the hard planes of his angular body; even the haggard face was softened in the mellow glow. Yet his mind could not be so easily diverted. Although there would be no immediate answers to these complex questions, there was one course of action Rudolph knew he *must* pursue. This decision had come to him, however, without the full realization that it was, in truth, what he *wanted* to do. He would propose marriage to Simone.

She had said she hated him. He now understood how this could be so. Had he not been an "egotistical fool"? How could he have been so reckless with her life, and not foreseen what his insensitivity would bring? She would not suffer again because of him. He moved from the side of the window to plant his palms upon the sill. Leaning forward, he gazed intently at the city's sharpening silhouette. He thought of the once living boy who now lay cruelly stilled beneath the cherub's mocking smile. What had he looked like? Had his eyes been blue, or had they sparkled with Simone's dark fire? Simone's child. My child. *Ours* . . .

Though his eyes remained focused on the wakening city, his vision slowly blurred.

"Simone, you must see him. He is so insistent, and I feel that he means you no harm. No matter what has happened in the past between you, you must not let it entirely color your judgment now. At least give him a chance."

"But you don't understand, Mother. Don't you see that the past does control the present? To see him again would only complicate things more."

"Simone, I refuse to allow you to hide behind these convent walls." The nun's firm voice was now laced with a hint of anger. "It is not that you are unwelcome here, but this is no life for one such as you. Simone, you are not one of us; you must resume your life in the world, no matter how painful it may be."

The words finally registered, and the young woman sat upon the edge of her cot and stared at her small hands. "You are right, Mother Angele," she spoke quietly. "But I do not trust myself where he is concerned."

"Simone, put your trust in Our Lord. He will help you." Mother Superior said no more, but she knew that the girl had resolved to see him.

For the first time in many months, Simone had felt the lack of a mirror, and was glad that Mother Angele had been kind enough to secure one for her. But now she was afraid to look. She peered down at her hands, so rough, so red. She feared what the glass would reveal of her face and hair.

How dead to the world she had been these last few months. It was a small, dressing-table mirror, but it was large enough for Simone to see the ravages that hard work and neglect had wrought. Her face was tanned, and where the edges of her blouse had been, there were the even demarcations of the sun's effect on her light olive skin. The raven hair was dulled, and a few errant freckles dotted her nose. "Oh, I look like a field hand," she said aloud to her reflection.

As Simone walked down the corridor to the bath, she hoped that Cassie had filled the basin with vast quantities of hot water. Closing the door behind her, she smiled as she gazed into the tub—red and white boats sailed across the surface of the water. Rose petals and gardenias. That Cassie, thought Simone, had the soul of a poet.

For a time she languished in the steamy pool, completely submerged, except for her dark head. She closed her eyes and allowed the liquid's soothing effect to temporarily immobilize her. Finally, she scrubbed her skin repeatedly with the rough cloth and pumiced her feet, knees, and elbows. She washed her hair with camomile soap and the yolk of an egg, rinsing it thoroughly with clear water and the juice of a lemon. When she had finished, she toweled herself briskly, and returned to her room. Immediately, she sought the verdict of the mirror. Her skin had taken on a healthy glow, and her hair, though still damp, held a promise of its former luster. Although her appearance fell short of aristocratic, she thought, perhaps her choice of attire might go far toward remedying this. But when she was dressed in her most elegant gown, her hair piled stylishly upon her head, she was unhappy with the effect. Removing the offending garment, she threw it carelessly upon the cot, and withdrew from the small cabinet a much simpler dress.

Of *mousseline de soie*, a gauzelike muslin, the white folds contrasted agreeably with her sun-darkened skin. The gown was trimmed with a ruching of Mechlin lace at hem and neckline, the wide ruffle draping her arms in a most becoming manner. Her pearl pendant enhanced the purity of the simple costume, she noticed with satisfaction. But one final adjustment. Purposefully, she removed some of the pins from her hair, allowing the black waves to cascade loosely about her bared shoulders. Some gardenias stood in a tiny vase by her bedside. She placed a pair of the sweet-smelling blooms behind one ear. She was ready.

No thought of why she had taken such pains with her appearance entered her awareness. She must simply look her best. As she finished arranging the flowers in her hair, Cassie entered to announce the arrival of her visitor.

The door closed behind the servant girl. Immediately, Simone became nervous, agitated. She regretted her decision to see him. How she hated his power to render her insecure and vulnerable! She glanced fleetingly into the mirror, as if to reassure herself. By the time she reached the first floor she had resolved she would not fall victim to his lethal strength.

"I am no longer a child. I will not allow him to impose his will on me. He cannot force me to go with him." Over and over she repeated these things as she drew nearer the parlor, her words in cadence with her measured tread. She hesitated only slightly as she gripped the handles of the French doors and swept them inward.

Rudolph stood in the middle of the room, where he had halted upon the flowered carpet. He was impeccably groomed in a Prussian blue cutaway coat and vest and lighter blue, fitted trousers. Gold and lapis studs adorned his starched white shirt front. The only incongruous note, Simone observed, was his thick golden hair, which tumbled across his forehead as if his fingers had recently brushed through the burnished locks. But it was on the eyes that Simone's own lingered. Again, the incredible blueness threatened to engulf her, and it was with some deliberate effort that she was able to remain standing before him.

Rudolph was not sure that his eyes were not betraying him. She stood framed in the doorway—a sylphlike vision, so very different from the smudged and ragged girl of only a few days ago. But she was not an empty dream that would mock him in the lonely mornings. It was Simone, of this there could be no doubt. No one alive could match her breathless beauty. She was gypsy and she was goddess; she was lady and she was wanton. It was all of these facets coming together that made her so complete, so satisfying.

No one else could ever make him feel as vital as he now felt. His simple desire was to go to her and crush her to him, to make her his, by force if necessary. But no, that was just what he must not do. He must handle the situation delicately and not allow his more primitive instincts to interfere with his well-laid plan. He chose his words carefully.

"Thank you for consenting to see me, Simone," he said softly. "I ask only that you listen to what I have to say." His conciliatory manner surprised her. "Simone, I do not believe that this is the kind of life you would have chosen for yourself, had the circumstances of the past been different. I cannot give you parents or wipe out the years of loneliness, but there is much I can offer you . . . want to offer you. As my wife . . ."

"*As your wife!*" Simone exclaimed incredulously. "Rudolph, you know well that we can never marry; your grandmother made that quite explicit. A Russian grand duke, and the bearer of the Balenkov *yarlyk*, must wed a woman of noble birth. I am hardly that!"

"My uncle has decided in my cousin's favor, Simone. The matter of the *yarlyk* is of no consequence. Will you become my wife, Simone?"

Simone had no answer. He had effectively foiled the only argument she could muster. Pressing his advantage he moved toward her. Looking directly down into her troubled face, he whispered, "It wasn't all bad, Simone." Without waiting for her affirmation, he drew her into his arms, and kissed her deeply. Moving from her open mouth, he ran his lips over her hair, her eyes, her throat, murmuring huskily, "Say *yes*, Simone. Say *yes*."

~ *Chapter 5* ~

The jeweled necklace sparkled in her palm, the diamonds surrounding the large emeralds focusing the sun's rays into a hundred dancing lights upon the bare walls. The bright rainbows seemed incongruous against the austerity of the tiny cell and the strange mood in which she found herself.

"*For you, Simone*," he had said, handing her the velvet box. "I have wanted to give this to you for a very long time."

When she had looked up to thank him she found that she could not. The words would not come; they were trapped deep within her, stayed by what she had seen in his eyes. And that which she had glimpsed . . . had it lasted but an instant, or was it an eternity? She could only remember that she had felt numbed by the experience. And what had she seen . . . ?

The lid snapped shut, entombing the shimmering stones within the luxurious interior of the small box. The sharp sound seemed to punctuate the incredible finality and import of her decision. She was to wed Rudolph Nikolaivich Balenkov. Involuntarily, she shuddered. The chill, the horrible chill—she thought it had left her body long ago. From some unknown icy cavern, it seemed to resurrect itself.

What is wrong with me? She chastised herself. Is this not what I wanted all along? To marry him; to be with him forever? Had I not long ago decided that I could accept Rudolph on his terms, knowing full well that to have him

338

would mean to have only a part of him, to relinquish any claim on his heart, to love him without being loved?

But why had he proposed marriage? She had no answer to this. It was like so much between them, words unspoken, intentions unrealized, promised unfulfilled . . . The baby . . . should she tell him of her beautiful, lost Rudolph . . . their son? No, she could not. There was too much pain. It was threatening somehow; it seemed to her a betrayal of Jalal.

Jalal, she had not thought of him in days, since she had seen Rudolph on that first morning. My dearest, it was you, only you, who made me feel that I was worthy of love. And now, am I to give your precious gift to another, to one who cannot ever return it? Can I give to him that which, in truth, you still might hold the greater part?

Jalal, oh Jalal. If you were alive, I would be safe, protected, loved. I and the child. *Rudolph's child*, a small voice reminded her. Oh, how had her life become so complicated?

But her decision was made, wasn't it? She would be his wife. They would live in Russia. She would see Mimka again and Yuri. But what of the others—Josephine, his Uncle Dimitri, Pavel—would his family accept her?

What had happened to cost him the loss of the *yarlyk*? Was it because her presence had been discovered? Had Josephine's plan failed utterly? If this was the case, how could she ever be one of them?

And Rudolph, how did he feel about this dire reversal? He had informed her almost casually about his disinheritance. But he cared, she knew, cared passionately for his land, his birthright. Above all else, she knew Rudolph to be a proud man. Proud of his heritage, the Balenkov name, the land. She knew that this fierce pride was somehow intrinsically bound up with his need to take that to which he had a natural right. Why was he not fighting for the *yarlyk* now? She knew that he felt that no other had the greater claim to the solemn investiture than he. What had happened?

And what of Ilse? She wondered suddenly. But somehow she knew that the contemptuous Ilse would reject a disinherited Rudolph. That explained why he was free. But why marry Simone Montpellier? A hideous thought arose to harrow her. Might he not deem marriage to her a consummate jest, a fitting vengeance against his family . . . against himself? Was he capable of such a contemptible mockery?

No, oh no! I can't believe such a thing. I won't. I won't, she cried to herself, her eyes shut tightly, her fists pressed against her temples.

Why? Why did he want her then? She gazed out of the window. Already, the small gray figures were bent over the rows of vegetables. She smiled. A vision of lively mushrooms sprouting, teased her fevered mind. Yes, there was a more basic, more primitive explanation, and one with which she could live, endure, even without his love. He wanted her as he had wanted all else, simply because she was his. His, because he believed that he did hold some perverse kind of claim upon her. From the beginning, she had always fought against this bondage, and she had always lost. But now she had accepted herself as Simone Montpellier. Jalal and Marie had led her to this. Yet she was now willing to accept Rudolph's claim upon her. She would fight him no more. Why? she closed her eyes. He had clothed that possession of her in a passion that caused her body and will to bend, her mind and soul to transcend all reality. Yes, she would accept his untamed desire, his unholy lust. True, it was not love, but it was so warm, so sweet . . .

She stopped. Her breathing had quickened, and she felt suddenly flushed. He had taken her then, just as surely as he had taken her that first time on his boat, in his dacha, before the fire at his lodge. But despite the beauty of their coupling, the void which this passion could fill, no matter what would happen between them, there would always be the hurt, the pain. It would always flow between them, an endless river separating them, dividing them. Each would sing to the other from within the reeds of the distant banks. But the truth of their songs would become hopelessly engulfed by the roaring music of the relentless coursing water.

~ *Chapter 6* ~

Her life had changed. Though she still rose early for Mass each morning and placed her offering of flowers upon the tiny grave, she worked no longer in the garden. Every afternoon he called for her. She looked forward to his visits. They seemed to have accepted each other with an easy grace. They smiled at each other often. Simone found herself laughing at the most improbable things. They strolled the avenue and shopped the Vieux Carré, danced and dined—one endless stream of mindless activity. Yet there seemed to be a hollow ring in the laughter, and the smiles came too often. It was only when the silence invaded the space of their days, did they dare look one at the other and know.

It was as if they had agreed to this charade, their secret souls well hidden behind the glossy black of the harlequin masks and the garish silks of their costumes. They had both accepted their roles; they never missed a cue or misread a single line of dialogue. There was no upstaging and no betrayal of character. It was the consummate human drama —*a masquerade of love*.

As Simone completed her toilette, a light knock sounded on her door, and Mother Angele entered.

"How lovely you look, child. That lush color suits you," said the nun approvingly, her alert eyes probing the girl's face.

"Thank you, Mother," returned Simone placidly. "I

hope that the lateness of my return from the opera will not be an inconvenience."

"There is no problem. Cassie is only too glad to wait up for you." Then she added, "Simone, all is well? You are content?"

"I am fine, Mother Angele," the girl assured her. "But I shall be leaving here very soon, and I do not know how I shall ever thank you for all your kindnesses to me."

"I shall be well repaid, my child, by your happiness. But I sense that you have not yet found peace. Are you sure about this marriage?"

"Yes, Mother, it is what I desire."

Cassie came into the room then, and announced Rudolph's arrival. The sister noted the heightening color in Simone's cheeks and the unnatural brilliance of her eyes. She smiled and kissed the girl's flushed face. "Do not keep your prince waiting," she murmured.

Simone retrieved her lorgnette, and placing it in a small reticule, floated from the room with a smile and a wave of her gloved hand. Mother Angele watched her go. Why were love and pain so often intertwined?

New Orleans was a city of music, and its finest expression was the French Opera House. The "lyric temple of the South" was built in 1859 by James Gallier, son of the famed architect of the St. Charles Hotel. Of plastered brick in the Italian mode, the elegant structure stood four stories high and could seat two thousand comfortably. The elegant foyer, bedecked with huge mirrors and glittering chandeliers, was reached by a wide double staircase. Patrons could alight from their carriages and pass directly into the theater from a colonnaded main entrance which reached to the street.

The interior was a fantasy in white, red, and gold. The seats ranged from plush upholstered armchairs on the first floor, to plain benches in the fourth floor balcony, called the *poulailler*, or peanut gallery. But so cleverly was the theater designed, that every patron had a clear view of the stage, on which appeared some of the finest operatic productions of all time.

New Orleanians, and in particular the French Creoles, considered the opera one of life's necessities; the city had been the first in America with a resident company. Interna-

tionally renowned singers often came for one or more
seasons. As one of the finest opera houses in the world, the
French Opera House stood as a monument to the Creole
dominance over the cultural and social life of the city.

They rode in silence for a time. The hollow clopping of
the horses blended with the wistful night voices of cicada
and katydid. The night was alight with stars, and a brilliant
moon poured her light upon the earth. She could see him
clearly, urbanely handsome in the dark evening suit, a
romantic figure from her girlish fantasies. It was all so
perfect, a fairy tale . . .

When Rudolph spoke his voice sounded vaguely strained.
"You're quiet this evening, Simone."

A gentle breeze fanned her face as the open carriage
wound its way toward the levee. "I was just thinking about
the young girl in the opera. She was so sad, so lonely. Why
is it, Rudolph, that life is so unequal in the dispensing of its
favors?"

He cupped her chin, and pulling her face upward, stared
into her eyes. "Do you think that life has been so unkind to
you, Simone?"

Abruptly, she turned so as not to look directly into those
penetrating, searching blue eyes. "No, Rudolph, for if I
measure the days of my life, and drown those separate
moments, submerge those pieces of time which hold the
real pain, then I would say that my life has not been
unhappy."

"*Has not been unhappy?*" he repeated her words. "Simone, that is far different from, *my life has been happy.*"

She did not answer him, but toyed with the tiny beads
which decorated the front of her small evening bag. "Simone," he spoke her name as no other, and she closed her
eyes against the sound as if to capture forever that sweet
utterance within her head. Her lids were still shut when she
felt his warm mouth close over hers. She opened her lips,
and felt herself sinking slowly into the sweet heady languor
of blossoming passion. She returned his kiss, all her desperate longing and quiet despair bound within that silent
communication. He seemed to sense something of her
need. He intensified his embrace, crushing her to him, as if
he would take her inside himself, that at last there might be
nothing to divide them. But she knew only the increase of

her hunger, and the frustration of her desire. It was words she needed, the simple words which were not in him to give. The moment passed.

Then his mouth found her ear beneath the heavy locks of hair. She shivered as she felt the soft tongue circling the delicate curves, and finally enter the small opening. A warm rush of breath, and then he whispered something softly, which caused Simone to pull away quickly and feign embarrassment. He laughed aloud, and drew her to him. She knew by the pressure of his fingers upon her arms and his accelerated breathing, that he had tired of their coy parlor games. She could hardly breathe as he bruised her lips with his mouth, his tongue, his teeth. She could feel the measured pumping of his heart against her. For a moment she had the horrible thought that he would die, so wild was the beating within his chest. No. Rudolph could not die, not like Jalal. Instinctively her arms tightened about his neck, drawing his hard body closer to hers. He had not failed to notice what he read as her mounting passion, and quickly he sought to possess one of her captured breasts. Suddenly, the hand moved from the rigid peak, and pulled one of her arms from around his neck. Holding her wrist tightly, he pressed her open palm against him. She could feel his hardness as it lay imprisoned beneath the tight cloth of his trousers. Her fingers closed over him, and as his arms once again encircled her, his voice came. Simone was shocked; there was so much pain, so much sorrow in it.

"Please, Simone, do not deny me. Please do not punish me for my sins, ma petite. Please, Simone, please."

Yvette had not questioned Simone when the young woman had told her of the engagement to Prince Rudolph Balenkov. Even now, Yvette could remember her friend's voice, so quiet, so even. It was almost as though she were making some idle comment about the sultriness of the New Orleans summer. She had looked into Simone's face, hoping that she would find there some hidden emotion that the calm delivery of her speech had refused to betray. But there was nothing. Yvette had felt stifled by Simone's unnatural manner, and the dry paucity of her words. "We are to be married here in a quiet ceremony, and then travel to Rudolph's home in Moscow." It was so final—a beginning and an ending, but all the pieces in between had somehow gotten lost or misplaced. Though she had not spoken, and only stared at Simone during her incredible announcement, Yvette's expression had desperately searched for the answers to the thousands of questions which raced through her mind. And when Simone finally looked at her, Yvette knew that her friend could read the unveiled confusion and worry in her face.

"I know, Yvette," she spoke softly, "it is all so strange to you. Perhaps it is yet a bit strange to me also. Please believe that I would tell you all that you wish, if I could. But I cannot, dear friend, cannot. Maybe someday . . . For now, you must be understanding, patient. Accept what I say, and do so without question, censure, or doubt. And know, Yvette, that I am happy now. I love you, my little sister."

With these last words, Simone had embraced her, holding her close for a time. And when Yvette had closed the door, she could hear the soft, muffled sounds of Simone's weeping filling the dark lonely corridor, and feel the emptiness in her own sad heart.

They had done what she had not been able to do. The Durands accepted Simone's unexpected betrothal without any real concern or misgiving. Of course, they had been more than surprised by their daughter's unbelievable announcement of Simone Montpellier's impending marriage to Prince Rudolph Balenkov. And Yvette remembered how her parents had searched each other's faces when she told of the engagement.

"But I don't understand, Yvette," Armand Durand finally said, his startled expression still unaltered as he faced his daughter. "How does she know the prince? When was she introduced?"

"Yvette, does this have something to do with Simone's mysterious disappearance?" her mother interrupted, her eyes wide with inquiry.

"Please, Mamma, Papa. No questions. I have told you all that I know."

"It is all so . . . so . . ."

"*Strange*, Papa. Yes, and that is exactly how Simone herself characterized this sequence of events in her life. But she asked that we all accept her decision without question, and to believe that she is truly happy. And this we must do."

And this they had done. Armand and Cecile Durand quickly dismissed the mystery surrounding Simone's approaching wedding, and concentrated on the joy and pleasure that such occasions engendered. Indeed, Cecile had almost immediately begun to make arrangements for a small party to honor the engaged couple. Simone was happy, and that was all that mattered.

But was she? Yvette wondered. She could not disregard Simone's seemingly unemotional manner, the disconcerting veil of secrecy and . . . the tears. What of the tears? A young woman's sentimental gesture, or the unburdening of a troubled and confused heart? Yvette did not know. However, she did take comfort in realizing that at least her dear friend would finally have an identity, a real future. But the enigma of Simone Montpellier, the riddle of her past, were ghosts which would yet haunt Yvette Durand.

Antoine Alciatore has the honor to announce to the public that his establishment will remain open one hour after the closing of the theater, and all night the evenings of the (Carnival) Balls. One will find the same quality of food and wine at a more moderate price.

Antoine Alciatore was sixteen years old when he left his native France for America. He had become apprenticed to the owner of the Hotel de Noailles in Marseilles when very young, and was already a qualified chef when he sailed to the United States.

From New York, Antoine made his way south to New Orleans, and was soon at home in the city, where the majority of the populace spoke French. He was first employed at the prestigious St. Charles Hotel, but in April of 1840, he opened his own establishment, a small pension on the Rue St. Louis. Here he offered incomparable French cuisine, adapted to the bountiful native products and catering to the Creole palate. Thus began the tradition of Antoine's restaurant and its matchless culinary history. The venture was immediately successful, and within five years Antoine was able to send to New York for Julie Freyss, the young girl he had met on the boat from France. They were married in New Orleans, and settled down to further develop the restaurant.

In 1860 and again in 1868 the establishment moved to larger quarters. The first relocation was to 714 Rue St. Peter, the second and final move to the seven hundred block of St. Louis. This last Antoine's, which included the Alciatore residence, had a few guest rooms, but the restaurant had become the main focus, attracting not only local clientele, but gourmands from around the world.

In 1877, Antoine would discover that he was dying of tuberculosis. Only then would he leave his adopted city, and travel to his mother's home in Marseilles to die six months later at the age of fifty-two. But he would leave behind a unique heritage, and Antoine's would become the oldest restaurant in the United States continuously owned and operated by a single family.

"I sincerely hope that everything is to your satisfaction, Monsieur Durand."

"Oh, Antoine, everything is superb. The *truite meunière* was *magnifique*—the best I've ever eaten. Merci, Antoine. Merci beaucoup. You have made it a most special evening for all of us, especially our honored guests."

"Mon plaisir, Monsieur Durand. I would very much like to convey my best wishes to Prince Balenkov and Mademoiselle Montpellier."

"That would be wonderful, Antoine. Please join us at our table when it is convenient."

As Armand Durand walked back to the small party, he smiled to himself. Everything had gone well. Poor Cecile, she had fretted all week. "Mon Dieu," he had exclaimed, as he regarded his wife only yesterday, worrying over some small detail of the menu. "You would think that we are entertaining six hundred instead of six. Remember, Simone insisted that we keep it simple."

"Oh, Armand, I know, but I want this little party to be just perfect for our Simone," she had replied.

And perfect it was, reflected the host, as he gazed at Simone. Simone, little Simone. In a curious way, tonight he had thought of the young woman as his second daughter. Maybe he had felt that all along, and had not fully realized it. After all, other than the good nuns, they were the only family she had ever known. He looked at Balenkov. It was a strange turn of events. Simone and a Russian prince. But oddly enough, it seemed quite natural to Armand. Certainly Simone had blossomed into a lovely, intelligent young woman, and the two missing years had only refined her incredible beauty. Yes, it was somehow right. Simone and her handsome prince were a perfect pair. Yvette was wrong to worry, anyone could see how much in love they were. For the third time this evening, Armand Durand decided that, indeed, all was going well.

He reached for his coffee spoon and tapped lightly on his water goblet. Rising, he lifted his wineglass before him. "To Simone," Armand Durand saluted, "our little daughter. May you receive the love and happiness which you have always so graciously given."

As Simone acknowledged the toast, her dark eyes misted. Tonight, she possessed what she had yearned for most earnestly all of the years of her young life. Tonight, she was blessed with a family. Sweet Cecile—Mamma; Armand, he would give her in marriage to Rudolph, she decided; Yvette, *ma soeur, ma jolie soeur*. And she had . . . absurdly she could not complete the thought.

Still standing, Armand continued, "Simone, Mamma loved you very much; before she died, her thoughts were of you. 'Armand,' she said, 'our Simone will return. I know this to be true. And when she comes home you must tell her to be happy always.'

"Simone, please accept this as an expression of the love which Mamma held for you, and as a token of our continuing affection." He reached out, and took the young woman's hand into his own, and placed an exquisite cameo within her palm. Bending forward he lightly brushed his lips against her moist cheeks.

~ Chapter 7 ~

My dear Simone,
 I hope this letter finds you well.
 Mimka has told me that Rudolph has gone in search
of you. Should he be successful in his quest, and attempt
to bring you back to Russia, do not give in to him.
 Our plan failed once when your presence was discovered, to Rudolph's detriment. However, there are new
circumstances, and Dimitri has somewhat relented. It is
my conviction that should Rudolph return to marry
well, and produce a male heir, the yarlyk will yet be his.
 Please forgive me if I have caused you further pain,
but I know that you, too, hold Rudolph's happiness
above all else.

                    I remain,
                    Josephine Bonneville Semolenski

Mother Superior looked at the young woman as the letter
fell from her hand onto the floor. The girl sank slowly into
the chair, her body rigid, her small face a white mask staring
ahead, seeing nothing. Mother Angele reached for the
innocent-looking sheet of parchment; as she read the fine
script, she knew that the singular premonition which she
had felt earlier, upon receiving the envelope, had indeed
been insidiously accurate.

My dearest Rudya,
 You must not be angry with Mimka for revealing to
me that you are in New Orleans, as I was able to
convince her that contact with you was of the utmost
importance.

*Pavel is in disgrace with Dimitri! I have been unable
to ascertain the nature of your cousin's misdeed, but the
breach is most grievous, and will not, I think, be healed.
Dimitri will say nothing definite, but it is my firm belief
that should you return to Russia and take up your filial
obligations—marry well and produce an heir—the yarlyk, my Rudya, will be yours.*

*I am aware that you have gone in search of the girl. I
can only repeat that this is madness, now more than
ever. No good can ever come of that misbegotten
liaison. Remember your name, your heritage, your
duty. Come home, my Rudya, to your destiny.*

*Yours as always,
Grandmamma*

He walked to the bed, his weight sinking deeply into the
cushions. The letter, held loosely in his long fingers, fell
impotently to the carpet. As he lay stilled, entombed within
a vault of his own making, the pink light of dusk filtered
through the windows, glazing the high planes of his taut
face. His chest rose and fell regularly, but the sound of his
measured breathing was barely audible. Slowly, the lumi-
nous angles of the stoic visage darkened. Night had descended, and yet he had not moved.

It came, almost an intrusion, resurrecting him from his
deliberative immobility. He opened the door and accepted
the sealed envelope and small package from the courier.

*Dear Rudolph,
    This is very difficult for me, and I can only hope that
you will understand why I feel this course of action to be
necessary.*

*Rudolph, I cannot be your wife; such a marriage is
impossible. There is too much between us, and there is
not enough.*

*I am aware of the honor you would bestow upon me,
and I do not reject that honor lightly. It is only that I
cannot believe in my heart, that a loveless marriage can
bring other than regret for both of us.*

*I am truly sorry that I led you to believe that I would
be willing to accept a life together, regardless of the price*

each would have to pay, how much each would have to compromise, how much each would have to forget. But I was wrong, horribly mistaken; you must forgive my naiveté, my utter shallowness.

Please understand that what I do is best for both of us. Perhaps in time the bitterness will leave us and in its place there will be only the warm glow of our happy moments together, our golden days.

Simone

He did not open the package; he knew what he would find within. He went to the armoire; it would not take him long to pack.

.

~ *Chapter 8* ~

Rudolph Jalal Montpellier, read the name on the baptismal certificate which Mother Angele held in her hand. Such a beautiful baby, so like the father: the same eyes, hair . . . And now Simone had lost them both.

Simone . . . that poor despondent child. One could hardly bear to look at her these last few days; so wounded, so vulnerable did she seem. It was always wrong to question the Lord's will, and yet, why did He ask so much from some of His children? What did he want for Simone? Not a nun's life, surely. A vocation was one of His greatest gifts, but the religious life must be embraced consciously, lovingly, and willingly. Properly conceived, it was a special way of experiencing life, not a negation of life in the world. No, it was not to be Simone's path. Mother Angele was sure of that. She knew that the Durands had offered Simone a home with them. When Simone was ready to give this due consideration, she would advise the girl to accept their kind invitation. It was obvious that the family loved her, and could provide her with the stability that she desperately needed.

As she thought, she flipped absently through the open file before her. Ah, *bien!* Here it was, the envelope containing Simone's baptismal certificate. She would file little Rudolph's here with his mother's. But what was this? From the depths of the folder, she retrieved a small packet. As she unfolded the cracked and yellowed paper, a slim heart-shaped pendant of heavy gold fell to the desk. Written neatly upon the parchment, she read:

Found pinned on the infant's clothing—September 23, 1854
Christened Simone Montpellier—September 25, 1854

Mother Angele had not been aware of the ornament's existence; she had not been head of the Order when the orphan was brought in. She weighed the charm in her palm. It was a lovely antique piece, with a soft rich patina, and decorated with intricate scrollwork. She must give it to Simone; it was certainly time she had it. Strange how it had lain within this envelope for almost twenty years, waiting . . . waiting . . .

But she was becoming fanciful in her old age, fanciful and romantic, she chided herself. She would give Simone the pendant after prayers, but she would be tactful. The girl was in such a state, that it was difficult to predict her reaction to this token from her past, this slender golden link to her origins.

The early evening sky ran with color; soft pastels washed across the horizon. A sharp silver slice of a new moon shone vividly against the suffused hues of lavender, pink, maize. She moved to the open window and gazed out. How often had she stood in this very place, taking in this quiet view of the convent garden? It seemed that all of the days of her life could be compressed into those brief moments in time that she had spent before this small window. Had she stood here forever? Had her life been a lingering eternity of gazing through this portal? She had seen tiny birds in their wondrous aerial flight across the wide expanse of blue. She had smelled the dusty earth as it suckled hungrily at the heavy rainfall of a late summer's day. She had seen the birth of green growing things, and their yellowed death, when one could feel September in the air. She saw morning and night and all the hours in between, and still it had not changed. And she . . . ? Yes, she had changed. She had learned that to give meant only to lose, and to love meant only to be hurt. But she had saved him, hadn't she? She had saved him from herself. Was this love? Being able to surrender what you desire most for its own sake? Was this the Christian message which she had been taught so many years ago? Suppress the being in selfless acts of love? *Greater love hath no man* . . . And what does one do with the empty shell when all of the essence has been drained? Death? Isn't the death of the self really greater than physical death? Oh, Jalal, my little Rudolph, you see I, too, am dead. And who will weep for me?

The rapping sound came several times before Simone moved from the window to open the door.

"Simone." Her soft voice filled the emptiness of the cell. "May I come in? I hope I am not disturbing you. If you wish to be alone, I will understand."

"No, Mother. Please come in. I have missed your company."

"Thank you, ma petite, and I have missed seeing you these past few days. But sometimes we all need to be alone. How else can we speak to the soul? How are you feeling, Simone?"

"Feeling, Mother Angele? I don't know. Perhaps I am beyond feeling. I am so empty, so cold."

"I know, my child, I know. Sometimes it is best that we do not feel, at least in the beginning. It is a way of protecting ourselves. But Simone, do not close out the emotions for too long, lest they die."

"Oh, Mother. I feel so lost, so helpless. Forgive me, but even prayer, even turning to God, doesn't seem to help."

"Please, Simone. Do not feel that this is wrong. It is only natural. You have experienced such pain, and that pain is still so sharp, so clear that it fills your heart, your memory. But in time, Simone, in time . . ."

They sat in silence for a while, Mother Superior beside the young woman, lightly stroking her dark hair. "Simone," the nun's voice seemed unsure, tentative.

"Yes, Mother?"

"Today . . ."

"Hail Mary, full of grace, the Lord is with Thee . . ."
Her fingers pressed against the beads. It was a familiar
ritual, and her hands moved mechanically over the hard
round crystals, but her mind floated beyond the walls of the
small convent chapel. ". . . pray for us sinners, now and at
the hour of our death . . ." She had never been able to
discipline her mind to the recitation of the rosary. But
tonight, more than ever, she found it difficult to say the
Aves and to contemplate the Joyful Mysteries. Yet she
needed to pray; she wanted to find solace in the holy words.
But there was nothing, only empty syllables. Why could she
not subdue her consciousness, keep her mind a blank? Why
did the old memories keep intruding? She did not want
them; they inflicted too much pain. It would be so much
simpler to surrender herself to the words. ". . . blessed art
thou among women, and blessed is the fruit of thy
womb . . ." She fingered the last bead of the decade. What
had she become? Was even her God lost to her? Only her
mind seemed to live, aflame with bitter reverie. Her heart
had died.

And what had he said about her heart? *You will not find
peace until the heart is open. He* . . . who was he? Her
fingers stopped their markings of the beads. The Russian
holyman . . . the fair . . . Why did she now conjure up this
bizarre visage . . . those unseeing eyes and his words.
Those mysterious words, they were suspended across her
brain, stretched against her awareness. She could not sever
that binding rope of words. *Open the heart,* his message
echoed.

No, she had opened her heart, and it had brought nothing
but sadness. But *peace,* he had said, *peace would come.* Oh,
God, if only I could find peace. But there is no heart . . .
no heart . . . Unbidden, the image of the small golden
pendant come to her.

She held the tiny heart in her trembling palm. She did not
move, but only stared blankly at the golden charm. Slowly,
she picked up the slender object and examined it for the first
time. It was *hers.* She held it closer to the small lantern. A
tiny seam was visible about the edge. On a portion of one

side, the line was broken, sealed, melded. Was it perhaps . . . ?

She opened the small desk drawer and rummaged through its contents. "Something sharp . . . something sharp," she mouthed, as her fingers rejected one thing, then another. She slammed the drawer shut. Walking across the room, she knelt before her trunk. As she lifted the heavy lid, she was immediately assaulted with colorful fragments of her life in Constantinople, her life with Jalal. She closed her mind, and opened a small tapestried box. She selected the longest and sharpest of the hat pins.

She returned to the light and began her tedious task. Placing the sharp point to the pendant's edge, she slid the pin through the seam. It held. Again she used the small tool as a lever, but the sealed edges fought against her effort. She knew that she would have to risk it. Removing the lantern's frosted globe, she brought the melted edge to the flame, and held it there for a brief moment. Again she inserted the pin and again the golden heart remained closed. The blue flame licked at the soft gold, and once again the hat pin went inside the small crease. But this time, Simone felt the pendant give under the pressure. Harder, harder she pried the slim needle upward. Slowly it opened. Like a tiny golden flower, the locket bloomed before her eyes.

She held it closer to the light. On the left side was some type of engraving, a crest perhaps. But it was to the right side of the heart that Simone's eyes were drawn. She was transfixed by the tiny portrait she beheld. It was a beautifully executed miniature of a young couple. The woman appeared small; her dark hair and eyes had come to life beneath the artist's brush. The man was fairer, although Simone could not determine the color of his eyes—blue, green? But as the young woman stared at his handsome face, she thought she had seen this man before; his features were clearly familiar—the straight nose, the soft curving mouth, the slightly upturned eyes. Everything about the face haunted her.

The lambent glow of the gaslight played upon the convex surface of the golden heart as it lay upon the green baize desk top. Armand examined it once again. The workmanship was of the highest quality, the hinges totally unobtrusive, the engraving still crisp where the heat had not blurred the fine lines. He opened it. The portrait was very small, but there was no mistaking the strong resemblance between the man and Simone. And the woman, surely here was the source of the girl's exotic coloring. Could there be any doubt that he gazed upon Simone's parents?

He turned his attention to the crest emblazoned opposite the miniature. This was the clue of importance, he realized. For all the painting's value as a human statement, a dramatic personal revelation, it was not nearly so useful as this graven emblem. Surely, his solicitors in Paris would be able to divine its significance. He trusted so. He did not like to think of the effect another disappointment might have upon Simone.

His brow furrowed as he reviewed their meeting. She had come to him in his office. Beautiful as ever, but so subdued. He had been excited when she revealed the discovery of the locket, far more excited than she herself. Was it that she was afraid to hope, or that hope was no longer possible to her? No, he would not believe that, Simone was too young to know such despair. She was cautious, that was all. And he, too, must be prudent, must not give her false hopes, lest his inquiries come to nothing. But surely this would not be the case. Dominique Ferrier was most thorough. Perhaps by December he would have the results of his investigation. What a lovely Christmas present for little Simone! With his characteristic ebullience, he imagined the sparkle returning to her eyes, and a happy smile on her pretty mouth. She would again be the sweet, enchanting child that had come to them from the convent six years ago. The news would be good—he was sure of it.

The weeks passed slowly; Simone closed her mind to all thoughts of the golden locket. She promised herself that she would never again be hurt. She would steel herself against any ploy to test her emotions. She would begin anew.

It had been a sad moment when she bid Mother Angele good-bye, and they had both wept. But she knew that the dear sister had been right. She could not hide behind the convent walls; she could not symbolically don the gray habit of the nun. She would have to move from behind the sheltering grille. She must now live within the naked open spaces of the secular world.

At first, she had been frightened when she walked

through the heavy black gates into the quiet patio. The courtyard was as it had always been; despite the oppressive heat of the late August afternoon, the enclosure was surprisingly cool. The lush palm fronds swayed gently within their glazed jardinieres, and the constant fountain babbled languorously into its large cast-iron basin. She was home.

Actually, it had been a very simple decision. She would resume her life with the Durands. And as each day merged easily into the next, she knew that her choice had been the correct one. She was truly made to feel a part of the family; there was no condescension, no artifice. Only a sincere concern and love. How long ago had he called her his little daughter? She realized now it was no momentary flexing of the emotions. It had come from the heart.

She struck upon a casual routine, and as her relationship with Yvette developed more fully, she realized how much she loved the sweet and gentle young woman. How wonderful it was to find someone who could understand your need to be alone, and yet, find a million silly tasks to distract you, when the burden of that aloneness became too great. So it was that Simone now sat at the small secretary, pen in hand, addressing envelope after envelope in her beautiful script.

She had been delighted when Yvette had come into her room, boxes of invitations piled high within her arms, pleading with Simone to rescue her from the arduous calligraphic undertaking.

"Mamma means to invite all of New Orleans, Simone," cried Yvette. "I hope that the cathedral will hold them."

"I don't think you have to worry," laughed Simone. "You can always usher the overflow into the upper balconies."

"Simone, are you sure you don't mind addressing all of these invitations? I'll certainly understand if you refuse."

"Yvette Durand, I would be hurt if you didn't let me do something for your wedding. You and your mamma have pampered me long enough. I feel like an invalid."

The blonde girl walked toward her friend and took her hands into her own. "Oh, Simone, I am so glad that you are here. I only wish . . ."

"Hush, Yvette, if you don't let me start addressing these, I'm afraid you won't have to worry that St. Louis will be large enough to accommodate your guests."

She scrutinized the name and address which she had just penned upon the face of the envelope. Her black cursive scroll flowed expertly across the vellum. She was satisfied with her work.

Celestin Adaberon looked about him as the elegant barouche traveled down the wide boulevard toward the St. Charles Hotel. So this was the Paris of the Americas. He found the sobriquet a bit presumptuous, and yet, there was much here that reminded him of his beloved city.

He had hardly expected to take up oceanic travel again at his age, but it could not be helped. This was one matter that only he could attend to. His nephews, those *jeunesse dorée*, could never be trusted with such a delicate mission. It could only be hoped that the law firm would not suffer irreparably in his absence.

Dominique Ferrier had assured him that his client was a man of unimpeachable honor, and Celestin was willing to accept that this was so. But given that Monsieur Durand's word was not to be doubted, still the man might have been duped by some clever little minx. From the information relayed to him, he concluded that Durand had readily accepted the honesty of his client; he himself would not be so easily convinced. Celestin's sharp blue eyes sparkled in his still handsome face. He chuckled to himself, realizing that despite the long winter voyage and Christmas in a foreign country, he was quite looking forward to this little *recontre*, this duel of wits.

There was, of course, the locket, which might be genuine. But given the tragic circumstances of twenty years ago, it could have fallen into the possession of anyone. No, he, Celestin Adaberon, had not lived sixty-eight years in this wicked world to be taken in by a doe-eyed gamin with a tale of woe.

"But I do not understand why Dominique did not apprise me of your visit, Monsieur Adaberon," Armand Durand addressed his distinguished guest. "Had we but known of your coming, Madame Durand and I would have offered you the hospitality of our home."

"*N'importe.* I am quite comfortable at your St. Charles. It compares favorably with the grand establishments of the continent," replied Celestin graciously.

"Ah, perhaps, but one can only wish that our St. Louis was in operation. There was an . . ."

"I have heard of its lost glories," interrupted the visitor gently. "But tell me, Monsieur Durand, do you have this locket here? I am most anxious to inspect it."

"Of course, Monsieur Adaberon, of course. I will send for it immediately."

Simone approached Armand's study, the golden heart, newly mended, hung from a fine chain about her throat. She wondered at the summons. Perhaps there was word from Paris. But no, she would not allow herself to speculate. When and if news came, good or bad, she would deal with it, not before.

As she passed the parlor, the pleasant scents of the fresh evergreens and clovestudded tangerines, which bedecked the mantle, came to her. Christmas was almost here. She had been in New Orleans a year. She could remember nothing of last year's holiday.

She hesitated a moment before the door of the study. As she was expected, she did not knock, but entered quietly.

To her surprise, Armand was not alone, but engaged in animated discourse with a patrician-looking gentleman. He was tall and thin and he sat erectly in the high-back chair before the fire, his long elegantly trousered legs crossed in front of him. His silver hair was close cropped, but curled in a loose cap about his high forehead and over his ears. Suddenly, he seemed aware of her presence, and turned his lively and intelligent gaze upon her.

Celestin, despite his avowed cynicism, and sang-froid, was totally unprepared for the vision which greeted him. His usually controlled countenance registered his shock.

"*Sacré bleu!*" he exclaimed beneath his breath, as he rose to his feet. There was no need to press the matter further. In spite of the difference in coloring, it was Eugenie Valois de la Villere. And who should know better? Had he not loved her with all the passion of a young man's heart?

BOOK VI
Paris

❧

"And how my birth disclosed to me,
Whate'er beside it makes, hath made me
        free. . . ."

"What deep wounds ever closed without a scar?
The heart's bleed longest, and but heal to wear
That which disfigures it; and they who war
With their own hopes, and have been vanquished, bear
Silence, but not submission: in his lair
Fixed Passion holds his breath, until the hour
Which shall atone for years; none need despair:
It came—it cometh—and will come,—the power
To punish or forgive—in one we shall be slower.

George Gordon, Lord Byron

~ *Chapter 1* ~

The Marquise Alana Eugenie de la Villere threw back her head in laughter; the high-pitched trill echoed musically through the small sunlit room. The bright yellow rays of the Argenteuil sun, filtering through the large expanse of latticed windows, had danced upon her smooth dark hair, and now it gilded the ivory column of her throat as it arched back in amusement.

"Oh, Henri, *vous êtes très drôle*," the young woman finally spoke, recovering from the comte's entertaining anecdote.

"Alana, ma petite *papillon*, you always laugh at my silly stories. Perhaps you are too kind, cherie."

"Non, non, Henri. Paris *tout entier* joins me! You are wonderful!" Her dark eyes sparkled as she readjusted the heavy lace mantilla, and once again stared ahead, her gaze fixed upon her handsome admirer. He was beautiful, thought Alana, the most beautiful man she had ever seen. Too perfect, she had first decided. But soon the chiseled perfection had softened, as the warm glow of Comte Henri Beaumont's personality began to radiate through the incredible, deep green eyes. Like a lush forbidden forest, they beckoned, and so willingly, so innocently did one enter the emerald depths. Yet, there were no dangerous gulfs, no caverns, dark and sinister, only the warm and gentle green fire. She examined critically the straight nose, the full sensual lips, the burnished chestnut hair. Yes, Henri was beautiful, she concluded again. And more, he was the most compassionate, tender man she had encountered in her six months in the French capital.

Alana stopped. Six months in Paris! Six glorious months! It was almost incomprehensible. The whole sequence of events was a fairy tale, a story woven by Scheherazade, a golden myth. There had been tragedy and triumph, love and hate, new life and . . . death. In the history which Celestin had told, there were all the fantastic elements which made life more complex, grander than the greatest of dramas. And Alana had been a principal player.

Celestin had been unshaken in his conclusion. From the moment his clear blue eyes had seen her, he knew who she must be. She was the granddaughter of the Marquise Eugenie Valois de la Villere. The only child of her dead son, Valeran, and his beautiful Spanish bride. Alana recalled how she had scarcely breathed as the old man recounted the strange narrative of her lost parents.

Valeran de la Villere had been cursed with an idealistic, sensitive soul, an inquisitive, probing mind, and a vulnerable emotionality which entirely betrayed the role which he was born to play. He was no bored courtier, no effete nobleman, who must by accident of birth portray the supporting character to his older brother's dominant lead. Valeran burned with passions that Emile had yet not imagined. Emile lived shrewdly and deliberately. Valeran lived by the gypsy's crystal, the paths of the sailing stars, and his own bright dreams. Gladly, joyfully would he have worn the rags of the street beggar, turned his back upon the title, the lands, denied all for one single moment of pure freedom—a brief space in time to master his own destiny.

Valeran knew from the instant that he made his decision that he would suffer. His father would hate him, his mother mourn him. Yet, he would endure the anger, for there was little else between this father and this son. Had the father not always made it known that he preferred the arrogant, realistic Emile to his younger son? But the pain in his mother's eyes, this he would always remember, and carry within his heart, until it became an old wound.

Eugenie had pleaded with her son to be patient with his father and Emile; she said that to be young often meant compromise and waiting. But Valeran was determined—he would travel to Nouvelle Orleans. He would invest what money he had in land; he would become a planter. But he had been most adamant about the use of slave labor.

"I will pay my workers, Mamma, and I will labor with them among the rows of cotton," he had proclaimed expansively.

But still Eugenie protested that he at least should wait until Micaela had given birth to their child.

"Poor Micaela," Celestin had sighed. Sweet, frail Micaela, how she adored Valeran. She would have followed him into the gates of hell. She would have died rather than darken his bright dreams, his glowing fantasies. And if his visions fell into charred ashes, it was her quiet strength that would rekindle him, phoenixlike. She would accompany him on the long voyage and hope that their deep love would sanctify their journey, carrying them safely to their destination.

Eugenie had crossed herself that day as she watched her young son turn from her and walk from the room. There had been few words spoken, and what was said seemed somewhat strained. They had avoided each other's eyes until the last moment, when he turned to her and said quietly, "I love you, Mamma." She had refused to see them to the ship, deciding that it would be too painful. She looked down at his tall form as he entered the waiting carriage. From behind the drapes, she saw him look up to the window where he knew she would be watching. It was the last time Eugenie de la Villere saw her son.

Alana moved her head; her back felt stiff. Running her hand across the nape of her neck, she massaged the tightening muscles. She straightened her pose. "Henri, you make it impossible for me to be a good girl and sit calmly. *Allez! Allez!*"

"Alana, you are the cruelest woman I have ever known, but you do have the most beautiful eyes, the most kissable mouth, and the most . . ." He nestled his head into the folds of the black lace, whispering against her ear.

"Comte Henri Claraque Beaumont!" she hit him lightly across the chest with her closed fan. "You are positively naughty."

"Till tonight, my angel," he laughed. "Please, Alana, be ready. I refuse to enter our box after the curtain has risen, although I know it pleases you immensely to make such grand entrances."

"And you adore it, Henri Beaumont. But I'll be prompt, I promise," she purred.

She watched the tall elegant young man through the window as he mounted his black stallion. Yes, Henri Beaumont, thought Alana, smiling to herself, you do please me. You are exactly what I need.

And, indeed, Henri was but a part of her new life. She was a marquise, with vast estates, a magnificent Parisian townhouse, and country châteaux. She had quickly acquired a circle of admiring friends, and an exciting life filled with days at Longchamps and nights at the opera and ballet. And there was Grand-mère Eugenie . . .

Marquise Alana de la Villere. It sounded natural. Yes, she *was* happy.

From its brass cage near the window, the tiny canary began to sing, the pure clarion notes rousing Alana from her reverie. Unconsciously, she had allowed the fan to fall into her lap. Quickly, she raised her hand, spreading the delicate folds carefully before her. Peering contritely over the lacy edge, she glanced across the room.

Her friend had not noticed her lapse, but sat frowning in concentration before the heavy easel, his brush moving in quick dabbing motions over the large canvas.

She smiled as he muttered under his breath, obviously unsatisfied with his efforts. His dark conservative suit, the neatly trimmed blonde hair and beard, his air of quiet earnestness—all belied the role into which destiny and his own wild talent had cast him. He looks, Alana thought fondly, more like a banker than a revolutionary artist.

As she watched, he seemed to attack the surface before him, his brush like a knife plunging, stabbing. With a low curse he flung the sable brush into its wooden tray. He sat back, his hands upon his thighs, his eyes moving over the sketch, following the paths his brush had taken scant moments before.

"What is it, Edouard? Am I proving such a difficult subject?"

"It is not the model that is deficient," he replied good-naturedly, "but the artist." He smiled as she rose and walked to his side.

"You are too modest, mon cher. It is lovely. It always

amazes me that you are able to infuse such vitality into your work. Even at this stage it is apparent. It is quite marvelous."

"Merci, Alana. I paint as I must," he said simply.

"But you are unhappy with this?" she indicated the sketch.

"I thought by posing you in Spanish dress to capture something . . ." he sighed.

"But perhaps it is all *this* that is the problem," she said, pointing to her elaborate gown and the stiff lace mantilla. "Would you not prefer to paint me like your Victorine?" she inquired slyly.

"You are wicked, little Alana," he laughed. "It is bad enough that you are seen in the company of such rogues as Claude, Edgar, and myself. Would you scandalize all of Paris by posing *au naturel?*"

"Paris need not know, Edouard. The portrait is, after all, to be mine. It need not hang in the salon."

"There is little chance of that, in any case, ma cherie, after the reaction to *Argenteuil* this summer," he answered, a note of bitterness in his voice. "And your offer is certainly tempting. We would have complete privacy in my studio in Paris. Perhaps there, I might succeed in rendering the truth of Alana de la Villere."

"What are you talking about, Edouard?" she said, looking at him sharply.

"Do you suppose that no one sees behind your mask, cherie? Charles said only the other day, 'Our little Alana plays the butterfly, but her soul remains hidden within its silken cocoon. And if her eyes constantly sparkle, it is only because they are ever filled with tears.'"

"Charles is a poet," she retorted, "it is expected that he say such things. But it is utter foolishness. Alana de la Villere never cries."

Alana stood resplendent in her daring wine-colored gown, a bright fantasy creature in peau de soie and plumes, surrounded by a coterie of young swains in dark evening suits.

Henri, a glass of champagne in each hand, pushed his way determinedly through the gay chattering crowd to Alana's side. "I see that my services were not required," he said, noting the sparkling glass which she already held.

"Yes, dear François kindly provided me with refreshment," she said, smiling to the man at her left, who inclined his dark head to the comte. "And I am afraid that Jean has gone to get me a glass as well," she continued playfully.

"I see. Well, perhaps François will be good enough to give your apologies to Jean. We must return to our box if we are not to miss the third act. If you will excuse us, gentlemen."

He guided Alana along, his hand firmly under her elbow, his jaw set.

"Please, Henri," she joked, as they moved toward their seats, "you must not go so fast. Monsieur Worth's latest creation was not designed for ease of movement. And don't look so grim."

"Forgive me, my sweet," he said, slowing his stride. "It is only that it enrages me to see those peacocks paying court to you. The truth is, Alana . . . I am jealous," he said at last.

They had reached the box, and as he helped her to her seat, she squeezed his hand and brushed his cheek with her lips. "Oh Henri," she murmured, "you are so dear, so very, very dear."

He would have spoken then, but the lights dimmed, and the orchestra signaled the beginning of the final act. He contented himself with watching the play of the flickering gaslights on the shining coils of her hair, and the vivid contrast of the claret fabric against her creamy skin.

Through the gold lorgnette, cold brown eyes assessed the pair in the ornate box. The Comte Beaumont was obviously besotted with the brazen hussy. They all were, even her blasé François. Would that this long-lost Marquise Alana de la Villere had remained undiscovered forever. She studied the young woman more intently, noting the revealing décolletage and the long graceful lines of the fitted bodice. Tomorrow she must call on her dressmaker . . .

And yet another pair of eyes beheld the Marquise de la Villere. If the previous pair had been alighted with the jade of simple jealousy, these were aflame with far deeper, more complex emotions. Their malevolent glow transcended the pettiness of Parisian drawing rooms, the gossip of salons. Their fire held something unearthly. A carefully controlled

evil seemed to emanate from the penetrating gaze. There
was something unholy in the naked appraisal, obscene in
the raking of her distant image. This intimate scrutiny raped
the woman in a way no fever in the loins ever could. He
smiled—such beautiful quarry.

It was still early when the last act had finished and the
curtain finally fell to the enthusiastic applause of the
audience. For some unknown reason, Alana now felt
strangely disquieted, restless. And the thought of a late
dinner with Henri and their friends became suddenly unbearable. Tonight she could not endure their artful sophis-
try. When she declined to join the party, she read the hurt
on Henri's expressive face, but as always he said nothing.
Alana sighed; he was falling in love with her.

As they rode through the narrow streets, they were
uncharacteristically silent. The ride became unbelievably
interminable, the unnatural solitude unnerving.

"Alana, marry me." Henri's voice broke upon the quiet.

The sudden sound startled her, releasing her from her
strange mood. Then the import of his words registered.

"Henri," she spoke, making her voice light, "you cannot
be serious. I would certainly not make a suitable wife. Do
you not see, mon cher, you are too good for me. Besides I
am afraid your mother, the comtesse, would not approve of
your wedding the scandalous Marquise de la Villere." She
laughed, but the sound was too high, too shrill.

"Alana, I care not what the world thinks, not even
Mamma. I know you as no other. You are gentle, and kind,
and good. I love you, Alana." The last words came
desperately, as if Henri knew that by uttering them, he had
already forfeited the prize.

"Oh, Henri, and I love you too, but . . . Please know if I
could give my heart, it would be to you. But you must
understand, mon cher, I cannot offer what is not mine to
give."

~ Chapter 2 ~

The history of France was a history of revolution. It became an historical imperative to rebel. If any lesson had been learned by the French, it was that power could be seized. By the late nineteenth century France was, more than ever, a place of ferment and excitement. The vast energy released through political and industrial revolution resulted in new cultural and social patterns, as well as great material progress. But this political and social upheaval also had the effect of further fragmenting French society. Republicans and Royalists, Socialists and Bonapartists, Jacobins and Legitimists—monarch, noble, cleric, bourgeois, worker, peasant—history was making French life increasingly complex.

The Revolution of 1848, forcing the abdication of Louis-Phillipe, gave birth to the Second Republic and to the rise of Louis Napoleon. By December of 1852, the nephew of Napoleon had declared himself emperor. Yet it was not to be internal pressures, but a foreign interloper that brought down the government of Napoleon III. If one single event determined the politic course of the 1870s, it was the French determination to recover from the embarrassing defeat in the Franco-Prussian War.

The Third Republic was proclaimed in September, 1871, despite the bloody uprising of the Commune of Paris earlier that year. The Republic survived, yet the pattern had repeated itself. The people would take to the street and fight behind hastily erected barricades. They would risk all—deportation, death. When the desperate fighting

ceased, twenty thousand lay dead. They had forfeited their
lives for patriotic, egalitarian and anticlerical ideals. In a
real sense, the sixty-two days of the Paris Commune encompassed the hopes and dreams of all French revolutionary
drama.

However, even after the suppression of the Commune,
the Royalist factions were unable to resolve their interne-
cine quarrels. They were never able to consolidate their
political power. Thus the Third Republic endured the
contest between two dynastic families for the restoration of
the monarchy. By 1875, the French Assembly had designated the presidency as the supreme executive office. In the
end, the Republic had triumphed, but not without major
concessions to the Royalists. Indeed, the government absorbed much of the form and substance of Royalism. And
although a new ruling elite replaced the hereditary nobility,
the old aristocracy was not totally impotent.

The nobles were survivors. Many had called them a dying
breed after the revolution, but this proved a premature
obituary. For despite the vicissitudes of the political and
social climate, they had clung tenaciously to their lands.
Their survival as a class was thus ultimately bound to the
continued integrity of their hereditary wealth. Their preoccupation with the preservation of ancestral lands was no less
than their obsession to marry well. Genealogy thus became
a means of insuring their survival as a class. From this
position of isolation, the aristocracy endured the plague of
centralization, the hatred of the masses, and the affectations of the bourgeoisie, whom they resented and feared as
"enlightened fools."

Although the complexities of nineteenth century life
threatened to overwhelm the nobility, they did not abjure
their *style*. Not surprisingly they adhered to the old social
dictum that life was made for the rich and beautiful.

The aristocracy continued to dominate the "sport of
kings." In the late 1850s, Longchamps was built west of
Paris on reclaimed wasteland. A beautiful racecourse,
bordered by trees and lush green fields, it attracted a gay
and sophisticated Parisian crowd.

The young man sat alone at the small, round table. Idly,
he watched as the silver bubbles within his glass rose, one
by one, to find release at the surface of the sparkling liquid.
Neither the excited exclamations of the crowd, nor the

determined pounding of the thoroughbreds, had the power to penetrate his consciousness. As was becoming habitual, his mind was absorbed with but one thought.

Comte Henri Claraque Beaumont was no different from other young noblemen of his day. Perhaps he was handsomer than most, and certainly his easy gallantry was incomparable. Yet behind the superficialities of his station, Henry was a gentle man with deep and tender sensibilities. He possessed a passion for life and living, and most desperately, a passion for the Marquise Alana de la Villere. This last, however, did not seem to separate him from his compatriots. To the young man's distress, it seemed that all of Paris was in love with the beautiful marquise.

His green eyes darkened as he thought of her—the radiant child, so alive, so uninhibited, running through the fields in the bright Argenteuil sun. Alana, the sensuous woman, so ripe, her lush beauty so promising in the enveloping shadows of the Parisian dusk.

He moved deliberately in his chair as he felt the uncomfortable quickening in his groin. Mon Dieu, he would not live without her. Her protestations of unworthiness were ridiculous. The de la Villere family, like his own, were of ancient lineage, tracing their origins back to the fifteenth century and beyond. He knew that he could easily meet the objections of his formidable mamma, who was at least not blind to Alana's splendid heritage. And, of course, Papa . . . Henri smiled. His father was as enchanted as every male in Paris. No, in the end, his parents would be very pleased with his choice of wife.

Yet he wondered why the Marquise Eugenie allowed her granddaughter such excesses. Oh, Alana, you are so determined to make the world think you the callous, cynical woman. But my love, I am not fooled by your little masquerade. Why, Alana, why . . .?

Henry knew precious little of Alana's past beyond the gossip current in Paris, and no doubt, half of that was fabrication. It was said that she was raised by the Ursulines, and after twenty years had found her identity through a picture in a locket. It seemed rather fantastic, and yet, she was never without the small golden heart. If only she would confide in him. He remembered a moment. It had been but a brief space in time. There was only a glimpse of the soul through the dark melancholy eyes. He could scarcely breathe at what he had seen. My sweet, my precious, who, what, has caused you this terrible pain?

Yes, he could very well understand Eugenie's pampering of her granddaughter, her unquestioning acceptance. The old woman sought to erase the suffering, the loneliness of Alana's childhood. She was endeavoring to sow the seeds of joy, of happiness. Yet the gaiety somehow seemed so false, so pretentious. Had the tragedy of her past, the little orphan life, been too much to bear, too much to forget? Henri wondered. Yet for some unknown reason he knew there was more.

He moved from the table. Somehow his winning the bet with Pierre on the last race no longer seemed of any consequence.

~ Chapter 3 ~

The bright sunlight streamed through the open French doors. A cooling breeze fanned the haunting fragrance of the last summer roses into the salon. It was a rather small chamber, but the very intimacy was its most alluring feature. *La petite fleur*, everyone called it. And indeed, it was "the little flower."

The faint blush of tea roses tinted the walls, and a wash of pastel mint stained the wood casings and trim. Each border of the room's twelve panels was laced with curving trails of wild roses. The artist's brush had latticed the high ceilings, where small lozenges of pale blue sky appeared only occasionally amidst the cascading shower of pink blossoms and lush greenery.

The small *bergères* and settees, upholstered in Beauvais

tapestry, accentuated the bowerlike illusion. Young virgins danced across the seats and high backs, their flowing blonde tresses knotted with curling vines. Each maiden held a small bronze bird cage in her hand; and as testimony to the artist's whimsy, each cage was empty.

A small writing table, *bureau plat,* stood against one paneled wall, its beautiful Coromandel-lacquer finish strewn with sprays of wild flowers. The magnificent fire screen, which spread before the carved green mantel, displayed an idyllic scene—round, red-cheeked peasant women balanced wide yellow straw baskets of freshly cut flowers upon their kerchief-wrapped heads. There was no concession to darkness or exotic opulence in the entire room. All of the precious wood veneers were light and finely carved. Ivory and mother-of-pearl marquetry graced the surfaces in simple, fanciful designs. Even during the long gray winter afternoons, when the white snow clung to the ground, and no coo of the gentle dove was heard, it was said, that yet the heady fragrance of roses filled the air in *la petite fleur.*

The two sat facing each other, their easy conversation intermittently punctuated by the sound of soft laughter. To any observer it was quite obvious that the women liked each other very much. Despite the forty-five years which separated them, the same casual onlooker had to note the astonishing physical resemblance between the two. The younger woman was but a more intensely colored model of the grandmother. Yet it was more than the similarity of feature or facial structure—it was the tilt of the head, the pout of the mouth, the laughing eyes. It was as though one viewed the charming scene through some magical mirror which reflected both past and present simultaneously.

And the women seemed to enjoy their physical kinship. Alana could appreciate the mellowed beauty of her grandmère, and know that the passage of her own years would hold for her a similar serenity and nobility. And Eugenie enjoyed gazing upon the vibrant beauty of Alana, remembering well the days of her own youthful womanhood, feeling no regret, only a poignant nostalgia. The relationship, though brief in time, was a special one between grandmother and granddaughter.

"Oh Grand-mère, it was very amusing. I laughed so

much. Poor Henri. I believe he thinks me quite mad. I'm afraid I embarrassed him."

"No, my sweet child. I doubt that there is anything that you could do that would distress Henri Beaumont—except perhaps break his heart. Are you breaking his heart, Alana?" she teased.

"Grand-mère, Henri is a grown man, and he knows very well how to defend himself against the wiles of Alana de la Villere. And besides, he understands that I care for him very much . . . But Grand-mère, beyond friendship, I simply have nothing to offer. Everything is just so gay, so wonderful. I cannot be serious. Oh, Grand-mère, life is so exciting for me now. I want to taste all of it!"

"I know, ma cherie, I know."

The old woman's clear hazel eyes looked closely at her granddaughter. How well she knew the urgency of the young, the rush to live as if tomorrow would come too soon. But it was more than the years of deprivation and loneliness, more than the exuberance of youth, that drove Alana. But what, Alana, what? Why do you want to live as if you must run from something or someone? What are you afraid of? What are you trying to forget? Eugenie stroked the side of her graying hair with her fingers. She knew that she should be more firm with Alana; some of her escapades were really quite outrageous. But she could not. Oh, my gentle angel, would that I could know what secrets lie within your heart, what pain, what remorse. She knew that her granddaughter loved her very much, and that there was nothing that the young woman would not do for her. Yet the revealing of one's soul . . . No, she would not press her. In time, perhaps, in time.

"My sweet," she spoke, "I have received another letter from your grandmother, Alana Isabelle. She and your grandfather, Miguel, are so very anxious to see you. When I first wrote to them, they wished to come to France immediately, but I insisted that they wait. We are all getting so old. But no matter. Does Christmas in Madrid with your Spanish *abuelos* sound exciting, ma petite?"

"Oh, Grand-mère," the young girl rose suddenly, and ran to her. She fell to her knees before the woman, her face childlike, open, the dark eyes moist. "I love you. And yes, Grand-mère, yes. Christmas in Spain sounds lovely." The girl rested her head in her grandmother's lap, and the woman began to play idly with the loose, dark curls.

"Alana," she spoke after a time, her voice soft. "There has been much for you to adjust to since your arrival in Paris; I know that it has not always been very easy. How does one discover a family after so many years, and begin to love them as if time and circumstance were meaningless? It is difficult, but the young heart opens easily.

"I know that you have wanted to write to your grandparents for some time. But I also understand that it was not something you could do until the heart moved the hand. But it is time, Alana, it is time. You will write to them and tell your grandparents that we shall travel to Spain in December to wish them *Feliz Navidad*."

When the two women rose, they looked deeply into each other's eyes and embraced. As Eugenie gently pushed her granddaughter from her arms, she spoke, her voice now light, casual.

"Alana, I must get ready lest Celestin fly into a rage. It seems, my sweet, that we have much in common. Neither of us is very prompt." She brushed the young woman's cheeks with soft kisses. "I will tell your Tante Bernice that you will visit her very soon, and that you send your love."

"Grand-mère, are you quite sure that you do not want me to go with you today?"

"Non, my angel. I am afraid that your aunt is in one of her most melancholy moods, and the poor dear would only depress you. She has not been the same since Emile. . . ."

"Oh, Grand-mère, I am so sorry. It has not been easy for you."

"Now don't worry about me. I am just fine, and so will Bernice be, as soon as I arrive at the château. First I will open those heavy drapes, and allow the glorious Auvers sunshine into every room. Now take care of yourself, little one. I shall not be away long . . . three days, perhaps. And Alana, miss me—*un peu*?"

"Oh, Grand-mère, more than a little."

The young woman watched as her grandmother left the drawing room. She marveled at the woman's beautiful elegance. Yes, thought Alana, I have much to look forward to.

Alana was thoughtful as she entered her bedchamber,

oblivious to the beauty of the room. The double windows, which led out onto the balcony, were open to a bright rectangle of blue, bordered by the tall tree whose leafy branches heralded the approaching season. Gold, orange, and yellow whispered among the dominant green of winter sleep to come; the September wind puffed importantly, its still-warm breath carrying soft undercurrents of coolness.

The young woman sat upon her canopied bed, her slim fingers caressing the golden heart at her throat. Slowly, she unfastened the fine chain, and allowed the locket to drop into her hand. The metal was not cool as expected, but still warm from the contact with her flesh. She opened the pendant to reveal the miniature of her parents. Her father, fair and classically handsome, stood, his arm resting possessively on the high-backed chair in which sat the small, dark madonna. This was her mother, Alana told herself. This lovely girl was the mother she had cried out for in her dreams, in her secret heart—all of her life.

Strange, even though she had been aware of the circumstances of her tragic entry into New Orleans, she realized now that deep inside was always the small unspoken belief that somewhere, somehow her parents were alive and searching for her. She had held on to this childish fancy for so long that she had ceased to recognize its existence as an integral part of herself. And now she must let it go, sweep it away with the rest of the broken promises of her life.

They were dead, these beautiful brave children. Dead for more than twenty years. She tried to feel the sadness that this terrible truth should evoke, but there was nothing. They remained unchanged, locked inside the tiny heart-shaped frame, a pretty picture from a past she could never share. She closed her eyes, seeking some flicker of emotion, some feeling to link her to life and the world of her present.

The face of her grandmother came to her. She welcomed the image, that kind face in which her own features smiled back at her in gentle benediction. Yes, there was Grand-mère Eugenie and her mother's family in Spain, her Grandfather Miguel and her grandmother, for whom she had been named.

Her breathing, which had grown shallow and constricted, relaxed. She looked about her at the creamy wood of the carved panels, the rich fabric of the bed curtains. She ran her hand along the thick silken fringe of the drapery, and weighed the heavy golden tassel in her palm. She was rich and beautiful. She had everything . . . didn't she?

Alana rose from the soft cushions and went to her desk. The secretary, like all of the furnishings in the large room, was exquisite, the lines simple, the proportions delicate. Its writing surface was an oval half, surmounted by a cabinet of small drawers and compartments. Graceful curving legs supported a smaller oval tray below the first, indented to allow the sitter access. The gleaming tulipwood was inlaid overall with the pleasing forms of vases, urns, and ewers, which echoed the elliptical motif. It was wholly feminine and clever, a jewel.

From one of the drawers, Alana extracted two envelopes. She had neglected her correspondence. It was always delightful to receive a letter, so difficult to pen an answer. But before writing her *abuelita*, Alana Isabelle, she must answer these. She took up one of the white rectangles —Yvette's letter. It had come months ago, not long after she herself had arrived in Paris.

Yvette was pregnant and so happy. She hoped her child would be a boy, a son for Etienne and a grandson for Armand and Cecile. The family missed her terribly, but Yvette most of all. But they were so glad for her; they knew she was happy and with her own grand-mère. Pappa was so proud of the part he had played in her adventure.

Etienne had promised they could visit her in France, but now there was the baby. Alana must think about returning to New Orleans for a visit. Perhaps in the spring. Meanwhile, she must write and tell all about her life in Paris, her family, her friends, everything . . .

It was not as hard to compose an answer as she had anticipated, Alana discovered. She pictured Yvette, the merry blue eyes, the shiny cap of soft blonde curls—her little sister in faraway New Orleans. She apologized for the tardiness of her response. There had been so many people to meet, the parties, the opera . . . Yvette's announcement, she wrote, was the most exciting however. A baby! It was wonderful news. Yvette must kiss Etienne for her and, of course, her mamma and pappa. And yes, perhaps in the spring . . .

The second missive waited. Covered with exotic postmarks, Marie's letter had arrived from Turkey only two days before. Alana had written to her friend twice since her arrival in France, but this was the first letter she had received in return. She had been a bit anxious over Marie's failure to reply sooner, but now she understood. Marie was deeply troubled.

Since Alana's departure from Turkey, Marie had come to know Razid. It had been natural for them all to become close after Jalal's death, she had explained. It gave them a certain comfort. But the unforeseen had occurred. Alana reread her friend's words.

. . . was imperceptible. André invited him to dinner. I was, of course, delighted. As you know, I always found him compelling. The evening went so well. There was no sadness, only happy memories and shared stories. We all laughed a great deal, and I felt gay for the first time since you left us.

After that night, Razid came more and more often. I found, unaccountably, that I began to think of nothing but his visits. Once I told André that I had a headache, and remained in my room. It was a lie, Alana. I wished only to prove to myself that Razid was, after all, not so important to my life. I tried to read. I even sat down to write to you. Your letter had come. I was terribly excited over your good fortune, and eager to tell you of our happiness for you. But I found myself, the pen in my hand, at the door of my room, ear pressed against the wood, straining for the sound of his voice. It was no use; I went to join them . . .

Alana turned to another page and picked up the narrative.

. . . months passed, Razid remained as ever—warm and humorous, charming André and me with his wonderful stories. It was difficult, but I think I managed well. Never by a word or a look did I betray myself. Not even my brother, I am sure, suspected the wretched state of my heart.

Then one night, André was called away to aid in a difficult delivery. Razid came. I was a little surprised that he stayed, for I was sure that he would not think it proper to remain alone with me. We sat together on the sofa and talked as always. Before long he began an amusing anecdote. But I found I could no longer hear him. The blood was pounding so in my ears, and a heaviness had gripped me so, that I could scarcely force the air into my lungs. I seemed to be in a black tunnel, and could see only Razid. I watched his lips move over his beautiful white teeth, and the gestures of his expressive hands as he unraveled the tale.

Then with no warning, his arms were around me, holding me close, his lips against my hair, whispering all the things I had believed never to hear. Nothing that happens can ever destroy the wonder of that night. It is this which sustains me.

But Alana, I have been so stupid. I have always played such games. Carefree, modern, sophisticated Marie. Nothing has prepared me for this. I love him, Alana. And he loves me. Incredible, yet I believe it. I must believe it. Yet what am I to do?

He wishes us to be married, but I must become Moslem. Oh, he does not demand it; he demands nothing. Yet, he is a man of high standing, and I would do nothing to jeopardize his position. Oh, it is impossible! I have always had such freedom. And though Razid certainly doesn't mean to keep me in a haremlik, there would, of course, be restrictions. What shall I do? My mind and my heart are enemies; there is no peace for me. Help me, dear friend. Advise me . . .

Alana took up her gold pen, and filled it from the marble well. Beside it stood the blue egg, a rich ornament completely at home on the ovoid desk. Alana ignored it, beginning the letter.

My dearest Marie,
Do not think, only feel. You must follow your heart . . .

~ *Chapter 4* ~

The chill evening breezes toyed with the high branches of the oaks. Above, the full moon rode in the vast cloudless Parisian sky. Within the townhouse, a fire burned in the marble hearth of the bedchamber. The orange tongues licked at the seasoned logs, adding a dry crackling note to the light tap-tapping of the twisted limbs upon the leaded pane. The only illumination came from the long thin tapers alight on the vanity in the adjoining boudoir. Like *dentenu* jinns, the yellow flames of the candles danced fitfully in the faceted bottles upon the small table. The apartment was of an unequaled architectural splendor, magnificently furnished, yet in the strange dark ambience of the night it had become an alchemist's chamber.

She stood before the cheval, the droplets of water clinging to her skin like a pave of tiny diamonds. The soft light of the tapers honeyed her skin beneath the glistening dew. She preferred candlelight in her boudoir; the interplay of light and shadow on her body pleased her. She moved closer to the small toilette table. The flame from the gilt candelabra burnished her abdomen and the curves of her full breasts, but her face was held within the dark shadows. Her hair was heavy with the moisture of the bath, and it lay pasted against her shoulders in sinewy black coils. She traced a finger down one of the wet swirls as it encircled and kissed the tip of one nipple. Reaching for a large cloth which Germaine had placed over her bath screen, Alana began to slowly dry herself. Ritually, she dabbed the end of the plush towel across each section of her body, patting, pressing the droplets until she had artfully removed the clinging moisture. Her measured movements appeared as a prelude to some mysterious Circean rite. Finally she allowed the soft, damp cloth to fall freely to the tiled floor. Retrieving a tall crystal flask from her toilette, she began to pour a quantity of its contents into her palm. Deftly, she massaged the golden oil into her smooth skin. Immediately, the anointing illuminated the raised planes of her beautiful body. She gazed once again into the full mirror. Her breasts rose high, and the balm more clearly defined their glowing ripeness. She touched her nipples; they had grown darker. Knowing what she had to do, Alana opened one of the drawers of her dressing table. From a myriad of pots and jars, she selected a small container of bright pink paste. She inserted a single finger into the rouge and playfully iced each brown aureole. She smiled at the effect. The blushing peaks were now clever imitations of tiny rosettes. Replacing the paste, she removed a heavy crystal jar. Carefully, she dipped the fluffy white puff into the mouth of the bowl, and began to shower her body with the silky powder. The flecks of gold, captured in the white dust, clung to the light coating of fragrant oil. She stood revealed, a golden moon goddess, a radiant nymph of the night.

"Mademoiselle?" the young girl's voice floated into Alana's boudoir.

"Germaine, hand me one of my wrappers, *s'il vous plaît.*"

Almost immediately, the maid returned, and held open an apricot satin robe for her naked mistress. Alana tightened the wide sash and pushed up the robe's long sleeves to prevent the ecru lace trim from falling to her fingertips. She then sat before the toilette mirror, positioning herself comfortably upon the small plump cushion of the boudoir chair. She examined the array of cosmetics before her. Tonight, she would enjoy her creation. Not unlike an artist, she was a clever woman with her palette of rouges and powders.

First she would need to whiten the skin. She ran the lamb's wool, laden with oyster powder, across her features. The dust clung lightly. She scrutinized the filmy finish and frowned. Quickly she reached for the crystal atomizer of mineral water. She misted the entire surface of her face, and waiting but a few seconds, she reapplied the silky powder. This time the layer of alabaster dust sharply chiseled her small face, and exaggerated each delicate feature. The effect was absolutely perfect.

Next, she worked bright red rouge high upon her prominent cheekbones, careful not to blend in the scarlet edges too smoothly, lest she lose the two distinct spots of vivid color. Again, she dipped one finger into the jar of red paste, and moved closer to the oval mirror. Tracing the rouged tip of her finger across her lips, she expertly extended the color just beyond the natural line of her mouth. She examined her work; the contrived bowed shape did not please her. Again, a spot of rouge upon her fingertip. This time she ran the crimson color in a straight line across the upper lip, erasing the heart-shaped appearance of the mouth. She looked at herself. Yes, she preferred the child-woman pout. It was precisely what she intended.

Now she removed the silver lid from another of her crystal jars. This one contained a dark smoky powder. Using a tiny sable brush, she smudged the kohl under her thick lower lashes. Again the brush went into the gray powder, picking up more of the soft dust. Arching her delicate brows, she began to paint dark smoky wings, fluttering gray butterflies upon her upper lids. She moved back from her reflection. Turning her face to one side, then another, she posed, pursing her rouged mouth, and drawing in her cheeks to create deep hollows. But something was missing. "Mais oui!" she exclaimed to herself, opening one of the lower drawers of the vanity and rummaging through velvet ribbons and hair combs. She knew that they must be in this compartment—her vulgar little purchase with which she had teased Henri so. "Bien." She opened the tiny lavender box, the glossy black shapes enticing her. She removed the small heart and gingerly covered one side with a sticky preparation. She held the provocative *mouche* to her face. Near the shadowed eye? Upon the rouged cheek? Non! Firmly she pressed the cupid shape to the side of the red pouting mouth. The gay painted image of the demi-monde was without flaw. And for no other reason than that it seemed quite appropriate, Alana de la Villere winked at herself.

She turned her attention to the dark hair. Oh, why had she not combed it while it was still damp? It had dried free in the warm room, and now it danced in a frenzy of waves about her face, an outward expression of the wildness that raged within her tonight. How should she ever coax it into submission? Impatiently, she began to work on the thick mane. Grabbing sections of hair and twisting them into large flat ringlets, she deftly secured each one with pins. The task complete, she reached for the wig. It was an astonishing shade of red, referred to by New Orleans ladies as "not any color designed by the Creator." Carefully, she fitted it against her forehead and pulled it securely over the pin curls.

The woman in the glass smiled slyly. The elaborate coiffure seemed to heighten the effect of the artificial blush of the cheeks, or perhaps it was only that the hot blood had suffused her face. She laughed, the dark eyebrows arching upward to meet the brick-red curls.

She called for Germaine, and was rewarded for her artful toilette by the girl's startled expression.

"Is it you, mademoiselle?" she breathed, her huge brown eyes grown even larger in her amazement.

"Oui . . . non!" The young woman laughed, the sound echoing from the paneled walls. _"C'est égal._ But hurry Mai-Mai, fetch me my gown, the emerald moire that I sent to Madame Didier for alteration. You will find it in the armoire."

The girl returned shortly, the heavy dress on one arm, a collection of lingerie on the other. Her mistress selected only the silken panties.

"Non, non, Germaine. I will have no need of these others. There is little enough room for me beneath the gown."

As the young maid fastened the tight bodice, the woman surveyed herself in the long mirror. Only the brightest tones and the darkest hues registered in the gloom: the bright wig, the dark irises above the pink cheeks, the red slash of her lips, the rich black lace outlining the low décolletage and the diagonal folds of the _tablier_. She seemed to be nothing but eyes and mouth, and a curving form against the darkness. She stood thus for a moment, poised before the glass, as if she expected it to speak of necromancer secrets.

But the spell was broken by the chiming of the gilt bronze

clock which sounded the hour. "Mon Dieu! *Je suis en retard!* Quickly, Germaine, my cape."

The maid retreated toward the armoire, and the titian-haired woman hurriedly nestled a black heron's feather aigrette upon her high pompadour. Impulsively, she removed the golden pendant from around her neck, and reached for a black velvet ribbon. Muttering softly beneath her breath, she fumbled in her jewelry case for some ornament to place upon the neckband. *The cameo!* It rested on the plush cloth like chiseled bone in the flickering glow of the candles. The woman's hand hesitated for a moment, then she grasped the brooch, and securing it on the ribbon, tied it round her neck.

"Your wrap, mademoiselle."

"Merci, Mai-Mai," she responded gaily. And flinging on the velvet cape, she stepped into her high pumps and was gone.

The man stood under the striped canopy before the doors of the music hall, his dark suit and high silk hat in elegant contrast to his blond hair and beard. It was obvious that he was waiting for someone—a woman—and that she was late.

The street surged with carriages and the comings and goings of the spirited Parisian crowd, eager for the exhilarating night life of the capital. In the gay confusion, the man was unaware of the discreet black barouche which had pulled up to the curb, or of the small caped and hooded figure who stepped from its interior. Joining the merry crowd, she moved toward the entrance of the imposing building.

"Bonsoir, M'sieur, may I join you?"

He directed a questioning smile at her; then, looking closer, his eyes widened. She expected some exclamation from his lips, which had parted in surprise. Instead, he bowed from the waist and spoke graciously. *"Je regrette,* mademoiselle, but I am afraid I must deny myself the pleasure of your most charming company. For you see, I await another *demoiselle,* a most enchanting brunette. And though she is not prompt," he said rather pointedly, "she has other virtues which make her tardiness endurable."

"But M'sieur," importuned the girl, looking up at him from beneath her thick fringe of lashes. "It seems to me that this other lady is a stupid creature to have kept waiting such a *distingué* gentleman as yourself, and little deserving of your loyalty."

"A clever argument, mademoiselle. I am convinced," he laughed, giving up the little game and offering her his arm.

"Well, well, Edouard. And who is this magnificent creature?" flourished Edgar. "She is certainly far more beautiful than the poor little brunette mouse that we expected. I have a passion for red hair, mademoiselle."

"Edgar, may I present Mademoiselle Francine Lascoux," continued Edouard, prolonging the charade.

"*Enchanté*, Mademoiselle Lascoux," he said, kissing her proffered hand with mocking gallantry.

"I have heard a great many things about you, m'sieur. I trust, for your sake, that they are gross exaggerations of the truth."

"Touché," the tall aristocratic man returned, bowing from the waist.

"Bonsoir, Francine," the third gentleman rose, and bent to kiss the young woman on both cheeks, lingering long enough to whisper rather audibly. "I can't say that I prefer titian-haired goddesses. Why, there is one exquisite brunette that I would relinquish my soul to the devil to photograph."

The young woman laughed gaily. "You are wonderful, Nadar; and perhaps, soon . . ."

"Absolutely not, she is my subject, Nadar," Edouard asserted jokingly. "I will not share her."

"Enough, you two are embarrassing me," she said, feigning modesty. "But where are Eugene and Berthe, Edouard? I had counted on their joining us tonight."

The man only shrugged his shoulders, the expression on his face revealing perhaps more than he wished.

"Edouard's dear brother, I'm afraid, thinks it scandalous for genteel ladies to be seen at the Folies," quipped Edgar, eyeing his friend. "He would not have his wife strutting as some demimonde, as a *poule*, replete with gaudy feathers atop her pretty head. Dear Berthe is not as liberated as you, Mademoiselle Francine. Yet I wonder . . ."

"If I would come without the wig, Edgar?"

"Oui, mademoiselle, without the wig or the face paint."

"Then it would not be as much fun," she said, touching the heart-shaped *mouche* coquettishly. "And one comes to the Folies-Bergère to have fun, to be whatever one wants to be. To lose oneself in the laughter and the music."

Edouard stared at Alana. He was disturbed, as always, by her hunger, her lust for living. Yes, he would enjoy painting the portrait, painting her as he really saw her this time.

A fanfare of blaring horns and clashing cymbals announced the next performer. He strode onto the stage, an elongated figure in black, his long flowing cape lined in scarlet satin. In the slender fingers of his left hand was a silver-tipped ebony wand. His deep-set eyes seemed to glitter in the reflected glow of the footlights, as he stared almost disdainfully over the heads of the assemblage.

"Maestro D'Allessandro," whispered Edouard. "He comes to us from foreign shores, and is quite the rage."

"I have seen him before," added Nadar, "and confess that I have little idea of how he performs the more intricate tricks."

"Perhaps, he is truly a mage," teased the young woman, as she continued to sip on her wine. "He certainly looks the part. Where do you suppose he comes from?"

"Most likely he is a grocer's son from far-off Lyon," remarked Edgar dryly from across the table.

There was no time for a retort. The lights were dimmed, and the four fell into silence as the magician began his performance.

Alana watched, becoming totally absorbed in the artful wizardry of the slender hands. They seemed to be endowed with the power to rescue all manner of objects from sheer nothingness, and to wave them away again with a motion of the shiny baton. After this virtuoso display of legerdemain, the swarthy man paused, acknowledging the acclamation of the crowd with only a slight inclination of his turbaned head. In thickly accented French, he requested assistance from the audience to aid him in his next demonstration. From the *promenoir*, the aisle behind the orchestra seats, came two young women, their dress and manner suggesting that they were of the demimondaines who habituated the Folies. All eyes followed their hurried advance to the stage.

The performance which followed involved two tall wooden cases, painted in strange glyphs and intricate designs, into which the conjurer placed the women. Chanting in his deep atonal voice, the master caused his subjects to vanish and reappear at will, first in one box then another, as if the seemingly solid women were both insubstantial and transmutable. At one last move of his imperious hand, both caskets stood emptied of their charming contents. The girls were discovered almost at once among the audience, magically returned to the *promenoir*. Here they stood, smiling broadly, the bright plumes in their hair waving and dipping as they bowed to the crowd. The magician exited to thunderous applause.

"What did you think of the maestro's prestidigitation?" inquired Edouard, noting the girl's flushed face and shining eyes.

"I thought him quite wonderful, though a trifle sinister," she replied. "He is the first stage magician I have ever seen."

"Then it is too bad," commented Nadar, "that our own Monsieur Alexander Herrmann has gone off to live in America. He was born here in Paris, and was taught his craft by his older brother Carl. They are both quite spectacular, but Alexander is unequaled in his mastery of the more elaborate illusions."

"Oh, I should have loved to have seen one of his performances," she assured her friend, as he refilled her glass from the decanter.

Almost hypnotically, Alana gazed about the enormous room. From above, the swirling gaslights set afire the moving sea of spectators with a pale verdant luminosity. The fleshy faces of the women became absurd anaglyphs —wet rouged mouths twisted below the violet smudges of eyes. Their pendulous breasts spilled upon the small ovals of glossy table tops as they bent closer to their foppish escorts. Mossy beards and curving wings of mustaches rolled easily over chalk-white teeth. The gentlemen matched the seductive posturing of the females, touching the women's white plump forearms as they spoke. Elegant black hats bobbed jauntily on the dandified heads, teasing the spreading plumes which grew in astonishing color from coiling pompadours.

She reached again for the claret. Sipping deeply of the red liquid, she gazed upon the gyrating kaleidoscope of humanity through the faceted crystal. Everything was suddenly severed—broken by the intaglios of the glass. The entire scene became one of sharp moving angles and bizarre abstract planes. Elongated forms and stunted shapes appeared and reappeared as she worked the stem in her delicate fingers. And where there had been the luminescence of green, a scarlet rivulet of wine now stained her view.

Then a purple haze swallowed the large hall, and the ribald laughter and clinking of raised glasses slowly dissolved. A haunting refrain raised its baleful voice against the lowering swell of the crowd. It wove its dolorous path round each small table. Then, without warning, the tempo switched violently—allegro! Faster the music raced, its jarring rhythm pulsating, on and on, higher and higher—its frenzied pace searching for some release. Then as suddenly as it began, it ceased.

The pall on the great room became almost tangible. A quick movement above, a rush of cool air, a soft metallic swish broke the spell. The queer sound repeated itself over and over, spreading above the arching heads.

Then they descended, like errant angels, running from an avenging god—rebellious misfits expulsed from the bowels of hell. Some rode the uncertain currents upon swinging trapezes of burnished gold, others spiraled downward upon long knotted cords of hammered silver. Downward, downward the unholy pantheon rained.

Dark-horned creatures with gaping holes for mouths and eyes; bright faeries with rainbow wings and white matted hair; cloven-footed satyrs; centaurs, snorting and pawing at the air; harlequins, checked black and white; chimeras and kelpies; gnomes and Nereids; and woolly *loups-garous*—all descended, their bodies angled toward the upturned faces below.

They sang Elysian melodies, and uttered obscene incantations; they pirouetted in mesmerizing spins and tumbled spectacularly from their high perches. It was the garden of Hesperides and the pit of Acheron.

She stared at the figure writhing above her, its wide mouth opened to reveal a lolling tongue, its eyes bulging white. The body was hideously deformed, a large hump protruded horribly from its back, and the bright shiny stripes of its satin coat gleamed incongruously. Then the ugly head snapped backward, and a manical laugh wrenched forth. Almost a material thing, it came from the mouth. She raised her hands to cover her ears, attempting to block out the awful sound.

Suddenly, the gaslights were fully ignited, the music hall was flooded with bright lights. Above the crowd, the creatures dangled, limp impotent things, benign in the room's illumination.

"*Les poupées*," laughed Edouard, as he reached to squeeze Alana's moist palm.

Alana became aware of the men with her at the small table. They were somehow at variance with the raucous crowd which filled the huge theater. Sitting here with them, she felt suddenly protected. It was as if some aura that they exuded had the power to hold at bay the stifling atmosphere, which a moment before had threatened her. Now she saw that they sat in a bubble of light, while around them the clamorous multitude moved within a dim gelatinous sea of arms and legs and moving lips—action and sound without sense or meaning.

She glanced at the faces of her companions. Like the others, they smoked and drank, talked and joked, but they were different. Each was consumed with a passion, obsessed with a purpose that was ironically liberating. They possessed a purity, a meaningfulness against which all that was tawdry and senseless in life was powerless.

Edouard had promised to paint her, to capture her *as she really was*. What was it he perceived behind the masquerade of her life—what was there left to see?

~ *Chapter 5* ~

He pushed lightly against the soft fabric of the white blouse, allowing the wide neckline to fall provocatively from one creamy shoulder. Stepping back, he viewed the subtle alteration critically. Something was still amiss. The model appeared too rigid, too unnatural. It was this very posture that had caused him to become frustrated with the first canvas. Of course, everything had been so contrived that day in Argenteuil—the stiff billowing gown, ribboned with yards of heavy black lace, and the mantilla framing that exquisite face. This was no Spanish madonna. He had cursed the blatant artificiality of it all, wishing desperately to release her from the pretentious trappings. He looked at her and thought, *Femme*! Eve bearing the red fruit, innocent Helen with a thousand dead at her naked feet, a woeful Persephone pining for the light. And more, Thais the courtesan, Artemis the virgin. Mother, sister, daughter, wife, mistress—gypsy.

Gazing into her black eyes, he anticipated rendering those dark pools. So alive, he marveled, smiling down at her. Slowly, he turned her to the left, and drawing one leg upward, allowed it to rest casually over the arm of the chair. He then pressed his open palm against her lower back, forcing her to arch upward. She had positioned her hands against the seat cushion for support, and the sweep of a decorous fan still dangled idly from one hand. Tilting her head backward, he ran his fingers through the masses of hair, which cascaded downward to her cummerbunded waist. She laughed at the wicked seduction he had created.

"*Très bien*, Alana, *très bien*. This is perfect. The head, the leg, the fan. And please, do not stop laughing. Don't ever stop laughing."

"Oh, Edouard, and what of the hidden tears? Or have you forgotten?"

"*Non*, cherie, my memory is not so poor. But is it that we laugh so that we do not cry?"

"Edouard." Her voice was quiet as she turned to face him. "You see me as no one else does. Is it the artist's eye? I am *naked* before you."

He laughed, "But if that were only true, Alana—oh, what a portrait! My new *Olympia* . . ."

"And make Victorine jealous, Edouard?" she returned playfully.

His manner growing more serious, he spoke, "Alana, if only . . ." He did not have to finish.

"*Oui*, Edouard, oui."

"You are sure, my dear friend?"

"Yes, Edouard, very sure." Slowly she stood, and walked to the faded screen.

From her new position on the velvet chaise, Alana watched in fascination, as an incredible transformation seemed to overtake her quietly elegant friend. A sort of frenzy seemed to possess him. As he sat before the large canvas, his brush flew from his palette to the surface and back again, his blue eyes intently fixed upon her, encompassing the space in which she reclined. His trance-like gaze seemed impersonal, yet all-seeing. Was he mad-man or god?

In contrast to the artist's furious energy, the model was utterly at ease, surrendering herself to the moment. For a while, she observed his frantic motions, but soon her mind became a pleasant blank, and she simply *was*. For the first time since her early childhood, she was totally relaxed—she was free.

The furious struggle had begun. Once again he had "thrown himself into the water without knowing how to swim." He must fight to wrest his vision from the world, and translate it into strokes of paint upon canvas. He never knew at the beginning if his effort would be successful. So often he failed. Yet he felt charged with a special power at this moment that seemed to connect his eye and hand. Boldly, he sketched in the broad flat planes of the background, which pushed the figure relentlessly forward. As always, he would hide nothing, neither the naked paint, which was his creative medium, nor the naked body, which clothed the soul of the woman.

~ *Chapter 6* ~

The Bois de Boulogne rose on the outskirts of Paris, a sylvan retreat for the ancient forest gods and the Roman deities who had once had their temples on the high banks of the Seine. It was refuge also, for those seeking a quiet haven away from the growing clamor of the city.

On this late September morning, the woods were at their most spectacular. The cloudless sky was an azure roof supported by columns of ancient elms. The bright sunlight filtered through the boughs, setting their autumnal colors ablaze. A golden silence, which was one with the crisp air and watching trees, was broken only by an occasional bird song. Stray eddies of wind ruffled the leafy carpet, which erupted suddenly into miniature tornadoes of whirling reds, yellows, and golds.

The brisk ride through the Bois de Boulogne had been invigorating for the young woman in the elegant riding habit. Beneath the brim of her high-topped hat, her eyes sparkled and her cheeks glowed pink from cold air and exercise. As she walked along the bridle path near a small pond, the indigo gauze veil wound about the crown of her *chapeau*, and streamed and rippled like a pennant in the breeze. She seemed absorbed in the beauties of the landscape, paying little attention to her companion, who was ardently expostulating at her side.

"But the Folies-Bergere, Alana! It is incredible. When Gilbert reported that he had seen you there, I protested that he was surely in error. But he insisted that despite the clever disguise, your beauty was unmistakable. Are you mad to go to such a place? To be seen everywhere with those . . . those . . . Impressionists!" Still the woman said nothing, and he went on earnestly. "Please try to understand, Alana, it is not just for your reputation that I fear, but for your safety. Can you not see that such places could be dangerous for one such as you?"

"For me, Henri? *Pourquoi?*" She spoke finally, surprise in her tone.

So he had gotten her attention. "Petite *papillon,* sometimes you are so naive," he said, his voice softening. "I do forget that you have not been in France long enough to understand how hated we Royalists are by some. And, of course, your Uncle Emile . . ."

"My uncle? What about my father's brother? Please, Henri, do not stop."

For a moment the young man hesitated, then he reluctantly succumbed to her promptings. When he spoke, his voice came in a monotone, and his gaze avoided hers.

"Your Uncle Emile did little to come to terms with the realities of the times. He believed that the masses should be subservient, that it was but their historical destiny. During the years of upheaval, many of the nobility lost their holdings, but many more were able to save their estates, and even increase their lands. The de la Villere family was most fortunate to be among the latter. When your grandfather delegated many of his responsibilities to his elder son, Emile accepted his ascendancy almost with a fanaticism. To Emile, the values inherent in the *ancien régime* were historical and moral absolutes. That it was the God-given right of the nobility to wield political and economic power over the people, he never doubted. And he lost no opportunity to make his views manifest. Emile, unlike many of the aristocracy, was not a good shepherd to his sheep, showing little human warmth or compassion. Perhaps it was this cynical indifference and unthinking cruelty which led to . . ."

"Led to what, Henri? What happened to Uncle Emile? Grand-mère has never told me, and I sense that I should not press her. Even Celestin would not speak of it. I must know, Henri. Please, can't you see that I am part of this too?"

Taking her hand into his, he faced her, searching her face with his deep green eyes. He knew she must, indeed, be told of her past. Was this not what he intended from the beginning, to impress upon her that Alana de la Villere must accept her legacy, however painful this heritage might prove? But beyond this, she must know that as the last of her line, she must fulfill the bright promise—she was the future.

He released her hand, and walked closer to the water. Slowly, he crouched upon the bank, and launched one after another of the fallen leaves which he found in profusion. As he watched the colorful armada glide over the rippling blue water, he began his narrative.

Georges de la Villere never understood his younger son. This antipathy went deeper than their incompatible temperaments and contrasting philosophies. Of course, the marked dissimilarity in their physical appearance only widened that awful breach. Unlike Emile, who was very much in his sire's image, there was nothing about Valeran which might mark him as Georges's son. It was as if man and boy bore alien souls incapable of transcendence.

Georges often castigated his younger son for being a dreamer and a fool. Emile labeled his brother a bourgeois Republican. Not that Valeran did not support the Restoration, but he saw the monarchy as the imposition of order against the chaotic forces which were destroying France. Georges and Emile saw it as a means of returning to the *ancien régime*.

And, of course, contributing to the dissension was Georges's suspicion that Valeran . . .

"Why do you stop, Henri?"

He stood avoiding her face. He had said more than he intended. "I should not have spoken so, Alana. All that I have said was but a tale told to me. Mamma and Pappa have always said that much of it is but vicious gossip."

"What kind of gossip, Henri? I have a right to know. What about my father?"

"That he was a bastard, Alana. Your grandfather often said that your father could be no son of his."

"I see," she breathed quietly.

Wishing to forestall further questions that he was loath to answer, Henri went on with the story. "Once your father had wed, it was an easy choice for him. He knew that he had but one destiny, and that it lay beyond his father, beyond Emile, far beyond all the bitterness and hatred that the passing years had brought. Pappa still recalls how excited your father was that day, when he showed him the tickets to New Orleans. He was so happy at the prospect of his new life, his new freedom. But your poor grand-mère, she was heartbroken. Had she fought so long and hard for Valeran but to lose him? And when the news came . . ."

He was quiet for a moment, understanding the pain that his words brought to her. When he did continue, his voice seemed strained and unnatural. "The years wrought further tragedy for your grandparents—the death of Emile, and with him any hope for de la Villere heirs.

"It was so strange. It is still difficult for Pappa to think of your grandfather, and not remember that day. Pappa was the one who accompanied him to the prefecture to identify Emile's body. As the carriage moved from the countryside toward the ravaged city, your grand-père sat staring out of the window, as if transfixed by the passing scenery. When he spoke, his words were firm and unemotional. 'So it is finished.'"

"Was it ever discovered why Uncle Emile went to Paris at such a time?"

"No, Alana, it is still a mystery why Emile should be in the capital while the rabble Commune mob still held the city. But it is highly probable that his murder was the plan of radical Blanquists or Jacobins."

"And the horrors of '71 are not yet to be dismissed. There are still those who harbor vengeance for the past. It is rumored that the Comte Joinville's death was not the accident it was reported in the press. I have heard from a friend of the comte's family that the body was marked in a most gruesome fashion, a bloody token testifying that his death was the work of some antiRoyalist faction. So you see, ma cherie, I am not being overprotective. There is just cause to fear for your safety." Taking her small oval face into his hands, he tilted her eyes up to meet his own. "Please, Alana," he begged, his voice impassioned with a quiet fervor, "promise me you will be careful. If anything should happen to you . . ."

That evening, Alana sat alone in her room, staring into the fire. All that Henri had told her echoed in her memory. She thought, too, of the gentle pressure of his hands against her cheeks, and the concerned look in his eyes when he spoke of the danger to her.

A sudden chill ran its icy fingers over her soft flesh. That night at the opera . . . what had happened to spoil her gay mood, to so unnerve her? Was it that eerie feeling that she was being watched, watched by someone whose very gaze seemed a thing of evil? Another fragment of memory stirred in her mind—the evening at the Folies-Bergere. It had been very late when Edouard escorted her to the waiting carriage. As she waved him good-bye from her seat within the barouche, she had observed a man standing a few paces behind her friend. She had noted that he was clothed in evening dress that seemed out of place on his square, inelegant frame. He was extraordinarily hirsute, with dark shaggy hair and brows. He was not wearing gloves, and even at a distance, the thick black hairs on the backs of his hands were discernible. As she took in his flattened, simian face, she laughed at the comical incongruity which he presented, a squat foreign creature amidst the bright Parisian landscape. But the chuckle had died quickly in her throat, as her gaze met the small black buttons of his deep-set eyes watching her from beneath the absurdly undersized silken hat. Was Henri correct? Was she in danger?

~ *Chapter 7* ~

"Grand-mère, I think your guest list is even longer than mine. I refuse to even count the names. It seems as though we are inviting all of Paris."

"All of Paris? Non, my sweet, all of France!"

"Oh, Grand-mère, I am so excited. I want to invite *tout le monde*. Everything must be perfect, the most magnificent *bal masqué* ever given. Oh, 'mère, am I so superficial, so selfish?"

"No, Alana, you are not selfish, only very young. And there is no greater virtue than youth, ma petite. Be happy!"

"Yes, yes," the beautiful girl cried, as she whirled about the parlor, whipping the crackling parchment about her as she pirouetted.

"And what have we here, a new ballerina for *Le Ballet Français*?" The man laughed heartily as the young girl turned to look into his wonderful clear blue eyes. There was no one quite like him, thought Alana. It was no wonder that her grandmother adored him. She watched as he bent to kiss Eugenie's smooth brow. It was obvious that he reciprocated her grandmother's affection. How much they enjoyed each other's company, how close they were. It was as if some special bond joined them. Unbidden, Henri's words came to her. *Of course, there was always the suspicion . . .*

"Well, Alana, I see that you and your grand-mère have been quite busy. And what kind of *fête galante* are you planning?"

"Why, a costume ball, Celestin, on the eve of All Saints' Day. Won't it be absolutely fantastic?"

"On the eve of *la Toussaint*," affirmed the man.

"Oui, dear Celestin, and I cannot wait to see you in some

marvelously romantic guise. Let me see . . . D'Artagnan, perhaps."

"Alana de la Villere, absolutely not. You will never see me strutting about in some dandy's costumes I am too old for such games."

"But you must, Celestin. It will be required that all of the guests wear costumes and remain masked till midnight. Really, I am surprised at you. Where is your spirit of adventure, your sense of fantasy? Is it not the wish of every man to once be what he is not?"

"Non, ma petite, I am afraid Celestin Adaberon is perfectly satisfied to be who he is," Eugenie de la Villere said, smiling broadly into his handsome face. And it was apparent, that she too, was satisfied with who he was.

Marie came into the salon to announce the arrival of Comte Beaumont. Henri entered *la petite fleur* looking pleased with himself, a square, beribboned box tucked underneath one arm. He greeted them all, bowing over Eugenie's hand, and lightly kissing her fingertips. Ceremoniously he deposited the mysterious package in Alana's lap.

"*Qu'est-ce que c'est,* Henri?" she asked brightly, looking up at the tall figure before her.

"It is a little mushroom that I picked for you this morning. It sprouted in my path on my visit to the farm at Gennevilliers, and Mamma agreed that you must have it."

As he spoke, Alana looked down in wonder as the box quivered slightly under her hand.

"Come, come, Alana, open it," prompted Eugenie. "I confess, I cannot wait to see this little *champignon*. Perhaps Nana can use it in the sauce tonight," she laughed, exchanging a conspiratorial glance with Henri.

"Yes, petite, please do hurry," chimed in Celestin. "I do believe that you and I are the only two here not privy to this little intrigue."

Eagerly, Alana slipped the large, flame-colored satin ribbon from the shiny white box. Looking up at the expectant faces about her, she removed the lid. Peering down, she reached in to pull back the pale yellow tissue, which still concealed the contents. Quite unexpectedly, there was a blur of motion as a small gray-brown shape bounded from the box to repose on the floor at the young woman's feet.

"Mon Dieu," cried Alana, catching her breath and

laughing at the same time. She bent down to stroke the ball of silky fluff which indeed seemed to sprout from the thick carpet. At her touch, a tiny head lifted to meet her caressing fingers, and enormous orange eyes regarded her.

"Oh, what a little darling!" Alana exclaimed, lifting the kitten into her lap. "She's beautiful, Henri. Indeed, she shall be my little Champignon."

Henri beamed at her pleasure in his gift, and sitting beside her on the settee, ran his fingers through the long downy hair behind the kitten's tiny pointed ears. Champignon purred her appreciation. Then opening her mouth in an enormous yawn that exposed her little pink tongue and tiny white teeth, she emitted a soft mewing sound. She curled deeper into the folds of her mistress's gown, and was asleep.

The formal garden of the Tuileries was a favorite retreat for the *flâneurs* and *boulevardiers* of Paris, even on a crisp October afternoon when the brown bones of leaves dotted the perfectly clipped lawns. It was pleasant to stroll the wide gravel avenues admiring the plashing fountains and the neoclassical statues amidst the topiary.

Beyond the garden stood the ancient Louvre, the origin of its name still shrouded in mystery. Perhaps the most charming translation was "a lodge for the hunting of wolves." In light of the succession of rapacious French monarchs, many proud Parisians might have rebutted sarcastically "were not those in residence, the true *loups des* France?"

As early as the thirteenth century, there was a royal fortress on the site with this name. The present Louvre Palace had served as the abode of the French monarchy for centuries, each king altering it to suit his taste until the reign of Louis Quatorze. The Sun King, fearing its proximity to his subjects and finding it too archaic and confining, built the isolated and incomparable Palais de Versailles. Even so, the Louvre continued to attract the nomad court. It was not until after the revolution, that the Louvre was converted to a museum.

"Someday my friends' works will hang in the Louvre," asserted Alana to Henri, as they meandered along the pebbled paths of the Tuileries. "The salon cannot always remain so blind."

"I wish my eyes were as open to their talents as yours, ma chère, but I prefer the works of Ingres and Delacroix."

"They too are quite wonderful, but men like Edouard and Edgar paint not with sight but with *insight*. They seek to capture the truth of the moment."

Henri smiled, enjoying her animated pontifications. She was so exciting . . . he loved her.

"It is a shame that the Tuileries Palace was burned in '71," he said after a time. "And I am afraid the bitter spirit of the Commune still lives. I do not like to frighten you, ma chère," he went on, his voice serious, "but there has been a second murder. And if there was any doubt about the perpetrators of the first crime, there is no question now. It seems as though the radicals take some sadistic pleasure in claiming their grisly deeds by leaving their gruesome mark upon the corpses."

"What is this mark?" she asked, her face pale.

"It is not so much a mark, Alana, as a mutilation. The victims have been men. I would not wish to think what they might do to a woman."

As they spoke, they had halted along the walkway. Now looking at her, he realized how strongly his words had affected her. "I *have* frightened you, petite *papillon*. Please forgive me. It worries me to see you like this." He took her into his arms and held her to him with a passion she had not known he possessed.

Gently, she pushed against the young man's chest so that she might look into his face. "Henri." She spoke the words in a whisper. "Someone has been watching me . . ."

～ *Chapter 8* ～

It was All Hallows' Eve. A large pumpkin moon grew low in the heavens, nature conspiring with human custom to produce a night of beauty and enchantment. The evening sky was a velvet cloak shading from deep black to indigo at the horizon. The crisp chillness of the October air was pleasant. Yet the intermittent wind was an augury of winter snow, the heavy gusts setting the naked branches of the oak to clawing at the leaded windows.

As bright flames licked hungrily at the dry crackling logs in the hearth, the shiny tongues of long black tapers winked against the veil of semidarkness which shrouded the chamber. The nude figure moved easily about the darkened salon, her slender shadow following her, crawling sensuously up the pale ivory walls. A thin ribbon of blue smoke curled from a small bronze urn, its exotic odor intensifying the room's cabalistic aura.

"Tonight, Champignon," the woman said, teasing the tips of her pet's small gray ears, "the gypsy shall live again." As soon as the words spilled from her lips, Alana saw his face, the one image which she had suppressed deep within her for so long. Wistfully, she moved her hand from the kitten to stroke the dazzling fabric of Madame Ravaillac's clever creation. The vivid colors of the costume burned brazenly, almost obscenely, against the creamy satin coverlet of her bed. Did not these fiery hues mock her also?

Without warning, the small kitten hissed, startling her mistress. Her long tail bushed, and the hair rose along her arching back. Quickly, Alana tossed the furry mushroom to

402

the floor, admonishing the feline for her suddenly uncharacteristic behavior. "Champignon, one overly sensitive female on this eve is quite enough. Tonight I must be gay. And see, I am not yet dressed. Of course, it is not fashionable for a woman to be early. But what a *faux pas* for the hostess to fail to greet the early arrivals! Yet I would not deprive the old crones of their gossip by failing to be typically myself on this night. The infamous Marquise de la Villere!"

She gazed deeply into the wide cheval. Even the muted reflection could not conceal the exquisite form which the mirror held within. Tonight she would forsake the satin undergarments. Somehow it seemed a curious betrayal to wear more than the filmy blouse and billowing skirt of the gypsy. As she pulled tightly on the long strings of her purple cummerbund, she almost regretted dismissing Germaine for the evening. Cinching the wide corselet about her waist proved to be more difficult than she might have supposed. Finally, the lace was tied; again she assessed her image. It was then that she remembered Edouard's hand on her arm, pulling the loose gauze over her shoulders. Her hand moved to recreate his seductive alteration. Now all that remained to complete her masquerade were the bright dangling coins for her ears and wrists. Impulsively, she shook her head. No longer did she curse the dark wildness of her long mane. The coins at her ears jangled, a soft sound against the growing darkness and the throaty laughter of the gypsy.

Alana had not been far wrong when she supposed that all Paris would attend her *bal masqué*. It was doubtful that any of the invited guests declined, and many managed to stretch their invitations to include relatives and friends, who would not be denied their chance to attend the grand fete. They overflowed the spacious ballroom and dining hall, and could be found on the balconies and in the lantern-lit gardens: nobility and high bourgeois, artists and scholars, young and old; gods and goddesses, satyrs and nymphs, knights and damsels; Hamlet was come with his Ophelia, Romeo with Juliet, and Manfred stood reunited with his Astarte.

On the long tables stood silver platters heaped with every type of delightful offering to tempt the palate. Interspersed among these delicacies were arrangements of dried flowers and wheat, bright gourds and nuts spilling from large

cornucopia. There were no gaslights, all illumination being
provided by an extravagance of candles, their guttering light
at war with the thick shadow. Servants in provincial costume passed among the guests with trays of hors d'oeuvres
and sparkling wine, while in the ballroom an orchestra of
black and white harlequins struck up a lively polonaise.

At the center of a large group stood the gypsy, scarcely
listening to the idle chatter which ebbed and flowed around
her. Her attention was focused on her grand-mère and
Celestin, who stood across the room sharing a quiet moment amidst the joyous confusion. Alana was pleased that
Celestin had surrendered to her whim. He looked quite
dashing in the velvet suit, high boots, and sweeping plumed
chapeau of a musketeer. And Grand-mère, her still-lovely
figure showed to advantage in the elaborate dress of a lady
of Louis XIII's court. How fond she was of both of them.

"Alana, come waltz with me," importuned a young
minstrel. "You cannot hide behind that checkered mask,
and I must seize my opportunity. Henri will soon return
from dancing with his mamma, and then we lesser mortals
will have no chance."

As they moved toward the dance floor, Alana glanced
again at Celestin and Eugenie. They had been joined by an
elegant figure in the high-peaked hat of a medieval lady.
There was something disturbingly familiar about the woman
who warmly embraced her grandmother. Who was she?
Someone she had been fleetingly introduced to at the opera
perhaps, or Longchamps, or . . . ? The music began; the
riddle was forgotten.

Across the room, a tall woman stood. Her long white-
blonde hair fell loosely about her milky shoulders, partially
covering the shiny ornamental breastplates which cupped
her small, high breasts. The pale-blue sheer of a flowing
skirt was drawn tightly about her narrow waist, its filminess
barely concealing her long slender limbs. She bore the
heavy behorned helmet gracefully upon the flaxen head. It
seemed that no fairer Valkyrie had ever ridden into the halls
of Valhalla. Yet the handsome pirate at her side all but
ignored her presence.

Sipping at a goblet of champagne, the man peered
disdainfully through a black stretch of a mask, which did
little to conceal his arrogant features. He wore the tight

breeches and loose silken shirt as though they were his
natural attire. The dark, calf-high boots and the bright sash
around his slim waist were no capricious affectations. And
the casual swagger of his powerful body only contributed to
the suggestion that this was a man playing no role, posturing
no romantic character. He was precisely what he appeared
to be.

"I don't know why I ever insisted that you attend tonight.
It is as though you are not even here." The blonde woman
spoke, her angry voice cutting bitterly into the pirate's
obvious detachment.

"When I agreed to accompany you, I did not promise to
enjoy it as part of the bargain."

"Or deign to be charming?" she spat viciously.

His dry laughter held no humor. *"Charming,* my dear
countess, when have I ever been so? I am afraid that if you
desire charm, you have selected the wrong cousin for your
husband."

"Sometimes I hate you!" As soon as she spoke, she knew
she had gone too far, because the gray eyes paled suddenly
beneath the black mask, and his next words were little
above a whisper.

"I do not belong in Paris. I am here only to please my
grandmother. I belong in Moscow. Already the harbor of
St. Petersburg is frozen, and we shall have to return through
the Mediterranean. So, my dear, if you still wish to marry
such a boor, I think you had best pack your trunks quickly."

Apart from the milling crowd, he stood obscured in the
shadow of a column, a strangely solemn jester in silver and
black. Idiots, he thought, puppets to dance on strings. Was
there no one in all the multitudes who was capable of
understanding? Are they happy? It did not matter. Only
power was important. Happiness was for fools.

How convenient that he should have found her months
ago at the opera. Was she not alluring bait for his trap? And
these stupid Frenchmen with their chaotic politics would
provide the perfect guise for his plan.

He gazed about him. Oh God, it was happening again!
The masks which had concealed the identities of the revelers were gone. And in their place was only a blankness, a
nothingness. This was worse than his nightmares, far worse,
because he was awake now. Wasn't he? The faces, those

hideous, eyeless faces! In horror, he looked on as they continued dancing, laughing, speaking—oblivious to their mutilation. Compelled, he watched thin lips forming words and the angle of heads tipped back in high silly laughter.

Somehow, he made his way to the garden, the incessant babbling following in his wake. When finally he returned to the ballroom, the incident had passed. He prayed it would not recur, knowing that its memory would haunt his hours. It was then that he saw that the quadrille had brought the pirate and the gypsy together.

Was it possible that she was tired of dancing? she thought. She who adored dancing, she who could seemingly move to the music all the night through? Perhaps it was the excitement of her debut as a Parisian hostess. So many introductions: "Marquise de la Villere, I would like to present *Duc et Duchesse* . . ." It was all but impossible for many of her guests to play her little game of anonymity. The masks were mere bagatelles. And if her brain was addled by the tedious litany of names, her feet caused her even greater discomfort. Oh, but she could not refuse dear Vicomte Verdurin. She adored the rotund little caricature of a man, and he had been waiting for "hours" to dance with the beautiful gypsy.

A turn to the right, and another partner claimed her. She did not even look up, but concentrated on the meaningless patterns of the parquet floor. The ball was a great success; Paris would talk of nothing else for weeks. Had it made her happy? A foolish question. She was having a wonderful time.

She turned again to the rhythms of the dance, and was surprised at the firmness of the hand which took her own. She gazed upward into the face of her partner. The blue-gray eyes behind the thin cloth seemed to bore into her. She tensed, and had it not been for his quick hand at her waist she would have surely stumbled. How strange she felt with his arms about her, his touch so intimate. But she had no further time to analyze the deep stirring of emotion within her, for she was propelled quickly to a new partner. And when the music faded into applause, her darting eyes sought out the tall stranger, but he was gone.

Alana stood out upon the balcony, the cooling breeze of the October night reviving her. She had no longer been able to endure the stifling closeness of the crowded ballroom, the raucous inane chattering. Indeed, she had fought against a sudden wave of nausea after the disturbing encounter with the handsome stranger. She gazed upward at the pale face of the moon almost completely veiled by the ragged wisps of clouds. It was fast approaching midnight; soon the masquers must stand revealed.

She sensed a presence behind her. She could feel a compelling strength, a power. Whirling around, she found the man staring at her intensely. He was so close she could scarcely breathe, and yet she spoke, keeping her voice light, her manner teasing.

"Strange you should be a corsair, m'sieur. I was once kidnapped by a pirate, a Russian pirate."

His hand flew to her face, ripping away the checked mask. "Simone!"

She laughed brittlely. "Mais non, Capitaine Balenkov. Marquise Alana Eugenie de la Villere. Welcome to my house."

He moved closer, his expression unreadable. Suddenly, Apollo appeared on the balcony. "Oh, here you are Alana. I was beginning to worry."

At the sound of Henri's voice, she looked toward him, accepting the proffered glass of champagne.

"Who was that man?"

She looked back to where the pirate had stood but a moment before. Recovering, she turned to Henri. "Now, now, my sweet Apollo. You know the rules. It is not fair to reveal anyone's identity before the stroke of twelve."

～ Chapter 9 ～

The woman gazed out of the window of the rolling carriage. It was a cold, ashen-gray day, and she tucked the lap blanket securely across her legs. Despite the utter somberness of the weather, she was home. Did one every truly journey from home? Did not the old memories one carried within the heart keep one irrevocably bound to home? A kaleidoscope of images flooded her consciousness; through them all, *his* face came to her—vivid, precious. He was the one integral fragment of her being that was not intimately woven into the French tapestry of her existence. He had never really been part of it. He had come to her on a beautiful clear morning, and simply possessed her. But he was not a Parisian, not a Frenchman, and inexorably her life became his in that cold, barren land.

As the phaeton approached the city, she noted flower sellers everywhere. It was *la Toussaint,* and the hothouses were overflowing so that the faithful might have beautiful offerings to place on the graves of their loved ones. She thought of him so far away. His grave would already be covered with its white winter's blanket. She shivered.

The gentle swaying of the coach over the wide boulevards was soothing. How she had danced last night! It was the first really large social gathering she had attended since returning to France months before. Eugenie had spared nothing to make the occasion memorable, but she supposed it was the influence of her young granddaughter. How wonderful that she had found this girl after losing everyone dear to her. She must hear the whole story from her friend. Until now she had heard nothing but rumor and conjecture. There had been so many people last night, and all in costume. She had thought to meet the girl after midnight, but her grandson had been so insistent about leaving.

Ah, the carriage was almost there. Her curiosity would soon be satisfied. She would meet the beautiful and high-spirited Alana de la Villere. The marquise was reported to be most unconventional. She smiled to herself. Had not the same been said of young Josephine Aimee Bonneville?

As the woman was shown to the sitting room, she regretted that her good friend had not yet returned from the *cimetière*. Marie informed her that the young marquise had not been awake when her grandmother left for early morning Mass. She was now, however, in the conservatory and would be told that the comtesse was waiting in the drawing room.

Josephine stood before a portrait of Eugenie. She had been an incredible beauty at that age—the luxuriant hair, the glowing complexion, the large expressive eyes. She had not studied the portrait for many years, and now she found it faintly disturbing. A movement behind her caused her to turn. The young woman who stood in the doorway was no stranger.

"Simone!"

"Comtesse Semolenski, how good of you to call."

The older woman seemed immobilized, and only when her hostess offered tea, did she move to take the proffered seat.

"Comtesse, do you take sugar? Merci beaucoup, Marie, I will ring if I require anything further."

"Simone, you are . . ."

"The Marquise Alana de la Villere."

"*Je ne comprends pas.*"

"When I returned to New Orleans . . ."

As the young woman related her story, Josephine contemplated the terrible irony of the situation. She tried to concentrate on the girl's words, but her mind was plagued with a myriad of unanswered questions. Yet when the young woman had finished, Josephine found that all she could say was, "I am happy my dear, that you have found your family." Then hesitantly, "Can you ever forgive me for the pain I have caused you?"

"Do not speak of it, comtesse. We do what we must. We

think that we control our lives, but it seems that we are ruled by a twisted destiny. What is done, is done, and cannot be changed."

Josephine might have formed an answer, had the door not been swept open.

"So you have met my granddaughter, dear Josephine. Is she not wonderful?"

~ *Chapter 10* ~

"It is most kind of you to call, Comtesse Durenchev. Regretfully, my grandmother is visiting her daughter-in-law in the country, but I will convey your thanks to her. I know that it was her pleasure to include you and Prince Balenkov in her invitation to the Comtesse Semolenski. Grand-mère and the comtesse have, after all, been friends for many years.

"I am sorry that we were not introduced the night of the *bal masqué*, but there was such confusion—so many guests and . . ."

Oh, but you found the time to meet with Rudolph on the balcony, thought Ilse, remembering how she had followed him, overheard their words from the shadows.

". . . and do you plan to remain in Paris?"

"I am afraid we have already stayed far too long. We will return to Russia very soon. We are to wed in the spring."

"In the spring?"

"Oui, we must wait till then, for of course you know how bitter our Russian winters are."

"Mais non, Comtesse Durenchev, Alana de la Villere has

never enjoyed cold climes. I have not had the pleasure of visiting your country."

How easily the hussy lies, reflected the blonde woman, her face a cool mask. But perhaps, after all, there was a germ of truth in it. The Marquise de la Villere had never been in Russia, but *Simone* had.

Simone. That night on the balcony, Rudolph had spoken this name with such surprise and wonder in his voice—and something else. It was incredible, but somehow his French harlot had become the Parisian marquise. And he had not known of it, of this Ilse was certain.

She had heard the story, all Paris still buzzed with it, how this unknown girl had been discovered in a New Orleans convent, the heiress to the de la Villere title and fortune. And this same *marquise* had, she was sure now, been the mysterious woman in St. Petersburg, Rudolph's *French cousin.* No, thought Ilse spitefully, his whore!

And suddenly, she *knew* that this liaison had been the source of Rudolph's problems with Dimitri. The old man had never before objected to his nephew's peccadilloes with the *filles de joie.* Why had this one been different? Ilse reasoned that it must involve more than Dimitri's demand that Rudolph settle down and assume his responsibilities as bearer of the *yarlyk.* What then had been Dimitri's real quarrel? Unbidden, the word *kidnapped* came to her mind. What had the bitch meant when she said she had been "kidnapped once by a Russian pirate"? Could Rudolph have actually abducted her? Had it been Dimitri who had sent her away, so that there might be no evidence of his nephew's crime? There were still so many unanswered questions, and she just did not possess enough pieces to the puzzle. But there was irony here, she mused, a marvelous irony. The strumpet had, in fact, been a marquise all along. The slut was royalty, and neither she nor Rudolph had known it then. How sad for them both. She would see that they did not get a second chance.

As she sipped her tea, Alana looked over the cup at the fashionably groomed woman who was soon to be Rudolph's wife. As when she had first viewed her from behind the shrubbery with Yuri, she received the same impression of ultracoolness and complete control. This was no polite social call. What did Ilse Durenchev know?

~ *Chapter 11* ~

Outside, winter had claimed the city, but within the glass-walled room, plants grew in profusion; the very air seemed green and alive. Henri entered the conservatory to see Alana totally absorbed in trimming a potted rose bush. Unaware of his approach, she started violently at his greeting, pricking her finger upon a wicked thorn. A crimson droplet bloomed upon her ivory flesh, blood red like the roses themselves.

"Ma chère, I am sorry," Henri exclaimed, taking her hand and soothing the small wound with his lips. "I did not intend to startle you."

"It is nothing, Henri," she smiled somewhat nervously, reclaiming her hand and returning to her work.

He looked at her as she moved among the rows of cache pots and jardinieres. Her fingers first touched the soil for moisture before she angled the long copper spout into the leaves. How beautiful she was, he thought. And yet, today, she seemed so pale, so tired, withdrawn. Indeed, it seemed to Henri Beaumont that Alana had undergone some subtle, yet all-pervasive transformation since the night of the *bal masqué*. What had happened that evening? The man on the balcony—who had *he* been? Was he someone who might harm Alana? Oh, Alana, Alana, his thoughts continued, why must you be so reckless? Why have you so little concern for your safety? Why do you not let me hold you, protect you—love you? If only . . .

"Alana." His voice was barely audible. "There has been

another murder. There is no doubt now that the perpetrators of these vile deeds are crazed radicals, political assassins. And I'm afraid, my dearest, that . . ." He stopped, his face strained, his words momentarily trapped by the cold fear that clutched at his heart. When he continued, his voice held a kind of desperation. "Alana, you must be careful. You must promise me that you will go nowhere unescorted. Have you seen that horrible man, the one who was following you?"

"No, Henri," her voice sounded shallow, distant.

"Mon Dieu, Alana," Henri cried, no longer able to restrain himself. His hands grasped hers, pulling her to him. "I cannot live this way. When I found you, the world became special, filled with meaning. I never thought to find someone who could make me feel as you do. I cannot live without you. Without you, there is nothing. Please, my dearest one, marry me."

Alana looked at the young man who had pulled her so closely to him. His eyes suddenly seemed a pale green mist, his face so tense, his body rigid. She could not bear to see him hurting like this. She loved this beautiful man, loved him as she had once loved Yuri. As she loved all bright and beautiful things.

"Oh, Henri, my dearest Henri," she whispered. "Please, do not do this to me, to yourself . . . to us. Do you not know how much you mean to me, how dear your friendship? It would break my heart, if I should ever lose you. But Henri, I cannot marry you. I will marry no one. I cannot love you as you wish. My heart is not mine to give." She brushed his cheek lightly with her lips, and ran her fingers through his warm chestnut hair, caressing the thick waves. "Henri," she murmured, her dark eyes clouding, as they looked upon his bruised face, "You are so precious to me."

"But you do not love me, Alana. You do not love me."

"What is it, Champignon?" Alana's voice rang out in the still air of her bedchamber as she entered from her dressing room. The small feline was no longer curled before the hearth, but had sprung upon the bed, her back arched menacingly, her long tail bushed wide. "Stop your hissing, you silly thing. I see nothing to upset you," she continued, her eyes sweeping the empty room. She sat upon the satin coverlet and took her agitated pet into her arms, soothing its ruffled fur. As she stroked the long silky hair, her gaze wandered to the large package which had been delivered earlier that day. Thankfully, her grandmother had been out with Celestin. She stared at it in an agony of indecision. Since its arrival, she had thought of nothing else, and yet it remained wrapped in the brown paper.

Why had she insisted that Edouard do this painting? Was she in truth the wild minx that all of Paris thought her? Was she as reckless as Henri said? I am being ridiculous, she told herself. It is, after all, only a portrait. Of what am I afraid? Without further thought, she set the kitten on the bed, and removed the loosely tied strings which bound the wrappings.

She looked closely at the large canvas, her eyes compelled to focus upon the shiny surface, to look at the reclining figure, the reposing odalisque. Whom had Edouard captured with his wide brush strokes, his naked paint? Alana? Simone? Marquise? Gypsy? Or someone who was both, and yet neither? Gone was the masquerade. All was revealed—the small black mask, a poor bagatelle of concealment. Here, at last, the young woman decided, was truth.

"Champignon, *qu'est-ce que c'est? Qu'est-ce que c'est*?" Alana exclaimed as the cat bounded from the bed, and ran like a gray streak toward the French doors to the balcony. Champignon stopped a few feet from the draperies, as if afraid to draw nearer. "Oh," laughed Alana, "it is nothing but the wind rattling against the doors. See, I will lock them, my little mushroom. Is this not better?" the woman offered, as she pivoted toward the kitten.

Without warning, a hand reached from behind the heavy damask, cupping her mouth and drawing her roughly behind the curtain. As she was crushed to a hard masculine chest, an image of the simian figure, the strange dark man, burned into her consciousness. Henri was right! They had come for her! She was going to die, and there was yet so much . . .

Abruptly, strong arms turned her to face her captor. She

gasped. In the pale light of the moon she beheld his blue-gray eyes.

Releasing her, he smiled, stepping from behind the curtain. Bowing slightly, he said, "Bonsoir, marquise. Since we were so rudely interrupted by your little gentleman when last we met, I have returned at a time . . ."

"My *little gentleman!* What would *you* know of being a gentleman?"

"And what do you know of being a *lady,* Marquise de la Villere?"

Her hand flashed out to strike his arrogant face. As always, she was no match for him. He laughed, and sweeping her into his arms, carried her to the bed.

He was still smiling as he looked down upon her, sprawled among the soft cushions. Her light wrapper had fallen partially open, and the soft light of the room caught patches of her honeyed skin. She made no move to defend herself against the sensual onslaught which she knew would come. Nor did she pull the silken fabric across her breast, to hide the dark peak, which had escaped the robe's concealing folds. She lay still and watched.

His hands had worked quickly, and soon he stood revealed, a naked golden god. How could she have forgotten his beauty? Or had she? The broad muscular chest, the hard flat abdomen, the taut columns of his thighs, and the strange white scar. His manhood was large, ripened. His physical need for her was the one thing he could never deny. It was the only power she had ever held over this man. And he needed her now.

He lowered his body to her. Simone pushed against him, not with the thought of escape, but for the pure pleasure of reveling in his superior strength. There was, at last, no room within her being for questions or thoughts. Having earned the freedom to simply feel, she was now a creature of pure sensation. She twined her arms about him now, her small hands pulling against the hard smooth muscles of his back, drawing him down upon her, welcoming the glorious weight of him. In the moment when his naked flesh pressed the length of hers, she took life. She was at last herself.

She lay in his arms. They did not speak; a deep peace seemed to have settled upon the room. For the first time,

Simone fully appreciated that when she and Rudolph came together, as they had done on this night, their perfect coupling transcended all. All the pain and hurt, all the fear and mistrust. It all dissolved into the pure, bright pleasure of the moment, disappeared within the circle of his arms. When he came to her, entering her, he fused himself deep within the core of her being. Then she was one with herself, one with him.

Champignon crawled from under the flowered chaise under which she had been hiding. Cautiously, she climbed up the padded coverlet, seeking her mistress, her sharp little claws digging into the silken quilt. As she reached the top of the bed, she encountered the blond giant who had so frightened her. Instantly, she sprang from the cushions, launching herself against the painting which leaned against the wall. The brown wrapping paper, which Simone had carelessly replaced, fell to the floor.

Rudolph had not missed this performance. And softly chuckling, he raised himself on one elbow, gazing in the direction of the kitten's clumsy departure. Suddenly he froze.

So they were true—all the rumors he had heard about her. There could be no mistake. It was she, even to the mole above her breast.

Simone had seen him tense. Slowly she drew herself up and looked to where he was staring. Mon Dieu, the portrait! What was he thinking?

He turned then, striking her face savagely with his open palm. "Slut!" It was a cry of anguish. "A perfect likeness, you shameless whore!"

The look in his eyes was beyond bearing. She blotted it out with her angry words. "And what then are you? Am I not what you have made me?"

His large hand, reaching for her face, pulled her lips up to his. Brutally, he raped the soft, delicate skin of her open mouth. His long tongue thrust so deeply that she gagged on its fullness. When his teeth cut sharply into her upper lip, she whimpered. He raised his head and smiled, seeming to gain some sadistic pleasure from her pain. Then he lowered his mouth to her breast, and slowly licked the small rigid nipple. Gently he lapped at the taut surface, his long tongue tracing small, precise circles about the dark peak. His suckling movements became more feverish, and when he seemed able to endure the tender nursing of her no longer, he bit deeply into the soft flesh. She screamed. This time he ignored her, and moved his mouth to torture the moist silkiness between her thighs—rubbing, biting, pulling.

He pushed himself upward, and kneeling, he offered himself to her. He pressed her head against him, his fingers twisting and burrowing into the tangled masses of her hair. His body rocked rhythmically until he threw his head back and groaned, a deep guttural sound. Suddenly, he pulled away, and turned her roughly onto her stomach. He was not yet satisfied. At the searing pain of his entry, her cries filled the room. Soon his desperate moans matched her crescendoing wails.

She lay abandoned on the bed. No, no, it could not have happened like this. She wouldn't let it be true. To have at last understood everything that he meant to her, and to have seen it destroyed in an instant.

Somehow she made her way to the vanity table, and sought the beautiful egg. The moon had not yet set, and it gleamed through the open doors. It was cold, deathly cold, and Simone shivered convulsively as she held the precious object before her streaming eyes. Horribly, the delicate ornament slipped from her nerveless fingers and shattered on the hard floor.

As the dark figure emerged onto the balcony, the tall blonde woman in the carriage below motioned for the driver to depart. She did not wish her presence known. She had seen enough, and knew where she must go. Tomorrow would not be too soon.

~ *Chapter 12* ~

10 November 1875

All goes according to plan. I have heard from Mother. She writes that the bishop has done his job well. The gift of a new church has sealed the peasants' lips. They no longer speak of "St. Sophia."

Dear Mother, how I hate her and her endless recriminations. But she is a useful tool. She has seen my uncle. The seed of doubt, which I so cunningly planted, begins to bear fruit. When the terrible tragedy strikes, I shall be welcomed home from my "sojourn in Italy" as my uncle's heir. There will be no other choice open to him. I have seen to everything.

His fingers tightened around the slender pen, then it fell heavily to the parchment. Desperately, the delicate hands clutched the dark head, the long fingers feverishly massaging the throbbing temples. The terrible pain, it had returned. Would it never leave him? Would it never cease? The fingertips pressed deeper into the hot flesh. Then suddenly, they tore into the damp matted hair, pulling at it in an impotent defense against the agony which ripped through his body. Stop! His mind screamed. Please, oh please, stop! His eyes tightened against the searing white-hot light that exploded in his brain, to ebb finally in his groin. And then it passed. Slowly the golden eyes opened —glazed amber, hollow in the ashen skin. He swallowed,

forcing the wave of nausea back into his throat. He retrieved the pen.

*I cannot fail. The Fates smile on me. Did they not
arrange that I find his whore at the opera, not two days
after my arrival in Paris on the heels of my accursed
cousin? Did they not provide the perfect spy? An ugly
creature, but good at his work. I know her every move.
She, too, has played into my hands. Her reputation will
lend credence to my little drama.*

*And not only the gods, but these idiot Frenchmen,
conspire with me in my work. Of what real matter to
these fools that the antiRoyalist cabal claim two more
victims? How simple it all shall be. My cousin and his
whore will be easy to manipulate. But aren't all those
blinded by love—ever like sheep, ever like children? She
will come to him, unselfish, free. And he, to save
her—so noble, so gallant. And both shall . . .*

The sharp knock was a jarring sound against the stillness
of the room. He rose from his chair, wondering why the boy
was so early with his bath water. He opened the door
without question.

"Bonjour, Pavel." Her voice was mocking in its sweetness.

"Ilse!"

"Well, aren't you going to invite me in?"

"But, of course, Countess Durenchev," he said, recovering. "Please do come in."

The tall blonde woman sailed into the room. As she
turned to face the dark man, she frowned slightly. Despite
her innate detachment, she was startled by Pavel's altered
appearance. *My dear Pavel*, she thought, *so thin and pale,
so . . .*

"How did you find me, dear Ilse? No, I should not ask
that. I know you have your little ways."

"And what of your 'little ways,' my cousin-to-be?"

Pavel laughed.

"What is so humorous?" she snapped.

"Nothing, my dear Ilse, except that I don't fancy being
your cousin. In fact, I have not at all accepted that I will
become your cousin."

Ilse looked at the man. Something was different about him, a certain wildness in the golden eyes. "You have no choice, Pavel. It seems that whatever had separated Dimitri and Rudolph is no more. So you see, there are now no obstacles to our marriage."

"Aren't there, Ilse?"

It was the way he had said it that convinced her that he knew of Simone. But how much did Pavel know? She was certain that he had discovered all that he needed. It was so characteristic of him.

He walked closer to her, and took her face into his hands. "You know, my love, it has always seemed to me that you selected the wrong Prince Balenkov to wed."

She tried to move her face, but his grip tightened, his eyes holding hers. "You're hurting me, Pavel!" He loosened his hold. "How could I have selected the wrong Balenkov? I chose the next grand duke."

"Have you, my sweet?"

"Of course. It is well known that your breach with Dimitri has not healed. Despite your cleverness and guile you have failed to enchant the old man. Indeed, what happened between you two?"

Pavel looked at her, a feral gleam in his eyes. She knew that their little game had suddenly grown serious. Pavel ignored her question. "I told you, Ilse, that I don't relish being your cousin. And I will not. I mean to have the Balenkov title, the lands, the *yarlyk*—all shall be mine!"

"I don't understand any of this, Pavel," she retorted, her voice losing some of its cool assurance.

"Well, I shall have to explain. Let us assume that something should happen to your dear fiancé. Dimitri would have no choice but to accept me as his successor. Thus, I would win by default. Of course, this injures my pride, since I was always the better choice. But I will accept this turn of events."

"What are you planning, Pavel?" the young woman asked, desperation creeping into her tone.

"Let us say that I don't believe that a wedding will take place in the spring."

She thought quickly. If Pavel succeeded at what he hinted, she would lose. And if he did not, would she not lose anyway? It was a risk, but one she had to take.

"And the Marquise de la Villere? What of her?" she offered archly.

Pavel threw his head back in laughter. "Yes, my dear Ilse," he spoke through his smiling mouth, "I believe we are well suited."

She was gone. He returned to his desk. He must record this interview with the Countess Ilse Durenchev. Everything must be accounted for. There could be no margin for error. How would this alliance with her affect his careful plan? All was a delicate balance.

But Pavel had not taken into account the fatal flaw in his character. There was that in him which yet resisted. He could not kill that which he regarded as his deepest perversion, but was, in fact, his greatest virtue—his ability to value that which was truly of worth. His love for Rudolph would not die.

~ Chapter 13 ~

She dipped the brush into the pigment, and tried to concentrate on the painting before her. It was not going well. The portrait of her grandmother would never be ready for Christmas. Even as she placed the brush stroke upon the canvas, her mind began to drift.

How foolish to think she could forget the past and begin anew. Even her feeble attempts at the gay, carefree life had failed, and now happiness was more elusive than ever.

She had come, at last, to the undeniable conclusion—that same conclusion she had unconsciously reached on that long-ago voyage to Russia. When had she first realized it?

That evening as he bent over the charts at his desk? Yes, she had loved him then. She had loved him always. When he held her tenderly, when he hurt her with his coldness and indifference. Yes, even in his violence, she loved him. Why had she never been honest with herself, with him? Why the *masquerade*?

She touched the golden heart at her throat. From the beginning, she had thought that if she could but know her identity, she would be happy, at peace. But now she realized it meant so very little. Far better had she remained Rudolph's mistress, than to become the Marquise de la Villere. Love was what was important. Love gave meaning to life. Her title and fortune meant nothing without Rudolph.

And yet she had had no choice. She had not had the right to love him before. And now that she did, it was too late. He hated her. And it was her own fault. There was no happiness for her. There never could be now.

— *Chapter 14* —

"If not Henri, my sweet, *who*? Who is he, Alana? Who is this man who disturbs you so, makes you so sad? Please, ma petite, I cannot bear to see the pain in your eyes any longer. Alana, there *is* someone, isn't there?"

The young woman stared at her hands. Had she really fooled anyone? Surely not her grandmother. Her feelings for him were so real now, so very honest. It was no longer a masquerade of love.

"Yes, Grand-mère, but he does not love me."

"Oh, Alana, my child. I cannot believe it is as you say."

The woman drew her granddaughter closer to her. "No one could not love you. You are so beautiful, so good.

"Alana, this man for whom you care so deeply, if he is worthy of your love, I cannot believe that he is insensitive to you. You must go to him, fight for him, even if you must fight him for himself. Do not make the same error I made so many years ago. Seek him, hold him close. Marry him, Alana, marry him. To deny the heart means only suffering and tragedy. I know, ma chère, I know."

Simone gave her dark green bonnet a final adjustment and threw her fur-lined cape about her shoulders. She must get out of the house, she thought, as she descended the stairs. She would visit Genevieve d'Albert. It had been some time since she had seen her friend; Genevieve was one of the few young women she had met in Paris who she truly liked. Later she would have Claude drive her to the Luxembourg Gardens. Perhaps there, she would be able to think . . .

"Marquise de la Villere!" The insistent voice rang out as she stepped from the house.

A man in a strange livery ran up the steps and thrust a note into her hand. Simone stared at Rudolph's bold script.

Simone,
I must see you at once. Leon will bring you to me.
Rudolph

How strange . . .

"Come, mademoiselle, it is urgent," implored the servant.

Simone hesitated but a moment, then allowed the driver to lead her to a waiting carriage. They were already pulling away, when the startled Claude brought Simone's own elegant barouche around from the stables.

Rudolph. Rudolph sending for her. She had thought after that horrible night that she would never see him again. But now, he wanted her. Was it possible that he had forgiven her . . . forgiven the portrait . . . forgive . . . forget . . .

But the missive. Something was wrong. Something was . . . Simone shook her head. No, I will not fight this. I will not allow anything to stop me. Rudolph wants to see me, and I will go to him. I will tell him how sorry I am for being so blind, so foolish. I will beg his forgiveness. I will tell him how much I care, how much I love him. He will forgive me, he will believe me. He will . . .

The carriage stopped sharply, jerking Simone forward. The door opened. "Marquise." The driver's voice came, punctuating his extended hand. "Prince Balenkov awaits you at the end of the path."

"Merci, Leon," the woman replied, alighting. "I am . . ." But she did not have time to finish her sentence. Leon had mounted the carriage and was swiftly pulling away.

For a moment she stared blankly at the retreating coach, its easy, swaying movements mesmerizing her. Then she turned, and breathed deeply. The crisp November air revived her. How she loved the Bois! A lush wilderness trapped within the city's bosom. So quiet, so secluded, especially at this time of the year. The trilling of the birds formed the solitary song against the peace of the late afternoon. Yes, she affirmed, her eyes closed tightly. Yes. Here we can find each other. Here we can learn what we have always yearned to know. Here we can discover our deepest secrets.

She had reached the end of the lane. A large pond mirrored the deep gray of the sky. The oaks had lost their leaves, but a thick shrubbery grew about the perimeter of the miniature lake. She saw no one.

A small gravel path diverged away from the water's edge, cutting through the hedge. She passed along the path silently. Indeed, the park itself was suddenly very still. The birds had ceased their twittering, and within the manicured forest the wind had dropped to a whisper.

He stood in deep shadow, his back toward her. She would have recognized the tall form anywhere.

"Rudolph!" she called to him, but he made no move to turn. She walked to him, reaching up to touch his shoulder. "Rudolph," she whispered.

Abruptly, he faced her, the yellow eyes boring into hers. "Pavel! I . . . I . . . Where is Rudolph? Is he not here?"

He smiled, but the intensity of his gaze did not lessen. "He will be here shortly, *Marquise de la Villere*."

He had spoken the words ironically. What was happening? This was all so strange and confusing. Where was Rudolph? What was Pavel doing here? And what of Pavel?

This was not the elegant cavalier that she had known in Moscow. Though still darkly handsome, this man was wild, desperate—bestial. Suddenly, an image of the wolf, so long ago on the white steppes of Russia, came to her. Was this the moment for which she had been spared? The ancient chill gripped her. She shuddered and took a step backward.

Pavel's hand shot forward, gripping the soft flesh of her arm. "Oh, do not leave, Simone. My cousin would not be pleased to come and find his little bird flown. Nor would it do for you to let it be known that Pavel is no longer in Italy."

"Italy? Please, Pavel. I don't understand any of this."

"But it is so simple, ma petite. My stupid cousin thinks me finished with my uncle because of . . . because of some unpleasantness with my serfs. What a fool he is to think that I would let it rest there. A true Balenkov lets nothing stand between himself and his birthright—nothing!"

As he spoke, his glowing amber eyes remained fixed upon her. At his last words, his look seemed to intensify. He searched her face, as if he sought in her features the solution to some problem, some ultimate answer which had yet eluded him. He went on.

"They all think me in Italy, gone south 'for my health.' How I am missed in the drawing rooms of Petersburg! But they have not long to wait for my triumphant return. Despite my 'ill health,' I will return home to comfort my uncle in his sorrow, and take my rightful place as successor to the *yarlyk*."

"But what of . . ."

"Rudolph?" he finished her question. "Do not be so impatient, Simone. We shall return to my cousin's destiny in but a moment.

"It is strange," he murmured, his tone suddenly introspective, "but even I could not have guessed that when I followed Rudolph to Paris, I would find his whore there also. It was but a stroke of luck that I found her at the opera."

Simone gasped. Had she not sensed his malevolent gaze upon her that night? She tensed. He was no longer aware of her—his grip had relaxed, his eyes were turned inward. She glanced quickly to the pathway. Could she escape him?

But the moment was lost. He smiled. "My spies kept me well informed of your activities. The Marquise de la Villere has hardly been a model of French maidenhood. Yet what could one expect of Rudolph Balenkov's New Orleans gypsy? What irony! I only wish there were more time, my dear marquise. I should wish to hear the whole of your strange little life. But alas, my cousin will soon arrive, and there is much to do . . ."

Simone quailed at his look. The golden eyes were merciless as they held hers, as his grasp tightened about her arm. And then, unexpectedly, he bowed to her, a courtly motion resurrecting the old Pavel, her companion at lunch in Moscow.

"It was a lovely *bal masqué*, ma cherie. I slipped in unnoticed—the jester at the feast, the trump card of fate. It was so kind of you to invite my dear cousin. Had you not made your presence in Paris known to him, I should have had to arrange your reunion myself. Just as I have arranged everything, everything. You do see that I cannot fail this time. The gods themselves are on my side. Have you not been provided for me, the sacrificial *virgin*, the harlot marquise? All has been arranged for Pavel by the gods.

"But you asked about Rudolph," he said, his tone changing once again. "When my dear cousin receives *your* urgent message, he will seek in vain for you here, calling out to his Simone, only to have the empty silence mock him. How well he will play the Orpheus to your Eurydice. And like unto Eurydice, my Simone, the darkness, and not the light, shall claim you. Rudolph shall find his beloved piteously dead upon the cold earth, *the bud plucked before the flower bloomed.*"

The words spilled like venom from his mouth. But still she could not speak, and perversely she listened, compelled to hear all of it, all of his madness.

"And how he shall cry out in futility and in such anguish. Wildly, he will seek the heinous assailant, the sickening revenge rising as bile to fill his throat. But alas, he shall find only his own dear cousin, and the sweet piercing bullet."

His eyes seemed to glow with a new excitement as he uttered this last. He was charged with a twisted passion, almost sensual in nature. Simone watched as a fine mist of perspiration coated his brow, despite the growing chill of the late afternoon. He ran a finger over her lower lip. His next words came forth as tiny gasps. "You will have been my perfect, my most alluring bait. Everyone will think the

Marquise de la Villere but another target of the antiRoyalist rabble. And your paramour? Only an innocent victim. And as much as I hate to mutilate your beautiful body, I shall leave no doubt that it was the grisly work of the radical mob."

So closely had he drawn her to him, that she could feel his hot breath upon her cheek. "No, Pavel. Rudolph will not come. You have made a grave error, a terrible miscalculation." Surprisingly, her voice sounded calm to her ears. "You see, Pavel," she continued, "Rudolph hates me."

Pavel's head flew backward, his laughter dry, hollow.

"Oh, Simone, how lovely. Your innocence and modesty still amaze me. Would a man such as Rudolph Balenkov risk all for a woman he hates? Would he have been willing to forfeit everything for such a woman—the lands, the title, the *yarlyk*? Besides, my precious, how could anyone hate you?" His chest heaved against her breasts, and to her horror, she could feel his quickening manhood pressed intimately against the folds of her skirt.

"Oh no, ma cherie, no one could hate you. Indeed, another time, another place . . ." His full mouth opened, and his long tongue poised between his white teeth. He lowered his head over hers.

"No, Pavel," she screamed, pulling violently against his tightening grip, and twisting her face from his warm lips. Yet her protestations seemed only to arouse him further. He pulled at her shoulders, dragging her to the ground.

Oh my God, no, not this, not this . . . I must escape . . . save Rudolph . . .

The clattering of the horses hoofs over the cobblestone streets of Paris formed a steady backdrop to Rudolph's fragmented thoughts. Long after the excited messenger had departed, the man's words reverberated in Rudolph's mind. "*Prince Balenkov, the Marquise de la Villere would speak with you. She says it is of grave importance.*"

He neared the outskirts of the city. It was a relief to spur the animal on, to substitute speed for thought. The cobblestones gave way to country lanes, and the metal shoes of the great black steed thudded heavily upon the hardpacked earth.

As he galloped toward the Bois, he again wondered at Simone's desire for seclusion. The Bois, it would be all but deserted at this time of the day. Why did she not see him at her townhouse? And why the urgency? *The Marquise de la Villere would speak with you.*

Simone. What is it, Simone? Another coy trick, my gypsy? But even as the thought had come, Rudolph knew instinctively there would be no game—no toying with him, as on that first occasion, when he stood below the inverted cross of Madame Ninon's. *It is of grave importance.* No —something was wrong. Deadly wrong. A primitive fear gripped him, and he dug his powerful thighs deeper into the horseflesh, pressing his mount to greater speed.

At last he had reached the Bois de Boulogne. The servant had been very explicit about the direction he should take. In a moment he would see her. The park was as he had imagined. The sunlight lay in pale shreds upon the dry grass, the mellow shafts emerging thinly between the dun-colored shadows of the arching trees. It was so quiet.

Rudolph reined his steed, and unconsciously, he smoothed the beast's long mane, as if to still its noisy breath and impatient pawing. Then he cantered down the long path toward the pond. He looked ahead. He knew she would be standing there, waiting for him. The cold, pale light of the day seemed to have gathered in the small lake, draining the surrounding air of any brightness. He could see her now, captured within the water's glassy depths, a glowing Nereid, her long black hair wet and curling about her shoulders and neck. Her silvered body entwined with swirling vines, her nipples and soft woman's down blossomed with fragrant hyacinth and lily.

He dismounted and walked quickly down the wide path, his boots crushing softly against the white gravel. The image was lost, and the imprisoned reflection faded as he moved to the water's edge.

Where was she? He tethered the horse and made his way down the small pathway which led through the bushes into the recesses of the nearby glade. As he passed through the shrubbery, he was faintly aware of the horse whinnying nervously behind him. But his senses were focused ahead, alert, probing. He stalked steadily through the darkling forest, his thick gold hair rippling in the soft breezes, his clear gray eyes seeking to penetrate the gloom of the wood.

There, but a few feet ahead of him, a movement in the hedge. The green-black leaves shivered as if touched by a violent wind, and the snapping of dry twigs sounded unnaturally loud in the stillness. Rudolph moved quickly forward, no conscious thought within his brain. He was the hunter primordial. And beyond the thick greenery lurked. . . .

"Pavel!"

The dark shape flung itself upward from the struggling figure upon the floor of the forest. He held a large pistol in his hand.

"You are early, Cousin, but no matter. I can finish with your whore as well after your death, as before."

Rudolph's reply was reflexive. He sprang forward, all muscle and sinew, his great golden body falling hard against his antagonist with a swiftness that forebore retaliation. They hit the ground simultaneously, the gun scrabbling across the dry leaves. Simone struggled to her feet, grasping at the rough bark of an oak for support. Rudolph, her mind chanted madly, *Rudolph*. She watched them in awed fascination. They rolled over and over in the dead leaves, light, dark, dark, light.

Then the motion ceased. Rudolph was astride his cousin, his hands grasping Pavel's throat, his strong white teeth bared in a grimace of effort and passion. Pavel battled to free himself with one hand; with the other he reached out in desperation—reaching, reaching. His finger's met the pistol's pearl handle. Through the purple gaze of his fury, Rudolph saw his cousin smile and heard Simone's agonized cry. The gun! He lunged forward, pinning Pavel's hand to the earth before he could take aim.

They lay sprawled body to body with no apparent movement. Only the straining in their outstretched arms, quivering with tension, betrayed their struggle. Pavel's finger locked about the deadly trigger; Rudolph's hand was like a vise upon his cousin's wrist. On it went, moment after unending moment. Finally the pistol began to move in a steady arc toward the intertwining bodies.

Simone watched as Rudolph strained against the motion of Pavel's arm, but the pressure was relentless. Pavel's strength was unnatural. How long could Rudolph keep the gun at bay? She looked on in horror; she could do nothing. If she should move, disturb Rudolph's concentration . . .

The gun moved closer to its target. He was winning! He could feel the dark power surging through him, filling him like cold steel. The moment was at hand. He would have it all. They would leave him alone. He could rest at last, be at peace. He looked into Rudolph's face, their eyes locked.

The gun continued in its resolute path. Suddenly, inexplicably, the weapon's path changed. Pavel's finger moved upon the trigger. An explosion, terrible in its finality, melded with the shrill scream which welled from Simone's throat.

Then there was silence, the hollow shot swallowing all within its death-echo. Rudolph felt the body heave violently against his own, and then . . . He lay very still for a time, his weight bearing down upon the motionless form. When did he finally move—a minute, an hour, an eternity? Slowly he drew his bulk upward, his arms tensing to brace his body. He gazed downward at the dark figure sprawled beneath him.

The head was turned away, but he could see that the eyes were closed and the mouth . . . the mouth . . . he was smiling. Slowly, Rudolph cupped the head with his palm, and drew it upward to cradle the man within his arms.

The eyes opened, the great golden eyes. And then he saw it—saw what he had refused to acknowledge, what Pavel had begged him to see. He knew their truth. "Rudolph," the pale lips whispered, "I . . . I . . ." His arm moved slowly upward, and with the tips of his long fingers, he brushed Rudolph's lips. The hand fell to rest upon the hard winter earth; the golden light faded from the amber eyes.

He lay within Rudolph's arms; the dark head hung limply, the black curls oddly bright and alive. The lustrous waves kissed the crackling dried leaves, capturing them within their silkiness. He appeared asleep, the wide mouth parted slightly in a childlike pout, the large man's body betraying the innocent countenance.

"Pavel," Rudolph breathed. "Pavel," his voice came again. But an impotent silence cursed his futile litany. His calling was no more than the whisper of the wind against the night. He crushed the body to his chest, and slowly began to rock, gently at first, then with a frenzied rhythm. His fingers raked through the dark hair, his lips murmuring in Russian against the deaf ears.

Suddenly he stopped, and looked into the serene face. When the words came from his mouth, they were as a tortured cry wrung from his soul, erupting from some primeval essence. It was a language that seemed to transcend all worlds, all times. It appeared to be a thing apart from the man himself, a primitive chant wrested from his Varangian past. As it ceased, he dropped his golden head. When at last he lifted his face, great tears rolled silently from his vacant gray eyes.

"Rudolph," Simone cried, her arms about his shoulders. "Rudolph, please, please." She repeated it over and over, like an ancient rune which had lost its efficacy. He could not hear her. The last of the cold gray light bled from the horizon into the hungry void; the night sounds rose unceasingly into the starless vault.

~ *Chapter 15* ~

Josephine held Pavel's diary in her hand. She would read it but one more time, and then . . . Her gaze went to the fire crackling in the hearth.

Again her eyes were drawn back to the words which so graphically detailed his hideous plan. Oh, how terribly sick he was, how tortured, driven by demons beyond his control. But could we not have helped him? If only we had realized . . . Dear God, forgive us all. Each of us has sinned in this horrid tragedy.

And Ilse. How could we not have seen her for what she was? Or had we, and simply chose to ignore it? Her hand trembled as she turned the page, her thoughts focused on the unholy alliance between the countess and Pavel. The police had wanted to investigate more fully after reading of

Ilse's involvement within the pages of Pavel's incriminating journal. But she, Josephine, had managed to discourage it. Her influence was still great. The incident would never come to public knowledge.

She had sent Ilse back to Russia, admonishing her that she should be grateful that Pavel's sordid intrigue, and her implication in it, had died with him. Of course, some story would have to be told concerning the severing of Ilse's and Rudolph's relationship. But that, she could leave to the countess. It seemed she was adept at deceit, and would no doubt manufacture a suitable tale.

If only all her problems were so easily solved. What was she to do about Rudolph? He seemed totally incapable of anything. He could not even manage living one day at a time. She had wanted to accompany Pavel's body to Russia, to attend the funeral. Dimitri and Natasha would need her. The letter she had written explaining Pavel's *accident* seemed so cold, so inadequate. But her first responsibility was to Rudolph. She had failed him once when he needed her many years ago; she must not do so again. He would not go, and so she must remain with him in Paris.

Would Rudolph ever accept Pavel's death? He had not been able to face what had happened. He would not speak of it. Since that day she had taken him from the police, he had said almost nothing. It was as if he, too, were dead.

Rudolph had been cleared of any crime. The official records would list Pavel's death as an accident. But Rudolph was unable to absolve himself. Oh God, she feared for his sanity!

And poor Simone, the girl too, was devastated, feeling somehow responsible for this tragedy. She would write her, and tell her that she was not to blame. It was they who needed her forgiveness, especially Rudolph, whose very life depended on her understanding and compassion. If she, Simone, could forgive Rudolph, could he not forgive himself? Josephine felt that something more than Pavel's death was destroying Rudolph—something which involved Simone.

She must convince the girl to come to Rudolph, and he must be persuaded to see her. Josephine knew that her grandson's only hope lay with Simone.

"Please, God," Josephine prayed, "give me the strength to do all that must be done."

~ *Chapter 16* ~

Tiny white particles whirled airily through the gray December day. Everything seemed to be peculiarly drained of color. A slate sky melted into the cold white earth. Oh, Edouard, Alana thought wistfully, what relief your palette could bring to this lifeless landscape. But the day was not unlike the woman herself. She had not felt happy, at peace, since the Bois.

Christmas! Like a tiny spore, the word germinated in her brain. Could the season be but two weeks away? Could she hope to endure the glossy holly and flickering tapers, the green pine smells, the orange-and-clove scents? Could she pull the velvet ribbon on a brightly wrapped package, or sing the ancient carols?

Even the joy of seeing her grandparents in Spain for the first time would be piteously muted. *Joyeux Noël*, she whispered, her breath frosting the glass of the carriage.

As she gazed into the haze of the falling snow, her mind drifted. She shivered. Through the descending powder, she seemed to see the wolf. The sculptured head, the ears pricked to points, the flaring nostrils, and the eyes—the great yellow fire-moons. The amber flames swallowed all but the black slits of his pupils. Then slowly, but quite perceptibly, the gray vision turned into the clear image of "his" face, "his" eyes. No! She would not think of him. For to think of "him" meant only to think of the "other." Mimka had been right. They were one, had always been one. And never had she really understood this until she saw Pavel in his arms. She held her breath for a moment. *Had*

433

always been one? Would always be one. Mon Dieu, could I ever hope to gain what even in death he still claims?

She had tried to forget that endless night in the desolate park. But as always, she was powerless against the on-slaught of merciless memory. Again she watched the slow ebbing of the wan light, and felt the increasing chill of the moonless night. Never had she been so utterly alone as there in the black wood, at vigil with death and recrimination. She could not remember the dawn, yet it had been late morning when the groundskeeper returned with Henri and the police.

She did not know if she could bear seeing him again as he was in the Bois. She wished fervently that she could somehow obliterate the hateful image of that haunted face, and see him only as he had been in Russia, and in New Orleans. She remembered the day he had proposed to her, his arms tight about her, his lips buried in her hair. Why? Why? she asked of the empty carriage, the chill December morning, the gray expanse of heaven.

What could she say to him? Why had Josephine insisted that she come? In the park he had not responded to her. She could not but believe that he blamed her in some way for Pavel's death. She had said as much to Josephine when they spoke after the tragedy. How could she help this man who hated her?

It was Josephine herself who opened the door. She was so changed—aged, haggard.

"Welcome, dear Simone, I am so grateful that you have come. Strange . . . once I sent you away because I thought you would bring ruin on him, and now I send for you as the only one who can save him. Help him, Simone. You must help him."

"I will do what I can, Countess Semolenski, but I ask that you do not place too much hope in my visit. I fear that I may only make things worse. I am afraid that . . . he hates me." Her voice, which had seemed steady, now broke. But she swallowed, and blinked back the tears. She was calm once again.

"Oh, no, Simone, oh, no. I am sure he does not hate you."

"But what can I say to him? There are no words . . ." There never had been, she thought.

"Simone," began Josephine, taking the young woman's

hand into her own. "I do not fully understand the nature of
Rudolph's melancholia. I know that Pavel's betrayal and
the manner of his death are integral to his illness, but there
is more. And you, Simone . . ."

They looked at each other. The sentence remained
unfinished. "Go to him, Simone," Josephine said at last.
"You will know what to say. Let your heart speak."

She walked slowly through the door into the darkened
study. He was seated before the dying fire. It was as she had
feared. He was thin, pale, unshaven; his golden hair, now
dulled, curled over the collar of his open shirt. She turned
her back to him momentarily, and idly stoked the charred
logs. She drew an ottoman before his chair, and searched
his face for some response to her presence. But there was
none. He stared ahead blankly, his eyes a strange clear
gray, almost white. She closed her eyes against the void.

The deafening noise exploded again in her ears. And the
sound of a woman's scream, her scream. Pavel was lying on
the ground, a crimson flower blossoming upon his silken
shirt, a kind of triumph in his smile.

"Rudolph," she said suddenly, looking once more at the
man before her, "it was not your fault. At the end . . .
Pavel . . . He did not want you to die, Rudolph. The
gun . . . he . . . He was sorry. Don't you understand what
I'm saying?"

He did not answer. It seemed so useless, but she would
try again. She looked into the glowing embers. Her voice
was level, her eyes, like his own, stared inward at the
unchangeable past.

"We all have our terrible ghosts to live with. There was a
time when I thought the awful memories of my past would
haunt me forever. Once there was such a deep sense of loss
within me, that I wanted to die. Life was too cruel. I hated
the glow of the morning sun, and the sweet song of the
birds . . . even the innocent laughter of children was painful to me. Especially the laughter of children . . ." She fell
silent for a time, transfixed by the gilded blue flames.
Suddenly, she looked at him; his gray eyes were upon her.

"Our child," he murmured, his lips barely moving, his
voice hoarse.

She started. He knew. How long had he known? And
who . . . Mother Angele? "Yes, Rudolph, our child," she
replied, controlling her voice. "When I left Russia, I did not

know that I carried your son within me. And during the long months when he nestled beneath my heart, so much happened, strange and wonderful things. Things which even now I do not fully understand. And when I gave birth to our child, I was happy. Something beautiful had grown within me, and something precious would remain. Our son made all the old pain of the past worthwhile, meaningful. But I did not anticipate life's cruelty. And when our baby was lost to me forever, I felt that I, too, had died. Yet I lived. I lived each minute, each hour, each day. And finally I faced the sun, the song of birds, and yes, the laughter of children. I understood that this death was beyond anyone's control."

She spoke of their lost child with a conscious detachment. In the only way she could, she was protecting him, saving him from the pain, absolving him from the guilt. He continued to look at her, but he did not speak again. But she could not stop now.

"I know that we shall never see each other again, but I cannot bear that you should hate me. Do you not remember what you once told me? 'It was not all bad.'

"Perhaps, our greatest sin is the walls we built about ourselves and the words we left unspoken. I never meant to hurt you, Rudolph. When I left Russia, it was because I believed my staying would bring you harm. It was no spiteful act. And then in New Orleans . . .

"Please, Rudolph, do not think harshly of me. I am not what you have called me. My life as Alana de la Villere is empty, a facade. It is but a masquerade to hide Simone Montpellier. You see, Rudolph, the discovery of my identity has brought me nothing, nothing. And please know, Rudolph, that the best that is Simone Montpellier is your creation."

She stood, and bending, lightly kissed his cool forehead. She walked from the room.

~ *Chapter 17* ~

It is true, entirely true, that Manet has almost unanimously been rejected. His two paintings, The Laundress *and a portrait, have been blackballed without a word of protest. Here is what we learned this morning: When the jury came to examine Manet's paintings, one of the members exclaimed, "Enough of this. We have allowed Manet ten years to turn over a new leaf. He has not done so; on the contrary he grows worse. Reject him!" "Let's reject him. Let him stay by himself with his two paintings," cried the other jurors. Only two painters tried to defend the author of* Bon Bock. *When they opened their mouths, they were interrupted. Manet was unanimously rejected, except for two votes.*

"Those fools!" Alana de la Villere exclaimed, as she flung aside the copy of the *Bien Public.* She stalked to the open French doors and gazed into the garden. The April breeze still bore the last remnant of winter's chill, and an errant zephyr teased loose tendrils about her face. Turning abruptly, she glared at her companion. "And I suppose, Comte Beaumont, that this bit of *journalism* pleases you. You have never liked Edouard's or Edgar's work."

"Alana, please, you do me a grave injustice," the young man pleaded, feigning indignation. No one was quite like Alana, he thought, smiling to himself. No one ever could be. Even the tragedies of the last few months could not long subdue her spirit. "I must admit," Henri continued, "that I do prefer the traditionalists to the Impressionists, but perhaps this is because I do not completely grasp their aesthetic philosophy. However, I have learned to appreciate some of their efforts. In fact, I do agree that the salon was unduly harsh in its judgment of *The Laundress*. I find it quite charming."

"*Quite charming*, indeed! Henri Beaumont, don't patronize me! Save your courtly manners for Genevieve. She adores your affectations."

Henri laughed. He took no offense at the young woman's remarks. She was enjoying herself, and he would never stop her fun. It had been such a long time since he had seen her this way. Even her comment about Genevieve was entirely pardonable. He knew Genevieve to be one of Alana's best friends. And more than anyone, Alana had been delighted to hear of his engagement to her.

So vehement had Alana been in her denunciation of the salon, that Champignon had sprung from her lap. Now Alana retrieved her indignant pet. Sweeping the young cat into her arms, she smoothed its long fur, and murmured endearments until its pique dissolved into contented purrs.

"Alana," Eugenie laughed, as she came into the room with a basket of freshly cut flowers. "Stop spoiling Champignon. She is already impossible. Here, help me arrange these. Ah, here is Germaine with the post. Thank you, my dear. A letter for you, Alana—from Turkey."

Alana folded the letter and held it against her breast. Marie and Razid were to be married. They had both been willing to compromise. Marie insisted she come to the wedding. Yes, Alana thought, perhaps I shall go. How she would love to see them all again, and there was nothing to tie her here, was there? "Be happy, Marie," she whispered. "Be happy."

"Marquise," Germaine called to her softly. "I am sorry to disturb you, but you have a visitor. The Comtesse Semolenski."

As the young woman slowly descended the staircase, she realized that Josephine had not visited for over a month. The two had formed a special bond, but they tacitly avoided speaking of Rudolph.

As she greeted the countess she noted that some of the strain had left her features. When they sat down to tea, however, an uneasy silence fell between them. Finally, Josephine spoke.

"Simone, I have received a letter from Russia. Although Dimitri has accepted Pavel's death as an accident, he seems unable to cope with the reality. He cannot forgive himself for the fact that they never reconciled. I have felt for a long time that I should be with Dimitri, but I could not forsake Rudolph. His need was greater. But in these last few weeks, Rudolph has seemed to come to terms with himself, though he will not speak of the past." For a moment they sat in silence.

"Simone," Josephine said at last, weighing her words. "We sail on the next ship."

Simone said nothing. The woman's last words had rendered her immobile; her mind was strangely blank.

Josephine, too, was silent. She embraced the girl. Then taking her face into her hands, she said, "I shall miss you, Simone."

~ *Chapter 18* ~

The full, bright moon sailed like a galleon over the City of Love. It was not yet midnight, and much of Paris was still alive with gaiety. But in the de la Villere townhouse on the Ile St. Louis, all was quiet.

Alana sat before her vanity. Champignon, her constant companion, was perched upon the marble top, her large orange eyes following the motion of her mistress's hand as she pulled the brush again and again through her long hair.

"Perhaps I should have accepted Celestin's invitation to

attend the opera with him and Grand-mère. But they did not need my presence, Champi. They are so . . . complete . . . together." She smiled. Celestin. She truly loved the old man. *If I could choose a granddaughter, Alana, it would be you. And I, Celestin, would choose you for a grandfather.*

If discovering her heritage had brought her anything worthwhile, it had been this, the love of her grand-mère and Celestin. And she must be honest with herself. Her new identity had brought her a certain freedom. Freedom from the unending questions of her childhood, and the freedom of security. The Marquise de la Villere could go where she liked, do what she wished. Could Simone Montpellier?

But ah, the irony of life. The Marquise de la Villere knew not where to go, or what to do when she arrived. What *would* she do with this accursed freedom? There was Turkey. Would it not be wonderful to see Marie? And New Orleans. Yvette would welcome her, as would Armand and Cecile. She would love to see Yvette's baby, a boy, named for Maurice.

"But what of you, Champi?" she addressed the cat. "Will you go with me? 'The Marquise de la Villere and her traveling companion, Mademoiselle Champignon, will depart in a month for the East. All of Paris will miss the popular *demoiselles* . . .'"

"Meowr!" the cat interrupted.

"You would not like that, Champi? Then you shall have to stay behind. For I believe I will go. Why should I not? There is nothing holding me here." She toyed with the dark, curling edges of her hair. The woman who now stared back at her was far different from that young girl who had questioned her womanhood so very long ago.

And what of being a woman? Was not a woman more than soft, glowing skin and warm, giving lips? More than full waiting breasts and fruitful womb? Was she not also soul and mind? Was she not also pain and sorrow, unspoken secrets, and hidden tears? Woman—for her, was not compromise inevitable? Did she not surrender much, to gain little?

And what of she, herself? She peered deeply into the mirror. The measure of her life, what had it been? What had she forfeited? And what of the prize? Grandparents in Spain, Grand-mère Eugenie, and dear Celestin. The Durands, Marie and André, Henri and Genevieve

Edouard and Edgar. And there was Jalal. He would always be with her, as would the image of *their* son.

And how could she ever forget her Baba Mimka, and Yuri, her dearest friend, her little brother? And Josephine, they had become close. No, her life was not without its shining rewards. And yet . . .

Alana de la Villere, you are a fool. You have what you have always wanted. You have an identity. As she thought the last, she placed the now idle brush upon the vanity table. With a single hand, she reached to touch her captured reflection. Her fingertips encountered only cold, hard glass. Quickly, she withdrew her hand. Am I but an image, a hardened, two-dimensional reflection, an unfulfilled vision of myself?

Looking down, she noted Champignon curled upon the vanity top, fallen fast asleep. "You are right, my mushroom, it is time for bed." She looked once more into the mirror, her dark eyes reassessing, refocusing. And then she saw him.

He stood just within the room, watching her, his legs apart, his arms folded casually across his broad chest. He wore high boots over his tight-fitting black breeches, and a silken shirt open at the throat. The soft evening breezes stirred his burnished hair, like pirate's gold in the glow from the sconces.

Through the open doors, bright rays of the moon shone against his back, and haloed his tall form. He seemed a thing of the night, an astral creature, charged with the luna-light. He did not move, but continued to gaze upon her. And she could not draw her eyes from his reflection, lest he dissolve into a pool of pure radiance. She dare not turn, dare not look at him directly. The silver moon-aura held her fast.

She watched as he walked toward her. He came to stand at her back. She felt his fingers in her hair, and then his lips whispering against its silkiness. "Hello, little gypsy."

At his touch, the chrysalis of pain and regret fell from her; her dormant senses blossomed anew. Was he real, or was she now part of the illusion? "Rudolph, I don't understand. I . . . I . . ."

"Not now, ma petite, not now."

He lifted her into his arms and carried her to the waiting bed, their eyes holding each other. Gently, he rolled the silken wrapper from around her. Her body was beautiful against the peach satin. The aureoles of her full breasts shone dusky upon the ivory skin, the nipples already budded, awaiting his caress. As he reached for his waistband, she touched his arm. Slipping her hand under the soft folds of his shirt, she felt the man-hardness of his muscled chest beneath the golden down. She undressed him, kissing where each button gave way under the pressure of her fingers. He lay against the cushions, beholding her, accepting her gentle attentions. And soon they lay naked, released to the magic of the Parisian night, not touching, not speaking, savoring their nearness.

When he touched her, his hand was warm, tender. She looked into the dark blue eyes. Within their depths she sensed a strange contentment, a kind of peace. She smoothed his cheek, and he moved his lips to her fingers, running his tongue over each fingertip. Then he pressed his loving mouth into her palm. Tracing his lips down her arm, he claimed the soft hollow of her throat. His beautiful giving mouth sought and found her full breasts, and here he lingered, suckling, kissing, drinking their woman-sweetness into him. She touched the sides of his head, and pulled him from her. Opening her mouth, teasingly she ran her pink tongue around her pouting lips. Quickly, he captured it. He kissed her, his wide sensitive mouth over hers, drawing her to him, body to body, soul to soul.

She lay beneath him, her hair spilling over the quilted spread, black waves shimmering in the moonlight, her body poised to receive him, each ready nerve sensitive to the pressure of his flesh upon hers. Suddenly, she arched her body up to meet his, a soft whimper escaping her lips. Opening her slender thighs, she pulled him to her. Her warm mound was soft and moist as it brushed against the taut muscles of his abdomen. Lowering her, he thrust his tight pulsing manhood into the warm, secret recesses of her beautiful woman's flower. Deeper, deeper he explored, and she met his sweet searching with the desperate longings of her own passion. His entering of her was a sacrament, the fulfillment of the unspoken promise which had always existed between them. Each yearning thrust brought its own deepening rapture, until the two were one in their ecstasy, nevermore to know the emptiness of their separate beings.

She lay cradled in his arms, and when at last he spoke, his sweet breath was soft upon her brow.

"Simone," he murmured, I . . . I . . . Have you forgiven me, Simone? Have you . . ."

"Rudolph, have we not said all that is necessary?"

"No, there is something more." He lifted her face up to meet his, his gray-blue eyes misted with his emotion. "I love you, Simone, my princess."

"I love you, Rudolph. I have always loved you."

Her words were his final absolution. He lowered his mouth to hers and kissed her. It was a kiss against all of the old pain, all of the suffering. A kiss for all of their Russian sadness, against the cold winds, the lost child. A kiss for Pavel. A kiss for all time.

Yet there was one thing more, one last question.

"Simone," he said softly, "in New Orleans . . . why would you not become my wife?"

"Because I was only Simone Montpellier. And you, you, my darling, could never have wed one such as I, if you were to gain your uncle's favor and become the grand duke."

"My little fool," he murmured, running his finger tenderly across her lower lip. "Did you not realize, I would have married you anyway."

As they lay once more locked within each other's arms, the dark night closed its heavy lids against the blushing horizon, against the promise of a new day. The rising sun spread its rosy fingers to touch the wispy morning clouds, and plant a pink cupid's kiss upon the blue bosom of the sky.

AUTHOR'S NOTE

From the end of May through the month of June, the "White Nights" come to Leningrad (St. Petersburg). During this time, the sun leaves the sky for but a few hours. In *Forget Me Not,* it has been chosen to ignore this phenomenon in order to preserve the delicate romantic ambiance of the novel. During the evening hours, it is felt that Simone and Rudolph would move more gracefully in shadow than in light.